TUESDAY NIGHTS

LINDA RAE SANDE

Twisted Teacup
PUBLISHING

Tuesday Nights

ISBN: 978-0-9893973-5-3

ALSO BY LINDA RAE SANDE

The Daughters of the Aristocracy

The Kiss of a Viscount

The Grace of a Duke

The Seduction of an Earl

The Sons of the Aristocracy

Tuesday Nights

The Widowed Countess

My Fair Groom

The Sisters of the Aristocracy

The Story of a Baron

The Passion of a Marquess

The Desire of a Lady

The Brothers of the Aristocracy

The Love of a Rake

The Caress of a Commander

The Epiphany of an Explorer

The Widows of the Aristocracy

The Gossip of an Earl

The Enigma of a Widow

The Secrets of a Viscount

The Widowers of the Aristocracy

The Dream of a Duchess

The Vision of a Viscountess

The Conundrum of a Clerk

FIRST IMPRESSIONS ON A MONDAY

April 23, 1810

Michael Cunningham, the second son of a viscount, was minding his own business as he strode toward The Ship. He intended to take a room at Shipley's only inn, the establishment promising a clean room and hot meals for the few days he would be in the Horsham District of Sussex.

Although his family's small estate, Cunningham Park, was just south of Horsham, he thought the daily trip to Shipley would take too much time away from his opportunity to meet with Harold Waterford. Sir Richard Waggoner had taken a risk in arranging for him to meet with the businessman, and Michael didn't want to disappoint either of the gentlemen by not being available on an hour's notice.

So it was a surprise and a bit of an annoyance when his attention was suddenly diverted. A young lady's scream, followed by a drawn out cry of "No!" stopped him in his tracks.

Michael glanced around, realizing almost at once that the sound had come from behind the inn. Hurrying around the whitewashed stucco building, he spied the source of the scream. A young woman, her back pressed against the inn's carriage house, was pinned in place by a taller young man, his bent arm pressed across her throat. Dressed in trousers and a wool shirt, he looked like he belonged at the edge of the flock of sheep that were grazing just east of town. But this wolf had his lamb at a distinct disadvantage, and Michael was quick to act on the lamb's behalf.

"Now, see here," he shouted, reaching out to grab the attacker's shoulder. He instead ended up with a handful of shirt, lifting it so the man was suddenly off his feet and facing him.

"Wh ..?"

Before the predator had completely turned to see who it was that had him pulled away from his prey, Michael's skills as a pugilist took over. His right fist struck the man's jaw, and then Michael let go of the shirt. Dazed from the blow, the young man stumbled backwards and landed on his bum, his nose dripping blood while one hand reached up to his cheek.

"The young lady said, 'no'!" Michael yelled, uncurling his fist and stretching his fingers to determine that, thank the gods, none were broken. He needed that hand to take notes whilst in his meetings these next few days. "You go near her again, and I'll see to it every bone in your body is broken," he vowed.

His eyes wide as saucers, the young man nodded. "Yes, sir," he mumbled, his hand still rubbing his cheek.

Michael's attention turned to the young lady whose back was still against the wall, her arms stretched straight and one palm pressed flat against the stucco while the other was curled into a fist around the strings of a reticule. Although her bodice was a bit askew, and her face had a look of astonishment, she seemed in one piece.

At least she hadn't had a fit of the vapours and fainted on him.

"Are you ... hurt?" he asked, careful to keep the tone of his voice as neutral as possible. He didn't want the girl as frightened of him as she was of the man who was scampering backwards like a crab toward his escape.

• • •

or the first time in several seconds, Olivia Waterford let out the breath she'd been holding. She was sure Eli Blaylock was about to kiss her. Perhaps about to have his way with her, although she still wasn't quite sure what that would have entailed. *Ruination, certainly!*

Her green eyes, still quite wide, took in her rescuer. Tall — at least six feet, she surmised—dark-haired and broad of shoulder, he had a rectangular face defined by a rather square jaw and straight eyebrows. Under those brows were blue eyes, eyes that had seemed full of mischief when he confronted her attacker but were now regarding her with a great deal of concern.

His broad nose was a bit crooked, but not so much that it looked out of place. And his lips made it rather difficult for her to remember what it was that had just come out of them only a moment ago. *Kissable lips,* she thought, just as she remembered how they were described in a novel she had finished reading only the week before.

Olivia blinked in an attempt to remember what it was he had asked.

y lady, are you unhurt?" Michael asked then, moving closer so he might determine if she really was about to faint.

Don't faint, whatever you do, don't faint.

He glanced down to her hands, noticed how one was flat against the carriage house wall while the other held onto a reticule and what looked like a terribly wrinkled hanky. One knuckle on her fourth finger was red; he reached out and carefully pried her hand away from the wall, lifting the finger so he could examine it.

The knuckle was bleeding from a deep scratch. He wondered if she had attempted to defend herself or had merely scraped it on the stucco. "You're bleeding," he murmured, before placing his lips over her finger. Sucking on the wound for a moment, an action that seemed to bring the young lady back to awareness, Michael tasted the iron tang of blood before he pulled away to examine the wound again.

He noticed how long and slender her fingers were, how pale and beautiful her hand was, despite there being no gloves in sight. Her fingernails were perfect ovals, trimmed short but not bitten off.

He imagined a ring at the base of that finger. *A sapphire would look most becoming,* he thought, *with a diamond or two on either side.* And then he chided himself. *Why am I thinking about jewelry?* he wondered, the thought nearly bringing a grimace to his face.

Once he determined that the injured knuckle had stopped bleeding, he dared a glance at his patient's face. She was younger than he'd first thought, but quite pretty, with mahogany hair caught up in a bun at the back of her head. Her smoky green eyes were tilted up at the outer corners, giving her a slightly exotic look despite her youthful cheeks and pert nose. But those lips—reddened a bit from her attacker's attempt at a kiss—were full and sensual.

Kissable lips, he thought, and was about to find out for himself when he remembered he had just rescued her from such an assault. He took a step back.

*S*taring at her rescuer, Olivia forced her mouth closed. She dared a glance beyond the man. At least the yard was still abandoned; no one had witnessed Eli's attempt on her virtue nor this man's unusual ministrations with regard to her finger.

She turned her attention to where his lips had just been and arched an eyebrow. Her knuckle, where it had intersected one of Eli's teeth when she attempted the same move this man had accomplished with a good deal more ease, was no longer bleeding.

A shiver passed through her as she relived the sensation of his lips against her skin, of how his warm hand had held hers with so much care. *Was the man a doctor?* she wondered. Well, whoever he was, he was giving her that look again, as if he expected her to say *something*.

"It appears I am now," Olivia answered finally, her eyes lifting to meet his. "And to whom shall I address my gratitude?" she asked.

Michael let out the breath he had been holding for that moment. "Forgive me." He removed his hat and bowed. "Michael Cunningham, at your service," he said formally.

Giving him a smile, Olivia pushed herself away from the carriage house wall and curtsied. *So this is Mr. Cunningham!* Her father had made mention they would be hosting the man for a few days—something having to do with a business venture he was considering.

Mr. Cunningham was certainly younger than she expected, given her father's typical business associates. "Miss Olivia," she replied finally, deciding to withhold her family name. She wanted to see if he appeared surprised when he finally learned she was the Harold Waterford's daughter. She reached out with her hand to shake his.

The man intercepted her hand with his own gloved hand and raised it to his lips. He kissed the back of her knuckles before she quite realized what was happening and had to still the sound of a gasp when the renewed dart of pleasure shot up her arm.

Either he was a gentleman or a bounder. She wasn't sure which just yet.

"Pleased to make your acquaintance," he said with a nod as he let go of her hand.

Olivia found that her hand suddenly felt leaden without his support. "And yours. Thank you, truly, for what you did." She looked toward where Eli had crawled off, disappointed that the boy had escaped.

In fairness to the would-be rake, Eli had been dared by his friends to kiss her. His first attempt the week before had ended when she'd managed to get a knee shoved up into his groin before he could get her against any wall.

His second attempt had been interrupted by his mother's shouts—the woman had no doubt been a Welsh milkmaid in her younger years.

This attempt, though, had been carefully calculated and timed for when she exited the mercantile with a package in one arm and her reticule and gloves in the other. She'd been unable to use her fists until she dropped her parcel, and by then, Eli had her in the inn's yard and halfway to the wall.

"You're welcome, of course," Michael replied before tearing his eyes away from Olivia. He glanced about the yard, rather surprised that no one else had joined them to determine the fate of the young lady. Certainly someone else had heard her cries.

"Mr. MacFadyen is at the mercantile. To pick up his weekly order," Olivia said, realizing her rescuer was probably wondering why no one had come out of the inn at the sound of her scream.

The comment reminded her about her package. She glanced about, trying to remember just where she had dropped her book. Somehow her reticule and gloves were still clutched in her uninjured hand. *My poor gloves*, she thought as she realized how tightly she'd been holding them.

Furrowing his brows, Michael regarded the young lady for a moment. "I take it Mr. MacFadyen is the ... proprietor?" he half-asked, trying to remember the name of the family that was supposed to be in residence.

Olivia shrugged as she regarded her gloves. "He runs the pub portion of the inn on behalf of the owners," she explained, as she moved away from the carriage house wall and walked toward the front of the inn. "Which is why Eli chose this particular place to try to ... kiss me," she explained, affording Michael a sideways nod. She spotted her bonnet and hurried towards it, surprised when Michael beat her to it and had it in hand before she could even reach the spot in the small lawn where it had landed. "Thank you," she added as she regarded the hopelessly crushed hat.

"Allow me," Michael countered, using the fist from one

hand and fingers of his other to pop the straw back into shape. He regarded the bonnet inside and out before holding it out for her inspection. "It's not perfect, but ..."

"It'll do!" Olivia interrupted, amazed that the man was able to restore the bonnet to a wearable state. She allowed him to place the bonnet on her head, adjust it, and tie the ribbons while she pulled her wrinkled gloves onto her hands. "Thank you again, Mr. Cunningham," she added, resisting the urge to add that he would make a good lady's maid. No need to embarrass the man. Especially since her mother was expecting him for dinner that evening.

"You're most welcome, Miss Olivia," he replied. Michael noted her increasing consternation. "Is there something ... else ... missing?" he asked finally.

Olivia sighed. "My book," she answered impatiently. "I dropped it when I tried to punch Eli."

*H*is eyebrows nearly rising into his hairline, Michael had to resist the urge to laugh. *So, she had tried to defend herself.* He held out his arm, intending for her to take it so he could escort her off the inn's lawn and onto the lane that led back toward the mercantile. He couldn't help but notice her hesitancy, but she placed a gloved hand on his arm.

"A fan of Minerva Press, are you?" he teased. He wondered if she would blush at his words, wondered if her complexion would turn a glorious pink whenever she was the least bit embarrassed.

He was not disappointed.

Despite her bonnet, he could see the flush of pink bloom on her cheeks. "I rather prefer more ... serious material," she replied quickly, her head dipping a bit. "As to Minerva Press novels, my sister has been known to bring some of *those* books home on occasion," she added, a dimple appearing in one cheek.

"Is she ... older?" he asked, hearing a hint of derision in

Olivia's comment. He wondered if Olivia found Minerva Press novels really so objectionable or if there was some sibling rivalry involved.

"A couple of years," Olivia answered carefully, before adding, "and quite out of place here in Sussex. I imagine she'll be headed to London before she's reached her majority. Although she has had some local boys come to court her, she is quite sure she wants a match to a more sophisticated gentleman."

Michael nodded his understanding. "And, no doubt, a man with a bit of blunt," he commented, wanting Olivia to think he didn't have much, which, come to think of it, was one of the reasons he had come to Shipley to pursue a business venture with Harold Waterford. Another had to do with how that business venture might become a boon for the local economy. "Is it large?" Michael asked suddenly. "The book, I mean," he added and then wondered why he had made the clarification.

Olivia shrugged as she scanned the area. "Somewhat. Rather thick, really, and wrapped in brown paper."

Even before she'd completed her description, Michael noticed the parcel on the edge of the dirt road. Some of the paper wrapping had torn away, and the book's cover was a bit scuffed, but the spine seemed intact.

He reached down to retrieve it at the same time as Olivia, so her bonnet nearly collided with his head.

"Oh," she managed to get out when she lost her balance and fell against his body as he stood.

His fast reflexes had her captured in one arm as he held onto the book with his other. Olivia's body was suddenly pressed against the front of his, her upturned face within inches of his own. A most becoming pink blush suddenly colored her face, and it took every bit of Michael's restraint not to kiss her right then and there.

What is wrong with me? he wondered suddenly. *She cannot be more than ... sixteen or seventeen years of age!* "Pardon, milady," he murmured before he removed his arm from her waist.

*O*livia continued to stare up at him, wondering if the man might want to kiss her. *I certainly would not object,* she decided. He looked as if he might, as if he was deciding whether or not he should; he had angled his face as he lowered his lips to hers. But then his arm suddenly fell away from her waist and he straightened.

Olivia had never before felt such disappointment.

"Oh, I am such a dubber," she whispered hoarsely. "It is *I* who should beg your pardon."

*M*ichael regarded her with mischievous eyes before he shook his head and turned his attention to the book. *The Flora of England.* The title was so unexpected, he had to use his gloved hand to uncover the book completely to ensure he had read it correctly. An eyebrow furrowed as he turned his attention back to ... *what had she said her name was?* Olivia.

Noting his surprise at her choice of reading material, Olivia swallowed. "I like to read. I thought it would be ... interesting," she said with a slight shrug, her face coloring up again.

"You are educated, then?" Michael half-questioned, a quizzical expression on his face. He didn't try to hide his surprise. Girls raised in the country were rarely taught anything beyond simple reading and mathematics.

Swallowing hard, as if she regretted leaving him with the impression she was educated, Olivia nodded. "It is my father's intention that I should be," she replied then, worried the man would think her a bluestocking. She glanced around, realizing she needed to be on her way home.

"Indeed?" Michael replied, wondering who her father might be. "And your ... siblings?" He began walking, noting the direction in which she was going matched where he'd left his gig and horse.

Olivia shrugged. "All of us, really, but my sister is not as inclined to it as I am. Eloisa would rather shop for ribbons and frippery and look at fashion plates," she explained with a shrug. "My father is of the mind that men have no right to complain about chit-chat if they have not properly educated their daughters so they might speak on topics other than gossip and Paris fashions."

Michael considered the comment for a moment. It was true that too many young women were uneducated, and those fathers who could afford to send their girls to finishing schools or hire a governess only wanted to see them learn French, elocution, and how to play piano-forté or do needlework.

"Is your intention to ... to employ your education some-how?" he asked then, suppressing the urge to remove her bonnet and pull the pins from her hair. There was a passing thought of how she might look in a thin night rail with her mahogany hair down past her shoulders and her rose-tipped breasts showing through the translucent fabric. He tried to erase the image as soon as it formed, his cock suddenly hardening at the carnal thought.

Olivia shrugged again. "If I am not married by the time I am one-and-twenty, then I shall become a governess."

Of all the professions a woman could claim in England, and there weren't many, *governess* was not the one Michael expected this young lady to mention. "A governess?" he repeated, not bothering to hide his surprise. Despite her apparent reading habit, the girl did not seem the least bit a bluestocking, nor did he imagine she would still be unmar-ried by the time she was of legal age.

There were obviously men of his age in Shipley who looked upon her with favor—besides the one who had accosted her—and who would no doubt line up at her father's door when it was time for her coming out. *And they'll probably be lined up behind me,* he reasoned, a bit startled by the thought. "You are quite serious?" he asked then, his brows furrowed.

Olivia paused in mid-step, as if she was surprised a man would question her choice of profession. "Is there something wrong with wanting to provide for myself?" she asked, her posture reinforcing her defensiveness.

Michael took a breath to answer and then let it out without saying anything, his head shaking just a bit.

"I do not wish to be a burden to my family," she added. At his sudden snort and the grin that changed his serious expression to one of delight, Olivia allowed a tentative smile.

"I assure you, Miss Olivia, you will never be a burden to your family," Michael said with a shake of his head.

Olivia regarded her rescuer with a small smile. "I really must be on my way now, Mr. Cunningham," she said as she curtsied. She reached out, intending to take her book from Michael.

"May I offer you a ride, Miss Olivia?" he offered, pointing in the direction of his conveyance. Olivia's gaze followed his line of sight, and her eyes widened when she witnessed a rather large Cleveland Bay pulling a gig in their direction, even though there was no one at the reins.

Shaking her head in amusement when the horse came to a halt just as it reached them, she glanced over at Michael and allowed a smile. "Well, seeing as how my father is expecting you, and my mother is planning to host you for dinner and has seen to it a bedchamber has been made ready for you, I suppose I could offer my services as a guide to our home," she finally answered, wondering if Michael would show his surprise at her identity. She was not disappointed to find him regarding her with a look of astonishment.

"You are Olivia *Waterford?*"

"At your service," Olivia replied, giving him another curtsy. With that, she turned and climbed into the gig, rather satisfied that she was the first in her family to meet Michael Cunningham. It wasn't often her father invited someone other than Sir Richard to their home, and neither he nor the others were as young and handsome as this man.

Michael walked to her side of the gig and held out the book so she could take it. "You might have given me your *entire* name when you introduced yourself earlier," he murmured, as if he was scolding her.

From his manner, Olivia realized he found the situation amusing. "Except that I am not in the habit of introducing myself to strangers," she countered as Michael climbed up and took the reins.

"Even if they have saved you from a rake?" Michael teased.

"Even then," Olivia murmured. The horse was suddenly moving, covering the half-mile to Waterford Hall in a few minutes.

Although the Waterford estate home wasn't particularly large, it was on par with the other country manor houses dotting the Sussex countryside, its Portland stone exterior half-covered in ivy. A large garden extended from the back of the house and along one side, while an expanse of parkland made the front of the estate look as if an aristocratic family lived there during their summers away from London. Given its half-mile distance from Shipley, the nearest village, Water-ford Hall had the advantage of seeming as if it was in the middle of nowhere and yet many amenities were either a ten-minute walk south or an hour's ride north.

Although Michael had grown up nearby, he'd never been to Waterford Hall. He admired the stately manor house from where he halted the horse in the semi-circular drive in front, trying to ignore the sudden nervousness he felt at the prospect of meeting Harold Waterford.

Jumping down from the gig, he hurried to the other side and assisted Olivia. "Have you lived here your entire life?" he asked, stealing another glance at the house before he offered her his arm.

Olivia noticed his nervousness. Of course, he would be anxious about meeting her father. "Yes. And my father doesn't bite," she remarked casually. "Barks a good deal," she admitted with a rueful smile. "But if you've come prepared and present your proposal in a straightforward manner, he will help you with your venture," she stated with a nod. "And all the others, should you decide to continue working with him. Shipley needs the jobs."

Michael paused to regard Olivia as she gave her opinion, surprised by her candor and by her comments. Without thinking, he leaned down and kissed her on the forehead. "Thank you, Miss Olivia," he murmured. "Truly."

As he expected, Olivia blushed as she bestowed him a glorious smile.

*L*ater that night

Wearing a long nightshirt and a cap on his balding head, Harold Waterford moved to the bed he shared with his wife. Louisa was similarly dressed in a voluminous white cotton nightrail with a mobcap covering her graying curls.

"So?" she said expectantly, her hands clasped together over the top of the counterpane as she leaned against a pile of pillows.

Harold paused before pulling down the bed linens on his side of the mattress. "So?" he repeated, feigning ignorance over his wife's desire to know what had happened during his meeting with the handsome, young man who was now ensconced in the guest bedchamber at the end of the hall.

"Harold!" Louisa scolded. "I have been quite patient these past few hours. Do not keep me in suspense!" she pleaded in a loud whisper. "Will he, do you suppose?" she asked, hoping beyond hope that her eldest daughter would soon be settled in an advantageous marriage.

Her husband got into bed and pulled the linens up to his chest. "Mr. Cunningham is far too young to be thinking about leg shackles," he stated evenly. "Unless Eloisa is willing to wait until she's on the shelf, she should be considering other prospects for husbands," he added in a tired voice. "Besides, I do think our eldest was behaving a bit ... fast this evening."

Biting her lower lip, Louisa regarded her husband for a moment. "She was a bit ... forward with the man," she agreed sadly. "But he didn't seem to mind," she continued, her countenance returning to a happier state.

Her husband gave her a quelling glance. "My sweeting, *I* was embarrassed for our guest. Eloisa's flirting was too overt. Even Olivia seemed embarrassed, although I suppose she was more embarrassed *for* Mr. Cunningham than on behalf of her own sister."

Louisa sighed a rather long, mournful sigh. "I rather hoped Eloisa would be settled in the next year or so," she murmured. "She won't even consider any of the local boys—"

"Can you blame her?" Harold shot back. "Can't say I'd give any of them my permission, although I hear Angus has a brother nearing thirty—"

"Don't you dare!" Louisa exclaimed, unable to consider her eldest married to a pig farmer.

A deep chuckle came from her husband. "I rather expect our Eloisa will be off to London to find a husband in a few years," he said before closing his eyes.

Louisa glanced over at her husband, knowing he spoke the truth. "And Olivia?" She sighed again. Earlier in the evening, her younger daughter confided that Eli Blaylock had once again attempted a kiss in The Ship's yard, but she insisted he wouldn't be trying it again. *Ever.* Louisa wondered what her daughter had done to the boy to be so sure, but she hadn't had the chance to ask.

His eyes still closed, a smile split Harold's face. "She'll be the one marrying Mr. Cunningham," he whispered, almost as if he didn't intend to share the information with anyone. "But you'd be wise to keep that to yourself, Louisa," he murmured, one eye opening to reinforce his suggestion. "I don't think either one of them has figured it out just yet."

Louisa allowed a rather large smile of her own. She rarely saw her husband smile, and the thought of at least one of her daughters married to the son of a viscount made her positively euphoric.

"Patience, dear heart," Harold whispered. "It may be four or five years before he'll be ready for a wife. I like this boy. He's determined to make his own way in life. He is convinced his older brother is bankrupting the Cunningham coffers, so he wants to build his own fortune and those of Shipley while he's at it. And that will take a few years."

He heard Louisa's gasp, knowing she would be rather happy to have a daughter married to a man of the *ton*, but not if it meant the girl would be living in debt for the rest of her life.

"Do you think he can? Build his own fortune? And Shipley's too, I mean?" she asked hopefully.

Harold rolled over and wrapped an arm around his wife's waist. "I shall do everything in my power to ensure that he *does*," he murmured as he reached up and began undoing all the buttons down the front of his wife's night rail. "He's got some excellent ideas, and he's done his research."

Once the last button was undone, he spread open the night rail and added, "Probably make us both rich." With that, he planted his face against one of her breasts.

"Oh, Harold!" she whispered happily, pushing herself down from the pillows. "I so love it when you're naughty."

CHAPTER 2

A PICNIC ON A TUESDAY

April 24, 1810

Anna closed her eyes as the sun peeked out from behind an afternoon cloud. Her left hand, firmly grasped by her best friend's hand, was lifted from where it lay in the grass. She smiled as she felt Edward's lips touch the back of her knuckles, his fingers gently kneading her palm and wrist. When she was sure the sun had ducked behind the cloud again, she barely opened her eyes. Edward stared down at her, his face a study of joy and his blond hair haloed by the rays of the sun.

"You are so beautiful," he breathed before lowering his lips to hers. The kiss, a mere teasing touch of his lips to hers, might have ended there, but Anna lifted her other hand to the side of his face. The ends of her fingers gently pulled his head down again and she kissed him. She opened her mouth and allowed his tongue to touch her teeth and her tongue before she used hers to do the same to him.

When Edward finally pulled away, he regarded his childhood friend and the love of his life for a very long time. "I am going to miss you terribly," he whispered.

Anna reached up and plucked a blade of grass from his hair. "Will I see you at Christmastime?" she whispered, bravely keeping tears from collecting in the corners of her eyes.

"Before that, I'm sure," Edward said assuringly. "I'll just be back at Oxford." He said this as if he would be doing research at a school on the other side of town rather than eighty miles away.

Swallowing hard, Anna nodded, her head still resting in the lawn behind the Earl of Eversham's country estate. The remains of their luncheon picnic were scattered over a blanket spread out beneath a live oak tree. "Father may move us to London before then," she whispered. "Do you suppose it would be acceptable for me to write to you?"

Edward frowned. "London?" he repeated. He lifted himself onto an elbow. "What are you saying?"

Anna seemed to shrug as she continued to lie stretched out on the manicured lawn. She had a passing thought as to how difficult it would be to get the grass stains out of her morning gown, but quickly replaced it with the consideration of how much she would miss the boy who had become a man whilst at Eton and Oxford.

Edward had been in school for several years, but he returned to Somerset so frequently, she barely missed him. But Oxford for research on antiquities? She rather doubted Edward would return as frequently. And it was more likely he would be tempted by the larger city's offerings, both in scholarly pursuits as well as other entertainments, and simply remain there during academic breaks.

The young men of Bath didn't always return after leaving for school. They were more likely to take positions as clerks or join the militia or a ship's crew. Edward was unlikely to undertake any of those occupations given his status as the second son of an earl; moving to London was more likely.

"There is a marquess in Mayfair who fancies Father's tailoring," Anna finally replied. "He has promised Father a higher commission than he can ever hope to make if he stays here. Oh, and a character if he makes himself more 'readily available' to the man," she quoted with a roll of her eyes.

Edward sat up, bending one knee and wrapping an arm around it. Despite his height—he was just over six feet tall—he still managed to look elegant in the pose. "I shall just have to take my vacations from school in London then," he said with a mischievous grin. "Not as far from Oxford, either," he added with a wink. He regarded her for a moment more. "Fancy your father being noticed by an aristocrat, though. He should be proud."

Anna covered her eyes with an arm to block out the sun. "He's a tailor, Edward," she stated sadly. "And even if every one of his clients is a member of the *ton*, he'll always be the lowest class citizen in this country."

Her best friend frowned again, surprised at Anna's assessment. It was true tailors weren't well regarded, but a good tailor was a necessity for any man who wanted to stand out among gentlemen, especially those who lived in London. "Still, to have a marquess notice his work and request that he move is an honor, I should think."

Retrieving her bonnet from the grass, Anna sat up and pulled it onto the back of her head. She thought of putting her hair back into a bun, but she would have to find the hair-pins Edward had pulled out of her carefully constructed bun, a rather difficult task given he had tossed them off so they were hidden somewhere in the grass.

"Perhaps someone will notice my sewing skills and request I work in their modiste," she said hopefully. At some point she would have to find employment. She was already one-and-twenty and still living at home. How much longer would she be welcome to do so? Perhaps the move to London would provide more opportunities.

Edward took her hand again, giving it a gentle squeeze. "I won't have you working, my love," he stated, apparently surprised by her comment. "I intend to marry you ... just as soon as my older brother is married and an heir is born."

Anna arched an eyebrow and regarded Edward. She'd heard his claim before. At one time, she believed she would one day be the wife of Edward Seward, the second son of the

Earl of Eversham. But as she grew older and learned more about the ways of the world—the ways of the aristocracy—the more she realized that Edward's fanciful claims were just that. She was sure Edward's parents would forbid such a match for the very reason that she was a daughter of a tailor. They would no doubt require Edward to marry an aristocrat's daughter. At least a baron's daughter. Anna could claim no ties to any wellborn family, let alone a family of the *ton*.

"If my father does move us to London, then I shall have to seek employment, Edward," she said quietly. "I will have to make my own way at some point."

Shaking his head, Edward gave her a look of impatience. "If and when you're no longer welcome to live with your parents, I shall arrange a small house or apartment for you," he insisted.

Anna's eyes widened. "You expect me to be your mistress?" she asked in alarm, stunned by his offer. No man arranged for a woman's housing unless he expected to pay calls on her— and not for the purpose of having tea and biscuits.

"No," Edward replied too quickly. "I ... Well, I suppose one would assume that, but ..." He allowed the sentence to trail off. Of course, he wanted Anna as his mistress. Especially if he couldn't have her as his wife right away. "I love you, Anna. I want you in my life. For the rest of my life," he vowed as he brought her hand to his lips and kissed the back of it.

Sighing, Anna nodded. "And I love you, Edward," she whispered. "But I will not hold you to your claim."

A grimace formed on Edward's face, making his long features a bit comical. "You think I will not honor my vow?" he asked, obviously offended by her comment.

Anna shook her head. "I know you would if you could. But this isn't just *us* we're talking about. Your parents have expectations. You're an earl's son. You cannot expect to be allowed to marry a tailor's daughter!" Tears suddenly streamed from her eyes, surprising her and startling Edward.

"Anna," he whispered as he gathered her into his arms, rocking her as he held her against his chest. Somewhere deep down, he knew that what she said was true—to a point.

Once his brother had an heir and the earldom's succession was secure, Edward would be free to marry whomever he pleased. But until then, he had a responsibility to his father—to the earldom—to make it appear as if he was biding his time in finding a suitable daughter of the *ton* to marry.

We have time, he reasoned. *All the time in the world.*

CHAPTER 3

MOMMA'S BOY ON A
WEDNESDAY

April 25, 1810

After two days of business meetings with Harold Waterford, Michael Cunningham paused just outside the front door of Waterford Park and took a deep breath. He recalled the comment Sir Richard had made before Michael traveled to Horsham. "Waterford will have a counter for every point you make. Be prepared with your own counter to his, and you'll do fine."

Obviously, Sir Richard had been through the same kinds of meetings with the venerable Harold A. Waterford as Michael had just endured. The two had met four times in those two days, their meetings ending only when Louisa insisted they join the family for a meal at the dining table.

Even the time the two men spent enjoying port and cheroots after supper was productive. Michael offered his ideas and Harold played devil's advocate until the older man was satisfied that Michael had considered all the possible pitfalls of their venture.

If additional financing was ever required during the next two years, Michael had a verbal assurance from his banker, Arthur Huntington III, that monies would be made available. Michael had sparred with the older man at Gentleman Jackson's salon only the week before, using the bare-knuckle mill as a means of bouncing his ideas—as well as his fists—off his friend.

He would have preferred to have the conversation over drinks at White's, but Arthur rarely attended the men's club. Besotted with his wife of ten years, the banker preferred to spend his evenings in her company. "If you ever marry a woman you love Cunningham, you'll understand," Arthur said as they left the boxing salon.

As Michael said his farewells to the Waterford family, he gave Olivia a nod and a wink, causing a blush to appear on the younger daughter's face. "If that Blaylock boy—"

"He won't," Olivia interrupted with a shake of her head. "You provided a rather convincing deterrent, I should think," she added with a surreptitious smile.

Michael nearly colored up when he noticed Olivia's expression, but he was forced to turn his attention to Olivia's older sister when Eloisa suddenly appeared from inside and bounced down the stairs. "Do have a good trip, Mr. Cunningham," she said with half a curtsy. "I look forward to seeing you tomorrow evening."

Nodding, Michael gave a leg and lifted his beaver to his head. "Thank you, Miss Waterford," he replied, not realizing the older girl expected him to take her hand.

Olivia elbowed her sister, controlling the urge she had to roll her eyes at that moment. "As would I, if I were allowed to attend," Olivia said wryly, her hands held behind her back.

Michael failed at suppressing a grin at the tone of Olivia's comment. *What the hell?* She was too young for him. And he wasn't in the market for a wife. Not for a long time. Maybe not ever if this venture didn't prove profitable for Harold Waterford. After all, the only way he would make money was if Waterford made it first. They were using the older man's capital for the initial investment; Michael had little to offer other than his ideas and a thoroughly researched business plan.

As he made his way back to Cunningham Park, Michael wondered at Olivia's intention with her comment and conspiratorial smile. Eloisa's had been pure flirtation. She had done nothing but flirt with him whenever they were in the same room, even with her parents present! But Olivia didn't seem the type to flirt, and until those smiles, he didn't think her capable. She was level-headed and well-read, her conversation during dinner about practical matters, while Eloisa's tended toward gossip and fashion and questions about London's entertainments.

His thoughts about the Waterford girls were soon replaced with business-related matters. He intended to spend the next few weeks working on the business venture he had convinced Harold Waterford to underwrite. They already had the land and a nearby pond, thanks to the Cunningham viscountcy. An experienced foreman had agreed to oversee the operation should Michael succeed in securing the financing. Given Sir Richard's additional backing, and the clout the man brought to any of his ventures, their iron smelting business could be in operation in just a few months.

Michael reached Cunningham Park later that afternoon to discover his mother, Lady Violet Cunningham, in residence. She had been on the Continent for at least six weeks and had just returned the day before with trunks full of new gowns and slippers and all manner of frippery. But her homecoming had not gone well.

Her husband, Mark Cunningham, a viscount, had gone off to London without a word as to when he would return to the Horsham District. And the butler informed her Michael was off to Shipley on a business venture. She had half a mind to head to Bath to visit her best friend. At least Temperance Seward, Countess of Eversham, would be in residence and happy to offer her accommodations until it was time to go to London for the Season.

"There you are!" Violet called from her salon on the second floor when she spotted Michael on the way to his bedchamber. "It's been an age since I've seen you, darling. Do let me have a look," she said as she stepped back from having given her younger son a peck on the cheek.

Michael obliged his mother after returning her kiss. "You've been gone a bit longer than usual," he accused. "Father was ready to send a Bow Street Runner to look for you." Violet Cunningham's visits to the Continent rarely lasted longer than a few weeks, so her absence after a month was a source of worry for her husband.

A look of surprise crossed Violet's face but was quickly masked. "I hardly know why. When I left he seemed quite at home with that ... that *trollop*," she spat out before lifting her fan from where it hung on her wrist to beat it through the air in front of her.

A bit stunned at her outburst, Michael set his valise on the threshold and followed his mother to where she usually held court with a bevy of visiting matrons. "What ... or rather, *who* are you talking about?" he asked, not aware that his father had any liaisons with prostitutes. Or had taken a mistress. And if he had, he certainly didn't entertain them at Cunningham Park.

Violet's eyes shot daggers at him. "There's no need for you to make excuses for your father," she countered, continuing to wave the fan below her chin. Had she been twenty years younger, she would have looked like a nervous chit at her first ball. "I saw her. She arrived just as my coach was leaving for the coast," she claimed. "She ran right into Cunningham's open arms," Violet added with a shake of her head. "You would think she could have waited until I was gone!"

Michael rolled his eyes and took the seat across from the viscountess. "Mother, the woman you saw wasn't Father's mistress. He doesn't have one, as far I know. The woman was Cousin Colette," he said quietly, realizing just then that the young woman had arrived at a rather awkward time. "His first cousin, come to stay at Cunningham Park.

Violet's eyes widened. "*That* was little Collette?"

Michael nodded. "She is all grown up now, but her fiancé threw her over for another," he explained with a deep sigh. He shook his head at the thought that his mother had been harboring her distrust of her husband for the entire time she'd been away.

The fan stopped moving and Violet stared at her son. "Truly?" she whispered, the hurt and dread she'd felt every day for over a month suddenly lifting. *How could I have thought he'd taken a lover?* she wondered then, thinking suddenly of Antony, the Italian count who had made it quite clear he was available for a liaison should she wish to have an *affaire* with him on her terms.

He had even offered jewelry.

But Violet had blushed like a girl still in the schoolroom and thanked him for his attentions, taking her leave of him before he could even kiss the back of her hand. She would never have the courage to take a lover, even if she discovered Mark's visitor was his mistress. She had no intention of cuckolding the man she had loved for over twenty-five years.

"Mother, all you would have had to do was simply ask Father," Michael said quietly, noting how his mother had turned quite pale with his news.

Violet, no longer near tears, finally looked up to regard him. "I don't know if I would have *believed* him," she replied with a shake of her head and a wan smile. "At least, not that day," she added with a sigh. After another moment of shared silence, she sighed. "So, where is your father now?" she asked, taking in a breath and holding it, apparently to keep herself sitting up straight on the settee.

Michael reminded his mother that Parliament was in session and that she shouldn't expect Mark Cunningham to return anytime soon. "I can escort you to the house in Mayfair," he offered, thinking she would quickly grow bored if she were to stay in Horsham. "I'm sure Father is in residence there. Or, you're welcome to use the blue room in my townhouse for the Season if you don't mind a lack of servants," he added, thinking she would attend enough Society events that she would rarely be in his home.

Given the lack of servants, she probably wouldn't take him up on his offer.

"But I must warn you that I will be quite occupied with a business venture and will be unable to escort you to many soirées," he added, deciding just then that he would probably stay at Cunningham Park for the duration of this first venture, at least until it was up and operating under the foreman.

The reminder of soirées had Violet's eyes widening. "I'll go to the house in Mayfair, of course," she answered quickly. "But before I leave for London, do you suppose you could escort me to the Fitzsimmons' ball in Crawley tomorrow evening?" she asked, her grief apparently forgotten as she remembered she had sent her response to the invitation the day before.

Most of the invitations Violet found on the salver upon her return were for events that had already happened. The early Season ball in Crawley was intended for those in Sussex who hadn't yet moved back to London, and the annual event was worth attending if only to see the new crop of young ladies making their debuts from the area.

"We could spend the night at Iron Creek. I haven't been there in an age," she murmured, thinking of the twenty-room "cottage" that her husband would give to Michael when he reached his majority.

"I suppose," Michael said reluctantly, not because he objected to spending time at Iron Creek—the house was his favorite Cunningham property—but because he remembered that one particular girl would be in attendance at the Crawley ball.

And the other would not.

Just before he'd left Waterford Hall, Eloisa had made a point of mentioning that her come-out would be at this ball. *Should I save a dance for you?* she'd asked, her lashes batting as if she had something in one or both of her eyes.

At the very moment Eloisa was addressing him, he was aware of Olivia, a hoop of needlework in her lap, rolling her eyes at her sister's boldness. Eloisa was certainly an accomplished flirt, although Michael couldn't begin to imagine on whom she practiced besides him.

Perhaps Eloisa wasn't really an accomplished flirt just yet.

"I have to pay a couple of calls and finish some paperwork tomorrow, but I'll do my best to be ready around seven," he offered, knowing the ride to the Fitzsimmons' estate in Crawley would take at least an hour.

"I'll be ready," Violet promised before she excused herself and headed for the door. "And I'll see to it we have a dinner this evening at seven," she added before she disappeared.

Michael watched his mother leave the salon, wondering if she had done something she now regretted because she believed his father to have a mistress. Had his father done something to make her believe he employed a mistress? Or was it just the unfortunate timing of Colette's arrival that had her believing the worst in Mark Cunningham?

Not wishing to dwell on the topic any longer, Michael moved to the escritoire, slid a sheet of his stationery into place, and took up a quill.

Dear Mr. Evans, he wrote in an even script. *It is my sincerest pleasure to formally offer you the position of foreman for the Shipley Iron Smelting Works ...*

CHAPTER 4

OH, THE JOYS OF CHAMPAGNE ON A THURSDAY

April 26, 1810

"We'll be back by midnight," Louisa was saying to Olivia just as Eloisa waltzed into the parlor, the skirts of her white ball gown billowing around her legs. A seamstress in Petworth had finished the muslin and tulle gown earlier that day, apologizing for her lateness when Eloisa arrived for her last fitting. Apparently, every eighteen-year-old girl in Sussex was planning to attend the ball in Crawley.

And all those older than eighteen, as well.

"Midnight?" Eloisa repeated in disbelief, her dancing coming to a complete stop. "Don't you mean two o'clock. Or three?" she whined, thinking that to get home at midnight meant they would have to take their leave of the ball by eleven.

"We'll be home at one-thirty. Maybe later," her father stated from where he stood in the threshold of the Waterford parlor. "I intend to enjoy the supper at midnight."

All three Waterford women turned their gazes onto Harold Waterford, their collective gasp rather loud in the suddenly quiet room. Their gasps weren't in response to his declaration, which was a rather welcome one, but rather to the sight of him dressed in his formal evening clothes. The man might have been in his forties, but dressed in satin breeches, a matching topcoat and silver waistcoat with his silvered hair pulled back into a queue, Harold could have passed for an aristocrat at any ball in Park Lane.

His wife straightened from where she stood next to Olivia. "You look rather dashing this evening," she commented appraisingly.

"And you look more lovely than usual, my sweeting," he replied, openly admiring Louisa's low-cut gown of scarlet tapestry. Although it wasn't of the latest fashion, it suited her figure better than the Grecian gowns the younger ladies were wearing these days.

Olivia could swear she saw her mother blush in response to her father's comment and had to hide her grin behind a hand. When she caught her father's suddenly stern expression, the grin disappeared completely.

"Why aren't *you* dressed, young lady?" he asked, his bushy eyebrows furrowing so they nearly joined together on his forehead. "We're due to leave in a few minutes."

Her eyes widening in surprise, Olivia glanced from her father to her mother and then to Eloisa. "I ... I didn't think I was ... invited," she stammered, straightening in her chair.

Harold rolled his eyes. "I'm not leaving you behind," he countered. "I know what the Blaylock boy is up to, and I'll not give him an opportunity to finally get what he wants."

Giving her mother a look of shock, Olivia took her leave of the parlor and quickly climbed the stairs to her bedchamber. Although she had a white gown, it wasn't nearly as fancy as Eloisa's. Her dance shoes were probably too small. And with only a few minutes, what would she do with her hair?

With the help of Caroline, the abigail she shared with her sister, she managed to get the gown on and fastened while her mother's lady's maid, Fitzgerald, brushed her hair and twisted the mass of mahogany into a simple chignon.

Olivia pulled a purple ribbon from her vanity drawer and was wrapping it around her midriff when she heard her father's call from the bottom of the steps. Before she could respond, ear bobs were looped through the piercings in her ears, and a string of pearls was secured around her neck.

Once she had replaced her slippers with a pair of dance shoes, she stood up and regarded her reflection in the cheval mirror.

"There," Fitzgerald said with a good deal of satisfaction. "Now, off with you before your father ..." Her mouth suddenly clamped shut at the sight of Harold Waterford standing in the open doorway.

Olivia followed Fitzgerald's line of sight to where her father stood. "I'm ready," she said as she gave her father a curtsy.

Harold cocked his head to one side as he took in the sight of his daughter in her simple gown. Perhaps taking Olivia was a mistake, he considered. She was only sixteen. Any young buck would overlook her virginal white gown, see her dark tresses, and assume she was ripe for the plucking.

He would have to keep an eye on her the entire night.

Or maybe he could trust Michael Cunningham to do that for him.

"Yes, I suppose you are," Harold said a bit sadly. After another moment, he turned and descended the stairs, Olivia following behind. "I'll explain the rules in the coach," he said as they joined her mother and Eloisa in the vestibule.

"Rules?" Eloisa repeated as she stared at her sister's gown, apparently satisfied when she realized it wasn't nearly as nicely embellished as the one she wore. Unlike Olivia's smooth hair style dressed with a simple ribbon, her own upswept hair was coiffed with several curls and adorned with tiny white flowers, and she wore an ornate pendant on a gold chain.

"Yes, rules," their father said again as he took his wife's arm and led them to the coach-and-four. "No flirting. No more than two dances with the same boy." He paused and turned to give Eloisa a direct stare. "No kissing in dark corners. Or behind a potted palm."

His oldest daughter gasped, one hand going to her chest.

"I wouldn't dare!" she countered as she stepped up into the coach and took a seat, stunned that her father would think she would. Of course, Mr. Cunningham could kiss her in any dark corner. Or behind a potted palm. Or out in the open, for that matter.

"What are the other rules?" Olivia asked, thinking the first few were obvious. She would probably be spending most of her night sitting with the older ladies or standing in a line of other girls too young to enjoy the dancing. Although she knew a few of the girls from around Crawley, she couldn't claim any of them as friends.

She took her place next to Eloisa in the coach, sitting so her back was in the direction of travel. Her father would expect to take the position, but she thought it better her parents sit side-by-side for the trip. And sitting across from him meant she had an advantageous view should he decide to tease her mother with a wandering finger. Or his whole hand.

Did other couples of their age indulge in such naughty behavior? Doing so in a dark carriage would mean no one else could see.

If only they knew what she had seen!

"You can each have one glass of champagne. Just one," her father replied as he took his place and closed the carriage door. Before Eloisa could protest, he added, "Maybe two, if you behave."

Olivia could feel her sister's smile in the dim light. Eloisa would probably drink far more than two glasses of champagne.

"Sit up straight. You don't want your gown wrinkling before you've even begun dancing," her mother said from the other side of the carriage.

Olivia turned to look at Eloisa, not sure which one of them her mother addressed.

"My back is as straight as a rod, mum," Eloisa answered, her gloved hands folded in her lap.

Olivia straightened but dared not let go her grip on the bench seat for fear she would be sent sprawling into the small space between her and her father. The coach driver was quite adept at hitting every pothole.

The thought of her fingers reminded her she wore no gloves. Her only pair was still in her abigail's possession. The poor girl was quite mortified when she took the wrinkled fabric gloves from Olivia the day before. The day she'd been saved by Michael Cunningham.

"Olivia, dear, do put on these, won't you?" Louisa spoke as she held out a pair of white kid gloves in her youngest daughter's direction.

Surprised her mother would have an extra pair of short gloves, Olivia reached for them and slid one finger along their smooth surface. "But, aren't you going to wear them?" she asked, looking up to find her mother regarding her with a smile. And sporting two gloved hands.

"I keep an extra pair in my reticule, of course," Louisa replied with a nod. Her statement was followed by a hastily swallowed gasp and a quick jerk of one leg, hinting that her husband was already being mischievous.

"Thank you," Olivia replied, wriggling her hand into one of the gloves. If she was a wallflower at tonight's ball, then at least she'd be an elegant wallflower.

*A*s Michael expected, it was nearly eight when he and his mother climbed into the Cunningham coach-and-four for the trip to Crawley. Despite the fair weather, the ball was not a crush. He hoped their hostess wouldn't be too disappointed as he escorted his mother up the stairs to the ballroom entrance. The lack of a crowd meant a quieter ballroom in which to converse and more room for dancing.

As he glanced around the room, looking for familiar faces, he remembered Olivia wouldn't be in attendance. A sudden melancholy settled over him at the thought. Not wanting his mood to affect his mother, he excused himself and returned to the vestibule to wait for his new acquaintances to arrive.

"Will we be announced?" Eloisa asked as she gave up her shawl to a footman just inside the vestibule of the Fitzsimmons' manor house. She glanced about, hoping they weren't earlier than most of the guests.

"No, dear." Her mother sighed from where she stood with her father. "We're not in London. And we're not at a *ton* ball," she added as she allowed Harold to remove her wrap and give it to a waiting footman.

Disappointed, Eloisa glanced around, hoping she would recognize someone. "What about dance cards?" she asked, hoping her come-out would include the opportunity for young men to sign their names next to the dances they wished to claim.

"No, thank the gods," her father replied as he held out his arm to her. "Come along. The orchestra is nearly done warming up," he stated.

Eloisa put her arm on his and straightened so she was as tall as she could be. Placing a hand on his other arm, Louisa fell into step as they made their way up the stairs to the ballroom.

Following behind, her eyes darting about in an attempt to take in all of her surroundings at once, Olivia marveled at the decor. So taken was she with calculating just how many candles sat in the chandeliers mounted in the fixture above the stairs, she barely noticed her arm lifting onto the sleeve of a black satin topcoat.

"May I?" Michael Cunningham whispered from directly to her right.

Olivia smiled, sure her face was blooming with color. "Since you're not breaking any of father's rules, then by all means," she whispered back, stealing only a quick glance in his direction. Given the level of noise in the vestibule and main hall, their whispers went unheard by any of the people around them, including her parents.

"From your comment yesterday, I thought you wouldn't be in attendance," Michael whispered back, his head leaning toward hers so he could be heard.

Olivia ducked her head. "Until an hour ago, I didn't know I was," she responded, finally turning so she could look at his profile. Her stomach did a little flip, and she found herself having to stifle the gasp she nearly let out. Michael Cunningham was a handsome man when dressed in his everyday attire. When dressed in black satin breeches, black satin topcoat and a red waistcoat, he was quite stunning. She barely noticed the ruby stick pin winking in the knot of his white cravat.

"You expect me to believe you were able to get dressed, travel from Shipley, and look as if you spent all day preparing for this ball in only an hour's time?" he asked *sotto voce*.

Olivia smiled as she kept her attention straight ahead, anxious for either her mother or sister to deign to turn their heads enough to realize the identity of her escort. "Well, it did take two maids. And four horses," she replied, sliding a glance in his direction.

Michael kept his attention on Olivia for perhaps a moment too long, admiring her simple chignon and elegant gown. And her sense of humor. With her cheeks still pink from blushing, Olivia looked like she was about to get married. The thought had Michael nearly stumbling on the stairs. "Be sure to give them my compliments," he said in a hoarse whisper.

"The maids? Or the horses?" Olivia asked archly.

Michael merely smiled. Lifting her hand from his arm, he bestowed a kiss on the back of her knuckles. "Do save me a dance," he said before he bowed and stepped away. Before Olivia could respond, Michael quickly made his way back down the steps along one of the railings. The middle of the stairs were too crowded with other guests.

Surprised by his hasty departure, Olivia paused at the top of the stairs and glanced quickly behind her. A sea of feathers and jewelry-adorned heads bobbed about as the other guests made their way up the steps. She scanned the crowd again, convinced she would be able to identify her escort, but Michael's head was lost at sea.

"Olivia dear, don't gawk," Louisa said as she leaned in her daughter's direction.

Smiling, Olivia turned to face her mother. "I won't, mum," she replied with a brilliant smile.

Sure she wouldn't be dancing much that evening, Olivia attempted to take her place among the young matrons and old ladies whose husbands were otherwise engaged in the card room. But a steady stream of young men saw to it she danced nearly every dance before eleven o'clock.

It was during a quadrille that she spotted a smiling Eloisa paired with Michael. Even though Michael appeared bored to tears, the sight of her sister with their recent house guest left her with a sour feeling. He hadn't yet claimed his dance with her, and it was already nearing midnight. Sadness settled in to dampen her mood.

So it was a bit of a surprise when Michael was suddenly at her elbow.

"I thought you were going to save one for me," he whispered, his lips so close to her ear she felt his warm breath wash over her neck. Something inside shivered, the sensation leaving a pleasant tickle in its wake.

"I did. I saved this one for you," she countered with a mischievous grin. The strains of a waltz were just beginning, though. She knew she wasn't allowed to dance a waltz.

However, Michael was apparently unaware of the rule. He suddenly bowed and then took one of her hands in his. His other hand went to her waist, and before she could protest, he had pulled her to the edge of the dance floor and was swirling her about in time to the three-count music.

"But I'm not allowed," she told him with a quick shake of her head, amazed at how easily he had them performing the steps. Her own feet must have been moving, but having never taken a lesson in how to do the waltz, she had no idea how her partner managed to keep them both gliding so smoothly.

"Oh?" Michael replied with a cocked eyebrow. "Hm." He moved them through another complete circle before pulling her off the floor and to the sidelines near a table filled with glasses of champagne. "Are you allowed champagne?" he asked, lifting a glass from the table and offering it to her.

Olivia nodded. "Just one. Two, if I behave," she added with an arched eyebrow. She took a sip and held the bubbling liquid on her tongue, almost closing her eyes as she swallowed.

Michael watched Olivia as she took her first sip and contemplated her words. "Youa flirt better than your sister," he stated before taking a long draught of his own glass.

Blinking in surprise, Olivia had to pull her glass away from her lips just as she was about to take another sip. "I wasn't aware I was," she replied, her rounded eyes coming up to meet his.

Michael regarded her for a second too long. "Which is why you're so much better at it than your sister," he replied with a grin. His attention was suddenly drawn to something — or someone—behind her. "My apologies," he said suddenly. "I must take my leave of you." Before she could ask if something was amiss, Michael had bowed and was moving quickly in the direction of the card room.

Glancing behind her, Olivia caught a glimpse of her sister making her way through the crowd in her direction.

"Where is he?" Eloisa asked as she reached Olivia, her breaths coming in short gasps, as if she'd been running.

Olivia blinked. "He, who?" she replied before taking another sip of her champagne. The stuff was rather good, and she was sure her knees were buzzing. She thought if she had another, she would no longer care how tightly her dancing slippers pinched her feet.

"Mr. Cunningham!" Eloisa responded with annoyance. "I was hoping I could claim my second dance with him."

Shrugging, Olivia regarded her sister before surveying the room. "Well, he was around here a few moments ago," she offered before giving her sister another shrug. "But I know if I were him, I'd be in the card room," she said as she placed her empty champagne glass on a footman's tray. "I'm off to stand with a potted palm," she added before surreptitiously taking another glass of champagne from the table.

A sense of dread settled over Harold Waterford as he observed Michael Cunningham bow to his younger daughter and then move quickly toward the card room. He was watching when the young man approached Olivia, apparently with a request to dance, despite the fact that it was the supper dance and was almost certainly a waltz.

Did the viscount's son deliberately flout the rules? Or was he unaware of how inappropriate it was for a sixteen-year-old to be dancing the waltz? At least their turn on the dance floor went largely unnoticed, and was quite brief. But Harold was sure he'd seen something between the two, some hint that Michael might not have his daughter's best interests at heart or that Olivia was a willing participant in what could have been a scandalous dance.

Well, he would have to speak to his new business partner. Not scold him, exactly. But warn him off a bit.

Trouble was, he rather liked the idea of his youngest daughter with the second son of Mark Cunningham. The viscount was well regarded in Horsham, as well as in Parliament. His wife, an elegant woman, would gladly claim their only daughter was a duchess, but only if she were asked. And she would only acknowledge her oldest son if she was in the same room with him. A rake and a poor gambler, Marcus Cunningham would drain the family accounts when or if he ever inherited the viscountcy.

Michael Cunningham, on the other hand, was a bit of a conundrum. Unlike any other son of a peer, he had apparently decided he had to work to earn a living, convinced his father's viscountcy would be left bankrupt by his older brother.

He seemed to genuinely care about Shipley's lack of jobs, knowing on the one hand it was due to the mechanization that made farming more efficient, but thinking on the other that mechanization would require even more laborers to see to the larger harvest.

He was never mentioned in the scandal rags, and the only disparaging comment Harold had ever heard was by someone bemoaning the fact that Michael wasn't seen in the company of Faith Seward. The daughter of an earl, Faith had set her sights on Michael during her first Season—just last year—and seemed willing to wait for him.

The girl would have to wait a long time, Harold considered.

Harold glanced around the room again, hoping he would find Viscount Cunningham in attendance. When he spotted Mark's viscountess instead, he gave her a nod and was glad to see her move through the crowd toward him.

"Good evening, Lady Cunningham," he said as he lifted her gloved hand and brushed his lips over the back of it.

"Oh, Harold, do call me 'Violet,'" she replied with a broad grin, curtsying to his bow. "I am quite sure you were looking for my husband, but he's already in London for the Season," she offered, opening her fan with a twist of her wrist.

Harold gave her a nod of agreement. "I was, my lady, but you're far prettier. And easier to ply for information," he teased as he held out his arm.

Violet regarded his arm and placed her own on top of it, wondering at Harold's comment. They began walking toward the edge of the room and then turned to follow the walls. "And what information might that be?" she asked. Violet noticed the Waterford girls standing across the room, their manner with one another suggesting they were engaged in an intense conversation.

"It's about your son," Harold stated, one of his eyebrows arcing up a bit.

"Oh, faith, what has Marcus gone and done now?" she asked in alarm. Last she knew, her oldest son was in London, haunting every gaming hell until his monthly allowance was spent.

Harold shook his head. "Not that son," he answered with a grin.

Violet smiled. "Michael, then. What has he gone and done?" She put the fan to use then, beating it through the air in quick flicks of her wrist.

"Well, besides becoming my business partner, nothing. Yet," Harold answered with a grin.

Glancing up at her escort, Violet had to suppress a gasp. "Business partner?" she repeated, stunned by his words. Michael had mentioned something the day before, but she hadn't realized the scope of his involvement. "I ... I had no idea," she murmured, mostly to herself.

"He's got a mind for it, my lady," Harold stated with a nod. "We hosted him at Waterford Park for a couple of days while he and I went over the details. Sir Richard recommended him to me, you see," he explained, noting how the viscountess gave him a quick glance before returning her gaze to the crowd. "I think we'll all profit from our iron smelting venture in Shipley," he added, slowing his steps so they eventually stopped near an empty alcove.

"Oh," Violet replied with a quick nod. "I suppose I am ... happy to hear it, given the situation there," she said with a bit of uncertainty. The economy of Shipley had long been in decline. More of the agricultural work was being done by machines, and jobs were scarce in the small Sussex community. Many of the younger men were moving to London for employment.

"Has your son ...?" Harold paused, not quite sure how to broach the subject of Michael's intentions with respect to any biddable young women. "Spoken of marriage?" he finally managed to get out, surprised the question would be so difficult to ask.

Giving Harold a sad grin, Violet angled her head to one side. "If he has, I was not in the room at the time," she replied coyly. "He is only three-and-twenty. And as much as I want another daughter, I do not think he will marry anytime soon."

Harold nodded his understanding. "I appreciate your answering my question," he offered before sending his gaze over the crowd. "I shouldn't want his attentions on anything other than business. At least for a few years."

Violet frowned suddenly. "Oh, I see," she replied, trying hard to keep her voice light despite how his words made her feel. None too happy with the thought that her son might remain a bachelor for several more years, Violet realized she might have to broach the subject of marriage with him later that night. If Harold Waterford thought for one moment that she would agree to his suggestion that Michael remain unattached, then he was mistaken. "Forgive me, Harold, but I do believe it's almost time for supper. If you'll excuse me?" she asked as she stepped back.

"Of course, my lady," Harold replied, bowing to her curtsy.

Harold watched as the viscountess made her way toward the ladies' salon, thinking he might have offended her with his suggestion that Michael should be remain unattached during their business dealings. Reminded of the young man's behavior with his daughter, he headed in her direction.

*M*oving through the crowd to the continuing strains of the waltz, Olivia was nearly to the palm plant when her father suddenly stepped in front of her.

"I take it you're behaving?" he asked as he slipped his arm under hers, forcing her to change the direction of her stroll. They continued walking, apparently in an attempt to circumnavigate the room.

"I am," Olivia replied with a straight face. "Are you?" she countered, her sudden grin causing a dimple to appear in her cheek. "I saw you with a woman on your arm," she accused in a delighted whisper. "And she wasn't your wife."

Harold Waterford regarded his daughter with amusement. "Your mother is not complaining," he answered with a cocked eyebrow. Despite his having combed the dark, bushy brows, one always seemed a bit out of control, giving the man the means to look sinister if he so desired.

Despite her attempt to maintain a straight face, Olivia giggled. "I should hope not," she said *sotto voce*.

The glass of champagne was lifted from her hand. "And that will be quite enough bubbles for you, young lady," he said as he downed the rest of the glass in one gulp. The glass seemed to disappear from his grasp as he took one of her hands in his and placed his other at her waist. Much like she had with Michael, Olivia found herself dancing the waltz, although she had to concentrate a bit more. Her father wasn't nearly as strong a lead as Michael had been.

"I'm sure it was you who said I was not allowed to dance the waltz," she said, finding it hard to keep a straight face.

"Did I, now?" Harold replied, glancing to his right to be sure their path was clear. "I suppose you're going to deny it was you doing just that with Mr. Cunningham only moments ago?"

Olivia considered how to answer. "Well, it was me, but once I informed Mr. Cunningham that I wasn't allowed to dance the waltz, he stopped dancing with me," she explained, failing to suppress a smile.

Oh, the joys of champagne!

"By the way, I'm not allowed to dance the waltz," she added, allowing a brilliant grin to appear.

Harold had to work hard to hide his amusement. "Livvy, my darling, you be careful," he said in a much more serious tone. "He's a young man. He's not yet interested in marriage, and probably won't be for several years. Which means that whatever he might do with you behind a potted palm would be your ruination."

Ruination?

Sobering quickly, Olivia nearly stumbled upon hearing her father's words. She managed to recover by doing a double-step to keep up, but her expression was more serious than it had been the day before in the yard of the inn.

The music ended, leaving the two of them right back

near the potted palm. Olivia glanced in its direction. "What is it you think he might have done?" she asked in alarm. "Especially when he was no where near this palm. He went to the card room."

Nothing in Michael's demeanor had suggested he had anything untoward in mind when he escorted her off the dance floor. Or when he offered her another glass of champagne. Was the man really a rake? Was it his intention to ... to *ruin* her? Olivia wasn't even quite sure what that meant, but from how her father had said the word, it couldn't be good. And it had to be worse than Eli Blaylock kissing her.

Embarrassed at her question, Harold put her arm on his and led her to the palm. "I ... I don't know exactly. Except he looked as if he wanted to ... to *kiss* you," he stammered, his face taking on a hint of scarlet.

Surprise showed plainly on Olivia's face. "Really?" she replied, perhaps with not enough alarm. With a bit too much delight, in fact.

"Olivia!" her father admonished her. "You can allow the man to kiss you when you're both sure he's about to ask for your hand in marriage," he stated firmly.

Olivia regarded her father for a moment. "I understand," she replied finally. After a moment, comprehension dawned on her face. "Did he try the same thing with Eloisa?" she asked suddenly.

Her father seemed to take a step back. "Not that I know of," he replied with a shake of his head. "In fact, I rather doubt he would. He's not ..." Harold stopped then, realizing what he was telling his sixteen-year-old daughter. "Just ... be mindful," he finished and then patted the back of her gloved hand. "And it's time for supper," he added, leading them away from the potted palm. "With all this dancing, I find I am famished."

Olivia allowed her father to escort her to the supper room, all the while pondering just what Michael Cunningham might have had in mind when he escorted her off the dance floor. And no matter what she imagined, she found she couldn't be fearful of him.

Quite the opposite, in fact.

For if she was pressed to say how she felt about their recent house guest, Olivia would have to admit she had a crush on the man.

Instead of feeling mortified by her admission, Olivia allowed a grin. *Oh, the joys of champagne!*

CHAPTER 5

A PROMISE IS MADE ON A FRIDAY

One o'clock in the morning, April 27, 1810
"Now, you really must tell me what you think of Faith Seward," his mother was insisting as she snapped shut her fan and regarded her son. She and Michael had just walked up to the coach-and-four and were about to get in for the trip to Iron Creek.

Michael regarded his mother with a rather stunned expression. She usually waited until they were actually *in* the coach before asking about the biddable ladies of the *ton* he might be considering for matrimony. And Faith Seward wasn't even in attendance at the ball they were just now leaving. She was probably still in Bath, or maybe in London for the Season.

Why would his mother bring up Faith?

"She's quite pretty, don't you agree? And her father is an *earl*," Violet said with a good deal of satisfaction. She didn't add that the girl was barely out of the schoolroom and his best friend's youngest sister. And *her* best friend's daughter. "I'm not so sure about the Waterford girl, though," she went on, not giving her son an opportunity to give his answer about Faith Seward. "She seemed—"

"Which one?" Michael interrupted, wondering if his mother had seen him dancing with Olivia. If so, he had every intention of letting her know Olivia had done the right thing in informing him she wasn't allowed to waltz. But the few moments he had spent with the girl simply reinforced his initial impressions of her. She was a delight to be around.

Violet raised an eyebrow before stepping up into the coach. "There's more than one?"

Michael held his breath for a moment, enough time to thank the stars she hadn't seen him dancing with Olivia. His mother had spent a good deal of the night in the card room.

"Well, only one out in Society," he amended.

Spreading her skirts over the seat, Violet settled back into the squabs. "That one, then. She seemed ..." Her voice trailed off, as if she was having a hard time describing Eloisa Waterford.

"Desperate?" Michael offered, thinking it was as good a word as any to describe Eloisa's behavior that evening.

"She is a pretty girl," Violet acknowledged, although the tone of her voice suggested she agreed with Michael's assessment. "But she's the daughter of a man engaged in trade, is she not?" She fluttered her fan.

Michael resisted the temptation to explain that he, too, was now engaged in trade with that very man, although in a very different business than Waterford's usual ventures. "She is," he agreed.

"So?" Violet said with a good deal of anticipation.

Michael furrowed his brows. He had hoped Violet had forgotten about Faith Seward. Despite his mother's desperate attempts to find a suitable wife for him, Michael had politely rebuffed all the young ladies she'd paraded past him during the past few Seasons in London, saying only that none of them suited him.

At soirées, she would introduce him to a few biddable girls with the hope that one of them would turn his head, intrigue him, or otherwise interest him in the idea of matrimony. But none did.

Truth be told, he really didn't want to get married. At least, not at this point in his life. He wondered why she even bothered, and then made the mistake of asking, "Mother, what does it matter?" with an air of indifference. He took the seat opposite her in the coach. When he heard her gasp of shock, he immediately regretted his comment.

"You are already three-and-twenty!" she declared, her voice rising a bit too much. At her son's widened eyes, she sighed and said quietly, "Even as the second son, you are expected to marry and sire an heir. You *must* for the sake of the viscountcy," she stated firmly, her impatience apparent in her reddened face and suddenly angry eyes. "Your older brother will no doubt end up in debtors' prison before your father meets his maker," she added under her breath.

They rode in silence to Crawley Down, the tension building until they were safely in the library of Iron Creek. Michael did not wish to carry on this particular conversation unless he could clearly see the viscountess.

She was truly concerned, for the viscountcy as well as for him, he realized as he took in the sight of her countenance.

And she was nearly in tears.

"I will marry, Mother," Michael assured her quietly, taking one of her hands in his. "I promise."

Lady Cunningham let out a long sigh of disbelief, as if she was surprised to hear her son make such a promise. "When?" she countered, her mood softening a bit but her hackles still up in response to his earlier insolence.

Michael's eyes narrowed, realizing now that tears were probably not so imminent.

Whatever answer he gave had to appease Violet but give him time to make his way in the world. At the rate she was spending his father's money and his brother was squandering his allowance, Michael wasn't counting on an inheritance when his father did pass away. And this new business venture, despite its lucrative nature, wouldn't pay out for a couple of years.

He took a deep breath and considered how much time he needed, how long it would be before he would have enough blunt to ensure a comfortable life for himself—and a family, as well as the assurance that Shipley and the surrounding area was economically viable. Four years might be enough, but five would ensure a cushion should the situation in Europe change in the next few years.

Michael took another deep breath and let it out. "If not before, then I will be married no later than on the eve of my twenty-eighth birthday," he answered firmly, holding up his broad chin. A forgotten bruise from his bare-knuckle fight with Gentleman Jackson the day before he left London was suddenly quite evident under his jawline. He remembered too late, and Lady Cunningham caught sight of it before he could hide it behind a hand.

Violet made a *tsk* sound and sat down in a Chippendale chair, her gown draping haphazardly over the arms. Michael thought the sound was in response to seeing the yellowing bruise.

"That's almost five years!" Lady Cunningham whispered, her despair apparent in her voice and slumping shoulders.

The bruise obviously didn't matter to her in the least.

"As I said, it might be before, but you must allow me time to build my own fortune, since it is apparent you will spend all of father's before he dies," Michael declared with just a hint of amusement, one gloved hand still holding her hand.

His mother's eyes shot daggers at him. "I assure you, my dear son. He can afford my little indulgences," she retorted defensively, before seeing the gleam in Michael's eyes. Then she sat up straighter, suddenly aware of the nature of her son's comment. "You are teasing me!" Her mouth pressed into a thin line as she tried not to smile in turn.

"And I must ask that I be allowed to marry whomever I wish, even if she is not of the *ton*," Michael added, thinking that to make clear the terms of the deal now would absolve him of having to attend the Marriage Mart in the future.

With a sharp intake of breath, Lady Cunningham pulled her hand from his grasp. "But, she *must* be!" she insisted, her face reddening again.

Michael sighed, knowing he had the perfect response for *that* demand. "May I remind you, Mother, that *you* were not?" he countered quietly, hoping she would simply drop the subject.

Even when he was a child, Michael Cunningham knew his father loved his mother, knew his father had defied his own father by marrying Elizabeth Williams, the daughter of a gentleman engaged in trade. Although it was a lucrative business involving expensive goods imported from the Colonies, it was trade nonetheless. But his mother had quickly learned everything she needed to know to be a viscountess, and before long, she was accepted by the *ton* as if she was one of their own.

"When you marry, Michael, and if she is not a daughter of a peer, I do hope she'll have a rather large dowry to make up for it. And if she is a daughter of the *ton*, I do hope she will help raise your station in life," Lady Cunningham commented quietly.

Michael nodded before he replayed her words in his head. He couldn't help but notice that neither scenario included another possibility.

What about marrying a woman because he felt *affection* for her? Because she felt affection for him in return? Wasn't that an option? Didn't anyone in the *ton* marry for love these days? Or were all marriages simply unions of convenience? *Or inconvenience?* he thought, as he remembered what had happened to cousin Colette. At least her dowry hadn't been wasted on a rake who would no doubt spend it at gaming hell tables.

Violet paused, but was apparently not finished imparting her wisdom. "And whatever the terms of your marriage agreement," his mother continued, "please, honor your vows and quit your mistresses," she pleaded, tears threatening to escape the corners of her eyes.

Michael's own eyes widened. "What mistresses?" he asked in surprise. How might she might be left with the impression he could afford such an indulgence? What man besides the most well-off aristocrat could afford more than one mistress?

Having a mistress meant having the blunt to cover the rent for a townhouse in Mayfair, not to mention pin money and modistes and tickets for the theatre. And jewelry! Just last week, he had overheard an earl complaining about his monthly bill at Rundell and Bridge and the amount of time he was spending making trips to Ludgate Hill.

"I have no mistress, Mother. Nor do I expect I shall ever be able to afford such an expense," he stated.

Allowing an expression of surprise, Violet said, "Oh. Then your brother must be the Cunningham who is employing one."

Not the least bit surprised his brother would have a mistress, Michael simply rolled his eyes.

And then he remembered his promise. *Five years. I have five years.*

CHAPTER 6

BIRTHDAY BLUES ON A SATURDAY TWO YEARS LATER

March 13, 1812

"Today is my birthday," Edward Seward announced happily, dropping himself into a chair next to the fireplace.

Michael Cunningham turned from the sideboard where he was pouring himself a glass of brandy and regarded his best friend questioningly. He and Sir Richard had just returned from another trip to Sussex, rather satisfied with how their joint business ventures were faring.

In just two years, they were seeing profits from their first iron smelting business, and twelve men from Shipley and West Grinstead were gainfully employed. Given their success, Harold Waterford had agreed to underwrite another venture, this one based on the coal industry in Somerset.

"Again? Didn't you just celebrate one of those a few months ago?" Michael asked, a frown forming on his face as he made his way to the chair across from Edward's. He let out a heavy sigh as he sank into the well-worn cushions. "At the rate you have birthdays, you'll be twice as old as me before I reach forty."

Edward cocked a blond eyebrow, raising his own glass of brandy in salute to Michael. "Not funny, Cunningham," he remarked dryly. "At least I know how to celebrate mine."

Edward had just returned from an evening with Anna Holdwalter. The young woman, a seamstress at a modiste's shop in Oxford Street, had moved to London with her family the year before. Her father, Justin Holdwalter, was now employed by several aristocrats who favored his tailoring skills. Although the man had built a respectable reputation and was much sought after for his fashionable waistcoats and tailored topcoats, he was still just a tailor. Since some in London considered tailors the lowest of the low in class, the daughter of such a man should certainly not have warranted the attention of an earl's son. But she did.

Anna, his childhood friend and confidante, had only grown more beautiful whilst Edward continued his studies at Oxford. Now that they were both in London, he had, earlier that month, set her up in a townhouse in Bruton Street. Edward would have married her the same day and moved in with her, but given his status as the second son of an earl, he knew he would have to wait until his older brother married and sired an heir before he would be free of any obligations with respect to the Eversham earldom.

At least his brother had someone in mind as his future countess. If they would just get married and have some babies, he and Anna could get on with having some of their own. He sighed as he remembered how their time together this afternoon had begun. With soft words, of course. And simple kisses.

But one thing had led to another, and before he'd quite realized it, he had lost control. Perhaps when he'd seen her naked and looking so much like a goddess of temptation, or perhaps when he'd recognized just how ripe and ready her body had been for him, how her spread legs had welcomed his touch and how willing she had been to simply let him pleasure her. To thrust his manhood into her warm, wet folds seemed the only thing he could do at that moment. And he had climaxed before he thought to pull out of her, although thinking back, he realized her body had such a tight hold on him, it would have been impossible to separate himself from her body's undulations.

He'd used the little bit of strength he had left to roll her onto the front of his body, stroking her back and arms as he did so. At the quiet sounds she made with each of his touches, he'd kissed her hair and temple until they both fell asleep.

Several hours had passed before Edward awoke. Embarrassed at having slept so soundly, he'd kissed her thoroughly. "I don't even have a *necklace* for you," Edward had whispered, thinking most women would insist on a bauble from a jeweler after such a satisfying evening. He'd pulled a ring from one of his fingers, a wide gold band featuring a square garnet. It had been a gift from his parents when he completed his time at Oxford, but it was all he had in the way of jewelry.

"Edward, you needn't, really," she'd started to protest, but his lips were suddenly on hers, kissing her until he had to take a breath. "But, thank you," she had whispered, admiring the ring by light of a dim candle.

What had Michael said? Edward had been so lost in thought, he'd lost track of the conversation.

Birthdays. They were discussing birthdays.

"I don't even know *when* your birthday is," Edward stated suddenly, as if he hadn't just been thinking of Anna and how he had spent his afternoon. He took a sip of the expensive brandy. "Ooh, can you taste the cognac?" he breathed, reveling in the warm sensation of the brandy as it slid over his tongue and burned down his throat.

Michael leaned back and allowed his first sip to do its magic. "April twenty-first," he whispered hoarsely. "And I no longer celebrate it." The comment came out tinged with bitterness, something Edward rarely witnessed in his long-time friend.

"Whoa," the taller man said as he leaned forward, placing his brandy glass on the pie crust table to his left. "Whatever happened to make you want to forget your birthday?"

Giving Edward a wary glance, Michael set his glass on the low table between them. "My mother," he finally said, a grimace crossing his face as he made the admission. "And Sir Richard made it worse."

Edward slouched in his chair, a look of amusement appearing on his lean features. As the second son of an earl, Edward Seward enjoyed a rather sedate life in London. Just that month, he had taken up residence in a room on the second floor of Michael's Grosvenor Square townhouse, choosing to sleep there when he wasn't at the townhouse he provided for Anna.

He hadn't intended to move into Michael's home, but having overstayed his welcome at his family's mansion in Cavendish Square and no longer able to tolerate his mother's frequent—that is to say daily—attempts to marry him to some poor daughter— or rather, some *rich* daughter—of the *ton*, Edward had spent the night and hadn't left. Although he paid little toward the upkeep of the Cunningham townhouse, he did see to it the wine cellar was stocked with the very best red wines, and the library decanters had a constant supply of French brandy. Given the current war against France, Michael never asked from where or how his friend managed to acquire the very best liqueurs. He merely enjoyed them as a sort of payment for Edward's presence there.

Edward's eyebrow cocked, giving his aristocratic features a haughty air that suggested he really could one day be the Earl of Eversham. His older brother, Arthur, would have to die before fathering an heir of his own, of course, but it could happen. Being the spare heir gave one a bit of leeway, though, and Edward was quite accustomed to taking advantage of his status. Not having to worry about his reputation meant he could live the life of a rake if he chose. He didn't, however; his one vice was gambling and his favorite form of exercise was a fencing match on a piste.

Well, second favorite, considering how much he had enjoyed the afternoon with Anna.

"What, pray tell, happened?" Edward asked then, sitting up straighter in the chair.

"I promised my mother that I would marry," Michael answered, savoring his latest sip of brandy, "by the time I turn eight-and-twenty."

Edward settled back again, taking another sip of the brandy and swallowing it. "Why ever would you promise your mother you would marry? You're the second son of a viscount, for deuce sake. You don't *have* to marry!"

Michael flinched at his friend's words, the motion causing sudden discomfort near his temple. His earlier bare-knuckle match with Lord Everly had ended in his favor, but Everly's knuckles had to be the sharpest amongst all the men who frequented Gentleman Jackson's salon. The punch the smaller man had landed on the side of his head threatened to leave him with a bruise that might last for four or five days.

He splayed out his broad fingers before him, noting the reddened, scuffed knuckles and the slight bruising around them. Unlike Edward's fingers, which were long and tapered to the perfect fingernails of a man of leisure, Michael's were broad all the way to the end. He was careful to keep them manicured, at least.

Despite not having the body of a typical aristocrat, Michael still understood the importance of keeping up appearances. He wore suits tailored by Weston and boots made by Hoby, employed a valet to keep his cravats perfectly folded, and had a membership at White's.

"Actually, I do have to marry," Michael replied with a sigh. "I never want to see my mother cry," he murmured quietly, taking another sip of brandy.

Edward sat up in his chair. "Lady Cunningham? *Cry?*" he asked, not bothering to hide his astonishment. "Forgive me," he said, shaking his head in disbelief, "but I do not believe your mother is capable of the act."

Michael regarded his friend with a grin. "Oh, yes she is," he countered. with a sigh. "Which is why I had to accept Sir Richard's wager."

Suddenly at attention, Edward stared at his friend. "Wager? *You?*" Other than during an occasional card game, Michael Cunningham never gambled.

Nodding his head, Michael groaned. "Sir Richard bet one hundred pounds that I wouldn't be married by the time I was eight-and-twenty years old." Unless Sir Richard had been told by his mother, Michael couldn't fathom how the man had even learned of the promise he'd made to her. Which meant she was probably telling everyone she knew that he would be marrying in three years' time.

"Can you afford to lose a hundred pounds?" Edward asked, his brows furrowed in concern.

Michael held up a finger, as if to make a point. "I didn't take the bet. At least, at first," he replied rather proudly. "Not until I got him to agree that I would only owe him *one* pound if I *didn't* get married."

Letting out a hearty laugh, Edward slapped one of his knees. "Leave it to you to make sure you profit from getting married," he teased. "And you'll probably get a dowry out of it, too!"

Michael considered that getting married wouldn't be all bad. As long as his wife didn't drain his accounts with frequent trips to the Continent and to New Bond Street modistes.

Like his mother did.

Edward knew that, given Michael's status as a second son, he should have some latitude as to whom he could marry. "And, since you promised, and you said you'll be keeping your promise, just whom do you intend to marry?" he asked. "Faith?" he suggested as he waggled one eyebrow, giving Michael his very best teasing grin.

Faith, Edward's youngest sister, had had a *tendre* for Michael Cunningham since she was still in the school room, and Edward had always figured Michael would somehow end up married to the girl.

"Oh, I know exactly whom I will marry," Michael replied coolly, draining his first glass of brandy after his pronouncement. "And it won't be your sister," he added as he got up to make his way to his bedchamber. He had three years. If she was still available, he had decided he would asked Olivia Waterford to be his wife.

He took a moment to consider how lovely she had appeared when she'd come running down to his coach as his favorite team pulled it into the drive at Waterford Park just a few days ago.

"Welcome, Mr. Cunningham!" she had called out, managing to meet him before her sister was even out of the house. "How was your trip from London?" she asked as she placed her arm on his and walked with him to the steps, only to find Eloisa glaring down at them. But Eloisa's expression softened in an instant, and Michael noted how much alike the two girls appeared.

"Good day, Miss Waterford," he'd said as he removed his hat and gave her a bow.

"And to you, Mr. Cunningham," Eloisa replied, her manner suggesting she no longer wished to flirt with him. Or that she was incensed at Olivia for having beaten her to his coach. He decided it was the latter when Eloisa tried to flirt with him again during dinner.

After his talk with Olivia about coal mining and gas extraction just before the meal—a rather surprising discussion given she was eighteen and had never visited the site— Michael found it easy to ignore Eloisa's overt manner in favor of continuing the conversation. Harold only occasionally chimed in, apparently impressed enough by his daughter's insights and her questions that he allowed her to talk more than she normally would.

While he had enjoyed a cheroot with Harold in the library after dinner, Michael admitted to the older man that he was a bit smitten with the girl. "Any woman who is comfortable speaking of gas extraction at the dinner table is a woman after my own heart," Michael had claimed before taking a sip of port.

Harold had merely given him an arched eyebrow and a

knowing grin. "But will you still feel that way in two or three years?" he asked.

Michael gave the comment a moment of thought. "If I do?" he countered.

Cocking his head to one side, Harold had replied, "If she is willing, she is yours."

Michael shook himself from his reverie to find Edward appeared not to have moved one inch, and his glass held about the same amount of brandy. "When are you going to marry Anna?" Michael asked suddenly, changing the subject.

He knew that discussing marriage to Anna was a sore point with Edward, although he always thought that once Edward reached his majority and Anna reached one-and-twenty, the two would simply head to Gretna Green and elope—the *ton* be damned—because Anna would make a perfect wife for Edward. But as the son of the Earl of Eversham, Edward Seward was all about his responsibility to the earldom and to his family. He wouldn't dare risk his family's disapproval until the line of succession was safely in place. Still, he was surprised to hear the determination in Edward's response.

"Someday I will marry Anna," Edward vowed, his words not the least bit slurred. "Someday, I will."

CHAPTER 7

BUSINESS OVER BREAKFAST
ON A MONDAY

April 12, 1813
"Well, I'll be damned," Harold Waterford said from behind a copy of *The Times* he had spread open and was reading during his breakfast.

Louisa set down the cup of tea she was about to bring to her lips and waited for her husband to explain himself. It was bad enough the man's breakfast was getting cold; now he was cursing in the presence of his younger son, George. "What is it, Mr. Waterford?" she asked.

Before Harold could give an answer, Olivia entered the breakfast parlor. "Morning," she said as she helped herself to a plate and some eggs and a rasher of bacon from the sideboard. "Will Mr. Cunningham be joining us this morning?" she asked, hoping her question didn't make her sound as if she was pining for her father's business partner.

Despite the fact that it had only been a month since his last visit, he was due to arrive for a few days of meetings and some fishing with her father. "I am curious as to his opinion of the news about the coal gas apparatus." She turned around to put her plate on the table, stopping short when she realized that both her mother and father were staring at her. "What is it?" she asked, slowly taking her seat.

"How did you know about Melville's device?" her father

asked, one of his bushy eyebrows cocked up on his forehead. The news of David Melville's patent for an apparatus to make coal gas had just reached England. "I just *now* read about it," he added, waving a hand at the paper.

Olivia craned her neck to see the page her father had indicated. "I read that yesterday, when it first arrived with the post," she answered nonchalantly.

Her father frowned. "Well, why didn't you say anything about it yesterday?" he enquired. "This is very important news."

Olivia was about to remind her father that he was in meetings with Sir Richard at the time, and she didn't think it appropriate to interrupt, when the butler appeared in the doorway. "Mr. Cunningham is pulling into the drive. Should I escort him here, Mr. Waterford?"

Eloisa appeared next to Smithers. "I'll escort him, father," she offered, her normally sullen expression replaced with one of delight at hearing her father's business partner had arrived. Before Harold could tell her to be seated for breakfast, his oldest daughter had disappeared from the doorway.

"By all means," he said with a shake of his head, knowing Eloisa was already out of earshot.

Louisa turned and said to Smithers, "Mr. Cunningham will stay in the guest room at the end of hall. Can you see to his things and offer breakfast?"

"If he's already eaten, you can take him to the study," Harold said before taking up a forkful of eggs. "And offer coffee. He prefers it over tea."

The butler nodded, disappearing in the same direction Eloisa had a moment ago.

"Would you like to tell Mr. Cunningham about the coal gas?" Harold asked, directing his attention to his youngest daughter.

Olivia's face took on a pinkish hue, but her mother spoke before she had a chance to respond. "Really, Mr. Waterford. Do you think it appropriate for Olivia to be discussing ... *gas*

... at the breakfast table? It was bad enough that she spoke of it at the dinner table last month."

George grinned, displaying a distinct lack of front teeth while his father rolled his eyes. "Louisa, really. If it wasn't for coal gas, London wouldn't have outdoor lighting," Harold admonished her. "And we wouldn't be as wealthy as we are."

"I rather suppose he's already read the paper," Olivia offered. "But if you want me to, I will mention it," she agreed, her stomach suddenly filled with flutterbies. She regarded the fried egg on her plate, deciding not to eat it just then. Perhaps after she'd given the news to their guest. "I do wonder if Mr. Melville's device improves upon the one that Mr. Murdoch invented," she said as an afterthought.

Harold regarded her with a bit of surprise. "Reading up on steam engines, are you?" he commented, a hint of amusement evident in the question.

Olivia shrugged. "Steam ships, actually," she admitted.

"Good morning," Michael Cunningham said as he crossed the threshold of the breakfast parlor. "Please do not get up on my account," he said as he patted George on the shoulder. The young boy was already half out of his seat upon seeing their guest enter the room.

"Good morning, Mr. Cunningham," Olivia said with a nod. "Would you like breakfast?" she offered, barely aware that she was taking over her mother's role as hostess.

"I can fill a plate for you," Eloisa offered, having just appeared in the room, apparently on their guest's heels.

Louisa grinned, amused at her daughters' dueling efforts to welcome their guest.

"Thank you, but no," Michael replied, standing behind his usual seat when he was in residence. "Just coffee for me."

Eloisa hurried to the sideboard, pouring a cup of coffee and adding a bit of milk before placing it on the table in front of Michael.

"Thank you, Miss Waterford," he said, waiting until Eloisa had filled her own plate at the sideboard and was seated before he took his own seat.

Harold gave him a nod. "Have you read *The Times* from last ... Wednesday?" he asked, pausing a moment to confirm the date of the paper spread out next to his breakfast plate.

Michael shook his head. "I have not," he answered quickly, thinking he had several days' worth of papers to read. "Not more bad news, I pray?" he responded, a worried expression darkening his face. After what his father had told him at White's the night before, he was prepared for the worst.

Marcus had apparently gambled away his monthly allowance in the first nine days of the month. When the rake had shown up at the house in Mayfair requesting an advance on his allowance, their father had refused to see him. Incensed, Marcus had stormed out of the parlor, hurling their mother's favorite vase against a wall in the vestibule as he took his leave.

Drawn from her rooms at the sound of breaking glass, Violet had hurried to the top of the stairs and watched her oldest son's poor behavior as he tried to kick a footman on his way out. Her lower lip quivering, she slowly descended the stairs. When her husband had emerged from his study, she begged that he forgive Marcus. "It was just a vase," she'd said in off-hand manner, the words at odds with the tears making their way down her cheeks. "Please, forgive him."

Mark Cunningham would have none of it, though. "Your favorite vase, as I recall," he countered, giving her a quick hug before summoning the butler. "Get the constable. I will be pressing charges," he ordered with a grim expression.

Marcus was arrested before he made it to White's. Perhaps a few nights in lock-up would make him regret his poor behavior. Or, perhaps it would make him worse. Michael had left London before his brother was incarcerated.

Aware the others in the room had their attention on him, he gave a quick shake of his head. "It's nothing affecting our business, I assure you. Now, what has *The Times* to say?"

When Harold nodded in Olivia's direction, Olivia took the cue to mean she was to speak. "Over in the States, a Mr.

David Melville was granted a patent on an apparatus he developed to create coal gas," she stated evenly. "Are you familiar with his work, Mr. Cunningham?" Olivia kept her gaze on Michael, well aware that her sister had just rolled her eyes and sighed audibly. Eloisa had no interest in matters of science.

Michael considered Olivia's words, nearly interrupting her with a request to call him "Michael." They had known one another for several years now. She might be his wife some day. If so, they would spend their mornings much like this, sharing news over breakfast, making plans for the rest of the day.

Perhaps they would ride through Hyde Park during the fashionable hour. Have dinner under the crystal chandelier in the dining room at his townhouse. Drink port and claret in the library afterwards. Share a bed for the rest of the night in a room lit by a single candle lamp. There would be no need for coal gas in his bedchamber...

He was suddenly conscious of everyone else in the room staring at him. *Concentrate,* he scolded himself. *David Melville. Coal gas.* He'd been aware of several inventions claiming to make illuminating gas from coal, but none that had been patented. "Is this Mr. Melville the same one who has the patent for the gas light?" he asked, his interest piqued.

Nodding, Olivia added, "And the gasometer."

Leaning back in his chair, Michael regarded Olivia with even more appreciation. *I'm going to marry this girl,* he thought once more. "Indeed," he whispered. He turned his attention to Harold. "We may be able to get what we need for the next venture," he suggested, *sotto voce.* How much more profitable their coal and smelting ventures would be if they could capture coal gas as a by-product! At some point, all of England could be lit by coal gas—indoors and out.

"Great minds think alike, Mr. Cunningham," Harold answered with a smirk. "I believe we have our next venture."

Michael nodded and took up his coffee cup. "I concur,"

he said, grinning. And then holding the cup in Olivia's direction as if he was making a toast, he added, "Well done, my lady."

A pink blush coloring her face, Olivia allowed a demure smile. "Thank you, my lord," she replied as she dipped her head.

*H*aving completed her assignment, Olivia took up her fork and ate her breakfast, her thoughts on what it would be like to impress Michael Cunningham on a daily basis. To be the object of his attention, even for just a few minutes. To find him watching her as she went about her daily routine. To share an evening meal and conversation about everything and nothing. To welcome him into her bedchamber. To allow him to undo the fastenings of her gown and watch as she prepared for bed. To help him unwind his cravat and remove his coats. To watch him as he climbed into bed next to her. To settle herself into his arms with her lips against his for what had to be the very best kisses.

Was a life with the handsome Michael Cunningham even possible? she wondered, her eyes lifting to find his regarding her with what appeared to be fondness. *Of course it was possible*, she considered as she gave him a slight nod and returned her attention to her plate.

A girl could dream, after all.

CHAPTER 8

HAPPY NEWS ON A TUESDAY

M ay 3, 1814

A year later, during the Seward's formal Sunday dinner, Arthur Seward announced he would be marrying Miss Penelope Winstead. The wedding ceremony, to be officiated by a bishop at St. George's, was scheduled for mid-June in the hopes that most of the *ton* would still be in London to attend the event of the Season.

Edward heard the words and smiled. With any luck, Penelope would give birth to a boy within a year. Once he was free of his obligation to the Eversham earldom, Edward would propose to Anna, they would marry, and the two of them could finally live together in the townhouse in Bruton Street as man and wife. As he'd always imagined life with Anna.

"You look rather happy," Michael remarked as he joined his friend in the library at Michael's townhouse. He poured a bit of brandy into a glass and leaned against the sideboard. "But not as happy as I am, I'll wager," he said as he held up his glass.

"I'll take that bet," Edward countered as he joined Michael at the sideboard, pouring himself a generous serving of brandy. "And raise you a hundred," he added as he took a sip.

Surprised at his friend's wager, Michael shook his head. "You know I'm not a betting man," he replied, curious what had his friend so damned happy.

Michael had just returned from Somerset with news that the coal gas extraction device was working. Although it had taken nearly a year to acquire the necessary plans and parts to build it, and another month to get the thing working, it seemed worth the effort. The type of coal mined in Somerset was optimal for the extraction process, and the plant was set up near enough to the shallow mine that transporting the coal to the device hadn't been an issue. His banker, Arthur Huntington III, had been in attendance at the demonstration, as were Sir Richard and Harold Waterford.

And Olivia.

She had ridden in a barouche with her father, her excitement palpable when she greeted Michael and hurried to inspect the device. Her enthusiasm had been infectious, especially when she rushed back to her father's barouche and returned with a bottle of champagne and glasses, insisting a toast was in order.

Michael had complied, of course, acknowledging all those who had contributed to the device's financing, building and operation. And when the spray of champagne had doused his favorite topcoat, he didn't mind a bit. Especially when Olivia's upturned face displayed a pink blush at having been somewhat responsible for the cork popping a moment too soon.

He smiled as he remembered how that blush had deepened after he leaned over and kissed her on the cheek.

Or perhaps it had because Michael winked at her.

Olivia had winked right back, giving him a brilliant smile.

Edward snorted as he took his seat in his favorite chair. "And this from a man who has one of the oldest wagers on the books at White's," he challenged, giving Michael a shake of his head.

Michael regarded his friend with a sideways glance. "I

was rather hoping that damned marriage bet had been forgotten," he allowed. Until Edward had mentioned it that moment, he had forgotten it.

After taking a sip of brandy, Edward shook his head. "Time only helps it take on a life of its own," he countered with a hint of satisfaction.

Alarmed, Michael straightened. "What are you saying?"

Edward shrugged with one shoulder. "Let's just say the bet is no longer just between you and Sir Richard. And the stakes are far greater. In *your* favor, should you marry before your twenty-eighth birthday."

Sighing, Michael closed his eyes. *Damnation!* What if word of the bet got out beyond the members of White's? He might be the laughingstock of the *ton* if the bet made the rounds of the gaming hells. Or not, as long as he kept his promise and married by next April. *I can do this,* he thought as he took another sip of his brandy. *Hell, I have to do this.*

And then he remembered why his bet had become a topic of conversation. "What, pray tell, has *you* so happy?" he asked, glad to put the attention back on his friend. Never mind that he hadn't been able to share the news of the success of the coal gas extraction device.

Smiling broadly, Edward stood up to make his announcement. "Arthur, my less-than-esteemed brother and future Earl of Eversham, has proposed. Lady Penelope said yes. And they're to marry next month."

"And you're probably thinking that once Arthur marries…" Michael began.

"Yes! My brother is getting married. If he gets a child on Penelope right away, and she has a son, then I'll be free to marry Anna next year," Edward explained quickly.

Edward had been so happy after Sunday's dinner, he had gone directly to Anna's townhouse and shared the news with her. Although her reaction hadn't been quite as euphoric as Edward's, she gave him a brilliant smile and kissed him quite thoroughly.

He was looking forward to another one of those greetings when he paid her a call the next day.

"Congratulations," Michael managed after a moment, allowing his friend a gracious smile. "I'm happy for you," he added with a nod and a raised glass. "To you and Anna," he said by way of a toast.

"To Anna," Edward countered as he raised his own glass and finished off his brandy.

CHAPTER 9

A RELATIONSHIP ENDS ON A WEDNESDAY

May 4, 1814

Edward Seward tapped the roof of his coach with the top of his cane and within moments the driver was slowing and then parking the conveyance in Bruton Street.

Edward took a deep breath and departed the vehicle, glancing about as if he was concerned about being seen. Hurrying to the townhouse he had let on Anna's behalf two years ago, he paused when he noticed a child's toy near one of the round bushes that flanked the front door. When he used the door knocker, there was a long wait before a young man opened the door just a crack. Startled, Edward glanced up at the transom to be sure he had the right house number.

"Sir?" the boy at the door said in a voice that confirmed he was much younger than Edward first thought. He was dressed in short pants, but seemed well groomed.

"Good day, my boy. I am looking for Miss Holdwalter," Edward said, a feeling of panic gripping him. Why didn't Anna open the door? And who was this boy?

The lad shook his head. "There's no Anna here, sir," the boy replied. "Used to be, I think, but she moved out so we could move here."

Edward glanced up and down the street, giving half a

thought to asking neighbors if they knew what had happened to her. "Do you know where she moved to?" he asked hopefully. But the boy's shaking head confirmed what he feared.

"How long ago?" Edward wondered, his heart racing. How had she managed to move out so quickly? He had just been here Sunday night to give her the news about his brother.

Then he remembered the house had been let with all its furnishings. Anna had little besides her clothes and a few sundries. If she had to leave in a hurry, she could do so.

She had *done* so.

But, why?

A myriad of thoughts flew through Edward's mind. Had something happened with her position at the modiste's? Had she been let go? Had something happened to her father?

Shrugging, the boy turned his head, as if his name had been called by someone in the house. "I have to eat now," the boy said and moved to shut the door.

"Thank you, my boy. Sorry for having bothered you," Edward said before he placed his beaver atop his head and hurried back to the coach.

Edward was forced to take a deep breath and then another before he opened the coach door. Taking a seat inside, he sat still for several minutes, wondering what might have happened. Why had Anna taken her leave of the house? The lease was about to expire, but he'd had every intention of renewing it.

Or had the landlord asked her to move out?

The landlord! Certainly, the man would know where she had gone. Probably her father's apartment above his shop, Edward realized. The agent was on the way to the tailor's shop, though. He tapped his cane on the ceiling, prompting the driver to open the trap door.

"Yes, my lord?" the man asked as he stared down.

"Oxford Street. Mr. Townsend's office at number thirty," Edward ordered, hoping the agent had a forwarding address for Anna. If he didn't, they would drive on to Mr. Holdwal-

ter's shop. And if Justin didn't know where his daughter was
…

But Edward couldn't think about that. The love of his life
had to be somewhere. She couldn't have gone far. Now that
his brother was about to marry, it wouldn't be long before he
could marry her without reprisals from his father. His mother
would no doubt disown him, but he couldn't think about her
reprisals right now. He had to find Anna.

Townsend had no word on Anna's whereabouts, claiming
she had left the townhouse in impeccable condition and
returned the key to his office the day before. "A rather desir-
able tenant," the portly man commented, giving Edward a
look through a pair of opera glasses that hung from a chain
around his neck. "No complaints from her or her neighbors,"
he commented lightly. "But she left no information as to
where she was headed."

Of course not, Edward thought sadly. And when he
arrived at Justin Holdwalter's shop, he found a team of tailors
cutting and stitching fabric, but no sign of the man whose
name was painted on the shingle above the door.

"He is paying a call on Lord Everly at the earl's request,"
one of the young men explained when Edward asked.

Edward considered this bit of news. He supposed a
tailor would make a house call given how much he could
earn. He knew Lord Everly, an explorer and scientist, had
just returned from an extended trip to somewhere on the
African continent. *He probably needs to refresh his wardrobe,*
Edward assumed. "Is his older daughter in residence?" he
asked, knowing his query would be met with curious
glances.

He wasn't expecting heads to shake.

"She is not here," the oldest man answered. "I do not
believe Mr. Holdwalter could accommodate another of his
children if she did return, though," he said *sotto voce,* leaning
toward Edward confidentially.

Edward frowned. "Why is that?" Anna didn't have *that*
many brothers and sisters.

"One of the daughters has had another set of twins," the tailor whispered, "And the father has fled."

Another set of twins? Which daughter had been breeding? Shaking his head, Edward thanked the man and took his leave of the shop.

He could visit every single modiste in London, he considered for a moment. He might have to if he really wanted to find her.

What has become of my Anna?

When Edward finally returned to Michael's townhouse, Jeffers, the butler, greeted him at the front door. "Good evening, Mr. Seward," he said as he took Edward's coat and hat. "Your correspondence is in the library."

Correspondence!

Edward rushed to the library, turning in a complete circle until he spotted the silver salver littered with a collection of notes. Rifling through each one, he paused when he spotted Anna's elegant script. His heart in his throat, he broke the plain wax seal and unfolded the letter.

My dearest Edward, My heart is heavy as I write what I must. Despite your happiness at your brother's impending nuptials and assurances that we will marry once an heir is born, I have known for some time that you will never be allowed to marry a woman such as me. You are an earl's son. You will always be an earl's son. As such, you are obliged to marry a peer.

I will always love you. You have been my very best friend, and I, yours. As such, I find it is I who must be the one to end our affaire.

Do not despair. I am employed. I have a room. Someday, perhaps we will see one another, when you are with a wife and your children in a park or in a street. I promise I will acknowledge you and hope you will do the same with me. Until then, be well.

Very sincerely yours, Anna.

Edward reread the missive twice before finally taking a

deep breath. *How could she think I would marry someone else?* He left the library as if in a trance. *How could she just ... leave?*

Truth be told, he had known for years that this could happen. But he thought *he* would be the one to have to tell Anna he couldn't marry her. Even if he was forced to marry someone else—a thought that nearly made him sick to his stomach—he never imagined they wouldn't be *together.*

His thoughts turned to his friend Michael. To how a lowly viscount's son had decided long ago that there might not be money for an inheritance, might not be funds for the everyday cost of living, and so had gone into business to make his own way in the world. And the man seemed to have the head for it, spending hours doing research and writing letters and traveling to learn more about whatever it was he did to earn his blunt.

Edward contemplated what he might do if Anna wasn't in his life. His studies at Oxford had been in antiquities, a field he thought he might one day pursue by traveling to countries like Greece and Italy and Egypt. But he couldn't bear the thought of leaving Anna again, and so he had remained in England.

And it wasn't as if he could earn a living studying pottery shards or unearthing ancient relics. In fact, the expeditions were usually quite costly, given laborers had to be paid and provisions had to be secured for treks into territories where supplies weren't readily available. Would his father agree to fund such expeditions?

Fighting back tears, Edward took his greatcoat and hat from Jeffers. He walked the entire distance to Eversham House, hoping to clear his head and, in the process, come up with a plan for finding Anna. And then, once he found her, he'd have to convince her she had to stay in his life.

CHAPTER 10

RESCUING A DAMSEL IN DISTRESS ON A THURSDAY

May 5, 1814

Michael regarded the notes scattered around the silver salver, surprised to find them in such disarray. Jeffers was usually quite fastidious when he left correspondence for him in the library. As he scooped them into a pile, he noticed one half-open. Not bothering to read to whom it was addressed, he noted the feminine script, thinking at first it might be from his sister, Elizabeth.

After he completed the first line, he realized that he was not its intended recipient, and since it was open, knew Edward had already read the missive from Anna.

He hoped Edward hadn't gone off half-cocked and done something stupid. He couldn't help but feel bad for his friend, though. Edward loved Anna. Had nearly his entire life. That she would simply end their relationship with a written note seemed ... lacking, somehow.

Although Michael had never been in love, he thought of how happy Edward had been only a few nights ago, happy because his brother was about to marry, thereby setting the stage for Edward and Anna to marry in the not-so-distant future.

Shaking himself from his reverie, he began opening the

other folded notes, mostly reports from foremen or clerks working at his ventures in Sussex and Somerset. One stood out, though, when he realized it was from his brother. *What the hell?* Opening it, he held it up to the fading light from the room's only west window.

Michael, It's been far too long since we shared a drink. Meet me at Lucy's in Covent Garden tonight at nine. My treat. Marcus.

Taken aback, Michael reread the note. Yes, it had been far too long since he'd seen his brother. They were last together when his mother hosted a family meal at the house in Cavendish Square. That had been at least a year ago. *Why now?* Michael wondered, helping himself to some walnuts from the sideboard. He pulled the bell to summon Jeffers.

"You rang, sir?" Jeffers said from the doorway.

Michael had to suppress a grin at how quickly his butler appeared, as if he had stationed himself just outside the library expecting to be called.

"Can you let Mr. White know I'll need the coach at eight-thirty?" he asked before returning his attention to the note. "And have you heard of an establishment called 'Lucy's'?" he asked.

Jeffers straightened, his hands disappearing behind his back. "Lucy Gibbons' house features ladies of the evening," he said, his eyes no longer making contact with Michael's.

"A brothel?" Michael asked in surprise.

"Aye," Jeffers said with a nod. "One with particularly beautiful women, I think. I don't mean to gossip, but another butler says his employer swears by Lucy's in Covent Garden. Says it's discreet and comfortable and has the very best brandy."

Michael had a fleeting thought that perhaps his brother was really looking for a card game, but the mention of brandy had him thinking otherwise. After a moment of consideration, he decided to join Marcus at the establishment rather than go to White's. But what if his brother's real intention was to share a whore? What then?

A few years ago, he would have acquired a French letter and joined his brother at a brothel. He had no attachments. There were no expectations that he remain faithful to anyone —although Edward had mercilessly teased him about his sister, Faith.

But now? A fleeting thought of Olivia gave him pause. Michael hadn't yet asked for her hand in marriage; he didn't owe her fidelity. But, for some unexplainable reason, he found himself uncomfortable with the idea of bedding someone other than her. Besides, as the son of a viscount, he had no intention of fathering illegitimate children, and he certainly had no fondness for women who wore cosmetics.

Michael decided that he would simply imbibe the excellent brandy but not partake of the other pleasures that might exist at Lucy's. Arriving a few minutes before nine o'clock, he made himself comfortable in a velvet couch in the upscale brothel's parlor.

A scantily clad harlot served him brandy and offered him her services, commenting on how he looked much like a man she had hosted just the night before.

"Oh?" Michael responded, off-handedly.

"Marcus, his name was," she said with a shrug.

Michael gave her his undivided attention.

"Came to meet his brother, but when the fellow didn't show, he met me instead." She said this last with a teasing grin.

Michael stilled himself, realizing that he hadn't read the date on the note from his brother and that he was supposed to have met Marcus the previous night. Well, at least his brother hadn't waited long.

When the girl again offered her bed, Michael politely declined, deciding he would simply finish his drink and take his leave of the place.

He glanced around the busy parlor, understanding why men looking for a tumble might favor Lucy Gibbons' place. The lightskirts were attractive, the furnishings were luxurious, albeit a bit feminine, and the lighting was subdued enough to provide a romantic atmosphere.

Although several happy harlots were wandering about, he couldn't help but notice an unhappy young woman in the far corner. She was nursing a bruised cheek with an ice-filled glass. And when she finally noticed him staring at her and turned in his direction, she recognized him.

And Michael recognized her.

Before she could turn to leave the parlor, Michael was out of the couch and across the room, removing his topcoat before he reached her. He quickly wrapped her in it. "Miss Waterford?" he whispered, as he turned her so that he could see her more clearly, hoping he had mistaken her identity.

"Mr. Cunningham," Eloisa replied quietly, her shoulders sagging under his coat. Even in the dim light, Michael could see her bloodshot eyes and tear-stained cheeks.

What the hell was she doing here?

He had several questions for her, but at that moment, Michael's immediate concern was how he was going to get her out of there before she was seen by anyone. "Lucy!" he called out, turning to look for the proprietor. Several girls gasped at the loud voice that carried over the din of the busy brothel. He motioned to a brunette. "Get my coat, please," he ordered, tossing a coin in the harlot's direction.

In a moment, the overweight madam hurried to stand next to Michael, her bright gold satin gown swishing with her movements. "Is she giving you trouble, Mr. Cunning-ham?" Lucy asked, her prim frown reinforcing her obvious displeasure with Eloisa. "She hasn't even been here a *day,* and she's already proving to be quite troublesome," she murmured with a shake of her gray-haired head, her arms crossing over her ample bosom as if to reinforce her opinion.

"No, Madame Gibbons," Michael replied, taken aback. "But it looks like someone gave *her* some," he continued, annoyance in his voice as he waved a finger toward the bruise on Eloisa Waterford's face. "Where did you find her?" he hissed, a flash of anger on his face.

At first indignant, Lucy increased her frown. Realizing she shouldn't displease a man of Michael Cunningham's position, she took a deep breath. "Well, I cannot be sure, but I believe this one came to London with the impression that she had a position as a governess, and, ... well ..."

Impression, like hell.

"*Damn* you!" Michael whispered hoarsely, not wanting to create a scene in front of her girls or their customers. Like so many other young women from the country, Eloisa had obviously been lured to the brothel by false correspondence implying she had a legitimate position in a respectable household. Once these young women were kidnapped by a madame like Lucy, they were trapped into servitude as a prostitute. "How much will it cost me to get her *out* of here?" Michael asked, his fury at Lucy apparent in his eyes as well as in the deep growl in his voice.

The madame's eyes, already wide from his having cursed her, widened even more at the insult. She quickly recovered when she realized he was offering blunt, though. "A guinea will cover what she's cost me," Lucy said in a huff, obviously displeased that she was being held in such contempt by a man who might have become a generous and frequent customer. "I could get more but for that bruise," she added for good measure, her plump hand waving in the direction Eloisa's cheek.

Michael fished a guinea from his coat pocket and thrust it at the madame. She palmed it quickly and tossed her head to one side. "Out with you then," she ordered and turned before Michael could insult her further.

With an arm around Eloisa's shoulders, he grabbed his great coat from the brunette who had fetched it from the coat check. But as he hurried Eloisa out the door and down to his private coach, she seemed to hesitate. "My things," she said between sobs. Even as he guided her out the back door, he could feel her body cringing under his arm.

"Forget them. I'll get you new ones," Michael replied brusquely.

Surprised at his master's sudden appearance, the coach driver hurried to open the door.

But Michael could tell by his shocked expression that he recognized Eloisa from their frequent trips to the Waterford's home. "One of Lucy Gibbons' victims," Michael whispered. "Your complete and utter discretion is *required*, Mr. White," he said with a hint of warning in his voice. Of all his servants, he knew he could at least trust his coachman. He didn't know yet how he would explain Eloisa to the others in the household.

"Of course, Mr. Cunningham. Where... where should I take her?" he asked, his voice kept low despite there being no one else in the alley.

Yes, where? Michael wondered, not having thought this far ahead when he'd seen to Eloisa's removal from the brothel. Sighing loudly, he got into the coach and said, "My town-house, I suppose."

Awkward couldn't begin to describe the situation in which he suddenly found himself. Other than the family house in Mayfair, where his mother and father were probably in residence, he had no other living quarters in London, and he could think of no friend to whom he could take a young woman who, from all appearances, was a harlot.

Especially at this time of the night.

"And your brother, sir? Shall we wait for him?" Mr. White asked, keeping the door ajar just enough to hear his master's reply.

Michael shook his head. "No need, Mr. White. Turns out, Marcus was here last evening," Michael replied.

If he could get Eloisa through the vestibule and up the stairs without Jeffers or another servant seeing them, he would put her in the blue bedchamber. There she could find a gown and slippers... but he was getting ahead of himself.

She needed a bath. She needed a good night's rest. She needed a lady's maid.

He'd have to pass her off as a visiting daughter of a friend. *Which is what she is,* he considered. But no woman in her right mind would travel to London without a chaperone —a maid, at least—and a valise. Eloisa had neither.

Sitting directly across from her, he tried to determine in the dim light if she was more hurt than she appeared. His coat remained clutched tightly around her with one hand while the other pressed against the side of her face. "Who hit you?" he whispered, hoping she would know so that he might practice his pugilistic moves on the man.

She shook her head. "Some baron, I believe. I do not know his name," Eloisa murmured, sniffing. "I was trying to get away. I ... he ... he *ruined* me," she sobbed, her tears flowing freely, smudging the black kohl beneath her eyes so that she looked as if she hadn't had any sleep in several days.

Michael didn't mention that she would have been ruined even if she hadn't been touched by a man. Just being *in* the brothel had done that quite effectively. He held out his handkerchief. She finally reached over and took it. "How long have you been in London?" he asked.

Wiping her unbruised cheek with the cloth, she sniffled again. "I only arrived this morning. On the postal coach," she whispered, a sob interrupting her statement.

This morning? She looks as if she had been here for days, Michael thought in dismay.

"*There* is no position ... is there?" she asked sadly, her tears finally subsiding. She had finally made it to London, sure she would have a respectable position and the opportunity to meet a man of means, and instead she was *ruined. Would life with Angus MacFadyen really have been that bad?* she wondered. For the barkeep at the Ship had been the one man she knew felt affection for her. And the one man she had allowed to kiss her all those years ago.

"No," Michael replied simply, his head shaking from side to side to reinforce his answer. "Tell me... tell me *exactly* what brought you to London," he insisted, his voice soft despite the simmering anger he felt deep in his gut.

This was his business partner's daughter!

Eloisa gave a shrug before she finally answered him. "Last week, I saw a printed notice for governesses and servants for London homes. It was in the window at the mercantile in Shipley," she explained before taking a deep breath. "It was all very professional-looking. It was a *printed* notice— not written by hand. I didn't want anyone else to see it—I have been desperate to find a position in London– so I took it out of the window. When I got home, I immediately wrote to the woman in the notice—"

"Mrs. Gibbons?" Michael interrupted, wondering if the madame actually used her name in the sign or if the notice was part of a larger sceme to get young people into the city.

"Mrs. Gibbons, yes," Eloisa said with a nod. "From the way the notice was written, I thought her to have an agency that placed governesses in the homes of the well-to-do," she continued. "I received a note back a few days ago saying she might be interested. She asked if I could come to London for an interview... and to provide a character." At this, Eloisa began crying softly. "So, I did."

Feeling a profound sense of loss on the girl's behalf, Michael considered her options.

What was she? Two-and-twenty years of age? Not exactly on the shelf, but there could be no hope of an advantageous marriage for her at this point. She was, by all consideration, a ruined woman. As such, she would have to return to her father's home or see to her own livelihood. "There will be another postal coach back to the Horsham District in a few days—"

"No!" she interrupted, shaking her head from side to

side. "I cannot go back there," she claimed, the haunted look in her eyes made more so by the smudged kohl.

Astounded by her comment, Michael sat back and regarded the young woman. "Returning to your home would certainly be safer—"

"I'll go mad, Mr. Cunningham," she countered. "There is nothing for me in Shipley. And I do not wish to be married to a barkeep. Or a pig farmer."

Michael regarded her quizzically. If she didn't go back home, she'd have to earn a living in London. What else could she do?

He leaned forward in the coach. "Have you ever worked in service?" he asked, thinking he could arrange for her to be hired in a friend's home, perhaps as a scullery maid or a chaperone.

Eloisa shook her head. "My father has always employed servants, so I have never..." She paused as she realized why he asked. Positions as a servant or a lady's maid or a laundress were possibilities, but she had never so much as watched how the servants in their household had done their jobs. She came from a middle-class household. A rather well-to-do house-hold, in fact. She didn't know the first thing about working in service. "No," she finally answered.

Michael nodded his understanding just as the coach pulled into the alley behind his townhouse. Mr. White seemed intent on helping him keep his passenger hidden from the eyes of gossips. "We'll talk more in the morning. Everything seems better by the light of day, after all," he added, sounding as if he was trying to convince himself more than his passenger.

"Thank you," he heard her say, her voice clear and her tears gone. "I owe you so much, Mr. Cunningham," she added before sniffling again. "I will do anything you ask. Anything you tell me to."

The implication of her words weren't lost on him. She might have come from the country, but she understood her predicament just as clearly as he did.

Once Michael had her out of the coach, through the garden, and up the back steps of the townhouse, he took a quick look around before hurrying her up the servants' staircase. He suddenly remembered the time he had saved another young lady from ruination. *Olivia!* Were no girls safe from the rakes of the world?

When they reached the second floor, Michael left her on the stairs and called out his greetings to the footman who manned the hall. "If there are still some servants about, I'd like to take a bath," he stated firmly. "Can you see to it?"

"Of course, my lord," the servant replied, hurrying down the main stairs to see to the preparation of hot water.

Michael used the few moments they would have to get Eloisa into his mother's bedchamber. "See what you can find in the way of a gown and ... under things," he whispered as he grabbed a hairbrush from the dressing table and a night rail and dressing gown from where they hung over a screen.

Sensing his urgency—the footman would probably return to his post in a few moments— Eloisa opened the wardrobe and stared at the vast selection of elegant gowns. She grabbed the first dress that looked like it might fit, a black gown made of bombazine, and a pair of black slippers. She pulled a few items from a dresser drawer and nodded in Michael's direction.

"I'll dismiss the footman for the night," he said as he gave her the items he had collected. "Stay here. I'll come get you once the bath is ready," he whispered.

Then he hurried to his room, relieved that the footman hadn't yet returned to his post.

Soon, cans of steaming water were brought to his room and poured into the copper tub. Once it was half-full, and several flannels were stacked nearby, he dismissed the servants, saying they could retire for the night. Although Edward probably wasn't yet home from White's or wherever he had spent the evening—Michael hadn't seen him for two days—Michael doubted his friend would need any assistance in preparing for bed.

When the house quieted and Michael was sure the servants were in their rooms, he found Eloisa and escorted her to his bath.

"When you're done here, just go back to the blue room and get some sleep," he ordered. "In the morning, we'll see to breakfast and get this all sorted."

Eloisa's eyes widened. "Where will you be?" she whispered.

Michael shrugged, not having given it much thought. He couldn't very well stay in his bedchamber with Eloisa using his bath. But there was another room—a salon of sorts that included a small bed—where he could spend the night. "I'll be in the guest bedchamber," he murmured. "Do you have everything you need?" he asked, seeing her arms clutching bedclothes and other sundry items.

"I think so," she replied, and then swallowed. "Thank you again, Mr. Cunningham."

Michael nodded and left the room, rubbing one side of his face as he made his way to the secret panel in the hall wall. He pushed a lever hidden in the panel molding before grabbing a torch from a nearby sconce. Once inside the small room, he lit a lamp and returned the torch to its holder.

Even in the dim light, the little room made him smile. *Whose idea had it been to hide a salon in the middle of a townhouse,* he wondered? And furnish it with nothing more than a bed, a dressing table, and an upholstered chair? *A room for trysts,* he thought as he undressed and settled into the small bed. *Olivia would look rather lovely in this room,* he thought wistfully. She could read books or do needlework by the light of the only window. Write letters or watch for him from the window when he was returning from his appointments. She could sleep in this room.

How lovely she would look in a thin night rail with the pins pulled out of her mahogany hair and her bare feet showing beneath the bottom ruffle! She would raise herself up on her toes to kiss him. She would wrap her arms around his neck and press the entire front of her soft body against his. She would invite him to spend the night with her in this room, sharing the only bed. And he would make love to her, slowly and passionately, until they were both satiated and sleepy. He would pull her body against his and hold her for the entire night while they slept.

Smiling, Michael was asleep before his imagination could furnish any further delights.

CHAPTER 11

A WIDOW ON A FRIDAY

*M*ay 6, 1814

The following morning, Michael returned to his bedchamber before Jeffers would normally arrive to dress him. He was intent on seeing to it there was no evidence a woman had used his bathing chamber.

He was surprised to find that, not only was there no evidence of a woman having taken a bath, there was no evidence that anyone had even been in the bathing chamber. His bed was still made, although it had been turned down. Messing up the bed linens a bit and even settling into the mattress for a moment to make it look as if he'd slept there, he stood up and stepped back to admire his handiwork. He was shedding his shirt and breeches when Jeffers knocked.

"Come," Michael called out as he pulled on his dressing gown.

"Good morning, sir," Jeffers said as he moved to pick up the clothes Michael had just tossed onto the bed.

"Morning, Jeffers. Did Mr. Seward ever return here last night?" he enquired, not having heard anyone on the second floor after he entered the salon. He moved into the bathing chamber so that Jeffers could give him a shave.

"He did, although I believe it's more appropriate to say that he arrived this morning," he commented lightly. "And just in time for your caller, I might add. I put her in the parlor. One of the maids is seeing to some tea and cakes."

"Caller?" Michael repeated. Who would be calling on him at—? He glanced at the mantle clock over the fireplace. Well, it was a bit after ten, but no one ever called on him.

"Yes, sir," Jeffers said as he placed a bath linen around his master's neck. "A Miss Waterford, I believe she said it was. Poor dear," he muttered as he spread shaving soap over Michael's face.

Attempting to control his alarm at hearing Jeffers' comment, Michael merely raised one eyebrow. "Oh? Why do you say that?"

Jeffers began shaving him, his strokes even and quick. "Someone must have died. She's dressed in a black gown and wearing a black veil. I do hope whoever died is not someone you know well, sir," he added as he completed the shave and began wiping Michael's face with a flannel.

Michael thought fast, realizing that Jeffers apparently knew nothing of their female boarder from the night before. Apparently, she had sneaked out the back door and come around to the front, acting as if she was paying a call in order to gain entrance. He had to give her credit for her ingenuity.

And then another thought struck. The gown she had borrowed from his mother's wardrobe was black. Of course, she would look as if she were in mourning. "Widows' weeds," he murmured.

It was the perfect solution to their problem!

He heard Jeffers' gasp as he stood to get dressed. "She's so young to have already been married and widowed," his valet was saying. "Husband must have been a soldier."

Michael regarded his valet with newfound appreciation. "Indeed," he agreed. "I believe he was in the infantry. An officer," he added embellishing his story. "But this is the first I've heard of his *death*. Her father is my business partner in Shipley. I have been a guest at their house on many occasions," he added, deciding it made her calling on him seem that much more ... legitimate. "I do not wish to keep her waiting," he continued, stepping into a pair of breeches. "What is the protocol should she need a place to stay?" he asked, hoping it would be within propriety's bounds to invite her to reside at the townhouse for a few days, at least until he could arrange a place for her. "Her landlord may not allow her to keep the house if her husband has died. I hear it can take some time before pension monies can be arranged."

Jeffers gave him a look of disappointment. "Sir, this is a household of bachelors. I cannot believe that it would be acceptable for her to stay here," he said as he tied Michael's cravat. "There would be *gossip*." This last was said as if it wasn't already scandalous enough to have two bachelors sharing a terrace. At least most in the *ton* knew that Edward was a friend and not a molly.

"Well, I'll see what can be arranged if the circumstances warrant it," Michael relied as he pulled on a waistcoat. The thought of Eloisa down in the parlor with Edward made him pause in his effort to button the waistcoat. What would they talking about? And how much of the story that he had just developed would fall apart when Edward heard it? "I'll see to our guest now," he said as he took his leave of his valet.

"*A*h, Miss Waterford," Michael announced from the threshold of the parlor. "I apologize for keeping you waiting so long," he said as he bowed.

Eloisa, her face somewhat screened by the veil on the hat she wore, stood up quickly from the Grecian couch on which she was seated and then performed a perfect curtsy. "And my apologies for calling too early, Mr. Cunningham," she responded. "But Mr. Seward has been kind enough to keep me company," she added as she indicated Edward. "He's been regaling me with stories of his youth in Bath." She lowered herself to the couch and resumed drinking from her teacup.

Michael nodded in Edward's direction, not surprised that the man would be talking about his days with Anna. He wondered if Edward had found the woman, and if so, had they made arrangements for their future together? If not, he half-expected to find Edward wearing crumpled clothes and sporting a pair of bloodshot eyes. But his friend was impeccably dressed and appeared as if he'd had a good night's rest.

"Please accept my condolences on the death of your husband," Michael stated, hoping she would realize what he had in mind.

The sound of a startled gasp came from Edward. "Oh, my apologies, my lady," he said as resettled into his favorite chair. "I should have asked as to your health earlier, but our conversation about Anna—"

"Quite all right, really," she interrupted. "You couldn't have known."

Michael took a seat near Eloisa and watched as she poured him a cup of tea. "How long has it been? Three... four weeks since you heard from the British Army?" he asked, hoping she would understand his meaning.

She gave him the cup and saucer. "About that, yes," she agreed.

"Forgive me, Miss Waterford, but I must ask. Has your landlord approached you about the rent?"

"Now, see here, Cunningham..." Edward broke in.

Eloisa held out a staying hand. "It's quite all right. I do so appreciate Mr. Cunningham looking out for me. I am sure my father put him up to it, didn't he?" she hinted, angling her head so she was facing Michael as she made the query.

"Of course," Michael replied with a shrug. "He is... concerned. You were married... what? Two months?" he asked.

Eloisa swallowed, trying to do some quick calculations. "Closer to three, I should think," she said. "But my husband was dispatched to France just as soon as we returned from our wedding trip," she added sadly. "And, in answer to your question, the landlord has stated that he expects the next year's rent to be paid by the end of the month. But I won't have Mr. Smith's pension by then."

Smith. A good choice for a new last name given it was

common—no one would question her. *Rent for a year.* Well, that was common enough for a house in a decent neighborhood. There was a rather small one for let down in Green Street, not too far away. He had considered renting it for Edward, just to get the fellow out from under his roof.

"I can see to it," Michael said with a wave of his hand. "How do you like living in Green Street?" he enquired.

Eloisa's eyes widened before she was able to control her reaction. "Oh, it's a fine neighborhood. Rather... quiet."

"And safe. I shouldn't want you any farther away. Your mother is quite concerned, you see," Michael said, more for Edward's benefit than for Eloisa's. "After your mourning period is over, we'll have to see about arranging an advantageous marriage for you." He turned his attention to Edward. "I'm sure Mr. Seward can help in that regard. Between the two us, we must know at least a dozen or so bachelors who will need to wed in the next year or so," he stated with a meaningful look at his friend.

Including me, he thought ruefully.

Straightening her back, Eloisa nodded. "That's very kind of you, Mr. Cunningham," she replied, obviously pleased at the possibility of marrying a man of means.

Edward stared at Michael and then at Eloisa. "I'm sure we can find someone... when the time comes," he agreed with a nod. "Now, if you'll excuse me, I must be on my way. I have an appointment with my tailor."

Michael and Eloisa stood and watched Edward leave the parlor, both exhaling heavily when they heard the front door close. They regarded one another for a moment. "Do you think he believed all that?" Eloisa asked in a hoarse whisper.

Shaking his head slowly from side to side, Michael sighed. "Not a chance." His hands on his hips, he sighed again. "My butler reminded me it would be inappropriate for you to stay here, so I think it best we see about that house in Green Street."

Eloisa's eyes widened. "You were *serious* about that?" she

asked, her eyes darting from side to side. "I cannot afford rent for a—"

"I'll see to it," Michael assured her, one hand waving as if the rent would be pin money. A year's rent would put a dent into his recent earnings, though. "It's the least I can do, given my meager fortune is mostly due to your father," he explained with a shake of his head. "I'll get my coat."

They spent the afternoon touring the property in Green Street, a furnished townhouse featuring two stories and a small garden. Once Michael had acquired the key from the proprietor, they stopped at an agency to arrange a part-time maid and finished their day at a modiste's shop in Bond Street to pick out a complete wardrobe suitable for the quiet lifestyle of a London widow.

"Are you comfortable with your new identity?" Michael asked as he opened the door to her townhouse. They'd discussed several options whilst they shopped, one having him act as an escort for a war widow who dared not venture out on her own. "Widow of an infantryman killed in France?" he added.

Eloisa gave him a wan smile. "He was an officer," she corrected him. "And I am, actually. It's like I am a whole new person," she declared, taking some of the parcels from him when they threatened to drop from his grasp.

"Near the end of your mourning period, say, eight months or so, we can reintroduce you into Society. After a year, certainly no one will recognize you as having been a prostitute at Lucy Gibbon's brothel—especially when you were only there one day," he reasoned. He pulled several pound notes and a collection of coins from his pocket and laid them on the small dining table. "You'll need some pin money, for food and whatnot," he explained when she seemed startled by the money.

"I cannot accept this, Mr. Cunningham. That is... I

cannot unless you accept something in return," she countered, her face turned up at a defiant angle.

Michael gave her a look of confusion, his head shaking slightly. "You owe me nothing," he stated firmly.

Eloisa stared at him, her eyes wide. "I... I can be your mistress," she offered resolutely. "It's only fair that you be... compensated... for your expenses in all this," she said as she spread her arms wide. "And I am already... *ruined*," she explained, her face blushing scarlet as she said the words.

Michael considered her proposition longer than he should have, aware that he would be bedding the daughter of his business partner—someone he respected—and the sister of the woman he expected to marry one day. *She looks so much like her*, he thought. *I could pretend she is Olivia ...*

But he declined Eloisa's proposal. "I cannot accept your offer," he told her. "I will be your *protector*—nothing more," he stated firmly, a bit relieved he was able to get the words out so they sounded sincere.

On the one hand, he thought Eloisa displayed a hint of relief, as if she had given her words further consideration and realized she had made a mistake in offering herself as his mistress. And, on the other, she seemed almost disappointed, as if she truly *wanted* him as her lover.

"I understand," she finally agreed, her embarrassment at having made the suggestion evident in her reddened cheeks and throat.

"You had best send a letter to your parents," Michael said suddenly. They would be concerned if they didn't hear from her soon. "Tell them... tell them you are employed in this house. That you have met an officer. A friend of your employer. A possible suitor," he went on, making up a plausible story that could result in widowhood.

"I will," she promised.

As Michael took his leave of the townhouse, Eloisa pondered her future. Aware of her lowered station in life and even more aware of how fortunate she was to have Michael as her protector, Eloisa realized she could never expect Michael to ask for her hand in marriage. Given her status as a widow, it would be another year before she could marry, but she could spend the year looking for a suitable husband.

In the meantime, there was a meager household to set up and gowns to put away.

*M*ichael arranged it so that he spent every Tuesday afternoon and evening with Eloisa at her townhouse. Despite his initial misgivings, Michael soon found himself looking forward to their visits. He could pretend she was the woman for whom he truly felt affection. When he took tea with Eloisa, he imagined he was taking tea with Olivia. When he spoke with her, he was imagining Olivia, although their conversations weren't nearly as diverting as they might have been had she really *been* Olivia.

When they dined together, he imagined it was Olivia who sat across from him. When he escorted Eloisa on walks in the park or for shopping in New Bond Street, he was thinking of what it would be like to have Olivia on his arm. There was something *right* about squiring a young woman about town, even if she wasn't the one he was imagining.

As to how Eloisa viewed their visits, Michael could only guess. She seemed eager to please, never making demands nor threatening him if he didn't bring her a bauble or buy her candies and perfume like a mistress might. He never told her about the promise he'd made to his mother. He feared Eloisa might offer herself as a means to make good on his promise, and then he'd have to admit he had someone else in mind to be his wife.

He didn't want to have to tell her he planned to marry her younger sister.

CHAPTER 12

CONFESSIONS ON A
SATURDAY

May 14, 1814
"Your business partner's daughter is quite the thing," Edward was saying as he helped himself to a drink from the sideboard in the library. He had just come from his daily trek to search for Anna, his attention on the modistes in Oxford Street. He was sure she was still in London, but in a town of a million people, she was proving difficult to locate.

Although his birthday had been earlier that month, Edward chose not to celebrate it. At the age of five-and-twenty, he had come into his majority. Funds were suddenly available to him, funds he could use toward an expedition to search for artifacts in Greece or Italy. But without Anna, he had no desire to leave England. No desire to do much of anything except search for her.

Despite his mother's latest ploy to marry him off to one of the Newton daughters, he had deftly avoided attending the ball where she would have made the introductions by sending a note claiming he was ill and would be spending the night at Michael's townhouse with a chamber pot nearby.

· · ·

*L*ooking up from his latest business plan, Michael regarded his friend for a moment. He didn't think Edward had believed any of the tale he and Eloisa had acted out the week before, but he decided to wait until Edward called their bluff before admitting anything. "I suppose," he said nonchalantly. "Not my cup of tea, but I certainly hope she will be for someone else," he added, well aware he had some time to find a suitor for her. At least ten months or more.

Edward took his usual chair. "Let's suppose you tell me what *really* happened," he suggested, challengingly.

Michael let out the breath he'd been holding and set aside his business plan. "I found her at Lucy Gibbons' brothel the night before you met her."

Nearly sputtering with the news his friend had gone to a brothel, Edward straightened. "What?"

"It wasn't like that," Michael said hastily. "I had a note from Marcus asking that I meet him there. Haven't seen the rake in... a long time." He still hadn't. Despite having sent a note apologizing for mistaking the night he was supposed to meet Marcus, he hadn't heard back from his brother. "So, while I waited for him to arrive, I spotted Miss Waterford standing in a corner.

"I couldn't get her out of there fast enough," he went on, his shoulders slumped.

Edward regarded Michael for a moment. "What the hell was she *doing* there?" he demanded.

Settling back into his chair, Michael frowned, realizing Edward thought she was in the brothel of her own choice. "She was the victim of one of madam's schemes to get young country chits into her brothel," he spat out with a good deal of disgust. "By the time I saw Eloisa, she had already been ruined by some baron, but I couldn't just leave her there. She's Waterford's oldest daughter," he whispered hoarsely. "Mrs. Gibbons made some excuse and demanded recompense, so I gave the bitch some blunt and got Eloisa the hell out of there."

Edward stared at Michael, his elbows resting on his knees. "It's even worse than I could have imagined," he murmured. "So, that entire time I was at White's waiting for you to make an appearance, you were dealing with Mrs. Smith?" His brows furrowed in concern. "I didn't know. If you'd told me..." Edward allowed the sentence to trail off, realizing almost immediately that there was nothing he could have done.

He hadn't returned to the townhouse until ten in the morning, but on his way to his bedchamber, Edward had spied the young woman coming out of the room the viscountess used when she was in residence.

From the crack in his doorway, he watched as she had tiptoed to the back staircase. Then, several minutes later, he spied her from his windows as the woman made her way out the back garden, down the alley to the street, and around to the front of the house.

Curious, he'd met her in the parlor shortly after Jeffers answered the door. Despite the black gown and the veil that covered part of her face, he could tell she was sporting a bruised cheek. "We could have made room for her here," he suggested and then noticed Michael's expression.

"A household with two bachelors cannot host an unmarried woman. The scandal would be untenable," Michael explained *sotto voce*. "I did the right thing," he assured his friend. "It probably wasn't right by her sister—I don't see how it can be, so Olivia can never discover the truth—but I only did what was best for Eloisa." He paused, wondering if he should admit the rest.

Michael had been intrigued by Eloisa's offer to be his mistress, tempted to the point of almost accepting because he was... curious. Because he knew he could always pretend she was Olivia, pretend he was spending his Tuesday nights making love to the only woman he had ever wanted.

But the arrangement would have been as unfair to Eloisa

as it was to Olivia. Even if Eloisa felt affection for him, as her incessant flirting suggested, at some point she would realize that Michael didn't feel the same way about her.

"I had to fabricate a story for her father," he stated suddenly, intent on taking his mind off the possibility of bedding Eloisa.

"Oh?" Edward replied, surprised at Michael's comment. "Wait. What are you saying?"

Michael shifted in the chair, thinking he might have to refill his brandy. He'd never made up such a story before, never lied to anyone as he would have to lie to Harold Waterford. "I have created a background story for Eloisa. To make her more... respectable," he admitted finally. "I've even started to believe it myself," he claimed. "And when I'm next in Sussex..." He thought of how long that might be and decided Eloisa would have had time to marry by then. "I plan to assure him I am providing protection for his newly widowed daughter."

Edward allowed his head to lean to one side, probably because he was unable to keep it upright. "Oh, this will be rich," he replied, wondering how his best friend would ever be able to pull off telling a bald-faced lie.

Michael Cunningham was not a liar.

CHAPTER 13

A FIB ON A SUNDAY

*J*une 19, 1814

Michael sat across from his business partner and wondered how to broach the subject of the man's newly "widowed" daughter. He had provided a stack of carefully copied reports to Harold Waterford, knowing the man would read everything. Then he would ask questions, especially if he thought some detail was overlooked.

"I do hope you weren't adversely affected by the recent floods down here," Michael began.

Harold shook his head. "We're far enough away from the river here, but it was hard on those down by the Arun," he admitted. "And it doesn't help that some bastards are fencing off land and selling it so it's not available for pasture," he added gruffly. "Local folk will revolt, mark my words."

Michael knew the man spoke the truth on that score. His father had complained about the very same thing just the night before. But Michael decided it was time he brought up the issue of Eloisa's "dead husband." "There's been an... unfortunate death recently," he finally said, resisting the urge to squirm in his seat.

"Are you referring to Huntington's wife?" Harold countered, looking up from the report he was reading. "Heard it was an awful fever."

Startled by the mention of Arthur Huntington, Michael frowned. "Huntington's wife died?" he asked. Arthur was one of his sparring partners at Gentleman Jackson's Salon. And his banker. "I hadn't heard," he said, shaking his head sadly. "I haven't sparred in a week or more, so I've had no news of Huntington lately," he added.

"He's beside himself with grief. Poor man. Really loved his wife," Harold commented as he returned his attention to the report. He glanced back up, though, when it dawned that Michael had meant a different death. "Who else died? he asked with concern then, sitting forward in his chair.

Michael took a deep breath. "Your daughter's husband. William Smith," he added. Hadn't Eloisa sent the announcement of his death to her parents? He hoped it would have been delivered to the house before he showed up, but given Mrs. Waterford's happy demeanor on his arrival earlier that morning, he realized he had beaten the postal coach.

It was Harold Waterford's turn to frown. "She's not even married a month, and she's already a widow?" he questioned, his eyebrows furrowing into one long, white brow.

Nodding, Michael explained the officer's situation to his business partner, secretly glad that at least Eloisa had done her part in letting her parents know that she had recently wed, and had done so with a marriage license. There wouldn't have been time for a reading of the banns, a wedding and a death on the battlefield given she'd only been in London six weeks. "If her wedding seemed rushed, it was, but only because Lieutenant Smith received orders that didn't give them time to plan a larger wedding."

"Leave it to my daughter to marry a military man!" Harold Waterford declared. He stood up from his desk and began pacing the floor of the study. There was already a well-worn path in the Aubusson carpet near the hearth where he had no doubt paced many times before.

Michael Cunningham gritted his teeth, regretful now of the profession he had chosen for Eloisa's supposedly dead husband. "Infantry officer, actually," Michael clarified, hoping that might help the situation. "Apparently, the man did not know he would be dispatched to the Continent when he proposed marriage, and, well, he died on a battlefield in Belgium shortly after they were wed."

Harold rolled his eyes and made a huffing sound. "That damned girl," he began, but trailed off, finally mumbling, "She'll never come to any good," as his fingers gripped the back of his overlarge desk chair. "Why didn't she just come back here?"

Michael had to fight down the urge to argue with Eloisa's father. After a moment, though, he thought it best he come to her defense. "Sir, your daughter is three-and-twenty. I believe she thought she was doing your family a favor by marrying," he explained calmly, hoping he would not jeopardize his standing with the man by his comment. They had been doing business as partners now for over four years, and their joint ventures were profitable. He hoped on this trip to begin another.

"True enough, I suppose," Harold agreed, taking his seat at his massive desk. "It's just that... well, she knows how disappointed I was when my son went off and joined the military..."

Michael immediately thought of George, the young boy he had only ever seen at the other end of the dining table during meals. Master George couldn't have been more than ten. "George has enlisted?" he asked, not bothering to hide his astonishment. He wondered if the boy would be relegated to playing a drum at the back of the regiment.

Harold snorted as he shook his head. "I was referring to Charles. My oldest. He's... five-and-twenty now, I suppose. I had high hopes for him, but he always wanted to be a military man. Been in the militia for at least as long as we've been partners," he explained. The elder man shrugged. "I am proud of him now, of course, since he's become an officer. Charles *earned* his commission," Harold stated quite firmly. "I didn't buy it for him, although I rather think he expected I might. He's at Brighton and doing quite well," he added wistfully, his eyes taking on a faraway look before he finally refocused them on Michael.

"But back to my eldest daughter. I know I should not be involving you in this, but once the wife finds out, she will insist that I have someone in town look in on Eloisa—to be sure she is safe." His face suddenly screwed up a bit. "What's become of her position as a governess?" the he asked. "Has she returned to it?"

Michael took a deep breath and reviewed in his mind what he and Eloisa had come up with as a story to cover her unfortunate situation. "She has not. The position was already filled by another governess by the time she learned of her husband's demise. Even so, it would not be proper for her... she must honor the mourning period," he said by way of explaining why she had not sought another position in service. "But do not despair," he added as he leaned forward to place a hand on Harold's desk. "As the widow of an officer, she'll be receiving a pension. She will not be a burden to you," he claimed in as calm a voice as possible.

Although Eloisa seemed to accept his self-appointed role as her protector, Michael knew the arrangement could only be temporary. At some point, he would have to find her a respectable husband. In nine or ten months.

About the same time Arthur Huntington would be out of mourning!

Stunned by the thought, he considered if the two might suit. She was certainly younger than Arthur's wife, by ten or fifteen years, but she was similar in appearance. Prettier, actually. Same height ...

But he couldn't think about that possible pairing at the moment; Harold was giving him a look that demanded his full attention.

"That is the least of my concerns," the man replied quietly, his stance finally softening. He shook his head but was apparently satisfied with this last bit of news about his eldest daughter. "I can certainly afford to support her. And Olivia, for that matter," he added, his eyes suddenly narrowing as he watched Michael. "And speaking of Olivia. Just what are your intentions toward her?" he asked rather bluntly, straightening in his chair. "You've shown interest in the past. Are you still...?" He allowed the question to trail off without finishing it.

Michael heard again in his head his own comment that any woman comfortable with speaking about gas extraction was a woman after his own heart. That was two years ago. He also recalled Harold's response.

If she is willing, she is yours.

Truth be told, he found himself more and more attracted to Olivia every time he returned to Shipley.

"Tell me. Is it true you promised your mother you would wed by the time you were eight-and-twenty?" Harold asked. "I apologize, but I was at White's last I was in town," he said, as if that explained how he knew about the promise. "The betting book was getting a good deal of attention."

Michael nodded, annoyed that Harold knew of the entry in the betting book. He would rue the day he and Sir Richard made that wager regarding when he would marry. "I did make such a promise, yes," he admitted, doing his best to keep his face impassive. "And I do intend to keep the promise, of course."

Harold's piercing blue eyes bored into him, and Michael found himself more than a bit uncomfortable. "But I hoped to see Mrs. Smith settled with a new husband... so as to avoid any awkwardness," he stammered, cursing as he tried to make excuses for himself. The reason he hadn't yet asked for Olivia's hand was because he wasn't yet ready to be *getting* married.

Harold sat back in his deep leather chair and regarded Michael, apparently knowing he had surprised the younger man with his insights. "But since Eloisa saw to her own matrimony, she is of no consequence to arrangements regarding her sister's marriage," he asserted lightly.

Michael winced upon hearing Harold's assessment. "Still,

I would be more inclined to ask for Miss Olivia's hand if I knew her elder sister was—"

"As a widow, her sister will not be allowed to marry for some time. Let us make a deal," Harold proposed. "If you truly intend to marry my Olivia, I shall ensure that no other man is allowed to court her. She'll be available for matrimony on the eve of your twenty-eighth birthday."

Trying hard not to gasp or show a reaction that would offend his partner, Michael nodded slowly. "I believe I would be amenable to such an—"

"I realize you are probably expected to marry on par with your rank," Harold interrupted, "But I hope that money—her dowry is quite substantial, I assure you—can serve in place of a title and lands," he said in a voice that was much softer than Michael was used to hearing. "I may not be a member of the aristocracy, but I have done well with our business ventures as well as with some others I have been involved with in the past. My Olivia is dear to me, and I would like very much for you to be her husband."

Michael could not hide his surprise at Harold's comment. "My *rank?*"

Harold Waterford smiled. He *smiled,* an expression that took at least ten years off his age and made him appear as friendly and as approachable as any man Michael had ever known.

"Your father and I knew each other as children, Michael," he confided. "I know what you stand to inherit, or not, because of that damned older brother of yours. I am most impressed that you work for what you have. You're not some rake who is spending his inheritance in gaming hells and brothels like your brother Marcus does."

Michael stared at Harold, not sure how to respond. How did he know that Michael didn't frequent brothels or gamble to excess? He was wondering if Waterford had some spy following him when another thought struck him.

Perhaps Harold Waterford wanted his daughter to be a

viscountess. But that could only happen if both his father and Marcus died before Marcus had an heir.

The elder man noticed his discomfiture and leaned over the desk. "I do not give a flying fig if my daughter becomes a viscountess," he intoned quietly. "I merely wish her to be happy." He sat back in his deep leather chair and regarded Michael, knowing he had surprised the younger man with his disclosures.

Another moment of silence passed between them before Michael finally nodded. "If you truly know my father, then you will know that he is likely to outlive even me," he said in reply, his lips thinning before he continued. "And you will also know that my mother and brother are displaying fine efficiency in depleting my father's accounts," he added with a heavy sigh. "Other than the entailed lands in Horsham, I am not counting on an inheritance. All I have is what we've made on these ventures. And a cottage in Crawley," he explained quickly.

Harold regarded him a little quizzically. "Ah, Iron Creek," he responded with an expression that suggested he was amused by Michael's use of the term "cottage" to describe the large country house. "A self-made man is a far better match for my Olivia, I should think," he added, his eyebrow lifting nearly into his wig's hairline.

Harold had done his due diligence prior to doing business with him, Michael now knew. And his business partner wasn't looking to gain social standing through an advantageous marriage for this daughter.

He doubted Olivia would prefer a husband with a title.

"I accept your offer," Michael replied, holding out his right hand.

Harold Waterford took his hand and shook it once with a good deal of force. "Thank you. I should like very much for you to be part of the family someday. If for some reason it does not happen, I will at least know that I did my best to make it so."

Michael nodded his understanding. "I will do my very

best to make Olivia happy," he said solemnly, a sense of immense relief settling over him.

With his choice of wife sorted and his certainty that Harold Waterford would inform his daughter of their deal, Michael went back to business dealings and put thoughts of marriage in the back of his mind.

Harold, however, kept the news of his deal with Michael a secret from his daughter. And his wife.

CHAPTER 14

SHOPPING FOR A POSITION
ON A MONDAY

February 20, 1815

At nearly one-and-twenty, and with apparently no prospects for marriage, Olivia was determined to find a position as a governess. For the past few years, she had been aware of a number of young men around Shipley who had seemed to show an interest in her. But then, in the past year, those she knew from her youth began to shun her, avoiding her whilst she shopped or took walks in the village.

She often wondered if Eli Blaylock had warned them off with tales of Michael Cunningham's fist. Eli hadn't come near her since that afternoon when she first met the bare-knuckle fighter.

And neither had any other young men.

Those who were new to the area would bow and introduce themselves, some even asking if they might escort her home from shopping trips to town. But soon, they too, would act as if they hadn't made her acquaintance, or they would ignore her completely.

The cut direct had her feeling offended.

Olivia often thought her mahogany hair might be the reason, but she had no freckles to suggest she had the French pox, if indeed, freckles really were a sign of the disease. From her reading, she rather doubted redheads with freckles were *all* afflicted with syphilis.

Perhaps it was her manner of dress. Her gowns were not of the most recent fashion by London standards, but then neither were those of the other girls in the Shipley area. And would boys in Shipley even know the latest fashions? She also doubted they cared one way or the other.

The only gentleman to show an interest in her was Mr. Cunningham, for he would always make time to converse with her when he stayed at Waterford Hall whilst doing business with her father.

Until last year, she had secretly hoped he might ask to court her, but it quickly became evident that he wasn't interested in her in *that* way. If he was, wouldn't he have asked her father for permission to court her? Her father hadn't said anything about Mr. Cunningham's interest—or not— in her.

As the second and youngest daughter, Olivia knew that her older sister should be the center of his attention— Michael Cunningham was certainly the center of Eloisa's during his initial visits—but then Eloisa had left for London the spring before and was already married and widowed!

Olivia was pondering all this and more when she was about to step into a draper's shop in Petworth. A notice in the window caught her eye. Curious, she read the beautifully rendered script on what had to be very fine parchment.

Governess position, Somerset Duchy. Two children. Must have experience or quality education. Send character and qualifications to the Duchess of Somerset.

An address in Wiltshire was printed at the bottom of the parchment.

Staring at the notice for several minutes, Olivia thought about the distance between Wiltshire and Sussex as she stared at the notice. Wiltshire wasn't so very far, she considered, but it wasn't adjacent to Sussex, either.

"Ah, what have we here?" Harold Waterford asked as he

joined Olivia in front of the draper's window. He held a long package under one arm and dangled a small case from the other. Reading the notice over Olivia's left shoulder, he gave his daughter a sideways glance. "The very position you've been searching for," he commented lightly, turning to regard his younger daughter's profile.

Despite the freezing temperatures and occasional snowy conditions, he had allowed Olivia to accompany him on the short trip to Petworth so that he might have someone to talk to whilst on the road.

The entire family had been a bit jumpy with the recent raids by the Shipley Gang, the group of thieves on horseback who had been terrorizing the area. Just the week before, the gang had robbed the Coomber's house, taking all the food in the pantry and a chicken from their coop. Harold had heard reports of missing sheep from the herds to the east and talk that the gang was based out of the Southwater Woods.

He knew they had taken to thievery in order to feed their families. Although his businesses had provided jobs to many in Sussex, there were still hundreds of men who were desperate for work.

Perhaps his attempts to provide positions would prevent his household from being a target for the gang. If they did raid his home, though, Harold intended to protect his family —he kept his hunting gun next to the bed stand. He'd had bolts installed on his exterior doors. Although he knew windows could be broken, the mullions in Waterford Hall would make breaking and entering time-consuming.

There was another reason to keep Olivia close, though. He had thought to tell her about what he expected would happen in the next month or so.

Having confirmed Michael Cunningham's birth date with his father, Harold was sure Michael would be asking for his daughter's hand in marriage during his next visit to Waterford Hall. He would have to; if Michael didn't plan to purchase a marriage license, he would have to propose to

Olivia so there would enough Sundays before his birthday for the banns to be read.

Although it had been over eight months since his discussion with Michael, there had been no further mention of a proposal, no indication that his business partner had even been courting Olivia. He wondered if Cunningham had told Olivia of his plans.

Or did he expect I would tell her?

Perhaps Cunningham changed his mind.

If that was the case, then it was certainly reasonable to allow Olivia to think she could apply for the position. What were the chances she would even be considered for a position so far away? "Maybe you could take the notice from the window?" he suggested quietly.

"I wonder how long it's been here," Olivia responded, turning to enter the shop with her father in tow. He conferred with one of the men behind the counter while Olivia admired the lengths of fabric displayed on the walls. When Olivia pointed to one made of yellow lawn, the other clerk pulled down the display and began measuring her order.

"The notice is yours to take," Harold spoke quietly. "Mr. Hermann says it was put there yesterday by a liveried footman, and he doubts there are any women in Petworth who would be interested in such a post given how far it is to Wiltshire," he murmured. He pulled out his purse and fished for a few coins to pay for the fabric.

Olivia nodded her understanding. "Thank you, sir," she called in Mr. Hermann's direction as she moved to the window and pulled the notice from its perch.

She spent the ride home thinking about how she would word her reply to the advertisement. Her character was already written. As to references, two of her tutors had provided her with glowing reports of her work ethic. She could cite her reading habit...

The thought brought her back to reality.

Reading.

Olivia often wondered if the local boys thought her a bluestocking. Ever since her sixteenth year, anyone who saw her in Shipley usually did so as she looked over the newest books in the local mercantile.

Just the year before that, she might have admitted to staring into the window of the confectioner's shop in the hopes of being given a piece of hard candy. But once she'd learned where books could take her, either in their fictional tales or their supposedly real-life treatises, Olivia had become quite taken with reading.

Remembering that afternoon when Michael Cunningham escorted her from Shipley, Olivia felt her face flush. They'd spoken of her favorite thing to do—to read books. She had half-expected him to tease her about her reading habit, but he never did.

After his lengthy meetings with her father, Mr. Cunningham usually found her with her nose in a book when he emerged from her father's study. Like the local boys, he probably thought her a bluestocking.

She remembered that at one time she had worried he might think her a wanton for reading books published by Minerva Press. But she hastened to assure him that those books belonged to her sister. Hopefully, Mr. Cunningham had taken her word for it.

A frisson shot through her body as she remembered that first afternoon, of how they'd met in the inn's yard, of how he had driven her home in his gig, their conversation so easy they barely noticed the weather or the conveyances that passed by.

And since that day, every time Mr. Cunningham came back to Waterford Hall for meetings with her father, Olivia had felt that same frisson, felt the flutterbies in her stomach, the other myriad sensations his very presence in the same room seemed to incite in her. None of the boys in Shipley affected her that way. Which, given they didn't seem too interested in marrying her, was probably just as well.

She glanced back down at the notice she held clutched in

her gloved hands. Michael Cunningham wasn't going to ask for her hand in marriage, she had decided. Better she see to her own future than to hope for something that wasn't going to happen.

As she read a book in the coach on the way home, Harold regarded his daughter and almost... almost mentioned his conversation with Michael. But if the young man had changed his mind about wanting Olivia as his wife... Harold kept his thoughts to himself and instead turned his attention to the latest newspaper from London

Before she retired to bed that night, Olivia completed her response to the notice and was ready to mail it from Shipley the very next day. Sleep didn't come easily, though. In making the decision to apply for the position, Olivia had also realized something she hadn't given much thought to in the past.

By taking a position as a governess, she might never have an opportunity to marry. *I'll be an old maid,* she thought sadly, as she drifted off to sleep.

A bluestocking old maid.

CHAPTER 15

CONSIDERING PROSPECTS
ON A TUESDAY

Over the course of the nine months following Eloisa's rescue, Michael Cunningham had settled into a regular routine. Every six weeks, he traveled down to Sussex to pay a visit to his parents at Cunningham Park—if they were in residence—and to spend a day or two at Waterford Hall going over business matters with Harold.

Most afternoons were spent pouring over reports from his various business interests. At least four days a week, he spent an hour at Gentleman Jackson's boxing salon, sparring with whomever would take him on, and on those occasions when none were willing or able, Jackson himself would be his opponent.

Most nights were spent at White's, reading *The Times* and enjoying a drink or a few hands of Pontoon or whist.

And every Tuesday afternoon, he took a walk with Eloisa before joining her for dinner at her townhouse.

March 21, 1815

"Have you ever considered that Eloisa might want *you* for a husband?" Edward asked one night as they enjoyed a glass of brandy before bed.

Having just returned from having dinner with Eloisa,

Michael took a deep breath and let it out slowly. "I did. For a while, but…" He paused, thinking back to when he had realized Eloisa no longer wanted him as a husband.

He couldn't explain exactly what had changed to make her stop pining for him, but it had happened. "She changed her mind," he finally murmured. "And I know I should have felt a bit of relief, and I suppose I did, but it's always a blow to a man's ego when a woman suddenly becomes… distant."

Edward nodded, thinking he understood. Had Anna had changed her mind about him? Her father still claimed no knowledge of her whereabouts, but Edward suspected he did so to prevent Edward from finding her.

Then his thoughts turned to his sister. "That happened to Faith," he offered, stifling a yawn.

At the mention of Edward's sister, Michael's head popped up. He knew Lady Faith Seward had pined for him, too, for several years, in fact. And then, suddenly, one day she was betrothed to another.

Michael had never felt such relief in his life.

To know a young woman wanted him as a husband enough to spurn every suitor until she was three-and-twenty and then to suddenly find out she was engaged to another— Michael had actually spent a long night on the town, toasting the impending marriage at White's and even dancing with Edward's sister at the next ball.

"I never knew what she saw in you," Edward commented, rising from the chair and steadying himself before heading toward the sideboard to refill his brandy glass.

Michael smiled, taking no offense at the statement. "I didn't, either," he said with a wave. Edward turned from the sideboard, holding up his glass in a salute. "To young ladies who don't know any better!" he called out.

Michael grinned, the first bit of amusement he'd felt all night. "To ladies changing their minds," he responded, downing the rest of his glass. "And speaking of young ladies, I'm off to Sussex and then to Wiltshire on the morrow," he announced, his grin broadening.

Settling back into his chair, Edward regarded his friend with a grin. "Do tell why," he replied before taking a sip and once again savoring the brandy.

Taking a deep breath, Michael nodded. "It's time for my meeting with Waterford, and I owe my sister a visit. Received a letter from her this morning claiming she has good news. Since I haven't been there in over a year, she's insisting she will only tell me in person," he explained. "I was thinking I'm about to become an uncle again, but..." He shook his head. "There was something *different* about the way she wrote it," he murmured.

Edward regarded his friend with a lopsided grin, his head nearly lolling on his neck. "I suppose she expects *you* to have some good news, too," he managed to get out before his head hit the back of his chair.

Michael stared at his friend for a very long time. "Good news?" he repeated, wondering what Edward could mean. And he was about to ask, but Edward's eyes were closed, and a soft snore emanated from him.

Sighing, Michael reached over and eased the half-filled brandy glass from his friend's hands, placing it on the pie crust table. "Good night, Edward," he whispered, draining his own glass before rising to stretch. "Sleep well."

CHAPTER 16

WONDERINGS ON A WEDNESDAY

March 22, 1815

The next day, Harold Waterford regarded the stack of letters he had just been given. The mail coach, delayed due to a late winter storm, had just pulled into Shipley as he was about to make his way home from the town's only bank.

He instead stopped at the Ship to have an ale while he waited for the driver to unload the coach. Angus MacFadyen, the barkeep, stood at the tap and gave Harold a nod. "I'd give you two pints if ya' brought some warmth with ya'," the man said with a teasing grin.

"And I'd pay for three if you could stop the snow," Harold countered. "Although snowy nights keep the Shipley Gang from raiding our homes," he acknowledged. The more well-to-do citizens of Shipley had grown accustomed to fearing the sound of hoofbeats in the night, for it meant their pantries and their pens were about to be emptied. Most knew at least a few of the Shipley Gang members, who fancied themselves modern-day Robin Hoods, but capturing the thieves with little in the way of local law enforcement was proving difficult.

"I heard the Laker house was broken into a few nights ago," Angus said quietly. "No one was hurt, but the bastards took everything from their root cellar. Mark my words, they will be caught, and they will hang for what they're doing," he vowed.

"Or transported," Harold replied, suggesting he didn't think the thieves would get a life sentence for stealing food. No one had been killed during their raids, after all.

Harold took a long draught and set his glass on the bar top, its surface varnished to a high gloss. "I had news from London a while back. Cunningham said my daughter's husband died in Belgium," he said, with a pretense of nonchalance, though he knew his new might be of special interest to the barkeep. "It's been, oh, I guess nine months since he died," he added, hoping Angus would realize Eloisa's mourning period would be over soon.

"Oh?" Angus replied, trying to appear uninterested. For more time than he could remember, he had been attracted to the Waterford girl, hoping one day she would notice him. He sometimes spent his late nights dreaming of Eloisa, remembering the one time, when he was twenty, and she was sixteen, when she had asked him to kiss her.

He could relive that night over and over as he remembered how he hadn't said a word, but instead had placed a finger along her jawline and lifted her head so that he could place his lips against hers. He had only ever kissed an older widow, but he knew how to kiss. Knew how to position his lips, how to take hold and suckle them so that it would be difficult for a woman to pull away.

For a few minutes, he had been able to hold the kiss with Eloisa. But she suddenly pushed on his chest with her palms, forcing him to end the kiss. He found her staring up at him, as if she was stunned that he was capable of such an intimacy.

"My lady?" he had asked, trying to focus his eyes so that he didn't look like some lovesick puppy. Eloisa had stood staring at him as if she was truly impressed by his kiss. But she had never again asked for another, and he had been too much of a coward to ask if she wanted another.

At one time, he could have kicked himself for not trying. Now, though, he was secretly glad she had opted to move to London. Hannah Coomber, one of the maids he employed to clean rooms at the inn, was proving she had skills in more than just cleaning; Angus planned to ask for her hand at the next district ball in Horsham.

Harold watched Angus as he wiped down the space behind the tap. He knew the barkeep had always had a *tendre* for Eloisa. At one time, Harold had thought the match would be a good one, except that Eloisa had always pined for life in the city and a man who could provide more than a business and a bed.

His thoughts were interrupted when the driver of the postal coach entered the pub, a swirl of snow and cold following him into the cozy tap.

"Here is your bundle," the man said, before giving Angus a nod as the barkeep held up a pint glass and an eyebrow in query. Surprised by the stack of letters, Harold gave the driver a nod and six shillings to cover the postage.

He thumbed through the correspondence, recognizing the script of his sister-in-law and two of his nieces. A bright white linen parchment with the red wax seal caught his eye, though. He flipped it over to study the seal embossed in the wax. *Ducal, but not Chichester's,* he thought with some puzzlement. He turned it over to see its addressee wasn't him but his daughter, Olivia.

Realizing immediately that it was a response to her application for the position of governess, Harold thought at first to simply discard the missive. But what if was a letter of rejection?

He doubted she would be turned down. He had seen to her education, after all. An education far too good for the life of a typical woman in England.

Sighing, Harold put the letter at the back of the stack and hoped it contained bad news for his daughter. Michael Cunningham would be turning eight-and-twenty this year, he thought with a wan smile. The man was probably going to ask for her hand when he was next in Shipley to pay him a visit and go over business concerns. *Next week!*

When he gave the letter to Olivia after dinner, she thanked him and held the folded paper in both her hands for a long time before breaking the wax seal and unfolding the missive.

Harold watched her surreptitiously, expecting to see an expression of disappointment appear on her features. Instead, Olivia seemed to stare at the parchment for a very long time before one hand went to her suddenly opened mouth to stifle a shout of, "Thank the stars!" From the way her entire body seemed to quiver, Harold realized his daughter had been selected for the position. *Damn!* he thought as he worked hard to keep his face impassive.

For the first time in all the years he had spent money on governesses and tutors, Harold regretted his decision to educate his daughters.

CHAPTER 17

TIME WITH A SISTER ON A THURSDAY

arch 30, 1815

"I know you have come with good news to share, but I finally have some good news, too," the duchess said with a happy sigh as she moved to sit on a chaise overlooking the large manicured backyard of the Wiltshire estate. A maid followed her carrying a silver tray with lemonade, crystal glasses and lemon biscuits, and a footman was behind the maid with a large parasol that he planted firmly in the ground behind the chaise. The shadow cast by the canopy perfectly enveloped the duchess right down to her slippered feet. Below them, several children played on an expansive lawn, their small voices and high-pitched laughter occasionally drifting up the grass covered hill. From the scent that filled the air, it was evident the lawn had recently been trimmed.

"Another niece or nephew on the way, perhaps?" Michael wondered, accepting a glass of lemonade from the maid as he took the chair adjacent to the duchess. He vaguely wondered what good news she expected *him* to have. This visit to Wiltshire was merely a brief stop on his way back to London from Sussex; he hadn't planned the visit much in advance, so his sister hadn't known he would pay a call on the ducal estate.

Michael took a moment to admire the woman he had known most of his life. As children, they had occasionally been playmates. As teenagers, he'd been her escort and some-time protector. But as adults, the two led lives that were so different, it was hard to believe they were brother and sister.

Elizabeth, now married to a duke and the mother of four children, was still radiant with her honey blond hair swept up in a mountain of curls and dangling ringlets. A pink pastel day gown made of fine lawn complemented her blue eyes and fair complexion, its not-so-modest bodice, which featured a ruffle lace trim along the neckline, just barely hiding her cleavage. Small rubies clung to her plump earlobes and hung from a fine thread of gold around her neck. Michael wondered if their mother had looked like her when he and Elizabeth were babes.

"Goodness, no," his sister answered with a shake of her head, her face coloring to match the gown she wore. "I finally have my figure back, and I've no intention of missing *another* Season of balls and soirées due to confinement." She blushed even more when she realized what she'd said and to whom she said it. "Oh, gracious, Cunningham. Pray, do not tell Jeremy. He's got his heir and a spare, but he still hasn't decided if he wants another," she said, a bit of concern tingeing her otherwise happy face. "And I haven't exactly broached the subject," she added in a voice barely above a whisper.

Her brother suppressed a smile. "My lips are sealed," Michael promised, helping himself to a biscuit and wondering if her statement meant she was no longer sharing a marriage bed with her husband. "If not news of more children, then what other good news can a duchess have these days?" he asked gently.

How different their lives were, he considered. Despite being the second son of a viscount, he had chosen a path of self-reliance, building his business of investments in iron smelting, coal, and coal gas. Those ventures were finally ensuring a fortune for him.

As the only daughter of a viscount, Elizabeth had fallen in love with Jeremy Statton, the second son of a duke. Their courtship, a fairy tale affair that captivated the London Season in 1809, led to a huge wedding at St. George's and a year of honeymooning on the Continent. With the deaths of Jeremy's father and elder brother in a boating accident in 1811, Jeremy was suddenly thrust into the role of Duke of Somerset, and his young bride, Elizabeth Cunningham Statton, was suddenly a duchess. The dowager duchess, overcome with grief but determined to remarry as soon as was socially acceptable, left her remaining son and England to accept an offer of marriage from an aristocrat in Italy. The new duke and duchess were left to run the duchy as they saw fit, managing to endear themselves to their tenants and the villagers by employing a competent estate manager, by paying their bills in a timely manner, and by being fair to their servants. And they had four young, boisterous children who were now happily playing on the manicured lawns below.

"I have finally hired a governess for George and Caroline!" Elizabeth announced happily, referring to her two oldest children. She didn't invoke the nicknames she sometimes used to describe the spoiled brats, deciding it better their uncle keep his good opinion of them (if, indeed, he had one).

Michael's eyebrow cocked at an awkward angle. "*That* is your good news?" he teased, trying hard not to laugh. "However do you react to really *good* news?"

Elizabeth pinched her lips together and gave him a withering stare. "Cunningham! I have searched for a suitable governess for those two *devils* ..." she said the word in a whisper, "... For nearly a year, I'll have you know. 'Tis not easy finding a well-educated woman who is not spoken for, and who is willing to move from her family and live in a drafty manor house whilst attempting to teach a duke's children everything they need to know to be decent peers of the realm," she added, a bit of impatience in her voice.

Suitably dressed down, Michael imagined an old maid, long on the shelf, with her hair caught up in a too-tight bun atop her head and wire spectacles resting on the tip of her hooked and crooked nose. He took a sip of lemonade before asking, "So, where did you find her?"

Beaming with her good news, Elizabeth bit into a biscuit and chewed quickly, not wanting to share her information just yet. "Our very own backyard," she finally hinted, giving him a sideways glance through her long lashes.

Michael's eyebrows furrowed. "Someone from Horsham?" he asked, intrigued by the thought that she'd found someone from back home. Even though he visited Cunningham Park every six weeks, he only spent a couple of days there, so he didn't know any young women from Horsham. Or even any older ones.

Elizabeth was nodding, obviously proud of her accomplishment. "She has the most wonderful surname," she enthused, her good mood firmly back in place. "Waterford. Like the gentleman who makes the beautiful crystal," she explained quickly. "But she claims she is not directly related, but only distantly ..."

Michael stared at Elizabeth, his mouth open and his vision suddenly graying at the edges. *Is this what it feels like to swoon?* he found himself wondering as he barely heard any of her words after 'Waterford'. *She cannot be serious,* he thought suddenly, a bit of panic settling over him.

"Michael?" The duchess was standing up from her chaise, concern etched on her face as she regarded him. "What ever is *wrong?*" she whispered, her hand coming out to take purchase on his forehead as if she suspected he might have a fever. "Is the heat too much for you?" she asked, and then rethought the question when she realized it was barely warm enough to warrant being out-of-doors. She waved to the footman, indicating he should move the parasol so that its shade would cover her brother.

Michael stared at her for a moment longer, taking a deep breath before slumping against the back of the chair and then waving off the footman. "*Which* Waterford?" he asked then, his face growing paler by the moment. *Not Eloisa.* She was in London, after all, and *she* certainly wasn't a candidate to be a governess. That just left ...

"Olivia Waterford." Elizabeth replied as she cocked an eyebrow, realizing just then that Michael must have some knowledge of the girl's family. "Daughter of ..."

"Harold A. Waterford," Michael completed for her, his head bobbing as if attached to a metal spring.

His sister sat back down and regarded him for a long moment. "Why, yes," she finally replied with a tentative smile. But her smile faded as she began to wonder if her information was not as accurate as she supposed. "Do you know him ... personally?" she asked carefully. "Is the family ..?"

"Yes, and yes," Michael responded with a sigh, one hand scrubbing the side of his face. Feeling a hint of stubble, he absently thought of shaving again before dinner. *What was it about being in the country that caused one's beard to grow so quickly?* "I have been doing business with Waterford for ... nearly five years now ..."

His sister gasped, a gloved hand coming up to cover her lips. Michael girded himself—he was sure she would scold him for 'doing business' when it was considered gauche for a member of the *ton* to do so. But Elizabeth's thoughts were still on the topic at hand. "So, you *know* the Waterfords?" she encouraged, hoping to glean more information about the girl she had hired.

"Oh, yes. Quite well, in fact. I just came from there. I am a guest in their home several times a year," he acknowledged with a nod, a frustrated sigh escaping. "But, Beth, why Miss Olivia?" he asked, his brows furrowing into a single line. *She actually pursued a position as a governess. Just as she said she would.* Michael couldn't fault the chit for following through on her plans, but hadn't her father said something to her? *Did she have so little regard for me that she would choose being a governess over being my wife?*

At least his sister's news meant there wasn't a rival suitor for Olivia's hand.

Elizabeth regarded him as she slowly took her seat on the edge of the chaise. "Well, she responded to my advertisement within a week of its posting date. Her credentials seem impeccable, her style of writing was clear, and her penmanship was very neat," Elizabeth explained, as if she felt a need to defend her decision. When Michael's pained expression didn't change, she lifted a shoulder in a shrug. "She replied to my subsequent correspondence very quickly. And she seemed to be the only truly qualified candidate," Elizabeth explained, making it clear she had given her decision a good deal of thought. She suddenly straightened. "Now, you must tell me. What do you know of her?"

Michael's sister seemed to hold her breath in anticipation as she cocked her head to one side. She couldn't help but notice how his expression made it appear as if he was in pain.

Michael took a deep breath, wondering what to admit to his sister. "She is ... " He bit his lip as he regarded Elizabeth. "I have thought for a very long time that if ... that is *when* I decide to marry," he corrected himself, "When it's time for me to take a wife, that I will ... well, that *she* will be my wife," he stammered, his face coloring to a deep scarlet as he gave his explanation. "But not until I *have* to get married," he clarified quickly. *When I'm about to be eight-and-twenty and have ensured my financial future,* he added to himself, not knowing if their mother had ever told Elizabeth about their agreement.

And then he remembered Eloisa. *I still have to find a husband for Eloisa,* he thought suddenly. *Huntington should be done mourning.* Hopefully, Michael's feeble attempt at playing matchmaker had at least resulted in Arthur noticing Eloisa as they shopped in New Bond Street. Michael had managed to learn Arthur's schedule during casual conversation as the two sparred at Gentleman Jackson's. Then he made sure he had Eloisa in a position to be seen by Arthur whilst the banker was on his way to his tailor's shop.

If Arthur showed no interest in Eloisa, other arrangements would need to be made for her welfare, he considered. He chided himself on how awkward *that* situation could get. *Why ever did I offer her protection?* Michael wondered absently, knowing full well why, while at the same time remembering his initial hesitation. It would have been far wiser to put her on a coach and send her back to Shipley. Simply set her up as a war widow and be done with her.

Stunned at her brother's words, Elizabeth sat back on the chaise. Not quite sure what to say, she took a sip of lemonade and pondered his announcement. "When you say you will marry her when you *have* to, are you referring to the promise you made to our mother?" she asked in a quiet voice, a look of defeat settling over her features.

Shifting a bit in his chair, Michael nodded and continued to do so. *So, Mother told her*, he thought, his misery growing.

Matching his nods bob for bob, Elizabeth gave Michael a long look before pulling her shoulders back and sitting up very straight. "That you would be married before your twenty-eighth birthday?" she added for clarification, her eyebrow cocked in a suggestive manner.

"Yes," Michael agreed, his head still bobbing a bit.

Elizabeth leaned forward and placed her glass of lemonade on the tray. "Well!" Elizabeth exclaimed, her bodice rising as she sucked in an indignant breath. "*Damn* her!"

Michael was forced to sit back on his lounge chair a bit, stunned at his sister's curse. "Beth!" he countered, his expression showing his astonishment. He was about to chastise her for her unladylike comment, but the duchess stood up suddenly, and Michael was forced by habit and courtesy to do the same.

"Why ever would she accept my offer of employment if she knows she's to be married ... in ...in..." She paused as she started to count on her fingers. "In less than a *month?*"

Michael's eyebrows furrowed. "What ... what are you

talking about?" He wasn't getting married in less than a month, so why would Olivia?

The duchess stared at her brother for several seconds, one eyebrow elegantly arching up and her arms crossing over her bosom. "Your birthday, you bounder," she countered. "You just told me you were going to honor your promise to Mother."

"And I will," Michael interrupted. "Before I turn twenty-eight."

His sister regarded him and began shaking her head. "So then ... you must already be courting Miss Waterford," she stated, frowning again as she wondered why a girl who was about to be betrothed to the son of a viscount would seek a position as a *governess.*

Perhaps the chit thought it amusing to play such a trick on a duchess ... *or on the sister of her would-be husband.* Was this some sort of joke? *How could she?*

"Of course not!" Michael countered quickly, his head suddenly motionless.

Her brows furrowing in confusion, Elizabeth shook her head. She blinked, and blinked again as if she was having a revelation. "She *doesn't* know you plan to marry her, does she?" Elizabeth murmured, rolling her eyes as she sat down in the chaise. *Well, that was a bit of a relief,* she considered. *I'm not the brunt of a bad joke.*

Michael slowly settled back into his lounging chair, his face reddening with the embarrassment he felt. He never intended to speak with his sister about his choice of wife, at least, not until after he had proposed to Olivia. "I .. I haven't told her of my intentions, no," he admitted in a small voice. "I thought her father would do that after our last conversation on the matter."

"Does she even *know* I am your sister?"

Rolling his eyes, Michael replied, "Of course not. At least, if she does, it's not because *I* told her." Harold Waterford probably knew. He seemed to know an awful lot about the Cunninghams, Michael considered.

Elizabeth regarded her brother for several heartbeats. *The chit doesn't know!*

Michael was about to add that he planned to tell Olivia when it was necessary, but he heard his sister's sudden titters and glanced up to find her covering her mouth with a gloved hand. "What now?" he asked in a voice that sounded a bit harsher than he intended. She was *giggling*, damn her. "Whatever are you giggling about?" he queried, taking umbrage at the sudden change in her behavior. "Duchesses aren't supposed to *giggle!*" he announced in annoyance, not really sure if they were allowed to giggle or not. A giggle certainly didn't seem to be suitable behavior for an aristocrat, though. Especially for one who was in possession of a rather impressive coronet.

The duchess rolled her eyes again. "*You* don't even know," she answered, her hands held up near her face. "Forgive me, but Michael, I am just turned six-and-twenty," Elizabeth claimed when she noticed his quizzical expression. "Your birthday is April twenty-first. Three weeks from this Friday, in fact!"

Michael stared at his sister for nearly ten seconds before he scrubbed the side of his face with a hand, felt the roughness of his afternoon beard and nearly swore. He suddenly realized the meaning behind Edward's comment just the week before.

I suppose she expects you to have some good news, too.

No wonder he had the distinct impression that something wasn't quite ... right ... when he left Waterford Hall to head to Wiltshire. The day he arrived at the Waterford's home, his business partner seemed especially happy, as if the older gentleman expected something monumental to happen, his anticipation nearly palpable. They spent a few hours going over reports, much like they did on all his other visits. Then, when Michael announced he wasn't staying for dinner—he had promised his mother he would have dinner at Cunningham Park—Harold suddenly seemed out of sorts, as if all the air had left his lungs.

Although Michael meant to ask what might be the matter, he was more concerned about getting to his sister's before a storm rolled in from the south. So he said his farewells and took his leave of Shipley, blissfully unaware of the calendar and of the events his forgetfulness set into motion.

"That can't be. I am six-and-twenty right now," he murmured, his heart suddenly racing and his breathing turning shallow as he realized that perhaps he really *was* seven-and-twenty and would be eight-and-twenty in three weeks. *Three weeks!* He leaned over, dropping his head nearly to his lap. *How could I have lost track of my own age?* he wondered, thinking at first that Elizabeth might be teasing him, that she really was just twenty-five. But, no, her youngest child was now nearly two and ...

Damn! How could this have happened? he asked himself. Of course, it wasn't as if he celebrated his birthday every year. He deliberately avoided doing so for this very reason! He hadn't given his age much thought—he hadn't *had* to. "Oh, my," he said again, his voice taking on just the very hint of panic. "Oh, Christ. Whatever shall I do?" he asked aloud, certainly not intending for his sister to hear his thoughts nor bear witness to his sudden distress.

Fighting the impulse to laugh at her brother's sudden discomfiture, Elizabeth moved to the edge of the chaise and considered her brother's dilemma. Although she found herself rather amused by the situation, she could see the panic in his face, in the set of his jaw and the deep furrow between his brows. "You *must* keep your promise to mother," she advised with as serious an expression as possible given the humor she still felt at her brother's expense. "You simply *must*. And, as far as Miss Waterford is concerned," she paused, trying to decide if she was willing to give up her new governess in the name of keeping harmony in the Cunningham family. "If you truly want Olivia Waterford as your wife, then you shall have to resort to drastic measures and see the Archbishop of Canterbury about a special license in order to be wed by your birthday. You haven't much time." She paused a moment, her lower lip caught by a tooth. "Since you apparently haven't been courting her, why is it you think Miss Waterford will even agree to marry you?"

Michael considered the question for only a moment. "Oh, I believe she will," he said hopefully. "Her father will insist on it. He practically promised her to me a year ago." He suddenly realized it was only nine months ago, but he wasn't about to admit *that* to his sister.

How could he have lost track of time? And no wonder Harold Waterford had behaved so oddly! The man had expected Michael to propose to Olivia! There would have been exactly three Sundays for the banns to be read, and then they could be wed the day before his birthday.

One of Elizabeth's eyebrows cocked mischievously. "He knows his daughter would marry well, then?" she questioned, thinking that Michael would have informed the girl's father of his station as the second son of a viscount.

Michael furrowed his brows in response, his head shaking from side to side. "Not ... not how you are thinking," he answered curtly. Although he had kept his full identity from the Waterfords, especially given his older brother's penchant for losing large amounts of money at gaming hells and spending the rest on whores, Michael remembered when Harold Waterford informed him he knew Michael was a member of the *ton*. It was the same day Waterford asked about his promise to his mother. The same day Waterford offered Olivia as a potential wife. The same day he assured him there was a sizable dowry. And the same day he claimed that he didn't care if Michael was a member of the *ton* or not.

Waterford probably knew all about Michael's situation long before he'd done business with him.

"Waterford only knows that I am a successful businessman involved in a variety of investments," he claimed, knowing the statement was only half-true.

Elizabeth's remaining humor quickly dissipated. "You've really gone and buggered yourself this time," she scolded him, her choice of words causing Michael's jaw to drop in disbelief and his face to once again turn scarlet.

"Your Grace!" he admonished her, his mouth still open in astonishment.

"Well, you *have*!" she countered, her humor completely gone. "And don't 'Your Grace' me!" She lowered her voice. "Statton told me what the word means when I caught him using it a few months ago," she explained as she held up her chin in defiance. "And it defines your situation *perfectly*. You've no time for a courtship, and the poor girl was probably hoping for a real church wedding," Elizabeth claimed with a frown, shaking her head as if she was ashamed of her brother. "You'll need a special license, of course," she said as she leaned forward. "You should plan to wed in Shipley. You'll want to line up a vicar or a bishop just as soon as you can. They can be notorious for being out of town when a wedding is required," she added, as if she'd had some experience with the matter. "Just as soon as you get back to London, you'll have to hire a decorator to create a mistress suite, or at least a decently decorated salon for her in your townhouse" she ordered, her mind racing with a list of things that must be done. "You obviously don't have the time or the blunt to buy a suitable house in Park Lane," she complained under her breath.

Frowning at her insult, Michael started to reply, thinking there was already a room on the second floor that would that would make a charming salon and he probably could afford a house in Park Lane, although not a large one. Before he could answer, though, Elizabeth continued her list of necessities.

"She'll need a wedding gown, of course ..."

"Well, I can't exactly buy that for her now, can I?"

Elizabeth frowned at him, not appreciating his interruption. "If her mother doesn't know about your machinations, then you'd better see to it her father knows so that he can arrange something. I rather doubt Shipley or even Petworth has a suitable shop for purchasing a wedding gown. She might have to go to *Chichester*." This last was said as if going to Chichester to purchase a gown would be a travesty.

Michael shoulders sagged as if he'd been burdened with the weight of the world. "What else must I do?"

"Let's see," Elizabeth replied as she took a breath. "She'll require a key to the townhouse, and a key to the house on Cavendish Square, and her own wax seal for correspondence, and you'll have to have some witnesses for the ceremony ..." She took a deep breath, remembering everything she had required when she married Jeremy Statton. And for that she'd had several months and a doting mother to help prepare! "It's rather doubtful that it can all be sorted in such short order," she complained, taking another deep breath. Then a thought struck her. "Unless you ..." She let the sentence trail off, her teeth firmly planted in her lower lip and a mixed look of disappointment and revelation crossing her face.

"Unless I what?" Michael prompted, wondering what she had in mind.

Sighing, Elizabeth shook her head. "It would be scandalous," she warned with a raised eyebrow. "Your reputation ..."

Michael's mouth opened. "How so?" he demanded, now very curious as to what his sister was devising in that devious brain of hers.

"You will have to *ruin* her," Elizabeth stated simply, an arched eyebrow daring him to argue the point. "Then she'll have no choice but to marry you. And quickly. And then I shall simply have to find someone else to be my governess," she added sadly, her shoulders drooping as she remembered what it had taken to find Olivia Waterford. After a long moment, though, her face brightened again as a huge grin split her face. "But then I shall finally have a *sister*!" she exclaimed happily, her hands coming together as if she were applauding herself.

Michael stared at Elizabeth for a very long time. "*Ruin* her?" he repeated in disbelief, stunned that his very own sister could suggest such a thing. Only men without scruples would dare to kiss or otherwise consort with an unmarried woman who wasn't a prostitute. And only rakes did it when they knew they'd be caught in the act, not caring about the consequences of their actions. *Olivia will think I'm a rake,* he considered as his brows furrowed. *She'll despise me for ... forever, perhaps.* "I cannot do that!" he exclaimed in a hoarse whisper, leaning toward Elizabeth so the servants would not overhear him.

His sister regarded him, a pout having formed on her lower lip as she watched her brother do his thinking. "Do *you* have a better idea, Cunningham?" she countered, a bit impatient with the stubborn man.

Even as he considered his alternatives—even considered *not* keeping the promise he had made to his mother all those years ago—Michael realized his sister might be right. In order to gain Olivia Waterford's hand in marriage, he would have to ruin her. There simply wasn't time for anything proper. "I do not," he finally replied. Sinking into his chair, Michael closed his eyes and groaned. *Three weeks,* he thought miserably.

And then he considered the true irony of the situation.

Eloisa had been ruined. Now he was working to arrange an advantageous marriage on her behalf. Meanwhile, he was considering ruining Olivia just to gain her hand in marriage.

Would she think marriage to him was advantageous?

He could only hope.

Will Olivia ever forgive me?

CHAPTER 18

ANOTHER FIB ON A FRIDAY

*M*arch 31, 1815

"You look as if you are a million miles away," an amused voice said from somewhere nearby.

Michael jerked upright as his eyes focused on his banker, Arthur Huntington III. "Beg pardon," Michael replied as he allowed a smile and stood up from his overstuffed wing backed chair. The cigar smoke had thinned a bit in the parlor of White's. He'd been enjoying a glass of port as he contemplated his next business proposal for Harold Waterford—and what he might do to ensure his marriage to Olivia. "You look well, Arthur," he said in greeting before motioning to the seat across from his. "Have you come for a game of cards or for a drink?"

He knew exactly why the banker had arrived when he did; Michael had arranged for one his sparring partners to make the suggestion to Arthur to go to White's and check the betting book.

The older gentleman, leaner than Michael but in excellent physical shape, sported a mustache and close cropped hair with just a hint of gray at the temples. Befitting his station at the bank, he was always impeccably dressed in well-tailored coats and waistcoats that were fashionable but tasteful. Like Michael, the banker boxed for exercise and was an occasional sparring partner at Gentlemen Jackson's.

Arthur took the proffered chair. "A drink is on its way," he said as he motioned toward a butler who was seeing to him. "But, actually, the betting book caught my eye."

Michael's right eyebrow cocked up, pleased to hear his suggestion had been heeded. Arthur Huntington wasn't one for placing bets at the men's club, although he knew the widower was the subject of one having to do with when he would find a suitable woman to marry.

When Michael reviewed the list of men he knew were in the market for a wife, Arthur Huntington's name worked its way to the top. He hoped the older gentleman would consider courting Eloisa. But how did one arrange it so the two could meet? How did one arrange for Cupid to make an appearance, for it was rather doubtful Huntington would consider remarrying unless he felt affection for his new wife. And Eloisa deserved a man who felt affection for her.

"Taken to gambling now, have you?" Michael teased gently.

The banker smiled. "Not at all, but I couldn't help but notice that several gentlemen stand to collect a hefty sum in three week's time if a particular member isn't married." The butler appeared from Arthur's right and set a glass of port on the small side table. "Thank you, Childers," Arthur said as he reached for the glass and held it out toward Michael.

The younger man lifted his glass and replied in kind, knowing damn well the banker was referring to *him*.

Michael struggled to keep his face impassive and took a quick sip from his port. "Ah, but how much do I stand to gain if I *am* married?" he countered quickly as he mentally counted the days until his twenty-eighth birthday, "In three week's time?" he added, a gleam in his eye that belied the familiar feeling of panic that was building in his gut.

Arthur snorted and appeared surprised by Michael's response. His gaze darkened a bit, though. "A few thousand pounds, I would guess," he replied quietly, the mirth suddenly gone from him. "I would be quite jealous, you know," he commented then, his attention on his port as he swirled the contents of the glass and watched the liquor slowly collect in the bottom of the glass.

Perplexed by the man's comment and a bit stunned at the mention of a few thousand pounds, Michael leaned forward. "What ever do you mean? You are not a betting man, Arthur. I can't imagine my winning a ..."

"It's not about the money," his banker interrupted, his voice a bit too harsh and his expression suddenly very serious. He quickly glanced around the room to see if anyone had overheard his outburst, but the club members playing cards were too engrossed in their game, and the butler was no longer in the immediate vicinity. "Your ... getting married. That is, if you truly keep your promise to your mother."

Taking a deep breath, Michael furrowed his brow and regarded the older man. *Did everyone know of the promise he had made to his mother?* "I was not aware that you were already seeking a wife," Michael replied quietly, lying through his teeth and hoping he sounded respectful of the widower's situation. The man had been in mourning for nearly a year. How many widowers mourned that long before remarrying? *Very few,* he thought.

Arthur regarded him and tried to shake off his melancholy. "I ... I *miss* her, Cunningham. I truly do. And I find myself wanting nothing more than to find a woman ..." He paused a moment and glanced away as if he was embarrassed by his emotional reaction. "I wish to find a *wife,*" he stated finally. "Many others would probably find my position enviable since it allows me to frequent brothels or employ a courtesan without reprisals from a jealous wife, but I don't want to *share* a woman. I wish to have a woman all to myself ..."

"You are a man of scruples," Michael commented lightly, appreciating his friend's candor. "There is nothing wrong in wanting a wife, Arthur," he said in a low voice, wondering if he would ever feel as his friend did. "Perhaps I can be of help?" he offered, not expecting the banker to suggest anything. Normally, finding a suitable wife for the man would best be handled by a matchmaker or one of the patronesses of Almack's. But in Huntington's case …

"Perhaps you know of someone … a young lady who may have been overlooked during last Season's balls … or a *young widow*, perhaps?" Arthur hinted with what looked like a pre-rehearsed shrug. "Someone who is seeking a gentleman for a husband?" The look on his face suggested that he had someone in mind, someone Michael knew—and that he knew Michael could provide the necessary introductions. *That is, if the woman wasn't already about to be claimed by Michael to fulfill his promise to Lady Cunningham.*

Michael considered the man's words and allowed a brow to rise as he feigned thinking over the situation. Having long ago decided to arrange an introduction to Eloisa and seeing to it that Eloisa was on display whilst they shopped in New Bond Street at the same time as Arthur was on his way to his tailor, it was now only a matter of suggesting a time and location where the two might meet.

"There is a widow I look in on occasionally," he answered carefully. "As a favor to her father, of course," he added hastily, wanting to be sure Arthur didn't misunderstand the situation. "Her mourning period is over," Michael added as he carefully watched his banker's face.

Would Harold Waterford be pleased to discover his eldest daughter had landed a well-to-do gentleman for a husband? A man with whom he had done business? Arthur had even been a guest of the Waterford's. Perhaps Arthur had already met Eloisa. Would he remember her from his brief stay?

For Eloisa to be wed to a banker was a far better situation than to be a ruined chit, he considered, thinking of the alternative should someone recognize Eloisa from Lucy's brothel. It had been nearly a year, though. Who would remember a terrified girl who had been at Lucy's for less than a day? The man who had taken her virtue was probably too drunk to remember anything about her.

"I would, of course, be happy to introduce you to the

former Eloisa Waterford," Michael offered. "Mrs. Smith," he added quickly. "Do you ever take walks near Grosvenor Square?" Michael asked with a cocked eyebrow, knowing he'd seen Huntington on foot near his townhouse on several occasions.

Arthur sat up straight and suddenly seemed most pleased. "I can. Just name the day and street," he said, unable to hide his anxiousness. "To be clear," he added suddenly, his eyes darting to his hands, "This is Harold's oldest daughter?" he half-asked. "The same woman I saw you escorting in New Bond Street a few weeks ago? On a Tuesday afternoon?" he quickly added, suddenly nervous. His eyes darted about, as if he was afraid someone might be eavesdropping on their conversation.

Michael suppressed the urge to grin. His tactic had worked. Allowing a quizzical expression to cross his face, he answered, "Yes, she is the one."

He had taken Eloisa to get a new corset and a morning gown, but the trip had been brief—they had only visited a few shops on a single block of New Bond Street when he noticed his banker watching them from across the street. "Did you find her ... pleasant to look upon?" Michael wondered, noting the man's nervousness.

Arthur took a deep breath and let it out before answering. "Indeed, although I must admit that when I met her at Waterford Park, it was only in passing, and it was a few weeks ago. And I saw her only ... briefly ... when you were shopping," he admitted with a nod. "And you?"

Blinking, Michael regarded Arthur, wondering at the question. "Beg pardon?" he replied, his brows furrowing.

Rolling his eyes, Arthur lowered his voice. "Do you find her ... *pleasant* to look upon?" he echoed, his nervousness still apparent.

"Oh!" Michael said with a bit of relief. "Well, she is ... pretty enough, I suppose," he answered with a shrug. He did not want to seem enamored with the woman and take the chance of scaring away a possible courting opportunity for

Eloisa. "In fact, now that I think about it, she looks a bit like your late wife," he said thoughtfully.

The banker seemed to breathe a sigh of relief, although he was still anxious. "And you have no claim to her?" he whispered, his tone suddenly suspicious.

Michael regarded the banker with an upraised brow. "No," he answered with a shake of his head. *Does he believe she's my intended?* he wondered suddenly. *Or does he suspect she might be my mistress?*

"So, when can I meet her?"

For a fraction of a moment, Michael was left with the impression of a cat pouncing on an unsuspecting mouse. And he wondered, in this case, if he was the mouse or if Eloisa had that honor.

Michael quickly ran scenarios through his head as to where he could arrange an introduction. He could see to it they met at a chocolate shop. *No, that would be too public,* he considered. Eloisa's maid had Saturdays off. He could arrange to meet her at noon and they could run into Arthur during an early afternoon walk. Green Street was not too busy in the early afternoon. "Tomorrow. One o'clock or thereabouts. Green Street near the square," Michael stated firmly.

Arthur cocked an eyebrow and allowed a smile to slowly spread over his face. "Thank you, Cunningham," he said with a nod as a sense of relief seemed to settle over the man. He took a sip from his drink and set it down. "Now, about that bet. Do you truly intend to keep your promise?" he asked with a cocked eyebrow. "I could enter my own bet in your favor and use the winnings to pay for a number of fripperies," he hinted with an amused expression.

Michael pretended to ponder the banker's question before he finally responded. "Oh, I do," he said with a nod. "And thank you for asking about it. I am reminded of a few items I must see to acquiring before the auspicious occasion," he added with a smile. He stood up, gave the banker a nod, and left the club.

Yes, it was quite fortunate that Arthur Huntington

appeared when he did, Michael considered again. When he left White's that Friday evening, Michael hurried home and headed directly to his study, intent on writing several letters. It was imperative that a certain duchess understand that the governess she had just hired was definitely about to become his wife. There was a bill to pay for the furnishings that had been ordered for the new purple and gold salon on the second floor. A missive to his father in Horsham would inform the viscount of Michael's intention to keep his promise to his mother. A note to his future father-in-law would request his hospitality so he could make his request for the man's daughter and schedule a quick wedding. A locksmith would be hired to create a duplicate set of keys. And an order for a wax seal with the initials 'OWC' needed to be placed with a local stationer.

The next business venture, nearly ready to present to Harold Waterford and Sir Richard, needed a hint of refinement and a bit more data to back up his claim as to its long-term payoff possibilities, but he was sure he could complete it before next week.

And he had to figure out how he was going to get Eloisa to take a walk with him tomorrow at about one o'clock in the afternoon.

CHAPTER 19

AN IMPORTANT INTRODUCTION ON A SATURDAY

April 1, 1815

Eloisa Waterford sat on the front edge of a yellow damask settee as she pushed a needle through fine muslin. Pulled taut in a wooden hoop, the muslin was still a bright white despite months of handling. The satin embroidery thread shimmered in the spaces where she had filled in the flowers and leaves, and the ribbons winding in and out of the foliage appeared to be made of silk. Another few days of handiwork and she'd be ready to insert the words of the wall hanging using delicate back stitches.

At one time, she thought the wedding sampler would feature her own marriage information, but now she wondered if it was likely she would ever wed. Perhaps she could finish it for Michael's wedding, should his mother ever coerce her protector into a suitable marriage.

The knocker on her front door rapped three times. Startled, she pricked her thumb with the needle. Sucking the edge of her thumb to stave off the droplet of blood that was about to appear, she placed the embroidery on the settee and hurried to the door, wondering who would be calling on her at noon. She opened the door to find Michael Cunningham, hat in hand, standing on the stoop of her townhouse.

"Good afternoon, Mrs. Smith," Michael said as he bowed, smiling mischievously at the name he called her.

Eloisa blushed and gave him a quick curtsy. "And good afternoon to you, Mr. Cunningham. To what do I owe this unexpected visit?" she asked with a grin as she stepped aside to allow him to enter the small vestibule.

Michael gave her a peck on the back of her hand once he was safely out of sight from the street. "I was hoping you would agree to a walk this afternoon," he stated as he glanced into the small parlor from whence she'd come. "That is, if you're not otherwise engaged."

Eloisa gave a very unladylike snort in response to the comment. "Embroidery is becoming very dull and boring. Of course, I will go for a walk with you. I should change into a mourning gown, though, don't you suppose?" she asked as she indicated the pale blue batiste gown she wore.

Michael allowed his eyes to travel the length of her gown before replying, "If you mean mourning gown, as in bereaved widow, then ... no," he said with a glint in his eye.

Although he'd never told Eloisa that he was the son of a viscount, there were those in London who did know. For the sake of discretion, and because he did not want his mother learning about Eloisa, it was imperative that no one know that he provided protection for Harold Waterford's daughter. Having her pose as the widow of a soldier killed in the war gave her some respectability and him an excuse to call on her when he didn't wish to busy himself with his business ventures. But today, it was more important that Eloisa be as presentable as possible.

Eloisa stared at him for a moment. "I have a blue walking gown and pelisse," she suggested.

"Perfect," Michael replied with a nod.

"It is my maid's day off ..."

"I know," Michael replied with another nod, implying that he wouldn't even be calling on her if the maid was present.

"It's just that ... I don't think I can reach ..." she motioned to her back, indicating the buttons.

"I will help with the fastenings of your gown," Michael offered, his manner quite serious.

Eloisa gasped, a shocked expression finally softening to one of acceptance at the idea of Michael buttoning her gown. But after another moment, her expression turned more serious. "It's not even Tuesday," she said as she headed to the stairs.

Michael colored a bit and followed her to her second-story bedchamber. "If today is not convenient for a walk, I can certainly ..."

"Today is fine, Mr. Cunningham," Eloisa answered brightly as she pulled shut the drapes. "You must know I would never deny you," she paused a moment, looking up suddenly as she considered why he might be there on a day other than Tuesday. "... Anything you wanted," she finally whispered, wondering if he had changed his mind about taking her as his mistress. Or had he come to tell her he would no longer be providing protection? A place to live. It had been ... eleven months! *Oh, dear.*

As she moved toward the dressing screen, Michael reached out for her arm and pulled her to face him. "Eloisa, what is wrong?" he asked, knowing enough from his time with her to realize that she was upset about something. "Truly, have I come at an inconvenient time?" he asked, his brows furrowing.

Trying to seem embarrassed, Eloisa shook her head. "It is only that ... it's my maid's day off, and I have to dress my own hair," she whispered.

Michael pulled her closer. "Which will be covered by a bonnet. We're only going for a walk," he reminded her, wondering what she was thinking. *Did she think he had come for a tumble? Good grief!* He was going to marry her sister!

But she doesn't know that.

Grinning at his persuasiveness, Eloisa reached up and smoothed his hair where the wind had tousled it. "All right, then, but you must really help to dress me. I cannot reach the buttons."

His eyebrow cocked in a most delightful arch, Michael reached around her shoulders and began undoing all the buttons down her back. He struggled for a moment. "If it's your maid's day off, however did you get these buttons fastened in the first place?" he whispered, his face betraying his concentration as he worked on the tiny fastenings.

"The neck opening is quite large enough that I can simply pull this gown over my head without undoing any of the buttons," she replied with an arched eyebrow, amused by his concerted effort.

"You minx!" Michael said suddenly, his hands giving up on the buttons and instead grabbing some folds of her gown and lifting them up. The dress was over her head and tossed to the bed before Eloisa could protest.

Despite Michael's assurances that she was a pretty woman and had a pleasant figure, Eloisa was modest, especially in the light of day. With Michael having removed all but her corset, chemise and stockings in a few quick moves, Eloisa blushed bright red. "Cunningham!" she scolded as she tried to cover herself with her arms.

She turned and lifted up the blue walking gown she'd retrieved from the dressing room. About to pull it on over her head, Michael took the gown from her and slipped his hands into the skirt, opening it with his arms. At her stunned expression, he rolled his eyes. "I said I would help!" he claimed, keeping his eyes on her face. He couldn't help but know she wore only a chemise, corset and stockings, though. He thought of how much she looked liked Olivia and wondered if Olivia would look like this when she wore only a few undergarments. He wondered if her skin would be as smooth and fair, if she had the same feminine curves, if her breasts were larger or smaller than Eloisa's.

Still bright red with embarrassment, Eloisa ducked into the gown and allowed Michael to turn her body so that he could fasten the jet buttons at the back. "I did not expect you would play lady's maid," she countered, accidentally bumping her elbow into his ribs. At the sound of a hiss, she turned to regard him. "I apologize. Did I ... *hurt* you?" she asked, not thinking she'd hit him that hard.

Michael frowned. Turning around so his back was to Eloisa, he moved toward the cheval mirror in the corner and unbuttoned his waistcoat. He lifted his shirt to expose his well-muscled chest. Curious, Eloisa peered into the glass from behind and around him. She let out a gasp. At the sound of her shock, Michael looked into the mirror and followed her gaze to a large bruise on his chest.

"Oh, it's nothing," Michael whispered with a slight grin. "Just took a hard punch is all."

Eloisa relaxed a bit. She'd seen far worse bruising on Michael Cunningham's body over the year since he'd become her protector. He'd taken up bare-knuckle boxing for exercise at some point in his past, and on the occasion when he required a plaster or bandage, he'd allowed Eloisa to see to his care. She seemed determined to provide some kind of service in return for his generosity. "I do hope you gave as good as you got," she murmured as she crossed her arms.

Michael grinned in spite of the pain he felt when he gingerly touched the bruise. "I did, indeed, although I must admit, I hesitated a bit," he said as he undid the fall of his breeches and tucked in his shirt. "He's my banker, and I'd rather not hurt him too badly. He has grieved quite enough as it is." There was a hint of a grin as he rebuttoned his waistcoat, but he paused as he noticed Eloisa. She was staring at his body, one hand held out but not touching him. "What is it, El?" he asked, his brows furrowing as he noticed her faraway expression.

"It's so brutal, isn't it?" she murmured, her gaze focused on something not there. "Men beating each other. And beating their women."

Michael's reaction was so quick, Eloisa was shocked when her face was buried in his shoulder as his arms pulled her body hard against the front of his. "I would *never* beat a woman, El, I promise you," he vowed into her hair as he held her. Then he remembered the bruise she'd had on her cheek the night he rescued her from the brothel. She had been hit at least once, maybe more.

Still stunned by the sudden movement, by the sensation of being held up against the front of his body, Eloisa nodded into his shoulder. "I know *you* would not," she whispered, her attention back on the present. "But ... But, what of your banker? Would he, do you suppose?"

Sighing heavily, Michael let go his hold on her and led her to the edge of the bed. He turned and sat down, pulling her down next to him. "I believe you have already met Mr. Huntington," he stated in a hushed tone." When Eloisa didn't respond, he added, "He is a widower. He worshiped his wife, and he is desperate to have a love in his life again. I cannot believe the man would lift a hand against a woman. Even a woman who might steal from him," he added, as if that might be enough impetus for a man to beat a woman.

Eloisa considered his argument, her gaze deliberately avoiding his. "So, why does *he* fight?" she asked, a crinkle appearing between her brows. She already knew that Michael did it for the exercise, or, at least, that's what he claimed when he first told her his reason for taking up the odd sport.

"I believe he does it so that he won't go mad," Michael whispered in reply, his eyes focused on the pattern in the Aubusson carpet at his feet. "I doubt the man would even consider taking a mistress. It would be like dishonoring his wife, I suppose. But when he finds a woman for whom he feels affection, I expect he will give up bare-knuckle fighting." He lifted his gaze to Eloisa's face, wondering if she believed every man capable of hurting a woman.

Eloisa regarded him for a moment before she nodded. "He needs the ... release, then," she said with a hint of question in her voice.

Michael regarded her for several seconds, surprised by her insight. "Exactly!" Michael replied, his eyes widening as he realized her comment could be true for Arthur. *She under-*

stands. When given the chance, Eloisa could astonish him with her insight.

She smiled then, realizing she'd pleased her protector. She stood up from the bed and stepped into a pair of black slippers before taking the small chair at her vanity. As she wound her hair into a tight bun and pinned it atop her head, Michael moved to stand behind her, fastening the rest of the jet buttons at the back of her gown.

Eloisa grinned at his reflection in the mirror. "Are we still going for a walk?" she asked, thinking perhaps he had something else in mind for the afternoon. *Maybe an ice at Gunther's!*

"Yes, we are," he replied, wondering what she implied with her question. *Did Eloisa think he was reconsidering her offer of becoming his mistress?* He wondered if he should tell her about his intention to marry her sister later that month. *What would her reaction be?* he wondered. "In fact, I need to tell you something," he said quietly.

Eloisa paused, about to attach an ear bob to one of her earlobes. "Oh?" she replied.

"This man ... Arthur Huntington ... we're going to meet him today. While we're on this walk," he explained, hoping he wasn't making a mistake by telling her what he had planned. "He asked for an introduction."

Her eyes widening, Eloisa turned from the vanity to look at him directly. "Why?" she asked, a bit of panic causing her stomach to clench. Was the man looking for a mistress?

Had Michael suggested her?

"He's ready to find a wife," Michael stated.

Eloisa's mouth dropped open in astonishment. *A banker has asked for an introduction to me!* "What ... What have you told him? About me, I mean?" she asked. *Did the man know ..?*

"You're a war widow, and you're done with mourning. Nothing more," he promised.

Letting out the breath she'd been holding, Eloisa slumped in her chair. "Oh." She started nodding. "Then, I suppose we should be going," she said as she turned and finished clipping on the ear bobs, her movements quick and efficient. She had her pelisse pulled on and buttoned before Michael had finished rebuttoning his topcoat.

Once he glanced out the windows and determined that the street in front of her townhouse was clear of pedestrians, Michael offered Eloisa his arm and they took off for the afternoon stroll.

Eloisa seemed lost in thought, and not wishing to interrupt the silence between them, Michael was soon lost in his own thoughts—so much so that he nearly missed Arthur Huntington as the man walked toward them.

"Good afternoon, Cunningham," Huntington greeted him as he hurried up to Michael with his right hand outstretched.

Smiling, Michael grasped the hand and shook it vigorously. "And good afternoon to you, Huntington. I see our earlier sparring match has not affected *you* in the least," Michael said jovially.

Arthur shook his head. "No, indeed. It was good exercise," he replied, his attention turning to Eloisa. The man's smile of greeting turned to one of appreciation as he nodded to Eloisa and removed his hat.

"Allow me to present Mrs. Eloisa Smith," Michael stated as he lifted the arm she held. He couldn't help but notice Arthur's gaze on Eloisa. He wondered how long the banker had known about the widow and if he remembered having met her at Waterford Hall. "This is my banker and sometimes boxing opponent, Mr. Arthur Huntington," he said by way of introduction. "The Third," he added, thinking the full name might seem more impressive to Eloisa.

Eloisa's eyes widened when she realized this was the very man that Michael had spoken of earlier. She performed a curtsy in response to the banker's deep bow. Even before their eyes met, she was aware of a frisson in her body, of her breath suddenly leaving and her face coloring a bit as the man seemed to openly admire her. "It's so very good to meet you,

Mr. Huntington," she said with a genuine smile. *So very good indeed.* She was sure she had never seen the man before; she would remember him if she had ever been introduced to him. And he was even more handsome than she could imagine from Michael's description of him! *He is debonair,* she thought happily. *A true gentleman.*

Michael noted Arthur's interest and immediately realized it was genuine. The man had obviously seen Eloisa more often than just the occasion of them shopping on New Bond Street. "Mrs. Smith's husband died last year," Michael explained quickly. "His infantry was quite battered in the war, I'm afraid. I try to see to it that Mrs. Smith gets some fresh air now and again."

Arthur's attention went briefly to Michael as he listened to the explanation, but it was directed back onto Eloisa almost immediately. "I am so sorry for your loss, Mrs. Smith," he said as he reached for her gloved hand and kissed the back of it. "I lost my wife last year, too, and have found life to be quite difficult without her. Are you ... out of mourning now?" he asked, noting the color of the gown and the pelisse she wore.

Eloisa wondered at the man's curiosity. "Yes, finally," she replied with a nod of her head. "I suppose I overdid it just a bit," she added, biting her lip when she realized her comment might seem flippant to the handsome banker. "Mr. Cunningham has been so very kind to look in on me. He and my father are business associates, you see," she added quickly, hoping she wasn't saying too much. "And please allow me to say that I am very sorry for your loss, Mr. Huntington. Were you married long?" Eloisa wondered, trying to determine the handsome man's age. The cut of his topcoat was exquisite, his Nanking breeches were tailored to fit over his knee in a most precise buttoned cuff, and his boots were polished to a near-glass shine. A neatly trimmed mustache gave his angular face a debonair quality, its jet black color contrasting quite nicely with the flecks of gray in his closely cropped hair. Her gaze drifted down to the ungloved hand that held his beaver and kid gloves. She noticed that his knuckles were scuffed much like Michael's. He, too, had carefully manicured fingernails.

The man seemed lost in a reverie of his own as he regarded the pretty woman who stood before him. Her face was beautifully flushed, *no doubt from their walk*, he considered. The strands of brown hair that had escaped from around her bonnet shown with a hint of red, and although her deep blue walking gown and matching pelisse were not the best color for her fair complexion, their fit promised a pleasant figure beneath. "Thank you. It would have been fifteen years this September," he answered with a nod, a flush coming over him as he realized he'd been staring too long. "And you?" he asked, hoping her marriage was not long.

"Only a couple of months," Eloisa spoke softly. "I was in mourning far longer than I was ever married," she added with a slight shrug of one shoulder, not caring one whit that she suddenly couldn't remember the details of the back story Michael had devised for her.

Michael cleared his throat, clearly aware of the attraction between the two. "Thank you again for sparring with me earlier today," Michael said lightly. "I look forward to a rematch."

Arthur tore his gaze from Eloisa and regarded Michael with a cocked eyebrow. "As do I. Next week, perhaps?" he offered, realizing he had kept them from their walk far too long. He was obviously satisfied with the introduction, though.

"I look forward to it," Michael replied with a slight grin.

Eloisa turned and placed her hand on Michael's arm. "Mr. Cunningham, do you suppose it would be acceptable for me to invite Mr. Huntington for tea tomorrow afternoon? My maid would be present, of course."

Although he hadn't expected Eloisa to want to host Arthur Huntington for tea—he thought Arthur would first offer a ride in Hyde Park—Michael found this arrangement more promising. "I think that would be acceptable," he answered. He turned to Arthur with a raised eyebrow.

"I would be honored to have tea with you, Mrs. Smith. At what time may I call on you?" the banker wondered, his enthusiasm barely held in check.

"Four o'clock would be perfect, Mr. Huntington," Eloisa answered with a heartfelt smile. "I live in the little brick house back there ... with the round bushes on either side of the front door," she turned and pointed to it as Arthur followed her finger.

"Yes, I know the one," he said with a nod, not bothering to give the place much of a glance. Michael nearly rolled his eyes as he realized Arthur had, indeed, been admiring Eloisa from afar for much longer than just a few days.

Eloisa nodded. "I look forward to seeing you again."

"And I you, Mrs. Smith," Arthur replied, lifting her hand one more time to kiss the back of it. He gave them both a bow and hurried off.

As Michael and Eloisa resumed their walk, a wall of silence seemed to build between them. Michael's attention was on his upcoming trip to Shipley while Eloisa considered the caller she would hosting the following day. After a quarter of an hour of no conversation, though, Eloisa could stand it no longer. "You are angry with me, aren't you?" she half-asked, biting her lower lip as she turned to regard Michael. But he showed a carefree expression and gave no hint that he was feeling anything in particular.

"Not at all," he replied lightly, his eyebrows furrowing at her comment. He wondered why she seemed upset. "I feel for Mr. Huntington, and you seemed to have cheered him up quite nicely with your invitation," he praised her, patting the arm that held his. "Now, if he tries anything untoward, you can be sure I'll beat his brains in," he added, a quirk crossing his face as he said it.

"You brute!" Eloisa gasped, realizing too late that he was teasing. She resumed her walk with him, humming softly as she thought long and hard about what kind of biscuits to bake for Mr. Huntington's visit. Perhaps several flavors so that there would be at least one he liked.

"Eloisa," he said then, his voice lowering so he couldn't be overheard by a passersby. "I must visit your father next week. We're working on another business venture," he murmured. "I've much to complete before the trip, so I think it best I forgo visiting you Tuesday. You won't mind terribly, I hope?" he asked, not sure of her mood just then.

Eloisa turned her face up to his. "Not at all, Mr. Cunningham," she replied with a brief shake of her head, a small smile touching her lips. *Mr. Huntington is coming for tea!* "You must give my family my regards."

"Of course," he answered with a nod. He had to keep from smiling at her change in mood since their meeting with Huntington. She seemed ... *happy,* he realized.

Although Eloisa might have at one time wanted a marriage proposal from Michael, she no longer seemed enamored with him. And he never said he would be her protector for the rest of her life. *Had she decided at some point during this past eleven months to search for a marriage prospect?* Michael wondered as they continued their walk. For if she had, he was hoping she was considering Arthur Huntington.

She wouldn't do badly with Arthur Huntington III. Not bad at all.

CHAPTER 20

A LETTER IS DELIVERED ON A MONDAY

April 10, 1815
Snowflakes fell in thick clumps and settled on the top of Olivia Waterford's bonnet as she walked quickly towards home. She wondered if there would ever be a real spring that year. The weather had been so cold, her mother's garden hadn't yet begun to show its greenery. Only the plants on the south side of the house had shown any signs of life. Tired of staying indoors, though, she'd made the chilly trek to Shipley and spent the afternoon shopping for sundries.

Given the weather, she was surprised when the mail coach arrived from the north just as she was about to make her way home. The driver, recognizing she was a Waterford daughter, entrusted her with a small bundle of letters. Most of the missives were for her father, but one bright white envelope was addressed to her. The elegant handwriting on the outside of the parchment was written in a feminine hand, but the crest embossed in the wax seal was that of the Somerset duchy. Olivia considered opening the letter right then and there in the middle of the street next to the coach, but she dared not take the chance that the other letters would fall onto the wet and muddy cobbles. It did not matter what the letter contained in the way of news. She was simply excited about receiving further word from Wiltshire regarding the position of governess for the duke's children.

Just seven weeks before, she'd sent a letter and a comprehensive list of her coursework and tutors along with a character to the duchy. Even if she wasn't considered for an interview with the duchess, she hoped her information might be passed along to another family in need of a governess. But then she'd received a letter from the duchess herself, informing Olivia that she had been chosen for the position and asking if she was still available. Olivia quickly replied, telling the duchess she was available at Her Grace's convenience and that she would await further word about when she should plan to travel to Wiltshire.

Certainly this letter contained that information.

And then she found herself wondering if she was making the right decision. If she left Shipley, she would probably only return to visit her parents on rare occasions. She would probably never see Mr. Cunningham again.

Marriage would be out of the question—had there ever been a governess who was married? But given she had no suitors, she was doing the right thing by accepting the position. She was sure of it.

Lost in thought about the move to Wiltshire and her lack of prospects for marriage, Olivia was unaware of a coach coming on the road behind her. The driver halted the matched Cleveland Bays and the coach ground to a halt directly to her left. Looking up, she waved when she recognized the driver, Mr. White, and then turned to curtsy when Michael Cunningham called to her from inside the coach. The door opened and Mr. Cunningham jumped from the equipage, calling out a greeting as he did so.

"May I offer you a ride, Miss Olivia? I believe our destination is the same," he said lightly as he held out a hand for her.

She's even prettier than the last time I saw her!

Olivia colored up a bit, surprised by the sudden appearance of the very man she'd been thinking of, as if her memories had somehow conjured him into existence. "I suppose it would be acceptable," she agreed as a footman set down the steps. *There should really be a chaperone*, she thought, but she'd known Mr. Cunningham for a long time. He was a friend of the family. Certainly there would be no harm in riding in his coach the rest of the way to the house.

"You have quite a burden there, Miss Olivia. Allow me," Michael offered as he took the bundle of letters from her grasp, leaving her to manage a small parcel under her other arm.

"Thank you, Mr. Cunningham. You are too kind," Olivia replied with a grin. She stepped up into the coach, a frisson passing through her as Michael grasped her gloved hand and helped her up the steep step.

Before he followed her into the coach, Michael's eye was drawn to the top letter on the stack he had taken from her. The crest of the Duke of Somerset was quite evident in the dark red wax seal, and he surreptitiously turned over the letter as he climbed up into the coach. He noted the addressee was not Harold Waterford but Olivia. And the beautiful handwriting was familiar to him. Michael's brows furrowed.

Elizabeth Cunningham, he realized immediately. Michael's younger sister and the only daughter of Viscount Cunningham understood why Michael did not wish to marry right away, but she also knew of his immediate need to do so. And she was grateful enough for Michael's introduction to the man who had become her husband, Jeremy Edward Statton, to bend to his wishes when the need arose. *Like now*, he thought to himself, hoping the letter was to tell Olivia the offer to hire her as governess had been rescinded. "You have quite a number of letters here," Michael commented as he took a seat across from her and settled back into the leather squabs.

"Indeed. The mail coach arrived from London just as I was about to leave Shipley," Olivia replied happily. "I am merely saving the driver from making the extra trip down our lane."

Michael pretended to notice the top letter for the first time. "And it seems you are the recipient of a rather pretty missive right here," he countered as he lifted the envelope from the pile and handed it to her. Depending on when it was sent, he was certain he knew its contents.

Olivia reached for the letter and bit her lip as she considered whether or not to open it. "Yes, and I have been most anxious to learn its message," she said with a sigh. "But we'll be to the house shortly. I can wait until then."

"Open it," Michael insisted. "Please. I will not see it as an offense if you open it and read it this very moment." He didn't want to admit that he was as anxious to learn its contents as she was. Perhaps, if it was the news he was expecting it to be, he would ask for her hand right then. Although he didn't know if a marriage proposal would be welcome upon her reading she was no longer in contention for the position.

"If you are certain?" Olivia queried, turning the letter over and breaking the seal. The bits of red wax scattered into her lap, and she gathered them into her other hand so they wouldn't litter Mr. Cunningham's coach. She unfolded the bright white paper and began silently reading the impeccable script.

> *My dearest Miss Olivia, I wish to thank you for your recent letter of reply and again for your previous letter of introduction and character in regard to the position of governess. My husband and I have been searching for a suitable woman for some time, and we find your qualifications to be quite acceptable. If you are still interested in this position, please make your travel arrangements to Wiltshire at your earliest convenience so that we might determine a mutually agreeable date for you to start. I trust you will be able to make the trip by coach with an escort, but if not, perhaps we can arrange a coach for your*

*transport. I look forward to your earliest reply. Yours,
Elizabeth Statton.*

Olivia's eyes widened as she realized she had been truly accepted for the position. *She would be the governess for the Somerset duchy!* She took a deep breath and let it out, smiling broadly.

"'Tis good news, I expect?" Michael wondered as he watched her reaction. *Damnation! What did my sister write?*

"Indeed!" Olivia answered excitedly. "The Duchess of Somerset has accepted me for the position of governess for her children!" she claimed happily. "This news is most welcome. I have been waiting to hear word for several weeks."

Michael, tamping down the sudden anger he felt toward his sister, smiled on Olivia's behalf. *So much for a marriage proposal!* "Congratulations are in order then. Your family will be most happy for you, I expect," he said with a nod, his expression not revealing his knowledge of the offer. He silently cursed his sister again, wondering why she would go ahead with hiring Olivia when he'd made his wishes quite clear, when his sister had agreed to rescind the offer given she'd be gaining a sister of her own.

Unlike the position of governess for which Eloisa had applied and apparently landed in London, Michael knew this position to be legitimate. Until his discussion with his sister the ten days ago, he had no idea Olivia would be resourceful enough to pursue the position and have the qualifications necessary to suit Elizabeth's requirements. "And when does she expect you in Wiltshire?" he asked, hoping his voice did not betray his disappointment at hearing her words. *Perhaps this letter from Elizabeth was sent a couple of weeks ago and was simply delayed in delivery*, he considered.

"I must make travel arrangements and let her know when I can start," Olivia replied, noticing the coach had come to a halt and the footman was opening the door. "It will be a few days before I can leave, I expect," she said as she stood up and allowed the driver to assist her. "Thank you, Mr. White," she said with a grin to the driver as she turned to wait for Michael to make his way out of the coach.

A few days, he thought, a bit of panic rising in him. *Well, that only gives* me *a few days,* he considered. He was prepared to present his proposal to Harold Waterford on this trip as well as carry out his sister's recommendation.

He would have to ruin Olivia before she made her way to Wiltshire. Ruin her and marry her and take her back with him to London.

She'll never forgive me.

CHAPTER 21

RUINATION ON A TUESDAY

April 11, 1815
Michael awoke with a start, his heart hammering in his chest. Glancing around, he wondered what brought him awake so quickly when the remnants of his dream had him relaxing back into the mattress.

Olivia!

Tonight would be the night, he realized, a bit of sadness mixing with the anxiousness he felt. Did every potential groom go through this agony when they knew they were about to marry? About to marry because they had done something to require a wedding to take place?

Tonight was also the night he was expected at the Ship. A soirée had been scheduled in honor of the latest business venture.

He would have to see to Olivia after he returned from the inn. A fitting place to be, he supposed, since he had saved her from ruination there and would be ruining her in her own bedchamber within an hour of his return to her home.

Would Olivia ever forgive him for what he was about to do? Even if she never wanted anything to do with him, he had certainly harbored feelings for her since that day they had met at the Ship.

Perhaps someday she would allow him into her bedchamber, or she would come to his. And if she ever submitted to him, he would take care to make their first time together as painless as possible. Then he would make love to her as he had imagined doing in his daydreams.

He was sure Olivia would not be shy about her body— not like Eloisa seemed to be. Olivia was so poised, so comfortable at conversation, and so very smart. She would challenge him, to be sure, but wasn't that part of why he was so attracted to her?

Michael shook himself a bit, annoyed that he'd allowed his thoughts to run away from him again.

He was even more annoyed that his cock was quite hard.

Concentrate, he thought. *Meetings.* He would be spending the day in a meeting with Harold. At some point, he would have to tell the man of his intentions. Until then, there was business to discuss.

Getting out of bed, Michael shaved, dressed and made his way to the breakfast parlor to join the Waterfords for their morning meal. "Good morning," he said as he entered the room, giving a bow to Louisa. Harold and George were also seated and just starting to eat as Michael helped himself to coffee at the sideboard.

The lady of the house grinned and offered a nod in return. "Good morning, Mr. Cunningham. And how are you on this fine day?" she asked, indicating the window with a wave of her hand.

Michael glanced out the window, surprised to see clear skies. "I am well, thank you. And you?" he replied, wishing he really did feel fine.

Louisa gave a wan smile. "I admit, I would feel better if my daughter wasn't about to leave us. I suppose Harold feels the same, although he won't be the one to tell you," she said with a quirk as she indicated her husband. Harold was mostly hidden behind the latest issue of *The Times*.

"Will Miss Waterford be joining us?" he asked, thinking it was unlike Olivia to be absent from breakfast.

Harold looked up from the newspaper. "She's already eaten and left for Shipley."

Alarmed, Michael hesitated at taking a seat. "Is that … safe?" he asked, thinking of the Shipley Gang. He was prepared to run after her, insist that he walk with her to provide protection.

"Mr. White took her in the carriage," Harold said, holding up a hand as if to stay Michael's sudden urge to leave the table. "She said she has to purchase a few things for her trip to Wiltshire," he added, giving his guest an arched eyebrow that suggested he was annoyed by the idea of Olivia becoming a governess.

Relaxing a bit, Michael turned his attention to his plate of eggs and kippers. "You would really let her go?" he asked, *sotto voce.*

Harold gave a one shoulder shrug. "She is of age. There's apparently nothing for her here," he replied sadly. "And that's the extent of what I'll say on the matter."

Michael realized the man was annoyed with him. *And he has every right to be,* he thought. He would have to tell Harold what he intended to do. Before the day ended, he would have to ensure that Olivia would marry him.

Eloisa arrived at Waterford Hall later that afternoon, her sudden appearance unexpected by even her mother. "I took the postal coach," she said as she hugged Louisa and Olivia. "And I don't have to return to London for several days."

Her happiness at seeing her family was infectious, making the evening a lively affair for the entire family.

"Do you ever see one another in London?" Louisa asked of her eldest daughter and Mr. Cunningham. They were having walnuts and coffee before dinner. "On your daily walks or whilst shopping, I mean, of course," she added as Eloisa's face turned a pleasant shade of pink.

"Yes, actually," Mr. Cunningham replied with a casual nod. "Once a week, I suppose," he added as he caught Eloisa's eye and then explained with a most innocent tone, "Her townhouse is very near to my own."

Louisa tittered and seemed happy that her Eloisa knew *someone* in the city besides the few relatives they could claim.

Michael noticed how differently Olivia and Eloisa behaved with one another compared to the time before Eloisa moved to London. *Mature young women*, he thought, noticing how they seemed to appreciate one another more, as if they no longer felt a need to compete with one another for his attention.

Twice during the meal, though, he was aware of Eloisa trying to do just that. He gave her a nod to indicate he understood, wondering why she seemed eager to meet with him privately.

He found out shortly after he and Harold finished their port and cheroots in the library. Michael stayed behind, pretending to look for a book to take to his bedchamber. Eloisa entered the room and quickly shut the door behind her.

Standing before Michael, she squared her shoulders and took a deep breath. "You do not have to be my protector any longer, Mr. Cunningham. Arthur has asked if he can court me." She said the words with such grace, Michael was left wondering if she thought he would refuse to allow the match.

But her words were a huge relief.

Michael smiled, of course, feeling relief for himself and happiness for Arthur. And for Eloisa, too, of course.

"Have you told your family?" he asked, thinking her good news would be a welcome counter to what he was about to do to Olivia.

"No," she replied as she shook her head. "I will speak with Olivia. In the event Mr. Huntington and I marry, I am hoping she will stand with me at my wedding," she explained. "But, I fear she will already be in Wiltshire before that happens."

Michael shook his head. "I have reason to believe she won't be," he replied carefully. "But, if so, I am sure her new employer will allow her a trip to London for the nuptials," he offered. "I can claim the Duke of Somerset a close friend," he added by way of an explanation.

Eloisa gave him a tentative smile. "Thank you, Mr. Cunningham. For everything you have done for me," she said quietly.

"You're welcome, Miss Waterford." He took Eloisa's hands in his, wished her happy and then kissed her on the forehead. At the risk of being discovered alone with her, he stepped away and gave her a bow before leaving the library.

A few minutes later, Michael excused himself from the Waterford home. Having received an invitation to a soirée at the Ship, he made his way to the village. On the way there, he realized he hadn't seen Olivia by herself all day. There was a point at which he thought if he had, he would simply pull her aside and propose. Perhaps she would agree to marry him without the benefit of a courtship and a planned wedding.

Michael was on his first pint of ale with Angus MacFadyen when they began sharing anecdotes about their childhood. Both from Horsham, the two knew one another from their youth, and several of the men in attendance were also familiar to him. Others he had met during his frequent visits to the Waterfords.

There was talk of the waning iron smelting industry and the jobs that would be lost if the newest ventures did not pan out. There was talk of Harold Waterford and his involvement. And there was talk of Waterford's daughters.

What of Eloisa? they wondered.

Angus seemed to ignore the question, but the barkeep watched Michael as he told them the story of her husband's early death in the war and explained that her mourning period was ending. Apparently, Harold hadn't told anyone but Angus about his eldest being married at one time. A couple of the patrons took that to mean that Waterford didn't think much of his daughter's husband, so it was just as well she was a widow now.

Michael regarded Angus with a frown. "Did you ever

court Miss Waterford?" he asked, remembering a time when the barkeep seemed to favor the young woman.

Shaking his head, Angus considered how to reply. "Except for the occasion when she asked me to kiss her, I have had nothing to do with the chit," he answered simply.

His eyebrows raised in surprised, Michael was about to ask for more details when a group of patrons captured his attention.

When will you be claiming the second daughter as your wife?

Surprised, Michael wondered why they thought he had a claim to Olivia. He didn't think he'd been overt about his affection for the younger daughter. He doubted Harold Waterford had told the villagers that a deal had been struck where he could marry Olivia if he was still without a wife on the eve of his twenty-eighth birthday.

The man hadn't even told his daughter.

If he had, she probably wouldn't have applied to be a governess for his sister.

At least, he hoped not.

"Waterford's warned off every other suitor," Angus stated, leaning in to give him a punch on the shoulder. "Says you made your intentions very clear when she wasn't yet old enough. Figures you were first, so you get the gel," he added with a wink.

Michael grinned, thinking at first the barkeep was joking. But as the evening went on and the story was corroborated by other patrons, Michael reddened with embarrassment. He wondered how many of those in the Shipley area knew of Waterford's declaration.

If Olivia Waterford was to be his wife, then so be it, he decided as he ordered his second pint. He had considered her the lone candidate for the position for several years. He wasn't impressed by any of the other young ladies he'd been introduced to over the years. His mother was desperate for a daughter-in-law. And there was the promise he'd made to her, and his own sister's suggestion on how he could have Olivia without courting her.

And, in the middle of his second pint of ale, Angus MacFadyen became the third person to remind him he was about to be twenty-eight. In fact, wasn't his twenty-eighth birthday just over a week away?

Michael felt a bit of panic on hearing the reminder again. But now that Arthur Huntington had asked to court Eloisa, he was sure those two would marry. He was nearly free of his obligation to Eloisa.

Now he could concentrate on his own wedding. He could concentrate on Olivia. He could concentrate on how he was going to make her his wife.

He remembered how he had awakened that morning, his only thoughts about Olivia. All his dreams about Olivia.

Olivia was the only woman he had ever felt any kind of

...

Damnation! he realized as he set down his tankard and stared into the mirror behind the bar. *I have been such a fool!* he thought suddenly. *I love her. I probably have since that day I rescued her from that kid who tried to kiss her in the inn's yard.*

This inn's yard.

Michael was still staring at his reflection in the mirror when Harold Waterford showed up at the Ship and took a seat next to him. Before Michael could properly greet the man that would be his father-in-law, he stated, "I need to marry your daughter before a week come Friday."

Michael would never forget the look on the older man's face—the perplexed but then very pleased expression topped by a set of bushy eyebrows that danced a bit before Waterford sat up straighter and finally replied, "Forgot your twenty-eighth birthday was this year, huh?"

Michael cocked his head to one side and gave the man an apologetic nod. "I lost track of time," he admitted sadly.

"Then you'd best get to it, son."

It was as if the man was giving him permission to simply take his daughter. There was no negotiation, no promises to be kept, no conditions.

At least, not that night.

And what was the quickest way to win a wife but to ruin a young lady's reputation? And be sure there were witnesses to attest to his overt behavior?

I am a rake! he thought suddenly. *How can do I this?*

Returning to Waterford Hall with Harold, Michael gave the man a heartfelt apology before making his way up the stairs. Pausing in front of the door to Olivia's room, he pressed an ear against the wood and listened, wondering what he would do if she were awake. When he heard no sounds, he unlatched the door and simply marched into her room, removed most of his clothing, and climbed into her bed.

Olivia was on her side, facing the wall, her breaths coming in soft sighs he barely heard. Michael enveloped her body with his, soothed by the feel of the smooth linen of the night rail that covered her. The scent of roses in her hair filled his nostrils. *Hair like silk,* he thought as his fingers gingerly stroked it.

He wrapped one arm over her arm, his hand cupping her breast as he pressed the front of his body against her back, his thighs cradling the back of hers. His arousal was suddenly apparent behind his smalls as his manhood tried to find the space between her thighs. In a voice almost too husky to understand, he said, "My beautiful Olivia, please be mine."

'Please, don't scream,' might have been a better choice of words, but then they wouldn't be discovered by her fore-warned father and three unknowing servants.

Olivia's body suddenly stiffened. He heard her sharp intake of breath and felt her hand atop the one covering her breast, her fingers gingerly rubbing his knuckles before her panicked yell for help filled the room and the hall beyond. Michael held her more closely, kissed the back of her head, and allowed his nose to take in the scent of all of her until the door flew open and he was discovered.

Having finally jerked herself away from his hold and spun her body around in the bed, Olivia stared at her interloper.

Michael was sure he would never forget the look of astonishment on her face. But with it, there was something else. Regret, perhaps? Disbelief, certainly. And definitely surprise.

Half an hour later, the house once again quiet as the servants returned to their rooms and her parents left hers, Olivia climbed into her bed as if in a trance. *I'll wake up in the morning, and this will all have been a bad dream,* she hoped as she pulled the covers over her body. In doing so, she caught the familiar scent of sandalwood and citrus. She couldn't help but allow the frisson that passed through her body, a frisson that reminded her of Michael's hand on her breast, of his body against the back of hers, of his kiss on the back of her head and ...

Indeed, it wouldn't be a bad dream at all, except she couldn't help but remember the words she'd heard him say just before they were discovered.

"My beautiful El, please be mine."

CHAPTER 22

AN ANNOUNCEMENT ON A
WEDNESDAY

April 12, 1815
    Eloisa approached her sister's bedchamber door, her footsteps deliberately soft. Knocking lightly, she placed her ear against the wood, hoping Olivia was awake.

"Come in," she heard. *She's awake.* After the chaos of the night before, which resulted in the entire household being up until the wee hours of the morning, she thought she might be the only one awake and about. But the rest of the family was at breakfast at the usual time; only Olivia was absent. Their conversation was light and varied, and, as usual, her father was mostly hidden behind a copy of *The Times*. When Michael appeared at the threshold, though, her father stood up and left the room, their house guest in tow as they headed for the study.

Turning the knob, Eloisa opened the door just enough to see Olivia sitting on the edge of her bed. She was fully dressed in a sprigged muslin gown, with her hair already pinned up in a bun atop her head. "'Morning," Eloisa murmured as she slipped into the room and took a seat next to her sister. "We missed you at breakfast. I wanted to be sure you were ..."

Olivia gave her a nod. "Is it a good morning, do you

suppose?" she asked, her face suddenly lifted to the ceiling, as if she had to stave off tears.

Eloisa clasped her hand over one of Olivia's and gently squeezed. "Of course, it is. Mr. Cunningham will do the right thing, you must know," she replied with a smile.

"I don't want him to do the right thing because … because he feels like he *has* to," Olivia countered. "I only ever wanted him if he felt *affection* for …" She paused, realizing she had just put into words something she had never completely admitted to herself.

Leaning her head to one side, Eloisa regarded Olivia with a half-smile. "From the first day you brought him home, you were smitten with him. And he with you, I think," she whispered, remembering the jealousy she'd felt at seeing her younger sister with the handsome man who was to be their house guest. *I had such a crush on him*, she thought, realizing it was only in the last year that she no longer held a candle for Michael Cunningham.

Having the man as a protector had taught her the importance of mutual affection. After nearly a year of Michael's regular Tuesday visits, she grew to realize he wasn't particularly attracted to her. And he seemed preoccupied, as if his thoughts were elsewhere.

Or were for someone else.

Olivia blushed, surprised at her sister's words. "I was, wasn't I?" she admitted, one tooth capturing her lower lip.

A quick rap at the door had the two girls jumping. Their lady's maid, Caroline, poked her head into the room. "Miss Olivia, your father wishes to speak with you. In his study," she said quickly. Before Olivia could even respond, the door was shut and Caroline was gone.

Sighing, Olivia gave her sister a glance. "Even the maid thinks I'm a ruined woman. And I didn't even *do* anything," she commented before taking her leave of her sister.

Eloisa stared at her sister's retreating back, realizing just then they had something in common. *I know exactly how you feel,* she thought with a bit of sadness. *But at least you'll be married as a result.*

Olivia descended the stairs and headed for the study. She passed their house guest in the hall as Michael left the study, his face unreadable as he nodded to her. But she could feel his eyes on her back as she entered the study to stand before her father. She found herself wondering if Mr. Cunningham would eavesdrop at the door. He had been in there with her father for at least an hour after breakfast.

"This is a most auspicious occasion," her father said with a genuine smile. *A smile!* Olivia couldn't remember ever seeing her father displaying such happiness as he did when he gave her the news. "You are to be married to Michael Cunningham. Tomorrow, if the vicar can be located."

At her stunned silence, Harold Waterford came around from the other side of his desk and did something he rarely did. He hugged her. He rubbed her back, kissed her cheek, and then held her out at arms' length. "I have been waiting for this day for a very long time," he said, his eyes bright with tears. "Mr. Cunningham will make the announcement to the family during dinner this evening. I do hope you'll agree this is an excellent match."

And then, as quickly as she was summoned, Olivia was dismissed from her father's study.

And she hadn't spoken a word.

Of course, it *was* an excellent match, Olivia decided as she made her way to the parlor. She should be ecstatic at becoming the wife of the only man for whom she had ever felt affection, innocent as it was. But she could not help but feel that the marriage was forced on their guest—that her father had demanded that Michael Cunningham marry her. And she knew that Mr. Cunningham had agreed due to honor and who knew what other code a man followed in situations like this.

As her father promised, Michael did make the announcement of the impending nuptials later that night. He stood up during the family dinner and announced that he would be marrying Olivia by special license the very next day.

Stunned, Olivia stared at Michael and wondered how was it possible that he could procure a license so quickly. She understood special licenses were only obtainable from the Archbishop of Canterbury.

And weren't they only good for three months?

Did he keep one handy for just this sort of situation? she wondered then, daring a glance in his direction.

The stunned silence that followed Michael Cunningham's announcement was most uncomfortable until her mother clasped her hands together and grinned like a school girl. And then George pushed his chair away from the table, walked to Michael, and took his hand to shake it, saying, "Congratulations. Glad to have another brother," as if he was several years older than his eleven years.

Her family should have been more shocked than they seemed that night. During Michael's recurring stays at the Waterford's, neither he nor Olivia had shown the kind of interest in one another that would lead someone to think that they might eventually marry.

That's not quite right, Olivia admitted to herself. When she was seventeen or so, she had once welcomed Mr. Cunningham as if he was a member of the family, hugging him when he stepped out of his coach. He had wrapped one arm around her waist that day and nearly lifted her from her feet. She was sure he had buried his face in the space between her shoulder and head, could almost imagine he had kissed her on the neck before she caught her mother's arched eyebrow and let go her hold on him. But, now that she thought about it more, her mother hadn't seemed shocked or angered by her display of ... whatever it was she was displaying when she hugged Michael.

Affection, she realized then, remembering the scents of sandalwood and tobacco and *man* when her head had been pressed against his shoulder.

From that very first day in the Ship's yard, she had found

him interesting. She occasionally conversed with him on a number of topics after dinner. But anyone from London would have been welcomed at their table, she considered, as remote as the Waterfords were from city life. Mr. Cunningham brought news of the latest theatrical productions, soirées, balls, books, and opera singers, but he doled out the information in bits and pieces that allowed him to contribute just enough to each dinner conversation to keep them entertained during the few days he would stay with them.

But he certainly hadn't *courted* her.

And from the time she'd first met him—*I was sixteen*—she thought him attractive. As a result of reading her sister's Gothic romances, Olivia spent more than a few nights wondering what it would be like to have Michael Cunningham's large arms wrapped around her, to be held against his broad shoulders and to be kissed by his mouth. To have those dark lashes brush her cheeks and his blue eyes look upon her with favor. And those large hands, with their long, broad fingers and beat up knuckles but perfectly manicured nails—how would it feel to have those fingers comb through her hair? To hold her cheek while he kissed her? To caress her body? A frisson suddenly passed through her as she gave her mind free reign to remember everything she ever thought of Michael Cunningham.

Did he have similar fantasies about her? she wondered.

Well, she supposed she would soon find out. By this time tomorrow, she would be Mrs. Michael Cunningham.

CHAPTER 23

A WEDDING ON A THURSDAY

April 13, 1815
Michael woke up with a start, his breaths coming in short gasps.

My wedding day, he thought suddenly. *And I have no ring!* How could his sister have neglected to mention his need to get a *ring?* In her list of everything he needed to do before he married, she never once mentioned a ring!

He dressed quickly, noting the sounds in the household indicated others were up and about. Making his way to the breakfast parlor, he found George the only Waterford at the table.

"Good day, Master George," he greeted the young boy. "Would you know where I might procure a wedding ring?" he asked nervously. The vicar was due at eleven. There wasn't time to make a trip to Horsham, let alone Petworth.

George regarded his future brother-in-law with an expression of concentration. "The mercantile doesn't have jewelry," he replied finally. "But Mr. Coomber can pro'bly make you one."

Michael's eyebrows furrowed. "Mr. Coomber?"

Nodding, George stood up from the table. "The black-smith. I can give directions," he offered, taking his leave of the breakfast parlor.

Michael watched as the boy made his way to the vestibule. Realizing George intended to go with him to the blacksmith's shop, Michael hurried to catch up. "Is he far?" Michael wondered as fell into step next to George.

"Not far," George replied. "Just the other side of Shipley," he added. "Are you nervous? he asked. "Father says you will be."

A bit taken aback by the young boy's question, Michael gave it some thought. "I am," he replied finally.

"Why?" George asked.

Michael nearly snorted. Such a simple question, he considered. "Marriage is a big step. I'll be ... taking responsibility for your sister. Providing protection for her."

George gave him a sideways glance. "Because you want to? Or because you have to?" he asked bluntly. "I heard one of the servants say you ruined Livvy," he added, as if that excused his having asked such a personal question.

Michael wondered if the boy even understood what ruination meant. "Well, I ... I do have to marry her because I ruined her," he admitted. "But I ruined her because I need to marry her," he added, the words sounding awkward to his ears.

"So, why do you need to get married to Livvy?"

Suppressing the urge to laugh, Michael considered how to respond. "My birthday is next week. I made a promise to my mother that I would marry before my birthday. And since I ... I love your sister, I need to marry her," he managed to get out, surprised he could admit his feelings to George.

I have to because I love her, Michael thought suddenly. Leave it to an eleven year-old to help bring things into focus.

"So she doesn't go to Wiltshire?" George reasoned, his faced turned up to the man who walked beside him.

Michael had to nod. "Something like that," he replied. "She would make a fine governess," he added. "My sister, the duchess, hired her, you see."

George shook his head. "But you want her as a governess for your own children," he said matter-of-factly.

Michael nearly stopped in his tracks. *Children?* "Well, of course, I expect she'll make an excellent governess for our children. When we have them," he reasoned, his grin broadening as he thought of Olivia with a child. With children.

My child. My children.

Before George could ask yet another question, he turned sharply, leading them to the blacksmith's shop just off the road. The smithy was wielding a hammer, striking blows onto a piece of metal that looked like it might end up as a horseshoe.

"Mr. Coomber?" Michael called out, not wanting to get too close to the open fire.

"Aye," the smithy replied, putting down the hammer and wiping his hands on his apron. "Hello, George," he said as he moved to shake hands with Michael.

"Michael Cunningham," he said with a nod.

"Robert Coomber," the smithy replied. "Aren't you about to get married?" he asked with a grin.

"I am," Michael acknowledged. *Did everyone in Shipley know he had ruined Olivia?* "But, I find I left the ring behind in London, and I'm in need of one. Today. The vicar is due at the Waterfords' at eleven. What might you have available?"

The blacksmith's expression changed to indicate confusion. "I only have iron," he countered. "No gold or silver," he added with a shake of his head.

"I understand. As I said, I have one in London, but I just need something I can use for today's ceremony."

Mr. Coomber nodded and disappeared into his shop, returning after a moment with a collection of iron circlets in the palm of his hand. "Any of these work?" he asked as he spread them out on his palm with a grimy finger.

Michael regarded the collection, a bit disappointed at the selection. But one seemed the right size, and its band was even and smooth. "That one," Michael said as he pointed to his choice. "How much?" he asked as he reached into his waistcoat pocket.

The blacksmith shrugged. "Five shillings," he replied. "And I'll polish it up a bit."

Michael nodded, thinking he was fortunate to find anything he could use this close to his wedding.

He and George walked back to Waterford Hall in companionable silence. When they were climbing the front steps, though, Michael paused. "Will you stand with me today?" he asked solemnly.

George blinked and then gave him a nod. "Of course," he answered. "I have to change clothes, though," he said as he glanced down at his dusty breeches. "My mum will make me wear my Sunday best," he explained.

"As do I," Michael agreed. The two disappeared into the house.

Olivia sat at her escritoire, a quill poised above the white parchment. She felt sick at what she was about to write. How did one go about informing the Duchess of Somerset her newly hired governess would be unable to make the trip to Wiltshire because she was getting married?

Deciding not to mention the sudden wedding, Olivia wrote a short note saying she was unable to accept the position due to unforeseen circumstances. Apologizing for the inconvenience she had caused, Olivia wrote that she hoped the duchess would have success in finding a suitable replacement. The very last thing she wanted was to insult a member of the aristocracy. One last 'thank you' and her signature, and Olivia set down the quill. *At least I won't be an old maid governess,* she considered, the thought not bringing her the comfort it might have the month before.

Folding the paper, Olivia dripped a bit of wax onto the back and sealed it with her 'OW' stamp. *This will the last time I use this,* she thought suddenly, admiring the swirl of the letters in the engraving.

When she stood up, intending to take the missive to the vestibule, she glanced out the window. The sight of two figures in the distance caught her attention. She was aware of Eloisa entering her room and moving to stand behind her.

"What are you looking at?" Eloisa asked.

Olivia didn't answer as she watched her brother and the man she was about to marry as they walked toward the house.

"Where do you suppose those two have been?" Eloisa wondered from behind her shoulder, following Olivia's line of sight to the lane that led to Shipley.

"The Ship?" Olivia guessed, trying to keep her response light. The flutterbies in her stomach were making it all but impossible to feel anything but nervous, though.

Eloisa gave a giggle. "I doubt that."

But Olivia convinced herself the two had been at the pub. The thought that Michael would have to have a drink before he said his vows only added to the heaviness in her stomach. But to have to take her younger brother with him?

Wasn't it bad enough that Michael was marrying the wrong Waterford girl?

As Olivia stood before the vicar, one arm resting on Michael's sleeve, she was suddenly aware that George stood next to Michael, his posture so erect he seemed much taller than usual. Eloisa was at her left, tears streaming down her face and into the bouquet of flowers she held. The sounds of her mother's sobs had her glancing in her direction, only to find her father watching her, his stance as tall and proud as the night they had attended the last district ball.

She tried to concentrate on the vicar's words. The rushing sound in her ears prevented her from hearing most of his litany. When it was time for her to say something, she heard herself say the words but barely realized she was saying them. And then as quickly as it had begun, her wedding ceremony was over.

A silver ring was on her left hand, and Michael was kissing her.

In a moment, she was being kissed on the cheek by her sister and her father, and even her brother, who had to tug on her sleeve so she that she might bend down a bit in order that he could reach her cheek. And then her mother shoo'd them all away and took her turn, her own cheeks stained by tears.

'Your father was right all those years ago," Louisa whispered in Olivia's ear.

When Olivia gave a shake of her head, not understanding the meaning of her mother's words, Louisa gave her a grin. "He always knew Mr. Cunningham would marry you."

They were only words, but they were the words Olivia repeated to herself the rest of the day.

CHAPTER 24

A NEW LIFE BEGINS ON
FRIDAY

*A*pril 14, 1815

Michael Cunningham studied his latest business plan as he held it in his gloved hand. Harold Waterford had given it his blessing, announcing his intention to fund the coal gas venture for another few years in exchange for a handsome percentage if the business made a profit. And if this one did pay off as Michael figured it would, he too, would profit handsomely.

He hadn't planned to make quite so much in fees. A few days ago, he had set his take at the usual five percent annual commission. And now it would be at least fifteen!

Michael looked up suddenly and glanced out the window of the private coach, noting the roadside marker for Coulsdon. His driver would change horses there; the stable at an inn just beyond the town housed his matched black shires. The shires were the horses that pulled his coach from London to Coulsdon when he made the trip to Shipley.

"Is something wrong?" a quiet voice asked from next to him.

Michael nearly jumped as he remembered who he had with him. *My wife,* he thought, a mixture of dread and relief and anxiousness returning to his thoughts. "Not at all. I was just ... reviewing my business plans, is all," he replied, trying not to stare at the pretty woman with whom he had exchanged marriage vows only the day before. *It had all happened so fast!*

"Will my father be involved in this particular venture?" Olivia Waterford Cunningham asked, mostly to make conversation. They had traveled in silence for most of the trip from Shipley, and the quiet was beginning to unnerve her. She had nearly finished the book she brought along to read.

Keeping his gaze in her direction, Michael nodded. He couldn't ignore the fact that she was pretty. She was, in fact, the prettiest girl he'd ever known, the most beautiful woman he could imagine. Now that she was nearly one-and-twenty, her features had lost some of their softer edges and were more refined, more elegant. The high cheekbones, the full lips, the large green eyes and long, dark lashes topped by perfect arching eyebrows—all those features had always appealed to him. The way she looked into him instead of *at* him might have unnerved him at times, but at the moment, it seemed to him that he was the center of her universe, and he wanted for nothing more. "Indeed. He was quite ... insistent that he be involved," Michael responded with a nod, not adding that part of her dowry was included in this deal.

As much as he didn't want to get married, or *be* married (at least, not yet), it was the best business deal he had ever brokered in his life. And given his wedding had taken place nearly a week before his twenty-eighth birthday meant that there was another payoff waiting for him at White's whenever he was next at the men's club.

How many men could claim that getting married would make them rich? *Only those who marry girls with large dowries,* he considered, knowing at least two of his acquaintances had done so in order to pay off gambling debts. But they had married chits who were the daughters of aristocrats. Olivia's father wasn't even a peer of the realm!

Olivia struggled to keep a pleasant expression on her face. It wasn't as if she feared her new husband. The man had been a guest in her house several times a year for five years. A very pleasant man, she knew, always very polite, always impeccably dressed. He was obviously well educated. *And very handsome,* she'd thought from the very first day she'd met him. That day when he'd rescued her from Eli Blaylock.

She smiled at the memory, thinking of how incensed Michael had been when he'd pulled Eli away from her, how intent he appeared when he'd punched Eli and let go his hold on the poor boy's shirt. And then how quickly his countenance had changed when he turned to regard her, to ask after her health, to take her bleeding finger and examine it ... she shook herself out of the reverie.

Olivia took a deep breath in an attempt to steady herself, reminding herself that Michael was sitting only inches from her. *He would make an excellent husband,* she remembered thinking when she was much younger.

And now he was her husband!

He despises me, she thought suddenly.

The thought brought her back to the present, realizing Michael had made a comment about her father's involvement in his business. "On how many ventures have you partnered with my father?" Olivia wondered, her curiosity suddenly piqued. If they could just converse a bit more, she was sure they would become more comfortable with one another.

Like they were when they were in conversation at Waterford Hall.

Michael shrugged and seemed to give her query some thought. "We have five ventures in the works—all coal and iron-related, and then this one that's about to start," he indicated by waving the sheath of papers in his gloved hand, "And two that have been completed. It's a good partnership, I think," he added, seemingly pleased with the arrangement.

She thinks I am a rake, Michael figured, doing everything he could to keep his face impassive. *And she had every right, given the circumstances that led to our sudden marriage.* All those years of behaving as a perfect gentleman, of easily conversing with her during family dinners, of listening to her play piano-forte after the dessert course, of complimenting her embroidery skills and her reading ability—all the goodwill he had banked over the years was gone in a few moments of apparent drunken stupidity.

Olivia tilted her chin and gave him a nod. "I do hope you two continue to work together." And thinking he no longer wished to converse, Olivia turned her attention to the window and the countryside beyond.

Michael scrubbed his face with a gloved hand and stole a glance at the woman who sat next to him. Although they were legally married, *for nearly an entire day now,* he realized as he checked the chronometer that hung from his watch chain, he actually knew very little *about* her. He knew about her family, of course, having stayed in their large house in Shipley several times a year. *For five years already,* he thought as he remembered how nervous he was the first time he met her father, the venerable Harold A. Waterford.

He reached out a hand to touch the arm of his new bride. "Are you ... comfortable?"

Olivia quickly turned her attention from the coach window and regarded her new husband. "Yes, thank you," she said with a nod, allowing a wan smile. It wasn't really the truth, of course, but what kind of response could be made to such a question when you found yourself married and in a private coach on its way to London when you expected to be a spinster and in a mail coach on its way to Wiltshire?

For at least the tenth time that day, Olivia wondered just how she had come to be on her way to London with a man she hardly knew—a man that was now her husband and who seemed not the least bit happy about it.

Pressing her aching shoulders into the fine leather squabs, she swallowed hard to stave off the tears that threatened to spill from tired eyes.

Turning her head to stare out the window, Olivia tried to determine if they were anywhere near London or perhaps already in it. Traffic on the road was considerably heavier than earlier in the day. Despite their late start, Michael promised they would arrive at his townhouse in the mid-afternoon.

Olivia had been prepared to leave very early in the morning, her trunk packed with all her gowns and undergarments and a smaller chest filled with a few household items and a case of wine that made up what she considered her dowry. However, her mother had put on a show of grieving and weeping that delayed their departure despite the fact that she had been so happy upon learning her daughter would be marrying Michael. And Olivia's older sister, widowed and a rare visitor to their parents' home, stood with a perplexed expression on her face that suggested she was either very relieved or most displeased that her younger sister had been to the altar with Michael Cunningham.

Olivia shook herself out of her reverie, reminding herself that the man next to her was only in Shipley this past week because her father had invited him for fishing and because he wanted news of their common business ventures. He had just been there a few weeks before—Michael usually came every six weeks. His stay in their home was to have been only a few days. But because he'd opened the wrong door in the middle of the night ... Tuesday night ...

Michael was quite content to sit in silence while the coach made its way along the fairly smooth road. Occasionally, he glanced out the window and tried to predict where they might be. If his driver could keep up the pace, they would arrive in time for him to make his late-afternoon appointment with Sir Richard. And, if he did not make it back in time, he could make another appointment without incurring any wrath on the part of the financier; Sir Richard was a friend first and business partner second.

When Michael finished updating the man on the news from Sussex, he would then inform him that he was a married man. He could hardly wait to see Sir Richard's reaction. *And the hundred pounds he owes me for that damned marriage bet.*

"We'll be stopping shortly to change horses," Michael

said suddenly. As if on cue, the coach slowed and turned off the road.

A coaching inn, its shingle a bit worn, appeared beyond Olivia's window. She studied the building and glimpsed the stables farther down the yard, recognizing the establishment as one at which her own family stopped when making the occasional trip to London. A flurry of activity commenced as several handlers hurried to unhitch the matched horses and bring out fresh shires.

"Are you hungry?" Michael asked as he stood up and reached to unlatch the door. A footman was already putting down the steps, ready to assist the passengers.

"Thirsty, I suppose," Olivia replied, not completely sure of her husband's economic means nor who owned the unmarked equipage in which they rode. Although she felt a bit hungry, she wasn't sure she could keep from casting up her accounts should she try and eat anything.

Nodding, Michael reached a hand in and assisted her from the coach. After a couple of hours of the constant sway and bounce of the coach, it was a moment before Olivia felt steady on her feet. She noted that her husband seemed to have no trouble gaining his land legs.

Hurrying to keep up with him, her hand barely wrapped into the crook of his arm, Olivia tried to gauge his mood. He didn't seem the least bit annoyed by her presence. Or even inconvenienced. In fact, his other hand had suddenly landed atop the one she held against his arm, patting it a few times as they made their way to the entrance.

Inside the inn's small eating area, several tables sat empty. Michael led them to one next to the front window. "What would you like?" he asked as he pulled out a chair for her.

"Tea, please," she replied quietly.

Michael shrugged and turned to the innkeeper, who was just coming forward with a menu board. "Hello, Portmouth. Tea and biscuits for the lady and one of your meat pasties and an ale for me," he said, the tone of his voice indicating he knew the place well and felt comfortable ordering the food.

The innkeeper nodded as he took the menu board from Michael. He stole a quick glance at Olivia before hurrying off to the kitchen, obviously recognizing the Waterford girl from her past travels.

Her gaze met Mr. Portmouth's, and Olivia gave him a slight smile, relieved that she recognized someone in her new life as a married woman. *Hopefully, he'll realize we're married and not assume I am traveling with a man and have no chaperone in sight!*

Olivia looked out to see a matched set of jet black shires being led to the coach. She gasped, her eyes wide as she took in the sight of such perfection; the animals were beautiful.

"They are my favorite team," Michael commented proudly when he saw the subject of her surprise. "Bought them at Tattersall's last year." He felt a bit of a thrill as he watched his new wife admire the pair.

Olivia turned her attention to him. "They are *yours?*" she asked, even more incredulous. *If they are his favorite team, he must have others*, she thought. *Horses are expensive!*

Michael suddenly realized Olivia knew nothing of his economic situation, and probably didn't know his lineage. Although he hadn't shared the information with her family, her father knew. But Michael was discovering that Harold Waterford wasn't one to share information. "Yes," he replied with a smile, happy to know she was impressed. "I traded them out here when I was on the way down to Shipley last Saturday," he added, wincing when he remembered that he originally intended to return to London Wednesday. *Two days lost*, he thought, a frown coming over his face. If he'd hadn't put off what he intended to do the day after he arrived ... *coward!*

He brightened a bit when the food and drinks were set down. Michael noted how carefully Olivia added milk to her tea. He watched as her small finger looped through the teacup handle, her thumb supporting the bowl as she sipped without making a sound. Michael stared at her hand, imagining what it would be like to have that hand rest on him, to have that hand held inside of his, to have it touch his cheek, to feel it trail across his chest and explore his body whilst they lay in the new bed he'd made sure was included in the remodel of the secret salon on the second floor.

He hoped the purple and gold fabrics and the elegant furniture in her salon would be to her liking. The decorator had been necessarily quick and efficient in creating the space, claiming he had just completed a room like it for Her Majesty the Queen, although the Queen's room had been much larger, of course.

One day, Michael hoped Olivia would invite him to spend the night with her in that room. He imagined undressing her, imagined taking the pins out of her mahogany hair and kissing her full lips and holding her bare breasts in his hands while she used her own hands to stroke and pleasure him, her finger tips trailing down to his groin, caressing his hardened manhood until he was sure he could no longer control himself.

His loins tightening at the thought, Michael caught sight of the ring on her fourth finger and grimaced. He would have to replace *that* just as soon as he could make the trip to Rundell and Bridge. How could his sister have neglected to mention his need to get a *ring?*

"Oh, I nearly forgot," he said as he set down his pint and reached into his waistcoat pocket, trying to get his mind off his sudden erection. "I have a set of keys for you. For the townhouse. And the mansion."

Olivia watched as he pushed the keys across the table toward her, his broad but long forefinger guiding them in her direction. "For me?" she replied in surprise, an eyebrow cocking into a perfect mahogany arch.

"Of course. As mistress of the house, you may need them on occasion," he said, wondering when there would ever be a time when his butler, Jeffers, or another servant wouldn't be at home to open the doors. His sister had seemed quite insistent that he give her keys, though, so he'd seen to it that copies had been made especially for her.

"Oh, thank you," Olivia said with a nod, taking the keys and dropping them into her reticule. *Did he just give me his only house keys?* she wondered. *He must have—he wouldn't have expected to return to his home in London as a married man!*

Unaware he had finished his pasty and Olivia had drained her teacup, Michael was surprised when Portmouth claimed the empty glassware. "It appears your coach is ready, Mr. Cunningham," the innkeeper said as he nodded toward the window and the sight beyond.

Michael glanced up, startled. "Of course. What do I owe for the extra days?" he asked, glancing out the window to see that the team was hitched.

Olivia excused herself and hurried to the door, wanting an opportunity to look at the horses more closely before she had to return to the interior of the coach. Standing in front of the left lead, she lifted her gloved hand to the space between his eyes and stroked softly, cooing as she did so. The right lead raised its head and regarded her. She moved to stand in front of him and repeated the stroking, smiling as the horse seemed to press his head against her hand. "You are a darling," she whispered. The horse nickered softly.

"Mrs. Cunningham," she heard from somewhere. It was a moment before she realized it was *she* who was being addressed. "Coming!" she called out. She gave the horses another stroke before hurrying to the coach door where her husband waited. Sensing dissatisfaction from him, *or is that just impatience? Or is he amused?* she got in quickly and settled into one corner, her attention only on what she could see outside the window.

Dozing when the carriage's sway was slight, Olivia was aware of Michael's soft snore from somewhere to her left. She finally looked in his direction, hoping to steal a glance while he slept. The planes of his face, defined by the square jawline at the bottom and the strong forehead above straight brows, were no longer quite so stern. His nose, obviously broken at some point in the past, was too broad to be considered aristocratic, but it suited his strong features, especially given the chin that extended a bit beyond the front of his face. And his mouth, with lips that hid straight white teeth and smiled easily—that mouth had her mesmerized until Michael's eyes suddenly opened and she was forced to look away or be caught staring at him.

The carriage came to a sudden halt and Olivia glanced out to see a fashionable square surrounded by beautiful townhouses and small, cropped lawns dotted with trimmed bushes and pots of colorful flowers. She turned to Michael to ask if they were indeed at Grosvenor Square when he suddenly stood up and opened the door before a footman could do so. He stepped out of the coach, and in his haste, nearly forgot to turn around and offer his assistance to her.

Holding up her skirt in one hand and placing her other in his gloved hand, she stepped down from the coach and took a quick look around. The terraces were neat and clean. Judging by the fashionably dressed ladies who carried parasols and walked the square with well-dressed men on their arms, she reasoned that this part of London was quite well-to-do.

"This way," he said curtly as he held out his arm for her. Olivia took it and hurried to keep up with him as he climbed the steps to the set of dark green double doors of a brick townhouse. Rapping the knocker, it was only a second before an older gentleman opened the door and gave his master a slight smile and bow.

"Mr. Cunningham. We expected you Wednesday ..." the butler started to say before he noticed the woman standing next to Michael. Quickly hiding a hint of recognition he felt upon seeing her, Jeffers said, "Forgive me," as he bowed in her direction and quickly stepped aside to allow the couple to enter.

A footman immediately appeared and offered to take Michael's topcoat and hat. When the master deferred, he paused to determine if Olivia would be giving up her mantle. She reluctantly shrugged it off her shoulders and handed it to the young man, nodding in his direction as she did so. Quite aware of the butler's gaze, she looked to Michael for an introduction and wondered why he didn't give up his coat and hat.

"Pardon me," Michael said in an off-hand manner. "Miss Waterford." He paused a moment before correcting himself. "Mrs. Cunningham. This is Jeffers, the butler. My wife, Olivia," he said as he turned his attention to the startled butler.

Michael knew that as the head of the household staff, Jeffers would see to it that all the servants learned of his marriage before the end of the day. He rather doubted it would take more than an hour for the news to spread to all those that worked for him.

Within another day, every servant on the square would know.

"Very pleased to meet you," Olivia said as she held out her right hand.

Despite his effort to hide his reaction, Jeffers stared at her in surprise before gently shaking her hand. "At your service, madam," he murmured as he bowed deeply. He suddenly realized why he thought he had recognized the woman when he remembered the young widow who had called on Michael all those months ago. *But this isn't the same woman.*

"Messages?" Michael questioned with a raised eyebrow.

"On the desk in your study, sir," Jeffers replied quickly.

"And Mr. Seward is in the library. He said he has good news to share with you before you retire this evening."

Michael gave a quick shrug. *Good news?* Either Edward had found Anna or his brother's heir had been born. "I have an appointment with Sir Richard. If I leave now, I can just make it," Michael stated evenly after a quick glance at his chronometer.

Jeffers looked surprised and did not try to hide it. "Don't

you wish to change from your traveling clothes first?" he asked.

Michael shook his head and opened the front door, intending to leave. Not sure what to do, Olivia stood in the large vestibule, wishing she, too, could turn and walk out the door. Or perhaps the back door, she considered as she sighed heavily and watched her husband descend the steps.

Jeffers, aware of her discomfort, called out to Michael before the man had made it to the coach. "And to which room should I have Mrs. Cunningham's trunks delivered?" he asked.

Michael stopped short and turned, a quizzical expression on his face. "Well, the purple room, of course," he called out, a bit of triumph in his voice. "The purple room," he said again before ducking into the coach.

The butler nodded quickly but soon frowned, his face displaying a look of consternation. *Purple room?* "Of course, Mr. Cunningham. I'll see to it right away." He turned to Olivia and gave her an apologetic glance. "If you'll follow me, I'll take you to your room. The housekeeper will see to it that the bed is made up to your satisfaction."

Gripping her reticule handle in one hand, Olivia gave the butler a small smile. "I'm sure it will be fine, Jeffers," she said with as much conviction as she could muster.

"Did you bring your own maid, madam?" he asked as he glanced back into the vestibule before he started up the stairs.

Embarrassed at the lack of an abigail, Olivia pinched her lips together. "I fear I was not able to convince her to make the move to London," she heard herself saying. The maid that served her and her mother—and her sister, when she deigned to visit them—would have gladly joined her. But her mother wasn't about to give up Caroline.

"Will you want me to hire one, or do you wish to vet your own?" the butler asked as he started down a short but wide hallway. Several closed doors surrounded the wide hall, and he paused in front of the one nearest the stairs, a bit of uncertainty apparent in his choice.

"I do not know anyone here in London, so if you could spare the time to find one for me, I shall be very grateful," Olivia replied as the butler finally opened a door to the first room on the right.

"I shall have a lady's maid for you by morning," he promised as he allowed her to enter the room.

The bedchamber was much larger than she expected and quite nicely appointed with light blue damask and silk covered furnishings, an elaborate canopied bed that was dressed and draped in sapphire blue, and large rosewood dressers. "Oh, my, this is quite ... beautiful," she murmured as she moved slowly into the room. *Certainly not purple,* she thought when she remembered Michael's direction to his butler. *Maybe he is color blind,* she considered. "Much larger than I would have had in Wiltshire, to be sure," she whispered, almost to herself. If a room could be called by its color, this one would be *blue,* she figured.

So why did Michael refer to it as purple? she wondered.

"Wiltshire?" the butler queried. Although it wasn't his place to converse with the various owners of the townhouse he had served for over twenty years, Jeffers was quite adept at ferreting out information that would assist him in his duties to the household.

Olivia turned and nodded. "I was to be the governess for the two oldest children of the duke and duchess," she said with a sigh. She tried desperately to smile but found the effort too much.

His eyebrows raised into the hairline of the white powdered wig he wore, Jeffers' expression showed his surprise before he could wrestle it back into an air of indifference. "Oh, my," he replied shortly, now certain that the lady was a bit more than just a chit from the country but definitely not a member of the *ton.*

But why would the woman who was to be Miss Cunningham's governess now be Mr. Cunningham's wife?

"Does anyone else use this room?" Olivia wondered as she put her reticule on a nearby dresser, removed her gloves, and gave the blue velvet counterpane a quick sweep with her hand. There was no evidence of dust or disuse in the room; the servants were to be commended for keeping it up if it was merely a guest bedchamber.

Jeffers nodded. "Lady Cunningham stays here on occasion. She's quite particular, of course," he said, his voice not giving any indication of his true feelings for Michael's mother.

Lady Cunningham, Olivia repeated to herself. *Lady? As in ... an aristocrat?* "Formidable?" Olivia wondered with a raised eyebrow.

Taken aback, Jeffers regarded her for only a moment before deciding on how to reply. "Very. I take it she was not at the ... wedding?"

Olivia shook her head, wondering if there was a *Lord* Cunningham somewhere. "No. Though my parents were in attendance, of course," she said quietly, feeling as if she needed to assure the servant that she and his master hadn't gone off to Gretna Green to elope. She resisted telling the butler anything more, however. As an unmarried man in London, Michael Cunningham had apparently met more than his share of debutantes and their conniving mothers, once making a comment over after-dinner drinks about his distaste for young women's tendencies to prattle on about nothing. *Present company excluded, of course, since you two do not seem to practice such conversation,* she suddenly remembered Michael saying as he made it a point of motioning to her and her sister Eloisa.

And yet, she also remembered that before Eloisa had moved to London, she did prattle on a bit too much, always wanting to know more about London than Mr. Cunningham was willing—or able—to provide. On this latest visit, though, her sister didn't flirt with Michael as she usually did. But Eloisa seemed most eager to speak with him in private.

Swallowing hard as she felt a rush of emotion coming on, Olivia blinked back tears. Noticing the look of expectancy on the butler's face, she turned and asked, "Does Lady Cunningham live here in town?"

The butler grimaced. "Not usually. When she is not in Sussex, she ... travels ... a great deal," he said with a bob of his head.

"The Continent?" Olivia half-asked with a knowing smile.

Jeffers lowered his eyes and nodded. "For some of the year, yes," he admitted sheepishly. "She requires the latest in fashion to maintain her status as a viscountess."

Had Olivia not been so very tired, a look of total surprise would have replaced her sad visage. *Viscountess!* She'd married the son of a viscount? Viscount *Cunningham*, no less, she realized, wondering if it was truly the same viscount that had lands in Sussex. Then she chided herself. *Could there be more than one?*

At no time during Michael's visits to her family's home in Shipley had Michael Cunningham *ever* said *anything* about being a member of the *ton!*

And what did that make her?

A pair of footmen appeared with one of her trunks dangling between them, and she pointed to a clear space along one wall. Relieved of their burden, they bowed and left the room as a pair of maids hurried in with ewers of steaming water.

"I take it that Lady Cunningham runs the household when she is in residence?" Olivia asked as she opened the trunk and pulled out several gowns.

"She has in the past, yes," the butler replied with a bit of hesitancy.

"And who runs the household when she is *not* in residence?"

Jeffers bit is lower lip and sighed. "I have been doing so, for the most part, Mrs. Cunningham, but I expect you will wish to from now on," he replied hopefully, avoiding her surprised look.

Sighing, Olivia considered his comment and knew he

was correct. Menus, staff, household bills, visitors, and receptions were the responsibility of a wife, she considered. Nothing she hadn't at one time prepared for before her position as a governess was secured. "All right then, I suppose we should begin with dinner then?" she offered, giving him a raised eyebrow.

Jeffers face took on a look of relief, perhaps even amusement. "Thank you, madam," he stated a bit too enthusiastically.

Olivia wondered if Jeffers really was happy to turn over authority to someone else, or if he resented her for taking over his domain. Servants would always defer to the butler and follow his orders, but having a lady in the house meant a level of authority that commanded just a bit more respect.

"How many servants in the house?" she asked as she sat down in a nearby chair and removed a small pad and thin charcoal pencil from her reticule.

"Ten. I ... I apologize for not having introduced you to them when you arrived."

Olivia cocked an eyebrow. "No apology required. How could you know, Jeffers? Name them, please," she ordered as she prepared to write.

"Cook, housekeeper, two maids, two grooms, an occasional gardener, two footmen, a scullery maid, and myself," he stated confidently.

Writing as fast as she could, Olivia considered the list and asked, "Do you serve as Mr. Cunningham's valet?"

"Yes, madam."

"Who serves dinner?" she asked.

When Jeffers didn't answer right away, Olivia looked up to find him perplexed. "Does Mr. Cunningham even eat dinner here?" she clarified, realizing that breakfast and luncheon were probably served from a sideboard in the dining room. *If there is a dining room.*

The butler sighed as he tried to control a bit of embarrassment. "My lady, this household is inhabited by two men who frequently dine at White's and who are rarely in residence otherwise ..."

Two men? Perhaps Michael's father lived here when he wasn't in Sussex. Olivia tried to remember where she had heard of White's and decided she would ask about it later. "Will there be a dinner ... or a supper served this evening?" she interrupted as she realized she hadn't eaten since breakfast. Although the carriage had stopped at the coaching inn earlier that afternoon, she politely refused Michael's offer of a luncheon and took just tea and biscuits.

I could have had a feast, she suddenly realized.

Jeffers gave a curt nod and turned to leave. "I will have Cook prepare something."

Shaking her head, Olivia put a hand out to stop his exit. "Please do not have him make something for only me. I merely wondered if ... when dinner might be."

Having hinted that she should *command* him to see to it there was a dinner served that evening, Jeffers tried a different approach. "The cook makes an evening meal for the staff every night. Shall I have him make one for you? I rather doubt Mr. Cunningham will be back from Sir Richard's by dinner time."

Olivia sighed. "Yes, thank you. I'll take it in the ... parlor?" she guessed, not wanting to eat in a dining room all by herself.

"Very good. And what about tomorrow? Shall I have Cook make you and Mr. Cunningham a dinner?" he asked, his eyebrow cocked as if hinting she should say 'yes'.

"Yes, that would be good. And who will serve dinner?" Olivia wondered.

"The footmen and one of the maids have serving experience. I shall see to it they are available for duty at dinner."

"Eight o'clock?" Olivia queried, remembering that people in the city tended to eat later than those in the country.

"I shall see to it," Jeffers repeated curtly. "And brandy and wine are served in the library at seven," he added, wanting to be sure she knew about the gentlemen's ritual of enjoying evening drinks before dinner, even if they didn't eat at the house. "Should I send up a maid to help you dress?" he offered, his face coloring up a bit as he made the suggestion.

Olivia considered the offer but shook her head. "I won't require one this evening, but thank you."

After a short pause, Jeffers bit his lip. *What has my master done to necessitate a marriage to this poor girl?* he wondered. *The man's mother has been trying to get him to the Marriage Mart for years, and he suddenly shows up with a pretty bride. And an unhappy one,* he considered.

Marriage of convenience, perhaps? Or marriage of necessity?

"Thank you, Jeffers," she said by way of dismissal, not quite sure what she was supposed to say.

The butler bowed and hurried out of the room. Olivia finished unpacking and chose a gown for her private dinner. She glanced at a clock on the nearby dresser and decided she had much to do before she'd be ready for dinner, let alone drinks. Having only three appropriate gowns for an evening meal, it would not be difficult to get dressed, she considered. A quick look at her mahogany hair in the oval cheval glass caused her to grimace, and the slight bruising under her eyes made her look as tired as she felt.

Her hair still smelled of roses when she undid the tight bun and brushed it out. With no abigail to assist her, she rolled it into a simple chignon and pinned it in place. The servants had filled the copper tub in the adjoining bath with enough hot water and lemon soap to rinse away the odor of travel.

Before long, she stepped into a simple periwinkle batiste gown. The cap-sleeved dress displayed the tops of her shoulders, but with buttons down one side under her arm, she was able to fasten them without the help of a maid. The color of the gown suited her pale skin and hair, and the bruising under her eyes was nearly gone by the time she pulled on long white gloves. Owning little in the way of jewelry, she had only a single strand of yellowed pearls to wear around her neck and small gold wires to thread through the piercings in her ears.

By the time she regarded her image in the cheval mirror at precisely seven o'clock, she felt revived and ready to face life in a London townhouse.

When Michael Cunningham returned from his brief meeting with Sir Richard, he slumped into the chair behind his desk and stared at the collection of pasteboard calling cards, letters and invitations that had piled up since he'd left for Sussex. *Has it only been seven days?* he wondered as he realized the date. A week ago, he was a confirmed bachelor.

And, now, he was a married man!

Am I really almost twenty-eight years old? he wondered for the tenth time that day as he pulled a letter out of the pile on the silver salver. The scent and handwriting on the outside were definitely his mother's, he noticed with a bit of indifference. Opening it slowly, he read of her latest travels in Italy and of her promise to be back in London for the start of the Season. The final line made him smile. *If you have kept your promise, and if it is the last thing I do before I die, I shall see you a married man,* she had written as a postscript. Well, she could die happy now, he supposed.

Or not, once she discovered his bride was not a daughter of the *ton.*

Leaning back in his chair, Michael suddenly remembered his bride's sister. *Damn!* he realized suddenly. *I haven't spoken to her since the wedding ceremony. What must she think of all this?* he wondered, hoping she would not be too cross that he hadn't included her in his plans to marry her sister.

I am a married man now, he considered. *I am married to Olivia,* he thought as his heart seemed to skip a beat.

Although it seemed apparent to him during their ride to London that Olivia Waterford wanted nothing to do with him, he had certainly harbored feelings for her since that day he'd met her in the inn yard in Shipley. *Hair like silk,* he thought as he recalled Tuesday night in her bed when his hand had touched it. And he remembered the golds and red that appeared in the mahogany strands of that silken hair when she was in the garden cutting the still-tiny flowers for the front hall of her father's house. He found himself wondering if she would ever do the same for this place.

Groaning, he sat back in the chair and wondered if he should write to Eloisa. She was in residence when he married her sister. She had already told him that he no longer needed to provide protection. But he realized that she still deserved an explanation, a closure of sorts for their relationship.

Opening the inkwell, he thought a bit about what to write in the short missive. An apology, certainly. Beg for forgiveness, of course. Provide assurances that she could continue to live in the townhouse he had let for her until she was married. And all would be well.

He folded the crisp, white sheet of stationery, sealing it with a few drippings from the nearby candle followed by a press of his 'MTC' seal into the round puddle. That missive complete, he took the next letter off the pile. When he read the return address, he was surprised to see it was from his banker. *Odd,* he thought as he broke the wax seal and opened the paper.

Cunningham, I do hope your trip to Horsham went as planned. Do let me know if any additional financing is required for this next venture with Sir Richard and Mr. Waterford. I would like the opportunity to spar with you at GJ's. Would Tuesday at 3 in the afternoon be convenient for you? Regards, A. Huntington.

Michael furrowed his brows. Arthur knew damn well that Harold Waterford would fund the entire project when given the opportunity. So the note wasn't really about financing the business deal, he considered.

Which meant it was all about Huntington wanting to take him on in an informal mill.

But why? Michael wondered briefly. They usually just sparred when they happened to be at Gentleman Jackson's at the same time. They had never actually *scheduled* a match. Sparring was informal ...

Eloisa! Michael realized, remembering again the short conversation they'd had in Shipley. There was nothing in the note about Arthur courting Eloisa!

This is about Eloisa.

Since Arthur had already asked to court Eloisa, then their afternoon tea must have gone well. *Very well, indeed,* Michael realized happily. And if that was the case, then perhaps Huntington was ready to ask for her hand! Michael considered the missive. He was certain the banker still thought he had some kind of claim to Eloisa. Michael had mentioned looking after the supposed widow the day they were on their walk together. Perhaps Huntington hadn't believed him that night at White's, when he'd assured the man he had no claim on Eloisa.

The man wants to fight me!

And what better bait to fight over than a beautiful woman?

He told Huntington he planned to wed before his twenty-eighth birthday, but he hadn't made his marriage public knowledge just yet. There was no notice in *The Times.* That meant Huntington might think he had a claim on Eloisa—that *he* planned to wed *her* to meet the deadline, even though he had assured the man he had no intention of doing so.

Well, if the man wanted to fight over Eloisa, then so be it. Because Michael knew he had nothing to lose.

Except, perhaps, a bare knuckle mill.

Deliberately.

Michael took a sheet of crested parchment from his desk and dipped his quill, writing a quick note that accepted the invitation to spar and declined the offer of financing. Folding it with a satisfied grin on his face, Michael dripped some candle wax onto the edges of the paper and reached over to pick up his seal. He quirked his lips as he nearly picked up the stamp with an ornate 'OWC' carved into it.

He had ordered the seal for Olivia the week after his visit to Wiltshire, remembering his sister's list of accessories he would need to arrange if he was truly going to marry Olivia Waterford. Exchanging the seal for his masculine 'MTC', Michael stamped the seal into the hardening wax.

The next letter he took from the salver had him sighing. The bright white parchment, folded just so and sealed with the Duke of Somerset crest, was from Elizabeth Statton. *Sister, you have some explaining to do*, he thought as he remembered the missive she had sent to Olivia, confirming that she had the governess position and to make arrangements for travel to Wiltshire. He broke the seal and unfolded the parchment.

My dearest brother, In the event you did not do as we discussed during your last visit to Wiltshire, I have sent a letter of hire to Miss Olivia Waterford. It is my sincerest wish that by the time you read this, you did indeed do what we discussed and are married to her. And if you did not, and you are not married to her, then at least she will soon be my governess. I promise I shall say nothing to her of our agreement. Sincerely, Elizabeth.

The minx!

Another rather uncharitable thought struck Michael as he read the letter, but he sat back and took a bit of satisfaction in the knowledge that he *had* done what he and his sister had discussed, and that Olivia was *not* going to be a governess. *At least, not my sister's*, he amended when he remembered the conversation he'd had with George. *My new brother*, he thought proudly.

Michael was about to read the last note on the salver when he heard a staccato knock on the door. A glance at the clock showed it was nearly seven o'clock. "Come in," he called out, opening an invitation to a ball at the Harvey's. *Next Thursday night*, he read before he turned his attention to the door.

Edward Seward opened the door only wide enough to allow his head to pop through. "Ah, Jeffers said you were back."

Michael smiled at the man who had made himself at home in his townhouse. "Indeed. I heard you have good news," he answered jovially, remembering that Jeffers had said Edward wanted to speak with him. "About time for drinks in the library, wouldn't you say?" Michael suggested as he stood up from the desk and stretched. "God, I ache," he murmured as he made his way around the edge of the desk. The constant jostle of the coach had his body complaining, and if he was uncomfortable, he suddenly found himself wondering how Olivia was faring.

"Someone's been missing his workouts at Gentleman Jack's," Edward teased as he opened the door completely so that Michael could join him in the hall. Taller and certainly more classically handsome than Michael, Edward wore only a shirt, breeches, and a pair of Hessian's that were either new or newly polished. His dark blonde hair was cropped short but left tousled on top while long sideburns made his long oval face seem even longer. "Penelope gave birth to a boy yesterday," he said suddenly. "Arthur has his heir."

Michael regarded Edward with a nod. "Congratulations! You're an uncle," he said with a huge grin. "And, you're no longer in line for the Eversham earldom. You must be so proud," he teased, wondering if Edward really was as relieved as he seemed at his lowered status in the order of inheritance.

Edward bobbed his head in several directions. "A mixed blessing, I know. But it means if I ever find Anna, I can marry her without reprisals from my mother," he said with a nod.

Michael gave Edward a worried look. "You still haven't found her?" he asked. Anna had been missing for nearly a year! What if she no longer lived in London? Perhaps she had gone back to Bath. Was Edward willing to broaden his search? Or hire an investigator to search for her?

"Not yet, but I will," Edward said with the kind of assurance that suggested he still had faith he would find the love of his life. "Did you just return from Sussex today?" Edward wondered then, his brow furrowing as Michael matched his step down the hall to the library.

"Indeed," Michael nodded and hurried to where Jeffers had set out the decanters and glasses on a sideboard. "I would have been home day 'fore yesterday, but ..." He sighed as Edward stopped suddenly to regard his friend. "Listen, I find myself in a rather awkward position," Michael started to explain as he poured the two of them rather large drinks.

One of Edward's eyebrows arced up as he took his glass and noted how full it was. "Who's the chit?" he asked with a serious expression replacing the light-hearted one he had displayed until they reached the library.

Sighing, Michael rolled his eyes. "Olivia Waterford," he said before taking a huge swallow of scotch. From Edward's quick take on the problem, Michael assumed the man had already met his wife.

Edward gave him a sideways glance. "I thought her name was Eloisa?" he countered, a bit of confusion showing on his face.

"Younger sister," Michael replied, opting not to take another sip of his drink just then.

Now more confused, Edward leaned forward. "You're involved with the younger sister, too?" he asked quietly, not wanting a servant to overhear their conversation. "Oh, now I remember. You told me about her. The night of my birthday," he claimed, his eyes glazing over.

Surprised Edward would remember anything from that night given the amount of brandy he'd drunk, Michael took a long pull on his own drink. "I married her," he finally stated with a nod.

"Eloisa?" Edward asked, stunned at the news of a marriage—especially of any marriage—involving Michael Cunningham.

"No, you dolt, the younger sister!"

Edward sat down hard on the edge of a chair and stared

at Michael. "*Married?*" he repeated before draining his glass. "*You?*" he questioned, his eyebrows nearly into his hairline. "You married your mistress's *sister?*" he asked in disbelief, just then figuring it out.

"You must have been very drunk the night I told you I would marry Olivia," Michael accused, his head shaking from side to side. "And Eloisa is *not* my mistress!" he added, his ire suddenly apparent.

Edward regarded his friend, his mouth moving much like the mouths of the tropical fish that Lord Everly kept in his library, although no bubbles or sounds came out.

And it was just as well, for there was a quiet knock at the door.

"Come in!" Michael called out, expecting a servant to enter with walnuts and coffee. When he saw *her* enter, though, he absently set down his glass on the sideboard and took in the sight of his new wife. The periwinkle gown she wore did wonders for her complexion. Her mahogany hair was pinned up in an elegant chignon, and she carried herself as if she truly was the mistress of the house.

And a member of the *ton*.

Edward was on his feet in an instant, his agile fencer's body bowing deeply to the lady's perfect curtsy. Upon seeing his friend's reaction, Michael bowed as well, suddenly not quite sure what to do when greeting a wife. *My wife.* Better to keep it formal until he knew where he stood with her.

"Oh, please forgive me. I did not know you were entertaining a guest," Olivia said as she moved to leave, a sudden blush pinking her face. The taller man was definitely a titled gentleman, she thought suddenly. Despite the lack of a coat, he exuded class and charm and sported the nose of an aristocrat.

"Oh, he's not a guest," Michael replied quickly, still a bit in awe of his new bride's appearance.

When Michael didn't make the introduction, Edward did so. "Edward Seward, at your service, milady," he offered, a click of his boot heels accompanying his bow.

Olivia moved forward with her right hand extended, intending to shake hands with the tall man she found to be rather handsome. He instead took her hand and lifted it to his lips, kissing the back of it as he surveyed the woman before him. "Olivia Wa ... Cunningham," she corrected herself with a quick shake of her head, realizing it was the first time she'd spoken her new name aloud. She also realized that Edward had been holding her hand a bit too long and gently tugged it out of his grasp.

"It's very good to meet my best friend's wife," Edward breathed, wondering how his friend was able to land such a pretty gel. The words were out of his mouth before he realized he said them. "How did Michael manage to convince such a pretty gel to marry him?"

Olivia regarded the man with a blank look, trying to decide if he was teasing. *How indeed?* she wondered to herself. "Thank you," she finally replied. "His approach was so unique I found I could not refuse him," she managed to get out with a wan smile, not sure what else to say. "Jeffers mentioned drinks in the library before dinner, but I must admit, I did not realize Mr. Cunningham had returned from his meeting," she explained, wanting Michael to know why she had come to the library. "I understand you two will be having dinner at White's," she added, hoping she wasn't prattling. "I am afraid the staff is not prepared to serve a proper dinner here this evening, but I promise you, they will tomorrow night," she finished with a curt nod.

Michael smiled and poured her a glass of claret, secretly pleased with her response to Edward's query. "White's sounds as good as any. But what about you? We should have the cook make a dinner for you. You've not eaten all day," he murmured, remembering her tea and biscuits at the inn.

Olivia regarded her husband, somewhat surprised that he remembered she hadn't eaten when given the opportunity. "I am having dinner in the parlor," she said with a smile.

"By yourself?" Edward wondered, immediately regretting

his reaction when he realized Michael was suddenly frowning at him.

"But, of course," Olivia countered, the forced smile still showing. "Once I have made some acquaintances here in town, I expect I'll dine with others on occasion." She reached out and took the glass of wine that Michael held for her. "Shall I expect you for dinner tomorrow evening, Mr. Seward?"

Edward gave Michael a nervous glance before he bobbed his head. "I will be sure to be present."

"And you, Mr. Cunningham? Will you be here for dinner at eight tomorrow?"

Michael had to swallow hard before answering his wife. Despite the long day of travel, she looked luminescent in her simple gown and pearls and far more sophisticated than he had ever seen her. "It will be my pleasure, of course," he said as he bowed his head.

Olivia smiled and sipped her wine. "Jeffers has assured me your coach will be ready shortly."

"Coach?" Michael repeated, pausing before taking a drink.

Nodding, Olivia said, "For your trip to White's."

Michael regarded his wife for perhaps a moment too long.

What did she know of White's? Had her father spoken of the men's club? And did she know what waited for him there? Michael didn't have another minute to think on it as Jeffers appeared at the library door to announce that the coach was ready.

Olivia continued to stand near the sideboard, sipping her wine as Edward bowed and moved to the door. Michael still stood before her, a look of uncertainty on his face. "I doubt we'll be gone long," he said, setting his empty glass on the sideboard. "Jeffers can see to whatever you may need. And," he paused, trying to decide what to say about later. "There's no need for you to wait up for me." He suddenly *wanted* to find her waiting for him. Waiting in his room, in his bed, devoid of a night rail and her hair out of its pins.

He had to erase the fantasy as quickly as he imagined it.

Olivia nodded and was about to curtsy when Michael reached over and surprised her with a kiss on her temple. "My beautiful," he murmured before he stepped back.

Trying hard to suppress her surprise at his endearment, Olivia could not help the rush of warmth that she felt cover her face. "Thank you," she replied, not quite sure how to respond. She suddenly wondered what she should call him.

Darling?

No, it was far too soon for endearments.

Michael?

Probably too familiar.

Mr. Cunningham?

Probably too formal. She was about to ask when Michael suddenly bowed and took his leave, his gaze not leaving her until the door was shut behind him.

Sighing, Olivia refilled her wine glass and found her way to the parlor. Before the night was over, she managed to eat a rather excellent meal and read a book, the combination a wonderful antidote to her first full day as Mrs. Michael Cunningham. And, although she tried to stay awake as long as possible, thinking that Michael would be paying her a visit when he returned from White's, she was soon sound asleep.

CHAPTER 25

SATURDAY HIS WIFE PLAYS HOSTESS

April 15, 1815

At eight o'clock in the morning, Olivia woke suddenly to the sound of a tentative knock at her bedchamber door. "Come in," she called out, careful to have the counterpane and bed linens pulled up over the front of her night rail.

A girl of sixteen or seventeen poked her head around the slightly opened door. "Excuse me, madam, but I do not wish to disturb you if you still wish to sleep," the young woman said quietly, the hint of a lilt in her voice.

"It's fine. I am quite awake," Olivia answered, motioning for the girl to enter.

"My name is Sarah White," the girl stated with a nod, obviously a bit nervous. "I have been hired to be your dresser and laundress," she said proudly, curtsying as she said it. "And I'll dress your hair, if you'll allow it." The lilt in her voice was clearly Scottish, and her fair complexion and strawberry blonde hair confirmed a northern origin.

Olivia regarded the girl for a moment. "I am Olivia Cunningham," she responded, amazed at how easy the new name came to her. "It is very good to meet you. And so soon! I would not have expected Jeffers to make a hire so quickly,"

Olivia stated, finding herself more and more impressed with Michael's butler.

The girl's gaze wandered off for a moment. "My employment may be only temporary. Although my father drives Mr. Cunningham's coach, Jeffers says I must prove myself before he's willing to add me to the household staff on a permanent basis," Sarah explained with a sad face.

Mr. White is her father! Olivia realized then, deciding she rather liked the daughter. "Then we shall just have to be sure you prove yourself," Olivia replied lightly. "Today, I must meet the staff, come up with menus for all the meals this week, and familiarize myself with the workings of the household."

Sarah quirked her face. "A simple muslin gown, then," she stated with a nod, hurrying to the clothes press to search for one. "And I'll put up your hair in a top knot and iron some ringlets for around your face," she added, pulling out a peach pastel gown and eying it favorably.

"Yes, what you said," Olivia agreed, stepping out of the bed and to the area behind the dressing screen.

"How can you have so little regard for marriage?" Edward asked of his best friend. He looked miserable as he sat in the corner of the library's settee, the festive floral pattern of its upholstery at odds with his mood.

Michael eyed Edward with a grimace. "I have a great deal of respect for the institution of marriage," he answered carefully. *I do, really,* he tried to convince himself. His parents had seemed quite happy in the early years of their union. His mother, Violet, had given birth to two boys and a girl in just five years. She was doted on by their father for many years, although these days she seemed to spend less time in Horsham, more time at the house in Cavendish Square, and was a frequent traveler to the Continent. Meanwhile, his father sequestered himself at Cunningham Park in Horsham when he wasn't in London for Parliament. "The timing, though ... I thought I had more *time*," Michael added quietly, remembering why he'd initially ignored his mother's pleas to marry.

By now, his brother had surely spent every pence of his allowance in gaming hells and at brothels and was probably working through the current earnings of the Cunningham viscountcy. At some point, unless his father cut off his brother or figured out a way to make their lands in Horsham earn more, the viscountcy would go bankrupt. And it didn't help that his mother was spending who knew how much to keep herself happy and fashionably dressed.

An undignified snort answered him. Michael gave Edward a raised eyebrow. "'Tis true," Michael responded. "I needed time to build up these investments so there will be some money in the Cunningham treasury," he said defensively. "And I'm of the opinion it's still too soon to *be* ... married." *And last night was a perfect example.*

Instead of dining at the men's club as they originally planned, he and Edward had treated themselves to a dinner at the Clarendon Hotel, Michael picking up the tab in honor of his business deal with Harold Waterford. He thought of the awkward moments when he wondered if he should have invited Olivia. He felt a bit of sadness at the thought of her dining alone at the townhouse. And yet, she had seemed quite satisfied to stay home, practically pushing them out the library door when Jeffers announced that the coach was waiting.

When Edward's eyebrows nearly disappeared into his hairline, Michael gave him a look of puzzlement. "What is it?" he asked.

"I know exactly why you married her!" Edward exclaimed, indignation thick in his voice.

He was sure it was about money.

Michael furrowed his brows and stared at his best friend. "I had a perfectly good reason to marry her," he finally answered, remembering the deadline he had set for himself to placate his mother. But when Edward's look of disgust didn't change, Michael's brows furrowed. "Wait. Why do *you* think I married her?"

Edward was up and out of the settee in an instant, his finger coming within inches of Michael's nose. "The *money* you'd make, of course," he accused, shaking the finger for effect.

Michael leaned back in an effort to avoid the fingertip that was about to make contact with his nose. "*Money?*" Michael repeated, a look of confusion on his face. "Her dowry was acceptable, of course, but by no means ... by no means was it a reason to give up my *freedom*," he countered angrily. Although he had to admit the dowry was far more generous than he would have expected from marrying a genteel woman from the country, especially one who apparently didn't have direct ties to the *ton*. Had it not been for him, she would have become a governess, for goodness sake!

Crossing his arms, Edward regarded Michael with the look of disgust still firmly in place. "Not her *dowry*, you dolt!" When Michael's look of confusion stayed in place, Edward added, "The money from the *bet!*"

Michael stared at his friend for several seconds, an uneasiness creeping over him. *Damn! He remembered!*

He already regretted the day he had entered into that damn bet at White's. He wondered why he had mentioned the agreement he had made with this mother to Sir Richard, but he did. Incredulous, and more than a bit amused at the claim, Sir Richard shook his head and said, "Any other son of a viscount would hold out until he was thirty," he stated with a smirk. Then he placed his name and a one-hundred pound wager in the betting book at White's—a bet that stated that Michael would miss the deadline and owe him one pound. If Michael did marry by the deadline, he would win the hundred pounds. Over time, several more members added their wagers to that bet, driving up the pot to what must be —*what had Arthur Huntington said?*—several thousand pounds.

Perhaps more, Michael realized, if word of his marriage

didn't spread very fast. This should be the night he would show his marriage certificate and begin to collect the winnings from the bet he had accepted so many years ago.

He wondered how he could keep news of the bet from reaching Olivia, though. The spirit in which the bet was made was quite innocent, he remembered, but she might be left believing that he had married her only to collect what could be a small fortune. He had forgotten about the bet for several years, but he was sure more bets had been added to those already in the book—he hadn't attended most of last Season's balls, nor had he publicly courted a woman. Ever.

He hadn't needed to, though.

Waterford had practically promised him his daughter, a candidate kept in reserve all these years and quite happily in the back of his mind until he conjured her for an occasional fantasy. None of his friends in London knew of her existence, of course. *No wonder the men at White's have been showing more interest in me than usual these past few months.* It wasn't because of the occasional bruises he sported on his jaw or around his eyes after a spirited round of bare knuckle fighting. They were deciding whether or not to add their names and wagers to the bet!

"I forgot about the bet," Michael lied, a slight smile coming on. Huntington had reminded him of it just a couple of weeks ago. "But, thank you for reminding me. I shall have to pay a visit to White's to show my marriage certificate and collect my winnings," he stated as his grin grew larger. *And somehow keep Olivia from finding out,* he thought suddenly.

Incensed, Edward took a step back and sank into the settee, his expression showing disappointment. "You are so lucky," he murmured, his elbows planted on his knees as he hung his head.

Rolling his eyes, Michael sighed. "There is nothing *lucky* about having to marry to win money," he stated as he moved to the sideboard and poured himself a brandy. He tossed the contents of the glass into his mouth and savored the smoky flavor for a moment before swallowing.

"You could marry whomever you wanted," Edward whispered, his sadness bringing a pall to the library. A sigh escaped him. "I could not. At least, not until this week." He said it so quietly, Michael did not hear him. Raising his head to look at his friend, Edward asked, "So, if it wasn't for the money, then, pray tell, *why* did you marry Olivia?"

Michael took a breath before he started to answer and then stopped. He had made a promise. He'd accepted a bet. She was still available. He loved her.

But would he have married Olivia if there had been no deadline?

Eventually, if she were still available, he supposed. *And when would that be?* Perhaps he would be more accepting of a marriage when he was past thirty, when all his investments were paying acceptable dividends, and he was sure his brother was no longer costing his father's estate.

But even as he considered the practical aspects of marriage, he remembered the most important reason. "She is the only one I have ever considered as a wife," he blurted suddenly, the words surprising him when he realized he'd spoken them aloud.

Edward sat up straight in the settee, equally surprised by the admission. "Indeed?" he questioned, not the least bit convinced. "You have a fine way of showing it," he murmured unhappily.

Grimacing at his friend's words, Michael sighed. "I will make it up to her at some point," he said quietly. "I am sure she despises me," he added with a bit more volume to his voice, his shoulders sagging a bit.

Edward frowned at the comment. "She hides it well, then," he stated, moving to the sideboard and pouring himself a brandy. He glowered at Michael just before he took a sip.

"Wait," he said as he regarded his friend with a raised eyebrow. "What makes you think she despises you?" Even as he asked the question, he considered the most logical explanation and his eyes widened. "Oh, God, no!" he shouted.

Michael took a step back, stunned by his friend's outburst. "No ... *what?*" he whispered, afraid of what Edward might know.

Or what incorrect conclusion he had jumped to at that moment.

"She knows you bed her sister!"

Michael visibly flinched and violently shook his head from side to side. "She does *not*, because I *do* not!" he argued with an annoyed glance at his friend. "How many times do I have to tell you that I was merely Eloisa's *protector?* And she has been quite accomplished at keeping our arrangement a secret from her family," he stated confidently, not bothering to add that Eloisa was no longer in need of his protection. Arthur Huntington had that honor now. "Olivia despises me because I ..." he allowed the admission to trail off as he moved to refill his brandy snifter.

Because I am a rake, he thought, not ever having thought of himself in those terms before. He'd never done anything to earn the moniker. Not until last Tuesday night.

Edward's eyebrow arched again. "Do tell. You know how I love a good story." He returned to the settee, obviously eager to hear whatever news Michael was about to divulge.

Rolling his eyes, Michael sunk into the nearest chair. "I didn't have time to court her. I didn't have time to properly propose. And I certainly didn't have time for a wedding to be arranged," he explained quickly. "So I took my sister's advice."

There. He could blame it all on Elizabeth.

The look on Edward's face was so comical that Michael had to suppress a grin. "Pray tell!" the taller man demanded, his eyes wide with curiosity.

Michael sighed, thinking perhaps he shouldn't give Edward all the details. He would never hear the end of it. "I went to Olivia's bedchamber, climbed into her bed, and waited for her to make my presence known to the rest of the household. Worked like a charm. We were married two days later."

When no sound came from Edward's direction, Michael looked up to find the man staring down at him. *Was that a look of wonderment? Adoration? Or astonishment, perhaps?* And how the hell had Edward managed to get up from the settee so quickly and make his way to stand before Michael in what could have only been *one second?* When he was quite thoroughly foxed?

"You *rake!*" Edward accused, his mouth opening and closing just like Lord Everly's tropical fish. "What a brilliant scheme! Perhaps I could do that to marry Anna," he suggested, his face taking on a decidedly happier expression.

Michael shook his head. "I doubt it would work in her situation. Anna isn't the daughter of a very wealthy business-man," he countered, a bit impatient with his friend's repeated confessions of love for a girl he had no hope of marrying given his station in life—and her lack of one.

And given the fact that she was missing.

"I love her."

"I know. Half of *London* knows. And now that you're no longer the 'spare' in the line of succession, you could marry her if you really *wanted* to," Michael offered, thinking that a second son of an earl should have a bit of latitude when it came to his choice of a spouse. Edward's status as the spare in the 'heir and a spare' scenario had changed with the birth of his nephew the week before.

His mother was rather fond of using the phrase when she described her handsome sons. The fact that there were three daughters in between the heir and spare was never brought up. At least none of *them* had been presented to Michael as contenders for the position of his wife, although the youngest had held a candle for him for several years before finally agreeing to marry another. The Sewards were quite choosy in who could be their sons-in-law, marrying off the girls to the heirs of two earls and a duke.

Edward took on an expression of misery. "I've no idea where she is," he said quietly, referring to the love of his life. "I have searched every modiste in Oxford Street, every modiste in Bond Street, and half the modistes in New Bond Street," he murmured quietly. "This week, I'm going to search the other half."

Michael sighed, thinking he and Edward had had this same discussion on more than a few occasions in the recent past. *Edward's birthday.* "You could hire a Bow Street Runner to find her," he suggested, despite figuring Edward would never go against his parents' decree regarding who he would marry. "Or you might try an advertisement in *The Times.*"

Edward shook his head and seemed to fall deeper into his depression. He had always put responsibility to family and the earldom first. "Perhaps she will find me," he said hopefully.

It was Michael's turn to snort.

Will he bed me tonight? Olivia wondered as she finished primping in front of the cheval mirror. She had dismissed Sarah earlier, wanting to spend some time by herself after a busy day of learning about the household, meeting the staff, and touring the house and grounds. There had been menus to plan and, given the condition of some of the common rooms in the house, a list of repairs and painting projects to compile.

Now she was feeling a bit anxious.

After their quick marriage ceremony before the vicar, Michael had gone off with her father to continue their business meetings and then spent that Thursday night in his guest bedchamber, never asking her to join him. Nor did he visit her in her bedchamber to consummate the marriage. *Probably didn't want to revisit the scene of the crime,* she considered with a quirk on her face.

She thought of his hands again, how one had cupped her breast while the other drew back the curtain of hair from over her face. Her entire body shivered at the memory. *He will have to touch me again sometime!* Glancing again in the mirror, she smiled and decided she would try to make the best of it.

How bad could it be? Her husband could one day be a viscount!

At precisely seven-thirty, she made her way down the steps and to the library for a drink she was looking forward to very much. Upon entering the room, she found her husband and his friend settled into chairs and looking as if they if they were both deep in their cups. Neither seemed to notice her entrance, so she moved to the sideboard and was about to help herself to a glass of claret when Michael's hand closed over hers as it gripped the bottle.

"My apologies, Mrs. Cunningham," he murmured quietly. "I did not hear you come in," he said, leaning over to place a kiss on her temple. His head remained very close to her for another moment, as if he was sniffing the scent of her hair.

Olivia could feel a flush rise when she remembered they were not alone. "I did not wish to disturb your reverie," she answered with a slight smile, admiring his profile in the dim light. "I trust you are well?" she added in almost a whisper, not wanting to be overheard by Edward.

Michael's breath caught just a bit as he considered the meaning of her words. "I am quite well, thank you. And you?"

"Very well, indeed," Olivia remarked, smiling as Michael poured her a generous glass of wine. She took the small goblet and moved to the center of the room. "Are you still planning to join us for dinner, Mr. Seward?" she asked, deciding it was acceptable to take on the role of hostess. And she hoped the cook remembered to make enough for three. She'd mentioned the possibility in her discussion with the woman earlier that day.

Edward exchanged a nervous glance with Michael. "I will, indeed. Thank you for asking," he replied, rather liking the sound of the invitation to dinner in his adopted home. Turning to Michael, he said, "You didn't tell her about me, did you?"

Rolling his eyes, Michael shook his head and moved to

join his wife. He offered her his arm and led her to the settee where he indicated she should sit. "May I get you a plate of walnuts?" he asked, ignoring Edward's comment.

Olivia looked over at Edward, a bit of nervousness returning. "Yes, thank you. And what did you not tell me about Mr. Seward?" she asked as she nodded her head in Edward's direction. It was awkward talking about a man who was in the room.

Sighing, Michael moved to the sideboard to pour another brandy for himself and to get the walnuts. "I own the townhouse, but Edward moved in a couple of years ago," he explained shortly, not realizing how the words might sound to a woman born and raised in the country.

Visibly reddening as she considered the possible implication of his statement, Olivia tried hard to keep her face impassive. She might have been a chit from the country, but she'd read enough books to know that some men preferred the company of other men as opposed to women. *That would certainly explain why my husband hasn't visited me in my bedchamber*, she thought, an odd sadness suddenly settling over her. *I did not even think of the possibility that he might be a molly.*

Her breath caught as she considered what her life would be like as the wife of such a man. She would be a wife simply for show, candy on his arm at various social events and an occasional dance partner at balls; appearances were everything in the *ton*. Would he even try to get a child on her? A bit of panic took hold and a tooth caught her lower lip in an effort to stave off the trembling she was sure would start any moment.

Aware of Olivia's sudden discomfort and the reason why, Edward gave Michael a glance filled with annoyance. "As *friends*," Edward added as quickly as he could. "We've known one another since our days at Eton." *Where we drank to excess and sowed our wild oats with fast women*, he almost added in an effort to make himself crystal clear. He gave Michael a sideways glance that displayed a bit of derision.

Olivia silently inhaled, not aware she'd been holding her breath. She smiled then, a wave of relief washing over her. *Wasn't it odd*, she thought then, *how I felt sad when I thought that my husband might be a molly?* And Edward! Such a tall, handsome man. She originally thought him to be a dandy, given his extravagantly embroidered waistcoat and perfect hair.

There was more than relief in the discovery that these two men were simply friends who shared a terrace. "And did you attend university together, too?" she asked, wanting to keep up her end of the conversation—and to avoid the awkward silence that might have descended just then. She hadn't realized how her earlier conclusion had made her feel until she was able to get her breathing back under control.

Michael gave her the plate of walnuts as Edward responded with a snort. Olivia noted Michael's look of exasperation and gave him a smile. "We were roommates at Oxford, but otherwise, we hardly saw each other," Michael explained as he took a seat next to her on the settee. Although he wasn't sure how close to her he should sit, he was relieved when his thigh nearly touched hers and she didn't readjust her position. And he was suddenly quite aware of the close fit of her bodice; the sight of the gentle swell of her breasts above the sweep of her neckline was more intoxicating than the brandy he'd already consumed. *Rising moons*, he remembered someone calling them. And he was suddenly remembering having held one in his right hand. His loins remembered, too, he realized as he felt them tighten.

The mischievous grin on Edward's face made Olivia glance at Michael. Rolling his eyes, more to hide the fact that he'd been staring at her bosom than to show his annoyance at Edward, Michael said, "Edward spent more time playing cards than he did attending classes. It was a wonder they saw fit to bestow a degree upon him."

Edward took umbrage at the comment and sat up straighter in the couch. "I believe *you* were the card player back then, old boy. I merely took more interest in off-campus pursuits." As if he had just realized that what he'd said could be misconstrued by the lady, Edward leaned forward and added, "Like riding and fencing and ..."

Edward was saved from having to continue the explanation when Jeffers entered the room and announced that dinner was served. The butler seemed pleasantly surprised at the sight of the Cunninghams sitting together on the settee as he nodded and left the room.

Michael stood, and when he didn't offer assistance to his wife, Edward stepped over and held out his hand. Not sure if she should take it, Olivia glanced in Michael's direction. But his attention was on the sideboard where he deposited his empty glass, so she gave Edward a nod and smiled as she allowed him to help her to her feet. "Thank you, Mr. Seward," she murmured.

Realizing his mistake, Michael quickly joined her and offered his arm. "Are you going to dinner dressed like that?" he asked of his friend, a hint of annoyance in his voice.

Edward looked down at his attire. His near-white pantaloons were topped with a snowy white linen shirt and crisp cravat. The silver waistcoat, embroidered with metallic thread, was expensive but not ostentatious. And his tasseled Hessians were polished to a glossy shine. "I think I need a topcoat, if you must know," be replied with a sigh. "At least you could have dressed for dinner. You smell like dust from your ride."

His face reddening in embarrassment, Michael pinched his lips together so that he would not say what first sprang to his mind. "You are right, of course." Pausing at the library door, he allowed Olivia to precede him and then shrugged off his topcoat and unbuttoned his waistcoat in the hall as Edward led Olivia to the dining room. Jeffers was immediately by his side, taking the coats while a footman was dispatched to his rooms on the second floor to get a fresh topcoat and waistcoat. Jeffers had his full shirt sleeves brushed out and his boots shined just as the footman returned with the coats. "I cannot recall having redressed in the hall before," Michael murmured as his butler buttoned the waistcoat.

"I don't recall there ever being a *need* to do so before today, sir," Jeffers replied, giving his master a thorough look over before nodding that his appearance was acceptable. "I'll draw a bath for you later, if you'd like."

"I'd like," Michael agreed with a nod before heading for the dining room.

When he entered the dining room, Edward thought he had somehow wandered into the wrong house. The room was certainly different than it had been at breakfast. The table was dressed, and complete place settings of chargers, silverware, and crystal were laid out in front of three chairs. The flames from a large candelabra lit the center of the table, their flickering light reflecting off the shiny surfaces and adding a dramatic flair to the table. Edward couldn't remember a time during his tenure at the townhouse when dinner looked so *formal.*

Despite the presence of a nearby footman, he pulled out a chair for Olivia. She thanked him as she sat down.

"So, tell me, Mrs. Cunningham, however did you get a confirmed bachelor to the altar?" Edward whispered loudly before allowing a footman to assist him into a navy blue topcoat that seemed to have appeared from thin air. He took his seat, buttoning the coat as he did so.

Olivia's back stiffened. *Confirmed bachelor? If that was really the case, then why did Michael have a special license?* She regarded Edward for a moment before deciding how to reply. Truth, it seemed, would be best with the man. But adding a light touch to the explanation would be better than a bitter sounding tirade. "After an evening in Shipley, Mr. Cunningham returned to our family's house Tuesday night ... three sheets to the wind, I believe the saying goes, ... and, in trying to find his way to his room," *Or, perhaps someone else's,* she thought, but didn't say aloud, "He found mine instead."

Stunned at the unexpected frankness in her explanation, Edward lowered his head and allowed the anger at his friend to wash over him. He frowned, though, wondering how simply entering a woman's room might be grounds for ruining her reputation. "I take it he did not just *enter* your room," he half-asked, wondering if she would describe the scene the same way Michael had earlier that evening.

Sighing, Olivia avoided the desire to rest her head in her hands, still trying to keep her response light-hearted. "Had I been awake and seen him enter, I assure you, I would have simply put on a dressing gown and escorted him to his room at the other end of the hall. However, he... undressed ... and proceeded to get into my bed. Which, of course, woke me."

Edward feigned surprise and gasped. "You ... screamed, I take it?"

Olivia shrugged. "Not at first. But when he lay on my bed, called me 'El', and said 'Please be mine', I became a bit ... vocal," she whispered, barely containing her sad and angry emotions at what had happened. She almost immediately regretted telling the story.

Rolling his eyes, Edward could only imagine the poor woman's plight. *Does she already know of her sister's relationship with Michael?* he wondered. And if not, did he suspect that Michael might want her sister more than her? "Who found him with you?" he whispered hoarsely, not considering that the question was entirely inappropriate.

Her face turning a bright pink, Olivia lowered her eyes.

"My father. Which wouldn't have been so bad, I suppose. We could have explained the situation, and I'm sure he would have understood. But ... several servants ..." She sighed audibly. "I was quite ruined without having done anything untoward," she said quietly, not quite sure what else to say.

Edward sat back hard against the chair and considered her tale. Not as salacious as how her older sister was ruined, Olivia's ruination was still just as potentially scandalous. And Michael had apparently ruined Olivia *at his sister's suggestion.*

Intending to say something to assuage her, Edward found he couldn't when Michael strode into the room, his waistcoat and topcoat replaced with formal dinner attire.

"Please excuse the delay," he said, not expecting anyone to reply.

"Of course, Mr. Cunningham. Shall I call for the first course to be served?" Olivia wondered as she began her duties as hostess of the dinner.

Michael and Edward exchanged a quick glance, surprised a girl from the country would know what to do in a formal dining room. "Please, do," Michael answered with a nod, trying to keep the uncertainty from his voice as well as his reaction to just then noticing the formality of the dining room. He glanced about to take in the details, the differences in the room since he had taken luncheon there earlier. With all the candles lit and the table set, it looked like a completely different room.

Olivia nodded and motioned to a nearby footman. It was as if a single wag of her finger controlled the entire household at that very moment. Waiters appeared with bowls of soup, a maid seemed to come from nowhere with carafes of two different wines, and coffee was poured into dainty china cups.

"Mr. Seward, would you do us the honor of tasting the wine?" Olivia asked after she'd surveyed the table and determined that everything was in order.

Michael gave his friend an amused glance, but Edward sat up straight and replied, "Of, course, my lady." He swirled the white wine in the glass, examined the liquid in front of the light from the candelabra, sniffed it, and finally took a small sip. "Ah," he said with a grin. "A thirteen Chardonnay, I believe. Very good," he stated before taking a longer drink. "I was not aware we had this in the cellar," he commented as he picked up a soup spoon and began his first course.

Michael glanced at Olivia and cocked an eyebrow. *When did she have time to order wine?* he wondered. She met his gaze and gave him a small smile. "I brought a case from Sussex in my trunk," she admitted with a nod, realizing right away that Michael knew it hadn't come from his stock. "And your butler confirmed that you only have reds in your cellar."

Nodding, Michael sampled the wine and seemed pleased. "Thank you for your generosity. It was most kind of you," he said humbly. *The woman is full of surprises*, he realized, and at the rate she was going, she would have complete control of the household within the next day. *If she didn't already.*

And is that really so bad? he found himself wondering. She was obviously competent, certainly more so than her elder sister would have been in the same situation.

Olivia, who had just sampled her soup, held his gaze for a moment. "I believe my dowry was rather limited, so it seemed the least I could ..."

"Your dowry was more than satisfactory," Michael interrupted, his voice a bit too harsh. *Especially given the circumstances.* Indeed, Harold Waterford had been most generous when it came to settling on the dowry for his daughter. Michael's share of their joint business ventures increased by over ten percent, its worth probably well over five thousand pounds a year, and a draft for one thousand pounds was in his hands before he left Sussex Friday.

Edward noted the sharp retort and made a note to ask his friend about it later. Seeing a break in their conversation, he asked, "Mrs. Cunningham, have you ever visited our fair city before?"

Olivia, still a bit startled by Michael's proclamation and wanting to know more about her dowry, reluctantly turned her attention to Edward. "Several times, of course. My father comes here for business and occasionally brings the family to visit," she answered, surveying the table to be sure all was in place.

"Do you then have family in town?" Edward prodded, noticing Michael's grimace.

Smiling, Olivia nodded. "Indeed. Two aunts and uncles in Mayfair and some cousins in Cheapside. And my elder sister must live somewhere near here," she finished, her attention on Michael as she mentioned her sister.

Keeping his face as impassive as possible, Michael nodded.

"Then you'll have ladies with whom to go shopping," Edward said brightly.

The comment had Olivia realizing she could go shopping in The Strand and Oxford Street and New Bond Street. She could borrow books from a lending library. She could walk in all the fashionable squares. Olivia tried hard to keep her sudden excitement in check and replied, "I suppose so." *This really won't be so bad,* she considered. She was living in London. In a house in a fashionable square in the West End. *I can do this.*

Putting down his soup spoon, Michael leaned forward. "I shall give you some pin money so you can do just that." He paused a moment, remembering the invitation to the Harvey ball he'd read the day before. "By the way, do you have a ball gown?" he asked. "The Season has barely begun, and we've already been invited to a ball."

Olivia didn't even try to hide her surprise. "Has an announcement of our marriage already been printed in the paper?" she asked, swallowing hard. Her attention was diverted for a moment as she nodded to a waiter near the kitchen door.

Edward and Michael exchanged glances. "No," they both said in unison. Edward realized her confusion. "Michael and I both received invitations to the Harvey ball, you see, and as his wife, you, of course, are included in the invitation."

Knowing he would no longer have to fend off mothers with their would-be-bride daughters, Michael grinned as he found himself looking forward to the ball. No more would he have to endure the parade of biddable girls at every social event. No more would he have to dance with girls he had no intention of spending time with after the ball was over.

He was a married man now. He was no longer on the Marriage Mart!

Edward was another matter, though.

"Poor Edward is still not betrothed, so he will be quite popular at this year's balls," Michael teased happily, his mood suddenly much better. A waiter swooped in and removed his soup bowl while another waiter placed a large plate of sliced beef, gravy and potatoes in front of him. The second set of wine glasses was filled with red wine and plates of sweetmeats and fruits appeared on the table. The same dance of plates occurred in front of Olivia and Edward. In just a few seconds, the room was empty of servants and a veritable feast was spread across the table.

Stunned at both Michael's teasing and at the quick change of courses, Edward regarded their hostess. "How ... How did you do that?" he asked in awe. "They've never served us dinner like this before."

Olivia gave him a questioning glance, not quite sure what he meant. Michael cleared his throat and said, rather proudly, "You'll find my wife is quite adept at running a household."

Blushing, Olivia gave her husband a small nod in response to his compliment. *And how would he know that?* she wondered, not sure if Michael really meant what he said. *What has my father been saying about me?*

"I can see that. But, tell me, Mrs. Cunningham, what would you be doing *right now* if you weren't married to this rake?" Edward asked, attempting to annoy Michael.

Olivia stiffened, her face taking on a look of offense. "I'll thank you not to refer to my husband in such terms, Mr. Seward."

It was Michael's turn to be stunned by his wife's defense of him. He stared open-mouthed at Olivia but then could barely contain his amusement, especially when he saw that Edward was doing his best to suppress a grin. "I apologize, my lady," Edward managed to get out before pressing his lips together in an attempt to stifle his laughter.

Annoyed by the mutual amusement the two men seemed be enjoying due to her rebuke, Olivia leaned back in her chair. "In answer to your question, I would be living in an estate home in Wiltshire, Mr. Seward," Olivia said lightly. After all those weeks of working out the particulars, she'd actually been looking forward to the move to Wiltshire and to beginning her position as a governess. It was only ten days ago when she'd received the good news she'd been hired.

Ten days!

So when Edward posed his simple question about where she would be if she wasn't married to his best friend, she wanted desperately to be angry.

She opted instead for forced lightness in her reply.

"Estate home?" Michael repeated, his fork clattering on his plate. His expression changed suddenly, as if he'd just then remembered that she was to have been a governess for a ducal family. *His sister's family.*

"Wiltshire?" Edward questioned when he'd just managed to avoid spraying the table with a mouthful of wine.

Olivia shrugged, remembering the butler's reaction. "I was to be the governess for a duke and duchess' children. I would have begun my position on the morrow," she added as she returned her attention to the meat on her plate.

Michael's face took on a serious expression as he considered the way in which she delivered her news. He couldn't mistake the disappointment in the tone of her voice. Was she bitter that she was married to him when she would have been a common servant in a duchy? Was she sorry she was married to him when the alternative was so beneath her? She probably didn't even realize that by marrying him, she had greatly elevated her social status as well as her financial standing. He would probably have more lands and a title someday. *Has her father even told her how lucrative our shared business ventures are and how much her family will gain in standing and wealth as a result?*

Or did Waterford keep the terms of his business deals from his family?

Like he did everything else? Michael realized just then.

"You sound .. disappointed," he said quietly, suddenly seeing her perspective but also wondering if she intended to offend him with her remarks. For, at that moment, he felt offended.

Olivia gave a shake of her head and dabbed the edge of

her lips with her napkin. "Not at all, Mr. Cunningham. I am at a bit of a loss. You see, I spent the past two years preparing to fill a certain role, and I am simply not ... I am not prepared for the role of w... wife ... just yet."

Edward eyed Michael, his manner a bit wary. He had witnessed the look of offense on Michael's face and wondered why, when he was sure the man had been bedding this woman's sister for over a year, he would think that he had done Olivia some kind of favor by marrying her. Especially when her ruined reputation had been entirely due to Michael's apparent drunken behavior. "I rather think you're doing a remarkable job given the circumstances," Edward announced, sending a frown in Michael's direction as he said so.

Olivia seemed surprised by Edward's support. "Why, thank you, Mr. Seward. I shall endeavor to learn everything I must know to ..."

But Michael ignored his friend's comment and his facial cues. "I do hope you realize you are in a far better situation?" Michael half-asked, not sure he wanted to learn her answer.

Surprised at being interrupted, Olivia realized Michael's mood had suddenly turned sullen. She nodded. "Of course, I do," she assured him, realizing the tone of her comment had been misconstrued. Or had it? *Do I really want to be here?* she wondered for at least the tenth time that day. "I just ... I have so much to *learn*," she claimed, her eyes downcast.

"Such as?" Michael prompted, not entirely convinced she realized her good fortune. *And what was left for her to learn?* She had probably read every book in Waterford's extensive library and been tutored in a variety of topics. She was an educated woman. But she'd been so quiet in the coach yesterday—not at all like her sister, who chattered on about everything and nothing to the point that he nearly ignored her. Why hadn't Olivia brought up these concerns then?

Feeling a bit defiant, Olivia angled one shoulder down and sat back. *Why is he angry with me? I am not the one who got us in this situation!* Thinking he was challenging her for a list, she took a deep breath and let it out slowly. "Having not lived here in London, I do not know whom to contact regarding the details for the reception that your mother or perhaps Mr. Seward should be hosting in honor of our recent nuptials. Should it be in Richmond Park or would it be more appropriate to have a tent erected in the back yard? Is there a back yard?"

"A small one, yes," Edward answered absently.

Olivia continued as if she hadn't heard him. "I do not know the available musicians, caterers, or florists, nor where to get chairs, tables, linens and invitations. And what of the names for the guest list? Should it be an afternoon affair or perhaps an evening dinner followed by entertainment for the ladies and a smoking room for the gentlemen? What would be an acceptable gown for me to wear to a soirée and where would I buy it? How do I get there? Is it acceptable for me to go there unchaperoned? Or will I require a paid companion? What is the household budget? With whom do I make menus? Who pays the household bills?..."

"I see your point," Michael interrupted, holding one hand up to stave off further examples. He swallowed hard. "And please ... accept my ... apology," he stammered, surprised at her already long list of concerns. He'd had no idea what she thought she was up against. Had no idea how out of her element she felt with the sudden move to London, with her sudden marriage to *him*. "I ... *We* have a butler who sees to much of what we've required as a bachelor household. Forgive me for not remembering what a ... larger household requires." *What a marriage requires*, he almost said.

Even though she didn't know who to contact for all the things she mentioned, Michael had no doubt she would learn, and quickly. And what about a companion? Perhaps she could take a maid. Did she really require one if there was a footman and a groom with her when she was in his barouche or coach? "There is a carriage you may use when you wish to go shopping, of course. Just let Jeffers know, and he will see to a tiger and footman."

Olivia nodded as she considered his apology and offer of the carriage. "Thank you." After a pause, she added, "And how should I address you?"

Michael took a drink of wine and pondered the question. Eloisa always called him 'Cunningham', which was well and good for their situation. *But what should Olivia call me?* he wondered. He finally smiled. "You should call me 'Michael', of course," he answered, deciding he didn't care for the more formal name when she spoke it.

"And when we're in public?" she prodded. "Should I refer to you as 'The Honorable Michael Cunningham'? Or simply 'Cunningham'?"

Michael stared at her for only a moment, trying to keep the look of surprise from his face. *Now, who the hell told her I was the son of a viscount?* he wondered, surprised at her question. *Did her father tell her?* "How long ... How long have you known?" he countered quietly, a look of guilt crossing his face. It might have been the first time in his life he was ashamed to be the son of an aristocrat.

Olivia drew her eyebrows together and wondered at his odd reaction. "Since yesterday afternoon. Jeffers mentioned it when I asked who else uses the bedchamber to which I have been assigned."

His eyes downcast, Michael shrugged. "My father's viscountcy is merely that. He is not the son of an earl." He thought of the rest of her comment just then. *The bedchamber to which she'd been assigned? Damn! Which room did Jeffers take her to?*

Olivia nodded her understanding. At least she wouldn't have to call him 'my lord'. "And when your father dies? Are you the eldest?" She took a sip of wine, hoping the topic of conversation would turn to something a bit lighter.

Michael scrubbed his face with one hand. "Second of only two. If he is not killed for owing so much money to so many people, my brother will end up in debtors' prison before my father passes, however. As such, I will likely inherit his title and the modest land he currently oversees in the south. But my father is of sound mind and body, and I do not expect to have that burden for many years," he explained, hoping to make it clear they wouldn't be living the life of luxury afforded to most earls. "In the meantime, I do quite well in my business dealings. I have a small place in the country ..."

Edward snorted and began to chuckle.

"It is small," Michael insisted, "Compared to Cunningham Park," he added, his own sudden smile a result of what was apparently an inside joke between the two men, Olivia realized.

"The estate or the home on it?" Olivia asked then, her own mood a bit lighter now that the tension was gone and the formalities were out of the way.

"Iron Creek," Edward interjected, "is a lovely little cottage of twenty rooms on twenty-hundred acres twenty miles from anywhere."

"With twenty tenants," Michael added for good measure. "All eking out a living on the land and in the orchards." He paused a moment. "And it's only *two* miles from Crawley," he added in a lowered voice.

Having ignored her meal in favor of the evening's conversation, Olivia took a bite of honeyed fruit and wondered if any of it had come from the orchards on Iron Creek. "It sounds lovely. How often do you visit?"

His smile fading a bit, Michael shrugged. "Not often enough, I suppose," he murmured. "I used to invite a group of friends to a four or five-day house party there. Haven't done that in over a year, though."

"Two years," Edward amended quietly, his mood suddenly pensive.

Olivia noted the longing in their voices and wondered why they didn't simply leave town for a visit to the country house. They could both afford such a trip, she considered. "I can arrange a week-long trip, if you'd like," she offered brightly. "When would work for you and whom should I invite?"

Both men glanced at each other and then regarded Olivia.

"It cannot be during the Season," Edward said, a look of consternation on his face.

Michael cocked his head and considered some possibilities. "Let me think on this a bit," he replied carefully, wondering what she had in mind. She seemed eager to please. *Or is she eager to have me gone?* he wondered suddenly. There was a fleeting thought that she might take a lover, and he nearly choked. *I will not be cuckolded,* he thought just then, wondering from where the sudden feeling of ... *jealousy* had come. "We can speak of it again when the Season is about to end."

Dinner continued with snippets of polite conversation and anecdotes, leaving Olivia in a much better mood and the men ready for port and cigars. When Olivia excused herself, she did so with a plea of wanting the men to enjoy their after dinner drinks and a smoke. As she passed Michael, he reached for her hand and caught it gently, forcing Olivia to spin around and face him. "Thank you for a wonderful dinner," he said as he lifted her hand and then kissed the back of it.

Olivia felt her face flush, and she curtsied, not sure what else to do. "It was my pleasure," she answered with a nod before leaving the dining room.

Once she was safely out of earshot, Edward leaned over the table. "You climb into her bed, ruin her reputation, and her father still comes up with a *dowry?*" he asked *sotto voce*, hoping there were no servants within earshot.

Michael sighed and rolled his eyes. "Yes," he hissed, realizing that Olivia must have told Edward the whole sordid tale. "And it was a very generous settlement, too," he added, a frown on his face.

Edward cocked an eyebrow. "But why would Waterford *do* that?" he asked, his hands spreading out in the air.

Shaking his head, Michael regarded his friend. "I ... I do not know. We spoke briefly of Olivia last year, but, although

I never divulged that I am the son of a viscount nor that I have land very near his home, he's apparently known my father since they were in leading strings." And Harold Waterford knew of his affection for Olivia. The man had warned him to steer clear of the girl when she was younger and then offered her as a possible wife when it was *necessary* for him to marry.

But even if the events of three nights ago had not happened, Michael realized at that very moment that Harold Waterford must have known long ago that Olivia would one day be his wife. The dowry he offered had to have been set well in advance. The bank draft and the details for the transfer of such a large part of the business were proof of that. "He knew I would one day marry Olivia, I suppose," Michael said slowly, biting his lower lip. *Before my twenty-eighth birthday.* The man had admitted to knowing about the promise he had made to his mother.

He probably knew about the bet, too.

Edward's eyes opened a bit wider. "Indeed? And would you do it if you hadn't been forced to?"

Michael stared open-mouthed at his friend. "I ... I do not know," he lied, admitting to himself that he certainly wanted to. Always intended to. He had made a promise to his mother, after all, and he always knew he would keep it.

Who else was he going to marry if not Olivia?

"I wanted to bid you ... good night," Michael stuttered as he took in the sight of his wife in her night rail, her mahogany hair loosed from its chignon and flowing over her shoulders just as he had imagined it so many times in his daydreams. Her bare feet peeked out below the ruffled hem of the gown as she stood before him.

He had gone to the panel door of the purple room, directly across the hall, expecting to find her in the salon. After knocking several times with no response, he softly called out her name and was surprised when the door to another bedchamber opened. *Did she decide she didn't care for the purple room?* he wondered, feeling more disappointed than offended. He'd had it decorated specifically for her, sure she was fond of purple. Perhaps it wasn't large enough to suit her, he considered.

Olivia blushed as her husband regarded her, suddenly wishing she'd had a dressing gown to put on over her night rail. "Do you wish to ... come in?" *Please, not tonight,* she pleaded silently. She'd spent the entire day learning about the household, meeting the staff, planning menus for the next week, and writing letters to her family. And then playing hostess for her first dinner as Mrs. Cunningham had been nerve wracking, although the service had gone off without a hitch and the food was more than acceptable. Now, though, weariness settled over her, and she did not know how she could bear the thought of him bedding her before she'd had a chance to bathe properly.

Michael nodded uncertainly. "Only for a moment, if I could," he replied, carefully stepping into the bedchamber. The blue bedchamber. *Damn!* he thought suddenly. *She didn't like the purple room, so Jeffers put her in mother's room.*

Olivia felt a bit of relief as she heard his words. "Of course," she whispered, stepping aside as he made his way into the room.

"I take it you ... you didn't care for the purple room?" he asked as he glanced around again, deciding he did feel a bit offended that she wouldn't like what he had arranged especially for her.

Her eyebrow cocking into a perfect arch, Olivia shook her head. "This ... this is the room Jeffers brought me to," she countered with wave of one hand, realizing that it must be Jeffers who was color blind and not his master. "I wondered about the color; I remember you said something about a purple room."

Michael sighed. He would have to have a word with Jeffers about the difference between blue and purple. "I'll take up the matter with Jeffers," he said with a nod. Glancing around the room, one he realized he'd never been in before, Michael spotted a settee in an alcove and motioned toward it.

"Could we ... sit for a moment?" he asked quietly, watching Olivia's face closely as she nodded and moved to take a seat on one side of the settee. He sat down next to her, angling his body so that he could better see her face as he spoke with her. *God, she was lovely.*

Noticing her hands folded together in her lap, he reached over and took her left one in his. There was no hesitancy on her part; she allowed him to touch her and lift the small hand to his lips. Michael kissed the knuckles as he watched her eyes widen. Still, she did not pull her hand away. The thin iron band that surrounded the base of her fourth finger glimmered in the lamplight, and his thumb absently brushed over the metal. "We shall have to get you a more... a more appropriate ring than this," he murmured quietly.

Her breath catching at the comment, Olivia regarded him with a frown. "What ... Why is this one inappropriate?" she asked, a bit of a crinkle appearing between her brows.

Because I can afford far more. Because you deserve gold. Michael smiled at her protest. "It was the best I could do on short notice," he stated, remembering the odd look Robert Coomber, the village blacksmith in Shipley, had given him when he asked what he might have available in the way of wedding rings. "Your brother helped me pick it out," he added. Of all the things he arranged prior to his latest visit to the Waterfords, the most important item had been, well, not forgotten as much as overlooked.

His sister had not mentioned him needing a wedding ring!

So he purchased the next best thing from the blacksmith, knowing he would pay a visit to his favorite jeweler once he was back in London. And he'd bestowed Olivia with the iron ring in the meantime.

"George?" Olivia responded, her brows furrowing. She remembered seeing Michael and George as they were walking back to the house. From The Ship, she was sure.

"Yes. He took me to the blacksmith's shop Thursday morning so I could buy a ring. But it's far too plain for a woman of your beauty," Michael commented, not mentioning the ring wasn't really silver and it would probably turn her finger green if she wore it much longer.

Olivia cocked her head and a look of surprise passed over her face. "You think me beautiful?" she asked in disbelief as she watched his eyes focus on the ring on her finger. *So, he didn't go for a drink at the pub the morning of our wedding!*

His grin broadening as a wash of red colored his face, Michael returned his attention to Olivia's face. His thumb, having abandoned her hand and the ring, moved up to slowly caress her jaw line and follow the curve down her neck and across her throat. "Of course," he whispered, his gaze sending her into a hypnotic trance. "May I ... may I kiss you?" he stammered in a quiet voice, his thumb working its way back up her neck and behind her ear to allow his hand to pull her face toward him. He saw panic in her eyes, though, and stopped his hand.

"I have never been ... kissed. Properly kissed, I mean," Olivia murmured. "You saved me from Eli Babcock, remember?" she added, her mouth left slightly open by the admission. She wasn't opposed to him kissing her, but if he expected her to know what to do, he would be sorely disappointed.

"Oh," Michael acknowledged, his eyebrow arching. *This is a pleasant surprise!* "Well, there's really not much to it," he replied. Leaning down, he allowed his lips to brush lightly over hers before he captured them in a light kiss. Quite pleased that she did not back away from him, Michael deepened the kiss, suddenly realizing that he rather enjoyed kissing her.

Olivia allowed his lips to caress hers until they very nearly thrummed.

The scent of roses filled Michael's nostrils. Her skin beneath his fingers warmed until he thought he might be branded by her heat. And then he was aware of the subtle change as his lips moved again.

Olivia's lashes tickled the top of his cheekbones as she

closed her eyes and returned the kiss, her lips eager to taste him.

Although he was tempted to use his tongue to further part her lips, Michael resisted and simply used his mouth to guide hers. She willingly followed, a small moan emanating from her throat when Michael nipped her lower lip. When he finally let go and slowly backed away from her face, mostly to catch his breath, the scent of roses wafted past his nostrils. *I could do this all night,* he realized, his senses suddenly on fire.

Stunned at the intimacy of the kiss, Olivia inhaled sharply and opened her eyes to find Michael staring at her with a curious expression. *Did I do something wrong?* she wondered, but decided after a moment that his look wasn't one of disappointment or disapproval. "Would it be acceptable for me to kiss you now?" she whispered, wondering why he was looking at her as he was.

Michael did his best to suppress a grin. *Well, that wasn't as hard as I was expecting it to be,* he found himself thinking. For obvious reasons, he figured Olivia Waterford wouldn't allow him to kiss her this early in their forced marriage. Nor did he expect that she would ask to kiss *him*! "I ... would be honored," he answered, suddenly breathless, barely able to hide his enthusiasm.

Olivia shifted herself on the settee so that she could better face him. Reaching up with her left hand, she combed her fingers into his dark hair until they were just behind his head. Pulling gently so that his face would come down to her level, Olivia angled her head up and brushed her lips against his eager mouth, the way he had done with her. A moment later, she had her other hand on his shoulder and her lips pressed against his, matching his moves one for one. At last, she pulled away, a slight gasp escaping her. Before she could sit upright, though, Michael had wrapped both his arms around her shoulders and pulled her against him so that her head lay in the hollow between his shoulder and arm. He felt her body mold into his, its comforting warmth seeping into the front of his body.

"Did I do it right?" she murmured, her voice muffled by his shirt.

Michael chuckled in response, the vibrations causing Olivia's head to bounce against the hard muscle and bones of his chest. "Oh, yes, my love," he whispered, his lips touching the hair along the top of her forehead. They sat in silence for several minutes. Michael finally took a deep breath. "I owe you an apology for what happened Tuesday night," he whispered finally. When he did not hear a response from Olivia, he went on, "My behavior was most unforgivable and very unlike me, I assure you," he explained in a whisper as he gently rubbed one of her arms. "But I must admit that I do not regret what happened and can only hope that one day, probably many years from now, you will not, either." He took a deep breath and let it out slowly.

There, I said it, he thought, not feeling the least bit triumphant about his confession. How long would she hold that night against him? How long would she regret having met him? Regret even knowing him?

And why wasn't she responding?

He glanced down at Olivia when he realized she hadn't made a sound for several minutes. Moving her so he could better see her face, Michael realized that her eyes were closed and she barely breathed. *She looks like an angel,* he thought, a grin spreading on his face. The grin disappeared, though, when he realized why she hadn't said a word.

Olivia was sound asleep!

Michael sighed, feeling a bit of relief that she probably hadn't heard a word he had said. But the thought that Olivia felt comfortable enough to fall asleep in his arms brought another smile to his lips.

Lifting her into his arms, he carried her to the bed, lowered her to the space above the downturned linens, and covered her. For a moment, he considered climbing in next to her. Then he remembered that his mother slept in this bed when she was in residence. Whatever thought he had of holding his wife while she slept immediately left him. Leaning over, Michael kissed Olivia's forehead and the back of one of her hands before he quietly left the room.

Olivia lay motionless for several heartbeats, surprised Michael had simply kissed her head and left the room. His apology, at least what she'd heard of it while half-asleep, seemed heartfelt. Humble, almost. Did she regret what had happened last Tuesday night? Yesterday, yes. She had to admit she had regretted everything that had happened since Tuesday night. But, now? Tonight? She wasn't so sure anymore.

CHAPTER 26

SUNDAY MORNING IN THE
GARDEN WITH HIS WIFE

April 16, 1815
Bounding down the stairs at precisely nine o'clock in the morning, Michael Cunningham came to a dead stop where the stairs ended in the central hall. The round table located in the middle of the hall, usually topped with an empty crystal vase, sported an enormous floral arrangement. Symmetrical in both form and color and featuring a variety of greenery and spring flowers, it appeared to have been created by a professional florist.

Or his mother.

"Jeffers!" he called out as he slowly walked around the arrangement, figuring Lady Cunningham had to have put it there.

"Yes, sir?" Jeffers replied when he appeared from the dining room, adjusting his sleeves as if he'd been performing some duty that required his sleeves to be rolled up.

"Where is she?" Michael asked gruffly, waving a gloved hand toward the flowers.

Jeffers' eyebrows nearly disappeared into his wig. "Mrs. Cunningham is in the garden, sir," he stated carefully, wondering why his master seemed so offended by the floral arrangement.

Michael started to turn and then redirected his attention

to the butler. *What did he say?* "'Mrs.'? Not 'Lady'?" he questioned, wondering if he'd heard Jeffers correctly.

The butler nodded. "Your *wife*, sir, is in the garden. If Lady Cunningham is here, she has not made her presence known. A rather unlikely event, I would venture to say," he stated in a quieter voice, one eyebrow still cocked in confusion.

Michael frowned but showed his relief regarding his mother's continued absence. "Then, where did the flowers come from?" he asked, the tenseness easing from his shoulders and his voice.

Jeffers did his best to suppress a sigh. "Some were delivered from a hot house yesterday. The rest are from your garden, sir."

Michael stood staring at the butler, stunned. "Did Olivia ...?" he waved his hand toward the floral arrangement and circled it in the air and then added his other hand in a pantomime that could have indicated the building of a rather large monument to Sir Nelson.

"Mrs. Cunningham did the florals, yes," Jeffers acknowledged with a nod. "A rather nice arrangement, if I may say. Very balanced both in color and structure. I believe she is working on one for the dining room right now." When his master didn't reply right away, the butler asked, "Are you displeased with the effort, Mr. Cunningham?"

Michael's eyes widened. "No!" he answered quickly, shaking his head vigorously. "Not at all. I am just ... surprised is all." *When had she had time to create such a huge display?* he wondered. After a moment, he asked, "Just how long has Mrs. Cunningham been up and about?"

Jeffers clasped his hands behind his back. "She came down at seven this morning and had tea, but she said she would wait to break her fast until you were ready to join her."

Michael colored a bit, not realizing he had married a woman who woke up before noon.

"Thank you, Jeffers. I think I will go to the garden then."

Hurrying to the back door, an entrance he hadn't used but for the one night when he'd been too drunk to climb the front steps and the night he'd sneaked Eloisa into the house, Michael opened it and did a quick survey of the back yard. The gardener had trimmed the bushes on either side of the door and cropped the bit of lawn around the statuary, but most of the plants surrounding the walk appeared to need attention. Although he saw no sign of Olivia, Michael started down the garden path, weaving his way through the islands of early spring flowers and admiring the riot of colors represented. *Are there usually this many flowers in bloom this early in spring?* he found himself wondering. *It's been rather cool this year.*

He came upon the derrière of his wife as she knelt over a clump of daisies, her dark green muslin gown shaping itself quite nicely around the globes of her bottom. Admiring the view, Michael did not immediately make his presence known. When Olivia leaned forward to cut some stems from the lower parts of the bush, he could stand it no longer. He reached out and placed his hands firmly under her arm and around her waist and lifted her from the ground, holding her solidly against the front of his body. He could feel her heart suddenly racing through the thin fabric of her gown. When his left arm rested just under a breast, he realized she wore no corset and his own heart began to race.

"Oh!" Olivia shrieked, the pruning shears dropping to the ground as she was pulled up and back against Michael. "Let go of me!" she demanded. Despite Olivia's feet being clad in only kid leather slippers, her solid backward kick into Michael's shin and sharp elbow into his ribs produced nearly the effect she intended. Michael stumbled, but instead of releasing her from his hold so she'd land on her feet, he pitched forward. His grip around her middle, already tenuous at best, gave way with her struggles. Olivia fell awkwardly, the wrist of her left hand twisting as she landed on the walking path. She continued to kick and squirm in an effort to get away from her would-be attacker.

"Damn it, woman, be still!" Michael exclaimed, crouching down in an attempt to lessen the impact of her fall. The words were out of his mouth before he realized he'd cursed at her.

Olivia let out an audible, "Ouch!" before she tried to sit up in front of him. As her left hand moved to support her, she winced and pulled her left arm against her body. Tears of pain pricked the corners of her eyes. She was glad of the wide-brimmed bonnet that hid most of her face.

Embarrassed by her outburst and by his, Olivia could feel her cheeks flaming even before she fully realized that it was Michael who had tried to lift her before she hit the ground. *What had he intended by lifting me like that?* she wondered.

"Good God, you're hurt," Michael breathed, his apparent anger replaced with genuine concern. *Oh, Christ, what have I done?*

Sighing audibly, she slumped forward, cradling her wrist with her other hand as the fight went out of her. Even before the tears began streaming down her face, Michael scooped her into his arms and was carrying her to the back door, shouting for Jeffers. And the way Michael winced as he took his first couple of steps told her she had succeeded in hurting his shin when she had kicked backward as hard as she could.

Her head suddenly pressed against the solidity of his chest, Olivia could hear the quick beats of his heart beneath his coats, smell the sandalwood of his cologne and feel the urgency in his step, the comfort of his arms as he carried her. When the startled butler opened the door, Michael called out, "Send for the physician!" Alarmed at the sight of his master carrying his prone wife, Jeffers nodded and disappeared back into the house.

Michael maneuvered himself and his burden through the door before looking down at Olivia. Seeing her eyes were closed, he at first thought she might have fainted, but her lashes fluttered and she looked up to meet his worried gaze.

"There is really no need for a doctor," she murmured as she attempted to shake her head. The bonnet she wore was crushed against his arm, but she managed to pull it off with her right hand.

"Hush," Michael spoke quietly in reply, moving into the parlor and gently placing her onto the settee.

"I think it's just a sprain ... "

Michael's hand went to the side of her face, holding her cheek as he surveyed her, his thumb brushing tears aside. "Was it just your arm, or did I ...?"

"It's only my wrist," she assured him, finding it odd that his look of concern was such a source of comfort. There was a moment of embarrassed silence between them. Olivia lowered her head and wondered what to say. An apology, certainly, despite his having brought this on himself, she considered. Her heart hammering in her chest, she took a deep breath and ventured to look up. "I apologize. I ... I did not know it was you," she started to speak, not knowing what else to say under the circumstances.

"I am the one who is sorry. It was most improper of me to have ..."

The two stared at one another for a moment before Olivia's gaze fell on his knee and his wandered over her. "Oh, dear. You've got dirt on your breeches ..."

"And you've got dirt on your gown ... "

The two stopped in mid-sentence and regarded one another in an awkward silence, bemused expressions on their faces. "May I?" Michael asked as he motioned to the space on the settee next to her.

"Of course," Olivia nodded as she shifted a bit to allow him room to sit.

Michael reached for her gloved right hand, his attention on her face. Lifting her hand to his lips, he hesitated when she suddenly tried to pull it away.

"If only I had known it was you ..," she stammered, her eyes darting between the back of the soiled glove and Michael's face.

Michael followed her point of attention and glanced at her glove, realizing she was attempting to prevent him from kissing a layer of dirt. He gently tugged on the fingers of the glove until it came free of her hand. Holding her bare hand with his other hand, he kissed the knuckles. "It was entirely my fault for having thought to ..." Michael let the sentence trail off.

What did I intend to do? Kiss her, certainly. Aroused by the site of her bent over the daisies like that made him think of other things he would like to do with her at some point in their marriage bed. Now, he realized it would be some time before she would even *allow* him in her bed. After this incident, he was afraid it might be a very long time before he was welcome in the same *room*. He removed his top hat and held the brim with both hands, his large fingers nervously brushing the beaver.

"If I'd known it was you, I would not have reacted as I did," Olivia explained quietly. *Although I still would have been startled by what you did,* she added to herself. *Whatever were you thinking to do?* She held her left arm in her lap, the wrist already swelling.

"I did not mean to startle you so," Michael countered lamely. "Our garden is safe from intruders, I assure you," he added, releasing his grip on his hat to reach over and carefully lift her left arm.

Our garden? she repeated to herself. *He means his and Edward's, of course,* she figured. Olivia allowed him to remove the glove from her left hand and survey the wrist, the fingers of one hand holding her arm as the fingers of his other hand gently manipulated her fingers, all while he asked where and if it hurt. When she could prove to him that she was able to bend every finger, he lifted her hand to his lips and brushed his lips over the knuckles. Her breath caught at the pleasant sensation that suddenly rushed up her arm and seemed to settle somewhere deep inside, but Michael misinterpreted her reaction. He quickly lowered her arm. "I am sorry. I shouldn't ..."

Not wanting him to withdraw, Olivia raised her right hand to the side of his face. "You did not hurt me," she whispered, her hand gently pulling his face towards hers. Nearly close enough to kiss, her lips parted and her eyelids drooped.

Michael held his breath, stunned that she was inviting a kiss. His lips brushed over hers for only an instant before they were both startled enough to turn and sit upright just as the parlor door suddenly opened.

A white-haired gentleman carrying a black leather bag appeared. "Good morning, Cunningham," he announced. Jeffers rolled his eyes as he stood behind the man, his hands clasped behind his back.

Michael quickly rose to his feet and then turned to place a hand on Olivia's shoulder to keep her from standing. "Doctor Ashcroft, so good of you to come," he said, his face coloring as if he'd been caught stealing something. *A kiss, I was sure,* he thought with a bit of annoyance.

"And so quickly," Olivia breathed as she nodded at the physician. "You must have a very fast horse." Despite the early hour, the man was well-dressed and sported a white cravat with perfect folds and an elaborate knot.

The doctor grinned at his patient as he stepped forward and gave a leg. "Proximity," he answered proudly.

"What an interesting name for a horse," Olivia replied, her eyebrows furrowing as she considered what the horse had been guilty of doing to have earned such an odd name.

The doctor cocked his head to one side, caught off-guard by her response. "Oh, there's no horse," Dr. Ashcroft stated with an even larger smile, his humor obviously at her expense. He lowered his black bag to the floor next to the settee.

"Dr. Ashcroft lives next door," Michael said in a quiet voice, taking a breath of relief as he did so.

"Oh," Olivia acknowledged, her face blooming with color. She held out her arm at the doctor's urging and he performed the exact same manipulations as had Michael, although he did so less gingerly.

"However did this happen?" the doctor asked as he examined her swollen wrist, turning her arm gently with one hand while holding her elbow with the other.

"I was cutting flowers in the garden," Olivia started to explain.

"I dropped her," Michael replied, not realizing how his words would be interpreted.

At the doctor's raised eyebrow in Olivia's direction, she said quickly, "He was helping me up from the ground."

The doctor turned his withering gaze on Michael. "She kicked me," Michael stated defensively, not wanting the doctor to think that he had *deliberately* dropped her.

"I didn't know it was him!" Olivia countered when the doctor turned back to look at her. "I was simply caught off-guard and thought only to defend myself."

When the doctor turned back to Michael, her husband simply shrugged. "I assure you, our garden is safe from intruders," Michael countered, his clipped words indicating he had taken offense at the implication his garden was somehow a bastion for miscreants.

"I did not mean to offend, I assure you," Olivia replied in a very quiet voice.

The doctor's eyebrows drew together to become one bushy white caterpillar.

Michael regarded her for a moment and the hardness in his features softened a bit. "You did a rather effective job of it," he said, a quirk at the edge of his mouth the only hint that he was teasing. He placed a finger under her chin and lifted it. "I am the one who should apologize," he said with a small smile, thinking he was having to do a lot of that, but at least she was awake to hear this one.

Aware of the doctor listening to their every word, he said, "I must assure you that I am not in the habit of accosting comely young ladies in their gardens so early in the morning. Or any time, for that matter," he added when he realized, too late, how his apology must have sounded.

Allowing a smile, Olivia bit her lower lip. *Last night he*

said I was beautiful, and now he thinks me comely, she thought, her embarrassment changing a bit.

Jeffers cleared his throat loudly and they all turned to look at him. "Dr. Ashcroft, may I present the Honorable Michael Cunningham's new wife, Mrs. Cunningham," he stated formerly.

A huge smile replaced the quizzical expression that had resided on the physician's face for the past few moments. "Ah! *Newlyweds.* No additional explanation is necessary," he said with a wink and a wave of his hand. Olivia's blush darkened to a deep red and Michael visibly swallowed, his face reddening as well. "Mrs. Cunningham, you have a sprained wrist," Dr. Ashcroft announced proudly. "I'll put some arnica on it and wrap it up for you. Keep your arm dry. You'll need to stay off it for a few days," he gave a pointed look at Michael as he made the proclamation. "And if you have ice, put some in a glass and hold it against your wrist. Helps with the swelling," he said curtly. "Then add some brandy and drink that. Helps with the pain." He had the wrist bandaged even as he was explaining what he was doing. "If there's nothing else, I'll be off," he said as he closed up his black bag.

"Thank you, Dr. Ashcroft," Michael said, relief evident in his voice. "Jeffers will see to your compensation." The two men couldn't leave quickly enough for Michael.

The butler nodded and ushered the doctor out of the parlor leaving Michael standing next to the settee. In the uncomfortable silence, he motioned to her arm. "Does it hurt?"

Olivia moved the arm experimentally. "No," she replied with a shake of her head, knowing that if she tried to bend her wrist, she would probably give away just how much it really did hurt when Michael saw her wince.

He nodded. "We've certainly made an impression on Dr. Ashcroft," he murmured, a sigh following his statement.

Olivia smiled, wondering what the doctor must have thought regarding how she sprained her wrist. "Indeed," she answered with a short giggle.

Seeing her amusement, Michael took a breath and allowed his smile to match hers. "Whatever do you suppose he was thinking we were doing in the garden?" he asked absently.

"Sowing seeds, no doubt," Olivia replied with a hint of amusement.

Plowing, Michael countered to himself, wishing he had been doing it.

When Olivia looked up, she caught sight of his flushed face and wondered what he might be thinking just then. "Did you sleep well?" she asked, noticing he appeared somehow different in the morning light. The planes of his face were not nearly as severe as in the evening lamplight, and his nose appeared straighter. The slight bend near the top of his nose reminded her that it had been broken at some point in the past; she remembered him telling her family of the bare knuckle fight when it occurred.

"Well enough," he lied. He couldn't exactly tell her he'd been awake most of the night due to a constant erection. And how many times had he left his bed and made his way to his bedchamber door with the intention of going to her room? "And you?" he asked.

"Very well, thank you. And ... thank you for putting me to bed last night. I ... I must have fallen asleep. The bed in the blue room is divine," she added with a smile.

Of course it is, he thought. *Any bed with you in it would be divine.* "Jeffers said you were waiting to have breakfast until I could join you," Michael ventured hopefully. He actually hadn't planned to eat at home but thought to get something at a chocolate shop on the way to his solicitor's office.

"Well, yes, if you can spare the time. You look as if you are leaving for an appointment, though," she replied as she indicated his greatcoat. Her eyes suddenly widened. "Or church," she whispered when she realized it was Sunday. *No wonder the doctor was up and already dressed!*

Michael smiled and shook his head. "Even though it is Sunday, I must see my solicitor this morning. But I can certainly have breakfast with you before I go," he offered, not bothering to explain just why he was about to see his solicitor. Marriage required certain plans be made and certain accommodations be put into place for his wife's future. He held out his arm in an effort to assist her from the settee.

Olivia remembered the basket of cut flowers and the fallen shears in the garden. "I should get the flowers into water," she said as she took his arm and allowed him to lift her up.

"Jeffers can see to them until you're ready to do your ..," Michael replied, waving his other hand into the air as he had done with Jeffers. "The arrangement in the hall is quite exquisite," he added with a nod.

Pausing in mid-step, Olivia regarded him. "You're not teasing me?" she half-questioned, wondering just how sincere he was with his compliment.

"I am not. In fact, I don't usually tease," he said carefully, watching her reaction. *Or do I?* he wondered suddenly. *I am not teasing about the flowers.* "You should know that about me. Edward is the one who delights in teasing."

Nodding her understanding, Olivia said, "Thank you."

Edward paced in front of the fireplace in his bedchamber, his anger at his friend building with each pivot he made. If Michael had learned to fence with a modicum of skill instead of spending his time sparring at Gentlemen Jackson's, Edward would have challenged him to a duel that very night over dinner, and then seen to it the cur was poked full of holes before he could even raise his sword in defense. *How can the man treat his wife so shabbily?* Sprains her wrist in a gardening accident? How dare he! *And how can he continue to keep the woman's sister as his mistress?* he wondered, ignoring the sudden thought that he might be a bit jealous of Michael's circumstances.

Michael Cunningham was no rake. Even before his arrangement with Eloisa, he wasn't a frequent visitor to brothels. Nor had he an arrangement with any other mistresses that Edward knew of. *He's probably never even bedded a virgin,* Edward thought, suddenly wondering if that might have something to do with the man's behavior toward Olivia.

Although Michael had claimed he didn't want to marry, at least not at this point in his life, Edward never believed the proclamations, thinking that they were merely made in self-defense to a mother who tried too hard to find him a suitable match. *Like my mother,* he thought suddenly. Now that there was a second heir to the earldom, Edward knew he could marry Anna.

He wondered where she was now, wondered what she might be doing. *And with whom.* The last thought had him grimacing as he imagined her in the arms of another man. Perhaps he would hire someone to find her if his efforts to do so in New Bond Street failed. And then he could send her a letter ...

Shaking himself from his reverie, he turned and passed the fireplace again, vaguely aware of the dying embers. Perhaps he could do something to make Michael see the worth of the woman he had wed. Certainly Michael felt *something* for Olivia. He claimed he did. Edward was sure he'd seen it when Olivia walked into the library; there was an instant there when his friend's guard was down, when he was expecting someone else and instead his wife had entered and the sight of her had taken the man's breath away. And didn't Michael always look forward to his trips to Sussex? And not just because it gave him an opportunity to visit his own childhood home in the Horsham District?

So, what would make a man like Michael take notice of his wife and realize her worth? Perhaps he already knew and simply took her for granted.

Or, perhaps, he showed her so little regard because he had never had to *fight* for her.

Harold Waterford had seen to it that no other suitors could seek Olivia's hand. He had made sure the gel was available when Michael was ready to be wed. By not having to compete for her affections, Michael hadn't dealt with other admiring gentlemen. He hadn't experienced the emotion that would make him truly appreciate Olivia Waterford.

Jealousy.

The man had never been jealous!

Well, I'll make him jealous, Edward thought suddenly. *I'll make him love her. Or, at the very least, feel affection for her,* he thought, his determination growing.

Edward stopped and stared into the dying fire, his plan forming in his mind's eye. *He may punch me in the jaw,* he thought for a moment. *He might even kill me.*

He'll at least hate me until I can explain myself.

After the broken jaw heals, and I can speak again.

The cons of the plan built up one by one until he had nearly talked himself *out* of intervening. But before he retired for the night, Edward had a very clear idea of what he could do. Taking a seat at his escritoire, he took up a quill, dipped it into the ink bottle and began writing a note on his finest stationery.

My dearest Olivia ...

CHAPTER 27

MONDAY HE AWAKENS HER
SLOWLY

April 17, 1815
At some point in the middle of the night, Olivia pushed the bed covers off her body. Still uncomfortably warm, she unbuttoned the front of her nightgown and pushed the fabric off of her right shoulder as she lay on her left side, her sprained wrist protected under the pillow. The cool night air of the nearby open window caressed her skin, and she drifted back to sleep.

The dream resumed where she left it. There was a warm, pleasant sensation of being cradled, of being held protectively whilst her head was tucked into the hollow of a neck, her back pressed against a man's chest, her thighs resting against stronger thighs. Even the bottom of one foot touched on another larger one. She sighed and wrapped her right arm around the larger one that held her, her hand resting softly on fine linen fabric of a shirt sleeve as her fingers caressed the softness.

Her body stirred as her bare breast was slowly covered by warm fingers, their touch so light her skin tickled and the nipple hardened to a small pebble. The sensuous caress continued, a fingertip gently circling her nipple, teasing it until it ached to be held and suckled. Turning her body slightly so that the hand could hold her breast completely, she was pressed further into the body behind her, and she smiled and sighed. She was aware of a kiss on her hair, of another on her ear lobe, another on her bare shoulder. Warm breath washed over her collarbone, the light kisses leaving behind just a hint of moisture that cooled her hot skin. The large hand moved to encase her entire breast, holding it and lightly rubbing until she felt desire rise from deep within her.

Her breath quickening, she realized her entire body ached for something more; the space between her thighs felt hot and wet, and it begged for attention. There was a light pinch on her nipple, and she inhaled sharply. She dare not stir more for she was sure if she did, she would awaken from the dream again and not be able to recapture the incredible pleasures that coursed through her body with every stroke on her breast.

A shiver passed through her as the fingertips made their way to the side of her other breast. There was a whispered sound near her ear that she finally heard as *beautiful Olivia.* Arcing her back just a bit, she gasped as another wave of pleasure rose and subsided. *This is a most wonderful dream,* she thought as she felt the kisses again. She purred and took a deep breath, inhaling the scent of him, the soft musk, a light whiff of sandalwood, the very faint odor of brandy, the scent of citrus laundry soap. Lifting her hand from the linen sleeve, she caught the side of his head, burying her fingers in a soft wave of silken hair.

Hair?

Her eyelashes fluttered and she slowly opened her eyes.

"Please, do not scream," she heard whispered in her ear before lips gently kissed it, bit it lightly. Turning her head slightly, she caught sight of Michael as he lifted himself onto his elbow to peer down at her with a look of adoration.

Olivia wondered if she was still dreaming, but when he leaned down to kiss her on the corner of her mouth, she closed her eyes and smiled. "Good morning," she whispered, slowly allowing her fingers to drop from the side of his head.

"Good morning, indeed," Michael whispered before he

kissed her on the mouth, a quick but thorough kiss that left her breathless.

"Did you ... did you sleep here all night?" Olivia asked, wondering when the dream had ended and the reality began. She was suddenly aware that he was dressed in a shirt and breeches, but his feet were bare.

Shaking his head, Michael sighed. "Just an hour or so," he replied, his eyes drifting down to her bared breast and shoulder. Even when she knew that he saw them, Olivia did not try to cover herself. "I was about to leave for Gentleman Jackson's, but I wanted to check on your wrist, and I wanted to ... to see you before I left." *And I'm seeing more of you than I thought I ever would,* he thought happily, his lips settling onto her shoulder to place a kiss there.

He bent down and suckled her hardened nipple. Olivia arched her body up and gasped as the incredible shivers of pleasure waves rolled through her body. She was ready to beg for him to take her. She wanted the sensation to continue. She wanted to feel his body pressed against hers with nothing in between them. She wanted to touch him and make him feel these very same sensations. She wanted him to do something about the ache that had developed between her thighs, the sensation of throbbing that seemed to demand he touch her there. And as he pushed her nightgown away from her other breast and placed his mouth over the nipple, she thought that perhaps this morning he would take her maidenhead. Her body seemed to shudder at the thought, as if it knew what was about to happen even before she did. "If I'd known it was you in my bed ..." There was a sharp rap at the door. "I would not have ..."

One moment Michael was pleasuring her with his mouth and tongue and a hand trailing down the front of her body, and the next, he was up and out of the bed, cursing softly as he moved awkwardly to the door.

Stunned at his sudden departure from the bed, Olivia clutched the top openings of her nightgown together and lifted herself onto an elbow. "Michael?" she spoke aloud. But even as she said it, she realized he had already left the room. In the doorway stood a very stunned Sarah, whose fair complexion was turning a splotchy crimson.

"Oh, Mrs. Cunningham, I am so very sorry," the dresser spoke as she raised her hand to her mouth. She had seen the flash of annoyance in Michael's eyes and his state of half-dress.

Olivia fell back onto the bed and moaned softly. "From now on, Sarah, I'll ring when I'm ready to get dressed," she said, trying not to sound too cross with the servant as she quickly buttoned her nightgown under cover of the bed linens, her left wrist complaining as she did so.

"Yes, ma'am," the girl replied, biting her lip as she entered the bedchamber. She waited a moment before coming further into the room and closing the door behind her. "I've a message for you from Mr. Seward."

Still flat on her back, Olivia considered the words and furrowed a brow. "Mr. Seward?" she repeated, finally reaching out a hand to take the folded notepaper from the dresser. She took a moment to admire the cursive writing on the outside.

O. Cunningham. She flipped the note and stared at the elegant wax seal that held the corners of the paper together. *Odd,* she thought as she broke the seal, unfolded the paper and read the missive.

My dearest Olivia, For the brief time you have graced our household with your presence, I have felt both great joy at your accomplishments and great despair on your behalf. I have for you a gift and news I must share. Please grant me an audience this afternoon in the library at 4 o'clock. Yours very truly, Edward.

Olivia stared at the note for several minutes, rereading the handwriting and wondering at its meaning. *Despair on your behalf?* she thought, her frown increasing on each reading.

"It is bad news?" Sarah asked as she stood waiting for her mistress to give her orders. "Mr. Seward seemed quite ... unsure when he asked me to give it to you."

Shaking her head, Olivia folded the paper and set it on the night stand. "I am not sure, either," she murmured as she moved to get off the bed. She caught the scent of Michael as she moved and inhaled deeply. Her entire body shivered at the thought of him and how he'd held her that morning. *What a glorious way to wake up,* she thought, her good mood returning. "I think I shall go shopping today," she announced suddenly, remembering the invitation to the Harvey ball. "I need a ball gown." *And a dressing gown.*

Sarah nodded and hurried to the clothes press. "Your navy walking gown, perhaps?" she suggested.

Olivia smiled. "That will do fine."

The shingle above the storefront of the modiste was painted in gold gilt, the name *Madame Suzanne's* in a script that suggested quality and femininity. Behind the window stood a mannequin decorated with a blue and gold walking ensemble, and surrounding it were swags of silks and satins in a dozen colors. Olivia stood before the store in New Bond Street and saw her reflection in the glass before she willed herself to go in and ask about a ball gown.

Madame Suzanne was arranging the skirts of a dinner gown on a sewing mannequin as a seamstress was pinning the arms into place. Upon seeing Olivia, she stood and curtsied, greeting her new customer with a warm smile. "Good morning. I am Madame Suzanne. Have you come for a special gown?" she asked without a hint of the French accent so many of the modistes used when addressing customers.

She moved to lead Olivia further into her shop, giving her customer a quick perusal to see if she could determine the woman's age, the likelihood she would actually order a gown, and how much she could afford. The modiste's cropped hair, stylish gown and the ostrich feather arcing out of a band around her head indicated she favored a modern mode of dress.

"Good morning," Olivia replied, her gaze sweeping the small shop. Unlike the modistes in Bond Street, this one had dozens of dresses already made up and displayed on the walls and in racks. "I am in need of a ball gown," she said, her heart pounding in her chest. *Why am I so nervous?* she wondered, chastising herself for being intimidated by the thought of having someone besides herself or her mother make her gowns.

There was a good deal of pin money stuffed in her reticule that would more than cover the cost of the most extravagant gown the modiste had on display. "And I'll need a dressing gown, as well," she added, remembering she really should answer her bedchamber door wearing something more than a night rail.

Madame Suzanne regarded her for a moment, thinking that at least this customer was planning ahead for one ball this Season. "Will you be coming out this year?" she asked, her eyebrow cocking expectantly.

Stunned, Olivia did not know whether to be flattered that the woman thought her young enough to just now be coming out or if the woman was teasing her. She did not have an escort or companion with her, after all. "I am far too old to be coming out," Olivia answered evenly, trying to make her voice sound as neutral as possible. "And I am a married woman."

"Oh!" the proprietor replied, apparently surprised. "Then you have the good fortune of marrying young!" she exclaimed happily. "Come, let me show you some samples of my work," she encouraged as she continued to regard her customer. "Now, what kind of ball will you be attending?"

Olivia bit her lower lip. "I ... it's at the Harvey's," she stammered, not realizing there might be different kinds of balls.

"Oh, but, of course," Madame Suzanne said as a hand went to her chest. "Lady Harvey is blossoming with child and wanted to host her annual ball before her confinement."

Glad to know the reason for the ball's timing, Olivia

nodded as if she already knew. "Then you'll understand why I do not wish to outshine the hostess," she hinted, hoping for a gown that would be elegant but not ostentatious.

"But, of course. Allow me to show you Lady Harvey's gown. It is not quite finished, though," she warned, leading Olivia to a back room where a sewing mannequin displayed an empire waisted gown of pastel yellow satin with cap sleeves of tulle. The gown had an overskirt of tulle and white ribbons that trimmed the skirt and bodice. A flounce with a hint of a train graced the bottom. "She'll not be able to eat a thing. One drop and the fabric will stain," the modiste complained quietly. "Now, for you, I am thinking a light cream satin ..."

Olivia followed Madame Suzanne back into the main shop and to a mannequin wearing the very dress she was describing. "Wear this with pearls or colored stones and cream kid dance slippers and you will be resplendent," she stated emphatically. "Would you like to try it on?"

Studying the gown, Olivia decided she liked what she saw. *But would Michael?* she wondered. A memory of earlier that morning passed through her mind. "I do not wish the neckline to be too low, but a bit of décolletage would be appreciated," she said with a lifted eyebrow.

Madame Suzanne regarded her for only a moment, a glint in her eye indicating she understood Olivia's meaning. "We shall see to it."

Olivia spent the next hour wearing the gown while standing on a wooden box. Three seamstresses pinned and positioned her as they worked their needles and thread and talked quietly amongst themselves. She overheard a comment about how unfortunate it was that Lady Worthington would not be wearing this gown for her wedding, but how fortunate it was that she discovered her fiancé's extreme gambling debts before marrying the man and losing her entire fortune to a gaming hell. And there was mention of Lady Harvey's dress still needing a bit of work because it was no longer large enough to accommodate her growing belly.

Olivia did her best not to let on that she overheard anything the seamstresses said, even biting her lip when the youngest asked, "And did you hear that the Honorable Michael Cunningham has finally married? I hear his wife is quite pretty, but no one seems to know who she is or where she is from."

"Viscountess Cunningham must be so relieved to see her son wed," another one said. "Madame will have to ask her about her new daughter when she comes in for her fitting."

Olivia inhaled sharply. "Lady Cunningham?" she whispered hoarsely, not intending for someone to actually hear her. If these seamstresses knew of the marriage, Lady Cunningham could certainly have heard something by now. And if Madame Suzanne was to ask her about her new daughter-in-law's identity, what would Lady Cunningham say? How embarrassing it could be for Michael's mother not to even know who her son had married, no matter that she was a formidable woman!

The seamstresses looked up from their work. 'Why, yes. We're very honored to have done her dress for this ball," one said before she stuffed a cluster of pins between her lips.

"Seeing as how she usually only wears gowns made in Paris or Italy," another said with a roll of her eyes.

"But I do not care how rich she is, I would not wish to be her daughter-in-law," the third said as she continued to hem the ball gown, her thumb sporting a gold band with a garnet embedded in the gold. The others murmured their agreement. "But I still find myself wishing that I could be married to her son's best friend. I miss Edward terribly."

"Anna!" another one hissed in surprise. "You don't really expect us to believe an earl's son feels any affection for you, do you?"

Sighing, Olivia tried to concentrate on what the girls had said about her mother-in-law and only half-heard what the youngest said of Michael's friend. She felt the grip of fear deep inside and tried to breathe normally. "Is Lady Cunningham really that...?" she started to ask and then clamped her mouth shut. *What am I asking?* she wondered suddenly. *I do not wish to come off as a gossip with these girls.*

"Formidable?" the oldest replied with a grin, her head bobbing even as she said the word.

"Oh," Olivia replied, feeling faint. Suddenly, a bit of gray appeared at the edge of her vision.

"Are you all right, Mrs...?" the one named Anna started to ask as she hurriedly stood up to provide support if Olivia fainted. "Mrs. ... I apologize, I did not hear your name," she whispered.

Olivia placed a hand on the girl's shoulder for support as much as comfort. The girl was quite beautiful, her curly raven hair framing a face that could have been made of porcelain. Her brown eyes were large, almost exotic with their long black lashes and up swept corners. And she was tall, her perfect posture emphasizing her height even more. "Cunningham," Olivia said quietly. "Olivia Cunningham."

Anna stared at her for several seconds, her gaze of concern changing to one of desperation and then fear. The other two seamstresses gasped in unison, the youngest pulling up a small chair for Olivia to collapse into.

"As in 'The Honorable Michael'?" the oldest one ventured, her eyebrows going up in a most worried manner. Her lower lip was caught by a tooth. She hadn't said anything untoward about whoever had married the man, at least. Whatever had caused their client to react so?

"Please, accept our apologies," the youngest seamstress said, biting her lower lip in an expression that seemed to match the oldest girl's. "We meant no offense..."

But Madame Suzanne had returned to check on her customer, shocked to find the woman extremely pale and sitting when she should have been standing on the wooden box in the middle of the small room. "What has happened here?" Her eyes widened even more when she noticed Anna's shocked expression.

Olivia shook her head as if to clear it. "Would you know when Lady Cunningham is due for her fitting?" she asked, quickly standing up from the chair and returning to her perch on the wooden box. The girls resumed their work on the hem, acting as if nothing had happened.

Madame Suzanne was taken aback at the question, but shrugged as if the impending appointment was of no consequence. "The viscountess comes when she is of a mind to do so," she answered, waving a hand in the air as if it did not matter.

Glancing down at the three seamstresses, Olivia swallowed and then took a deep breath. "When she does, please let her know that Mrs. Michael Cunningham is looking forward to meeting the woman who bore the magnificent man that is my husband. She is certainly to be commended," she stated with as much conviction as possible.

Madame Suzanne stared at Olivia for a long moment, her expression sobering until she gave her customer a deep curtsy. "I shall convey your words exactly," she promised, the heads of the seamstresses nodding in agreement. "And may I say, Mrs. Cunningham, it has been an honor for me to do the gown for your first ball as a married lady," she added, her ostrich feather bobbing with her curt nod.

"Thank you," Olivia replied, her relief evident to anyone who looked her way. And as she stood very still for the hemming of her dress, she found herself regarding the beautiful seamstress who claimed to miss her husband's friend. *So this is Edward's Anna,* she thought with a bit of excitement. Such a beautiful, exotic woman! *Why is it so unacceptable for the second son of an earl to marry a seamstress if that is what he wishes to do?* she found herself wondering. After all, Michael had married her ... *because he had to*, she remembered with a suddenly heavy heart and a memory that made her think his attentions were meant for someone else.

Less than a half-hour later, Olivia paid the modiste with some of the pin money Michael had given her. Very satisfied with the ball gown and a long dressing gown in deep gold satin, she left the shop with her parcels. A quick visit to a shoe seller and she had her matching cream dance slippers.

By the time the private coach brought her back to Grosvenor Square, her worry over meeting Michael's mother was replaced with concern when she realized she might be late for her appointment with Edward.

From the back sewing room of Madame Suzanne's, Anna watched Olivia Cunningham take her leave of the shop. She couldn't help but feel sorry for the young woman. To have married a man with a mother who was considered difficult to please ... Anna shook her head. She could only hope Viscountess Cunningham wouldn't make trouble for Mrs. Cunningham.

Anna suddenly inhaled as she realized that if she were ever married to Edward, her situation would be the same. Except she knew already Lady Eversham personally—had known the woman since she was in leading strings. Although Lady Eversham had never treated her poorly, she also never treated her as she would a lady of the *ton*. The woman wanted her son wed to an aristocrat's daughter, the higher the rank, the better.

Perhaps it was better that Anna wouldn't be spending her life with Edward. That didn't mean she wasn't concerned about him, though. Had she been the only seamstress in the room with Mrs. Cunningham, she would have asked the young bride more about her dear Edward. She wondered if the man ever spoke of her. Did he still pine for her as he claimed he did when they were younger and he was off at school? Or had he begun his search for a suitable wife? A debutante eager to marry and give him children?

As she felt hot tears stream down her cheeks, Anna shook her head and vowed to put away thoughts of Edward. *If he cannot be mine, than he shall no longer be on my mind.* The thought, of course, only made her cry harder.

Jeffers met her at the front door with a message from Michael, saying he was meeting with Sir Richard but would be home in time for drinks before dinner. Leaving the gown and matching slippers with Sarah, she took her embroidery and headed toward the library. On her way, though, there was a loud knock at the front door. Jeffers hurried to answer it, and Olivia stood in the hall so that she could catch a glimpse of their visitor—a liveried footman who now stood before the butler.

The footman bowed and handed Jeffers a letter and a parcel. "I am to wait for a reply," the rather tall man stated with a nod. Beyond the door, Olivia could see to the street where a black Thoroughbred was hobbled. The blue and white silks under the saddle matched the footman's uniform.

Jeffers read the address on the outside of the parcel and turned to Olivia, his eyebrows nearly in his wig. "A package and letter have arrived for you, Mrs. Cunningham," he said, and then he motioned for the footman to take a seat in the vestibule. The footman moved to the chair but stood in front of it, bowing as Olivia hurried to take the package from Jeffers. "Who is this from?" she asked, addressing the footman.

"Her Grace, the Duchess of Somerset," he replied with a nod. "I am to wait for a reply, milady," he added as he stood at attention.

"Of course," Olivia replied as she stared dumbfounded at the white wrapped package. She turned to Jeffers. "Could you see to it that he has a meal and refreshment? And have the groom see to his horse, please. I'll be a few minutes writing a suitable reply," she explained as she took the letter and parcel and disappeared into the library.

"I will see to it," Jeffers replied, even though Olivia had left the vestibule.

The Duchess of Somerset sent me a letter!

Here! Olivia realized suddenly, wondering *how* in the world the duchess could know *where* in the world she could be found! She hastily unwrapped the stationer's paper from around a pasteboard box. Inside another layer of tissue paper wrapping was a cut crystal bowl of exquisite detail. Olivia nearly dropped it, so surprised was she by the sight and weight of it. Placing it on the fireplace mantle, she studied the bowl and its decoration and wondered at how much it must have cost. She put the empty box on a nearby table and tore open the wax seal from the back of the folded letter. *My dearest Olivia*, the missive began, the familiar handwriting a perfect script in a feminine hand.

> *Words cannot describe how happy and how sad I was all at once upon learning of your marriage to the Honorable Michael Cunningham. Happy for you, of course, for you have married a man who is highly regarded by this duchy (and we have long wondered whom he would choose for a wife since his deadline was nigh). And sad for me since you will not be educating my children. Yours was a most complete and qualified application for the position, but I have it on good authority that another governess of nearly your qualifications will begin in your place next month.*
>
> *I so look forward to the day we can meet, perhaps in London at a ball or at the theatre, or the house in Cavendish Square, so that I may wish you happy in person. In the meantime, please accept this wedding gift as a token of our best wishes on your fortuitous marriage (I thought it only appropriate that your first piece of crystal be from Waterford's studio.) Yours, Elizabeth.*

Staring at the paper for several minutes, Olivia reread the letter and wondered—*how had the Duchess of Somerset learned of her marriage to Michael Cunningham so quickly?*

Olivia remembered the short note of apology she wrote prior to her wedding Thursday morning; but there could not have been enough time for a mail coach to deliver it to Wiltshire and for a footman to be dispatched with a gift so soon!

She sat down at the escritoire, finding a sheet of Michael's stationery with his crest and a simple 'C' embossed at the top. Steadying her hand, she dipped the quill and wrote her reply as neatly as she could.

> *Dear Duchess of Somerset, I am most humbled by your words and by the beautiful gift of Waterford crystal that arrived only*

a few moments ago. Please accept my heartfelt thanks for your best wishes and for your kind words about my husband. Although I made his acquaintance many years ago (he is involved in business ventures with my father, Harold Waterford), I found myself a bit surprised when I was told I would be marrying Mr. Cunningham. I was, of course, even more surprised to learn he is the son of a viscount! Instead of the honor of educating your young children, it is I who must be educated on how to be the wife of a viscount's son, and sometime in the distant future, perhaps a viscountess. I shall endeavor to learn all that I must to be a suitable match for my husband. And, like you, I so look forward to the day when we can meet in person. Thank you again for your best wishes (the first we have received) and for the exquisite crystal. Yours in service always, Olivia Cunningham.

Reading her script one more time before sprinkling sand on the ink, Olivia considered her words and hoped she did not sound as if she was too familiar with the duchess. This was her fourth correspondence with Elizabeth Statton, but she hadn't really believed the duchess herself had written the other missives she'd received regarding her impending employment as a governess. This note was written in the same handwriting, though.

When she was sure the ink was dry, Olivia folded the note and dripped melted wax on the edges where the paper met in the middle. Her husband's seal, an 'MTC' in a bold font, lay on the edge of the desk. Another seal, with an 'OWC' in a more elaborate font, rested in a small wooden box next to the inkwell. Olivia studied the seal, wondering why there would be a seal with her initials carved into it in Michael's library.

How can this be? Realizing the wax would be setting hard in a moment, she stamped the seal into the dark red wax and admired the flourish of her new initials.

Olivia hurried to the kitchen where she found the footman eating. "Please, do not get up," she ordered before the footman could rise from the trestle. She took a seat across from him and handed him the note. "Tell me, sir, exactly when were you dispatched with the letter and package from the duchess?" she asked in a pleasant voice, hoping the man might know something of when his duchess received word of her marriage to Michael.

"Why, very early this morning, milady," he answered, putting his fork on his plate and averting his eyes. "The duchess was quite ... impatient, seeing as how the crystal she commissioned took nearly a week to be completed. A servant from Waterford's studio delivered it only last night," he explained, almost apologetically.

Olivia stared at the footman. *A week?* "Still, it's quite timely ..." *as I have only been wed since this past Thursday*, she thought to herself. "I cannot imagine how the duchess could have learned of my marriage ..." *Before I did!* "So quickly," she finished, her head suddenly spinning.

The footman shrugged and seemed eager to return to his meal. "If I may, milady, I believe Her Grace received a letter from Mr. Cunningham a bit over a week ago with the news of the impending nuptials." And when he realized he shouldn't have known such details, the footman colored up and averted his eyes. "Pardon, milady, I assure you, I did not read the letter. I cannot read, in fact, but I overheard Her Grace speaking of it with His Grace, the Duke of Somerset, over dinner."

For a moment, Olivia was very glad that the footman could not see her face, for the look of shock was most unladylike. *Michael sent a note to the duchess more than a week ago to inform her of his upcoming nuptials?* But how did *he* know? And from Elizabeth's letter, it was quite apparent she was informed as to *whom* Michael would be marrying. *The letter is addressed to me!*

Olivia excused herself from the footman's presence, intending to determine the whereabouts of her husband. While on her way to the vestibule to ring for Jeffers, she recalled him saying Michael was with Sir Richard. Then she remembered her appointment with Mr. Seward. Sighing, she instead stepped back into the library. Finding it empty, Olivia took a seat near the fireplace. Anxious to learn more, but knowing she would simply have to wait for Michael's return, she began stitching on her embroidery. She wondered after a time where Mr. Seward might be, and *just how did Michael know that she would be marrying him before last Tuesday night?* Intending to reread the note from the duchess, Olivia was about to get up and move to the mantle where she'd left it when she realized she was no longer alone.

"Olivia," Edward said a bit breathless as he entered the library. He gave a slight bow as a slightly startled Olivia stood and curtsied. "I am honored that you have come," he said quietly, his manner indicating a great deal of nervousness.

Edward was dressed impeccably, as usual, and his hair was perfectly combed into place. Just once, she considered, she would like to see the straight-laced man a bit *rumpled.*

"Your note was most cryptic," Olivia replied as she set aside the embroidery, her thoughts still on the timing of her marriage to Michael and the seal with the letters 'OWC' and her correspondence with the duchess. There was something else in the note she wanted to reread. *Something about a deadline.* "What is it you despair in telling me?" she asked, a look of curiosity crossing her face.

His hands behind his back, Edward regarded her and took a deep breath. "If you are not otherwise engaged, I would ask you to accompany me to the second floor. I have something I wish to show you," he stated, hiding his nervousness as best he could.

He'd been rehearsing this moment in his head for the entire day and was sure he was prepared for whatever Olivia's reaction might be. For this to work, he would have to be sure his supposed feelings for her seemed genuine and that she did not feel anything for him in return. A possibility that he hadn't considered last night suddenly crossed his mind. *What if she feels affection for me?* he wondered. *No, she cannot,* he quickly countered. She had not shown the least bit of interest in him in that way, he did not think. He expected her to outright refuse his offer. Hoped she would, in fact.

"Of course," Olivia answered without hesitation, her curiosity apparent. She joined him near the door and took his offered arm. "Will you give me a hint?" she asked lightly as he led her past the dining room to the stairway.

Edward smiled down at her, his heart beating a quick tattoo as he replied, "Not yet." They climbed the stairs and barely passed her room in the broad hallway before he turned to stand before a panel in the hallway wall opposite from her room.

The same panel that Michael had been knocking on just the night before, Olivia realized.

Turning a piece of molding and then pressing the flat of his hand against the raised paneling, Edward gave a sigh as a doorway in the wall appeared from the seams of the molding and swung inward. Olivia gasped in surprise as Edward surreptitiously glanced toward the stairs to ensure no servants had seen them. He ushered her into the space beyond the door and quickly closed the secret panel behind him.

"What ... what is this place?" Olivia asked in awe, her voice lowered as she glanced around the room, trying to take in all the details of the decor—the colors, the furnishings, the fabrics, the carpeting. She hadn't noticed Edward closing the door behind them.

Edward paused just inside the doorway before he replied, "Your salon, my darling." He stood very still as he allowed her to stand next to him, her attention drawn to the door he had just closed. From inside the beautifully appointed room, the door was just part of the wall, its seams not readily apparent.

Turning around to follow Edward's gaze, Olivia inhaled as she gazed at the elegant fabrics and ornate furnishings of the salon. Golds and purples shimmered in the walls, in the carpet, on the settee, and in the coverlet and pillows that adorned a large bed. A purple velvet overstuffed chair sat next to a gilt table, and a gilt vanity stood against one wall covered in purple satin. But with only one small window, light came from several lamps and a set of sconces on either side of the vanity.

The purple room, she realized with delight.

"Do you like it?" Edward asked hopefully, swallowing hard as he watched Olivia turn slowly to take in the room.

"Of course! 'Tis beautiful!" she breathed, her hand reaching out to touch the fabric on the bed. "So royal ..."

"Suited for a queen, of course," Edward stated quietly. He practically held his breath as he watched her. He closed his eyes and hoped his plan would work.

Olivia turned her attention back to him, a quizzical expression crossing her face. "What did you say?" she asked, her brows furrowing.

Edward straightened and then led her to the settee. "It is suited for a queen," he stated again as he sat down and motioned for her to do so. He took one of her hands in between both of his. "In fact, it is patterned after the recently created Queen's purple salon," he explained in a quiet voice.

Surprised at his impropriety, Olivia nearly pulled her hand away. "But I am not a queen," she answered, the wrinkle between her brows deepening.

"You are to me," Edward replied, realizing immediately that he may have spoken too quickly. He bit his lip. At Olivia's raised eyebrows, he continued, "I had this room decorated for you to use whenever you wish," he lied. "I just ask that you tell no one else of its existence."

Shaking her head, Olivia studied Edward's face. Michael obviously knew of the room—at that moment, she realized it was the room Jeffers was supposed to have taken her to when she arrived. *Doesn't Jeffers know about this room?* How could a room like this exist without the entire staff knowing, especially if it had been recently installed? "But ... *why?*" she asked, her head feeling a bit light and her breaths coming in short gasps.

Edward sighed and then cupped a hand along her cheek.

"Because ... because, I love you," he whispered. "I have since the ..."

Olivia gasped harder and tried to stand, but Edward quickly moved his hand to her shoulder and gently forced her back down onto the settee. "I have loved you since the moment I first laid eyes upon you, my dearest Olivia." He took a deep breath. "I wish for you to be my mistress."

Olivia stared at Edward, stunned by his words. "But, Mr. Seward, I look nothing like your dear Anna," she stated quietly, wondering why the man would consider her for the position of his *mistress.*

What had the young seamstress said earlier? And the other seamstress had called her 'Anna' when she rebuffed her comment about wishing to marry the friend of Lady Cunningham's son. *Edward! She had said 'Edward',* she remembered. It *was* Anna in the modiste, it had to be!

Edward frowned. "True, you do not," he answered, his eyes darting away from her for a moment as he nearly lost his nerve. "But, what ... what has *she* to do with this?" he asked suddenly, immediately regretting the question.

Cocking an eyebrow, Olivia regarded Edward for a moment. She had to live in the same house as this man, so she dared not offend him. "You have already given your heart to another, Mr. Seward. I have no intention of becoming a mistress, even to a man as handsome as you, especially when I know you cannot feel true affection for me," she reasoned, trying hard to keep her heart from pounding too hard. And then she remembered the most important reason she had to deny his offer. "Besides, I cannot ...," Olivia heard herself saying as she shook her head. "I am a married woman ..."

Edward took a deep breath. *So, at least she did not seem to share my supposed feelings of love,* he realized with a great deal of relief. He had to make her believe he wanted her more than any other woman, though. And just one night would not be enough to satisfy his supposed hunger for her. He had to make her believe he wanted her often. And he would do whatever it took. "Surely you know of Michael's mistress," he stated calmly. *Damn! I wasn't going to play that card this soon,* he chided himself as Olivia's expression seemed to turn to one of shock and then anger.

"How *dare* you?" she whispered hoarsely. Olivia swallowed hard and stared at the tall man. What would Michael do when she informed him of Edward's proposal?

"Your husband has a mistress," he countered defensively, his voice soft and quiet, and very effective as its message made its way to Olivia's comprehension.

"I am well aware that my husband has a mistress," she admitted with a nod of her head, tears threatening to form in her eyes. Although she did not know for certain, she was fairly sure Michael had a mistress based on what had happened last Tuesday night. *Breathe,* she thought quickly. *Do not cry.*

Edward's brows nearly reached his hairline. "You do?" he questioned, a bit of surprise in his voice.

"My sister, I think," she whispered, almost hissing the word between clenched teeth. At his surprised expression, she explained. "I have suspected since before the night he ruined my reputation." When Edward continued to look confused, she added, "I am quite sure he wasn't looking for his bedchamber when he found mine that night, Edward. He was looking for my sister's room. He even called me 'El'," she claimed, not able to meet his gaze as she admitted what little she knew. She did not add that she had seen the two in the library the day before, Michael holding her sister's hands whilst he kissed her on the forehead. *Had he just asked if he could court her?* she wondered then, her stomach suddenly churning. She forced herself to remain calm. Nothing of what Edward said was really a surprise, after all.

Staring at her, Edward swallowed and then lowered his eyes. *She knows more than I thought she would.* "Certainly you will notice his repeated absences on Tuesday night."

Putting a hand on her bosom, Olivia forced herself to smile and gave a sigh. "Then I shall not expect him to be home on Tuesday nights," she replied quickly, wondering what else she could say in her husband's defense. *And why am I even trying to defend him?* Edward was merely confirming what she had already guessed before she'd married the man.

Edward simply stared at her, his expression one of sympathy. As Olivia watched his face, hers took on a look of dismay. "Oh, my," she whispered. Turning away from him, she covered her mouth with one hand and took several breaths. "How long have you known?" she whispered hoarsely.

Trying to contain his growing nervousness, Edward paused a bit before answering, "He has been seeing your sister since her move to London, I believe."

The confirmation of what she'd suspected hit Olivia as if she'd taken a solid punch to her chest—a punch that could have been delivered by Michael in that it landed so precisely, it took her breath away and left her heart aching so badly she thought she would die. For in the that moment, besides finding out her husband and sister were indeed lovers, she also realized she was undeniably in love with Michael. She had been for years, she admitted to herself. How could she not be? How could this news brings such pain—such a deep ache that threatened to prevent her ability even to take another breath—if she did not truly feel affection for him?

If she was not in love with him?

Her eyes had become blurred by tears that welled up so quickly she was blinded to Edward's look of regret at having told her what he knew. And from somewhere far away, she heard him say, "And I promise you, my darling Olivia, that I shall never do such a thing while we are together," as he raised her left hand to his lips and kissed the back of it.

Pain radiated from her sprained wrist, giving her mind something concrete to concentrate on as she continued to review everything in her head. She still could not quite believe what Edward was proposing. Suddenly hearing Edward's last words in her mind, Olivia looked up at him. "Together?" she repeated, her head spinning and her breath held in disbelief.

"I want you, Olivia," Edward whispered. "I love you. I wish you only happiness and hope that by agreeing to be my mistress, you can find some happiness in this life. And provide me with some as well." For a moment, he found himself believing his own statement. "I assure you, I will be a most generous lover," he added, still trying to convince her. *She is a rather pretty gel, even if she doesn't have black hair*, he thought absently.

Olivia heard his words before everything in sight began to go gray. And the last words she heard were, "Oh, dear, you need to breathe, Olivia," just before everything went black and she felt herself falling.

Edward caught her head with one hand before it could hit the wood frame of the settee, and he pulled her body against his. The scent of roses from her hair filled his nostrils, and he smiled a bit as he lifted her from the settee and carried her to the bed. Lowering her, he arranged a pillow under her head and supported himself on one elbow as he used the other hand to brush a ringlet of mahogany hair from her face. He leaned over her and kissed her forehead and her eyelids, his lips barely touching her skin. *Damn! That wasn't supposed to happen*, he thought, a bit of panic welling up inside him. *She really is a pretty woman*, he admitted to himself as he felt his loins stir. *But she is not my Anna.*

Sighing, he stood up from the bed and quickly made his way out the panel door, leaving it ajar so that she would be able to find her way out. With any luck, she would run straight to her husband with news of his improper behavior. Then Michael Cunningham would show his true feelings for his wife.

And if not, Edward Seward was going to have a lot of explaining to do.

"Might I have a word with you?" Olivia asked quietly as she stood in the doorway to her husband's bedchamber. Her heart was beating so rapidly, she barely heard his, "Of course," as he waved her in and motioned to a chair near the fireplace. *Was that a look of surprise she saw on his face?* It was there and gone so quickly.

Michael nodded to Jeffers, who had been helping him dress for dinner, and the butler left the room, closing the door behind him. *This is unexpected,* he thought, surprised she would visit him in his bedchamber when they were due for drinks in the library in a few minutes. "What's wrong?" he asked when he saw how distraught she looked. Her red-rimmed eyes were evidence of a good cry, and a very recent one at that. He was buttoning his waistcoat but stopped and moved to stand in front of her.

Olivia found herself unable to speak. Should she first tell him about his mother? Or about the wedding gift from the duchess? Or about Edward's proposition? She took a deep breath and set her shoulders.

In order of discovery, she decided.

"I bought a ball gown today," she started to explain, not making eye contact with her husband.

Letting out a breath he'd held too long, Michael said, "Oh," with a profound sense of relief. "You told them to have the bill sent to me, I hope?" he added lightly, thinking that perhaps she was concerned about the cost. Or perhaps she had decided she didn't like the gown or thought that he wouldn't like the gown. He was about to ask when Olivia raised her eyes to meet his.

"The same modiste is making a gown for Lady Cunningham for the Harvey ball."

Michael stared at his wife, his mouth closing suddenly. He swallowed hard and nodded. "I was not aware my mother would be back in town ... at least, in time for the Harvey ball," he said quietly, his tone of voice not indicating if he was pleased or not with the news.

"So, then the seamstresses were discussing ... Michael Cunningham's new wife..," she stammered, trying hard to make sense. "And they made a comment about needing to ask Lady Cunningham who she ... who I was." When Michael's expression didn't change, she added, "I would rather your mother not be put in such an awkward position," she finally got out, still having a hard time raising her eyes to meet his.

Her husband regarded her for a moment, suddenly realizing how awkward it had to be for Olivia to be the subject of a discussion among gossips at a modiste. Leaning over to kiss her forehead, Michael gave her a reassuring pat on her shoulder. "I sent a note to my mother last Saturday letting her know of our wedding, but I rather doubt it's had time to reach her," he replied quietly. "You have nothing to be concerned about, though," he added with a shake of his head. "Even though I promised her I would be married by this Friday, she will be so happy I have married, she will hardly give you notice."

Damn! That didn't sound right, he realized before he even finished the sentence.

Olivia bit her bottom lip and nodded. "Oh," she replied, hoping that would indeed be the case. *But when had he made the promise that he'd be married by Friday? And why Friday?* she wondered. *What had the note from the duchess said about a deadline?*

"I will be sure my mother is informed this very evening," he promised, *although she probably already knows everything,* he figured. Now that the seamstresses were in the know, news of their marriage would spread quickly.

"Thank you," Olivia said with a watery smile. "I understand from Jeffers that she usually is accommodated in the bedchamber that I am using ..."

"She'll stay at the house on Cavendish Square, of course," Michael interrupted quickly. "There's no need for you to vacate your room," he assured her, thinking that was her only concern. He was tempted to ask her why she wasn't using the purple room when he resumed buttoning up his waistcoat.

"Oh. Thank you," she replied with a bit of relief. *One down, two to go,* she thought. "We received a wedding gift from the Duchess of Somerset today," she stated, forcing her voice to sound light. "She commissioned a crystal bowl from

Waterford's studio." She watched for Michael's reaction and was not disappointed by his look of surprise.

Michael turned to regard her with a raised eyebrow. "And it's already *arrived?*" he asked in disbelief. "Well, Elizabeth is quite resourceful," he murmured as he turned his attention back to his reflection in the cheval mirror.

Elizabeth? He'd used the duchess's first name as if he knew her intimately. *Had she been a mistress of his in the past? Were they still involved with one another?* "Yes," Olivia nodded. "'Tis quite beautiful. I left it on the fireplace mantle in the library. The footman who delivered it said it took Waterford a week to fill Her Grace's order," she added, hoping he would understand why she seemed disturbed. "Which is quite interesting since I only wrote her a note last Thursday morning to inform her I would not be able to fill the position of governess."

Pressing his lips together, Michael looked away, suddenly realizing why Olivia was so concerned. *And probably confused.* He wondered how much to tell his wife. *Do I tell her I've known for years that she would be my wife? That I simply ran out of time and ruined her in order to gain a quick marriage without having to court her and take time to plan an elaborate wedding?*

"I wrote Her Grace a note when I made arrangements...," he started to say and then stopped. "I made a promise and ..," he stammered, trying to figure out how much to tell her. *Don't be a damned coward,* he thought, still not sure where to start.

"To my father?" she asked, remembering how happy the man had been after his meeting with Michael the morning after he'd found them together in her bed.

"Arrangements with him, yes, and the promise to my mother that I would be married before I turned twenty-eight," he admitted finally, not elaborating on either.

Still a bit confused by the timing but realizing he wasn't going to tell her more, Olivia sighed. "The footman waited while I wrote a thank you note," she commented. "I hope it was all right that I used a sheet of your parchment."

Michael pulled a long white length of linen from the counterpane and began folding it. "Of course," he replied absently, placing the cravat around the back of his neck and arranging the folds evenly.

"There was a seal on the desk with the letters 'OWC' carved into it," Olivia continued, holding her hands as still as she could in her lap. "I hope it was all right that I used it to seal the letter."

Pausing in his wrapping the cravat around his neck, Michael regarded Olivia for a moment. "Of course it was. I bought that seal for you several ... when I was last at my stationer's," he faltered, not wanting to admit it was the first item he'd purchased for her after his talk with his sister.

"It was very kind of you to do so. Thank you," Olivia said, a bit heartened that he would do such a thing. She suddenly remembered the keys to the townhouse and to a house in Cavendish Square he'd given her at the coaching inn. *Had he given her his own keys then? Or had he already had them made for her?* She shook her head, needing to ask him one more question. "May I ask what arrangements you have with your mistress?" she asked then, trying to make her voice sound as calm as possible.

Michael stared at her, a red flush coloring his face. He looked away and then scrubbed his face with a hand. "I don't have any arrangements ..."

"Tuesday nights?" she countered, *With my sister,* she almost added, but she set her lips in a thin line before the words could come out.

"I will not discuss this with you," he stated quickly, feeling a bit defensive and suddenly very embarrassed. He began the task of tying the ends of the cravat into some kind of acceptable knot. *Eloisa promised she would not say anything about our arrangement,* he fumed. *How could she?* He remembered an appointment he'd made at the jewelers, though, and thought it best to tell Olivia now so she wouldn't think the worst if he didn't show for dinner. *Tomorrow is Tuesday.* "I probably will not be home for dinner tomorrow," he said more calmly. "I have an appointment in Ludgate Hill and may not make it home by eight."

Olivia swallowed hard, finding it hard to believe that Michael would deny having a mistress and then tell her in the next sentence that he was going to be late on the very night of his weekly *affaire!* Feeling spiteful, she countered, "I only wonder because Mr. Seward has asked me to be his mistress." She almost immediately felt regret at having made the comment, sure it would incite anger in her husband.

Michael pulled on the ends of the cravat so tightly he nearly choked himself. He stared at Olivia for at least five seconds before he said, "Come again?" A rather large weight had suddenly fallen somewhere inside him, and he was having a very hard time breathing even as he loosened the cravat from around his neck.

Sighing, as much to calm herself as to take in a breath, Olivia repeated, "Mr. Seward has asked me to be his mistress." After a short pause, she added, "Tuesday nights. I do not believe he was ... sincere in his request, though," she started to explain, but Michael was out the door before she could finish. "Nor do I intend to take him up on his ..."

Olivia followed her husband through the hall and down the steps, careful to hold her skirts up so that she wouldn't trip in her haste. "Michael, he is your friend. Please, do not hurt him," she pleaded as she hurried to keep up with his long stride and quick descent down the staircase.

"And why shouldn't I?" he responded, his agitation increasing as he landed at the bottom of the stairs. He turned to look up at her. "You are my wife! I love you, and he has *dishonored* you. And he was my best friend!" he continued, his voice rising with each point he made. "Whatever possessed him to think he could take you as his *mistress?* You don't even *look* like Anna!"

Olivia stared at him as he turned to go down the hall in pursuit of Edward. "Oh," she whispered as one hand went to her mouth and another went to her stomach; she held it as if she'd been punched with a roundhouse blow.

His words had been that forcibly delivered.

"Well, in that case, I suppose you should have a word with him," she said uncertainly, backing up against the wall across from the library door and slumping into the nearest chair.

I love you.

Had he really just said that? she wondered as she tried to remember all the words he had spoken since they had left his room. *He loves me.*

"Jeffers!" Michael called out. As usual, the butler was nearby, trying hard not to overhear his master's tirade.

"Yes, Mr. Cunningham?"

"*Where* is Mr. Seward?"

The butler's lips pressed into a thin line. "In the library, sir. I believe he's expecting you," he said quietly, wondering if he should offer to retrieve a glove or ask about sending for a doctor.

Michael nodded, gave Olivia a quick glance, and then burst through the library door. "I have a mind to beat you to a bloody pulp!" he yelled, his face red with anger and his fists balled up as if he would follow through on the threat with the least provocation.

Edward stood up from where he sat in an overstuffed chair next to the fireplace. He crossed his arms and regarded his best friend, a spiteful grin on his face. "And why is that?" he asked, obviously proud of himself. At Michael's stunned expression, he added, "Because I made you face the fact that you love your wife?"

Michael fumed as he moved closer to where Edward stood and then stopped quite suddenly, aware that the man was right next to the fire poker. Given Edward's fencing skills, he could use it very effectively if need be. Edward stood his ground as Michael replied, "I am very aware of my feelings for my wife," he whispered hoarsely. "What you did was ... *reprehensible!*"

Rolling his eyes, Edward shook his head. "It wasn't as if she was going to *agree* to the arrangement I proposed, you dunderhead," he countered, his humor disappearing.

"And what if she had?" Michael replied quickly, wondering if maybe she had considered it before coming to him with the news. He certainly hadn't shown her any interest beyond the few stolen moments in her bedchamber that morning.

It serves me right if she went looking for affection in some other man's bed.

Edward stared at Michael for a brief moment, remembering that Olivia might have taken him up on his offer. *What would I have done then?* he wondered. "I would not have continued the charade, I assure you," Edward replied with a shake of his head. "As you said, she doesn't look a bit like Anna, and she knows it, and, well, ... she is not a wanton woman...." He allowed the sentence to trail off as he hung his head. "I am sorry," he said finally. "But, I fail to see why you would keep a mistress ...

"For the last time, Seward, I *do not have* a mistress!"

"... When you have this very pretty wife who I believe loves you dearly." He paused a moment, just then realizing what Michael had said. "You don't have a mistress?" he repeated in surprise.

Michael sighed audibly. "*No!* I never *did!* And even if I did, I wouldn't have one *now*. I am a married man!"

Edward took a step back, nearly falling into the fireplace. He struggled to maintain his balance and regarded Michael with a raised brow. "Oh. Then ... Then why do you treat her as if she is merely a part of a business deal?" he accused, finally making eye contact with Michael.

At his friend's suddenly guilty expression, Edward's brows furrowed as he realized something. A puzzle piece in his head seemed to drop into place as he studied Michael. "She *was* part of a business deal, wasn't she?" he queried, his own anger suddenly surfacing. "You *bastard!*" And after another second, his face screwed up in confusion. "You no longer have a mistress?"

Michael caught his breath as he heard his friend's words, regretting having told Edward the details of his marriage deal with Harold Waterford. His large hands flexed and he sank into the nearest couch, the fight going out of him. "Her dowry ..." he started to say and then stopped, redirecting his attention to Edward. "What did she tell you?" he asked suddenly, wondering if perhaps Harold Waterford had told his daughter about the financial arrangements he'd offered as part of the deal to marry her off. But knowing what he did of the man, he was sure he hadn't even told Olivia about his plans for her to marry Michael, let alone any financial arrangements.

Cocking his head to one side and a bit relieved that Michael wasn't about to pulverize his face, Edward took the chair he had vacated earlier. "She told me *nothing*, my friend." When Michael gave him a confused glance, he added, "She didn't have to. It's apparent every time she looks at you. She adores you, probably even loves you ... you dunderhead," he continued, hoping to drive home the point.

"She does not ... despise me?" Michael whispered, thinking the woman had every right. He had been her sister's protector. His insistence on keeping his promise to his mother had forced Olivia into this marriage without benefit of being courted. He hadn't even asked for her hand in marriage! His behavior since their wedding was ... *What was Olivia trying to say when we were interrupted this morning?* he wondered as he scrubbed his face with his hands.

Edward sighed loudly. "She should," he claimed angrily. "She has every right to despise you, you *rake*. She should go straight to the nearest magistrate and request your marriage be deemed null and void."

A hurt expression suddenly on his face, Michael stared at Edward. "But, she cannot. I ... I ruined her," he stated with a curt nod. "She cannot marry another," he insisted with a shake of his head. "I will not allow it."

Edward's face took on a look of surprise. "You say that as if you ruined her *deliberately*," he accused, obviously not remembering when Michael had explained what happened that night. Edward was quite drunk, after all. Edward's eyes widened and he stared at Michael for a long moment. "Oh, my God, you did do it deliberately, didn't you?" he whispered, not quite believing that his friend could do such a thing unless he was completely foxed or a candidate for an extended stay at Bedlam.

Michael stood up, his anger returning. "Take that back," he threatened, his fists coming up.

Edward remained in the chair and kept his gaze on Michael. "I will not," he countered, feeling a sense of bravery he hadn't felt in at least the past week. He'd rehearsed over and over in his head how he was going to take the punch to his face.

Well, he was prepared, he decided.

He hoped his jaw wouldn't break. His nose, well, it would heal, he figured. And he had no appointments scheduled for the coming week, so there would be time to be bedridden with a broken rib or two.

When he returned his attention to Michael, he found his friend staring into space, as if he was deep in thought. *Planning my funeral already, is he?* Edward thought quickly, wondering if he could make it to the library door before one of those fists made contact with his body. *I can outrun him,* he thought with a smile. *I don't know where I'd go...*

"I have to take a walk," Michael announced before he turned and left the library, closing the door behind him.

Edward stared after him, the stunned expression on his face remaining for several minutes after he heard the distant click of a front door closing.

When the library door opened again, he looked up to find Olivia staring at him, her hands wringing together. He stood up quickly, intending to bow.

"You took a very risky chance for my benefit," she whispered, a mixed look of shock and relief on her face.

Edward tried to appear calm even though he knew that he had barely escaped Michael's retribution. "Indeed. But I think it was worth it. And for your sake, I hope it was," he said with an impish grin, his face coloring as he realized Olivia and probably half the household staff had overheard the entire exchange.

The library door was wide open during the argument.

"I think ... nay, I am quite sure that I met your Anna today," Olivia stated as she moved to take the chair across from his. "She is a very beautiful woman."

Stunned at the comment, Edward stared at her. "Indeed?" he replied, his breaths suddenly coming faster. He sat down. Hard. "And did she ... did she seem to be in good health?" he asked, his eyes darting about the room.

"She did. She mentioned wishing she was married to you, in fact," Olivia said quietly. She took a deep breath, not sure if she should say what she'd been thinking while she waited in the hallway. "I know it is none of my business, Mr. Seward, but may I inquire as to why you are not already married to her?"

Edward slumped in his chair and finally glanced at Olivia. "My family ... As a second son, I had an obligation to the earldom," he replied with a sigh, his eyes leaving Olivia's to focus on other objects in the room. "At least until my brother married and sired an heir." He could not bring himself to make eye contact with Olivia, his embarrassment at his earlier charade still apparent.

Olivia nodded her understanding. "Has your brother taken an acceptable wife?" she queried, her voice very gentle as she continued her line of questions.

"Oh, yes," Edward answered with a nod. "About a year ago, in fact. Lady Penelope, the daughter of the Earl of Heatherington. Very suited to the role, and very pretty," he stated enthusiastically. "But not as beautiful as my Anna," he added in a whisper, his gaze full of fondness and longing.

"And is Lady Seward with child?" Olivia wondered.

Edward's gaze fell on the fireplace. "She bore a son last

week, so my obligation as a spare heir has ended," he stated firmly.

Olivia leaned her head to one side. "So, you are free to marry your choice of bride now."

"I am," Edward agreed. "But my Anna disappeared a year ago, and I have been searching for her ever since," he explained.

"And, if you found her, would you marry her?" Olivia asked as she moved to the sideboard and poured him a glass of brandy.

Edward finally made eye contact with Olivia. "Of course," he answered simply as he took the glass and gave her a nod.

Olivia smiled then. "She is a seamstress at Madame Suzanne's modiste in New Bond Street. Go there now. Ask for her hand. Get a special license ..."

"I have one of those," he interrupted, holding up a finger in the air. At her raised eyebrow, Edward shrugged. "I believe it is common practice for sons of earls to have such things," he explained proudly. "They are sort of issued to us so we're spared the reading of the banns. They last three months, too!"

And apparently they're issued to the sons of viscounts, as well, Olivia thought with a smirk, remembering that she and Michael had been able to marry because he had one.

He had to get married before next Friday, he'd said. But given what she'd seen in her father's library the day before Michael's visit to her room, she was sure Eloisa was his intended. *And yet, just moments ago, he'd announced that he loved me.*

She was suddenly aware of Edward's attention on her, as if he was waiting for the rest of her advice. "Marry her, Edward." She poured a glass of claret for herself. "I would like very much to have another woman around with whom I can learn how to be an aristocrat's wife."

Edward nodded. "What else do I need?" he asked suddenly.

"A ring," Olivia answered, giving her own a quick glance when she remembered Michael mentioning he had to go in search of one. "Or use the one she wears on her thumb ..."

At Edward's sudden inhalation of breath, Olivia paused and gave him a brilliant smile. "And ask her for her hand and visit the bishop," she finished with a curt nod.

Edward took a sip of brandy and considered Olivia's words for several moments. *What do I have to lose?* he wondered when he considered what there was to gain from such a union. A woman who loved him, for he knew she did, and Olivia had just confirmed it. He closed his eyes and imagined a life with Anna—they could travel the Continent during their first year of marriage, visiting the sources of ancient civilizations and looking for antiquities, live in London during the Season attending balls and musicales, live on his family's estate in the summers, raise their children wherever they chose. They would have a happy life, he decided.

Anna!

When he opened his eyes, Olivia was gone.

Meanwhile

Michael descended the steps to the square and began walking east. His mind replayed Edward's accusations over and over. He had to admit the business deal that included Olivia's dowry was the best deal he had ever brokered in his life, but Harold Waterford had been the one to propose the terms. Who was he to turn down an increase in his management fee?

Before he had rounded the corner to the next street on the square, he was instead thinking about the night he'd entered Olivia's room. It was not as if he was in a drunken stupor; he knew exactly which room was his, which room was Olivia's. *What had she started to say to me this morning?* "If I had known it was you..."

Just because he wanted her as his wife didn't mean Olivia wanted him as her husband. *But perhaps she did,* he thought hopefully. Had she seriously considered Edward's offer? *She thought I had a mistress,* he remembered her saying. How could she have known about the Tuesday nights he spent dining with her sister, unless Eloisa had told her? But Eloisa had promised him she wouldn't tell anyone, and what would she gain by saying anything, especially now that she was being courted by Huntington?

So, if Eloisa didn't tell Olivia that Michael was her protector, then how had she found out? Who had told her? There were only a few other people who knew about Eloisa. His coachman, Mr. White. Eloisa's maid, of course. And ...

Damn!

Edward told her, he thought angrily. He took a deep breath and shook his head.

If things were going to plan, then Eloisa would not be an issue. He had received Huntington's invitation to spar on the morrow—that was certainly confirmation that his banker intended to ask for her hand if he hadn't already done so. Michael vowed then and there that he would no longer see Eloisa in any capacity but that of a brother-in-law. And he hoped the next time he saw her, she would be betrothed to his banker.

As for everything else, perhaps it was time to have a talk with Olivia. She deserved to know she was his intended all along. She might despise him for a long time to come.

Or she might not.

When he had completed the circuit around the entire square, he climbed the stairs to his townhouse, still contemplating what to do about Olivia. *Court her,* he decided. *And get her a decent ring!* That he planned to do the following evening.

But first, he had to write another missive to his mother, he decided.

"Is it true, then?" Olivia wondered when Michael finally entered the hall from the vestibule. He had come into the townhouse wearing an expression that suggested he was deep in thought, his attention drawn so completely away from the present that Jeffers made no attempt to greet him. He hadn't taken a coat nor a hat when he left the hour before; he had simply left the house.

Olivia knew that, as her husband, Michael could do with her what he liked. She was his property now. But he also had an obligation to provide protection for her. She was sure her father would have required it of him before he would have made whatever business deal it was that included her. Michael had said over dinner that her dowry was quite—how had he put it? *Quite satisfactory.* And weren't some marriages predicated on convenience? A merging of two families or two businesses or two countries? *Why should mine be any different?* she wondered, a heavy sense of dread settling into her belly. Was that all she was to Michael, then? A by-product of a business deal? Perhaps she should have accepted Edward's proposal and become his mistress, if for no other reason than to have a sympathetic man with whom to spend her Tuesday nights.

The thought sickened her, though, and when her stomach suddenly threatened to cast up her accounts, she took a deep breath and looked up at the ceiling, closing her eyes to steady the spinning sensation she felt at her very core.

A slight waft of a warm breath washed over her just before lips brushed against hers. She opened her mouth a bit and accepted the gentle kiss, keeping her eyes closed just in case the kiss was in her imagination. The kiss deepened as a hand rested against her cheek, the fingertips barely making contact with her jaw and the back of her ear. She moaned softly as she pretended it was Michael who kissed her, who held her with such care.

"Is what true, my sweet?" Michael whispered, his lips now near her ear.

So startled was she by the sound of his voice next to her ear that her eyes shot open. She found herself staring up into his eyes. "Oh!" she gasped, realizing Michael really was *right there*, standing over her, supporting himself by leaning on one forearm that was propped against the hall wall.

A small smile quirked the edge of his lips as he watched

her. "I did not wish to startle you," he whispered, his lips moving to her forehead, where he kissed the space just below her hairline. "Is what true?" he repeated quietly, his brows furrowing a bit when he noticed the crease between her brows deepen.

Olivia took a breath, realizing she no longer felt as if she was spinning, her eddy suddenly anchored by Michael's very solid presence above and in front of her. She swallowed hard and finally found her voice. "Is it true that I am part of a business deal you made with my father?"

Michael sighed and cursed to himself, angry that he'd allowed Edward to say aloud what he hoped he would never have to admit to himself. "Yes, as a matter of fact," he replied with a nod, wincing when he realized how awful the news must have sounded to her.

Olivia bit her lower lip as a tear collected at the corner of an eye. She nodded, her face taking on the expression of someone trying very hard to maintain control when, in fact, the world was quite out of her control.

"A deal that has been in the works for five years, I might add," he said quietly, his right eyebrow cocking in amusement at the last moment. "Your father drives a very hard bargain, you must know."

Olivia continued to stare at him while the tear at the corner of her eye finally spilt and trailed down her temple. Michael quickly caught it with his lips, tasting the salt and kissing the space around her eyes.

"Are you teasing me now?" she whispered, a sob catching her breath before she could get out the last of the question.

Shaking his head slowly, Michael closed his eyes. "No," he said as he pushed himself away from the wall. He placed his hands under Olivia's arms and lifted her to her feet, surprised at how easily he was able to get her to stand, although she seemed to need his frame to stay standing.

Wrapping his arms around her shoulders, Michael held a hand on the back of her head and drew it against the crook of his shoulder. "You are part of the most lucrative business deal I have ever made with your father," he claimed, a hint of pride in his voice. "And, I am of the opinion that you are the best part of the deal," he added before leaning down to kiss her on the lips. It was a quick kiss, as much a kiss of reconciliation as it was of affection.

Olivia allowed him to hold her for several minutes as she considered his words. "And for this deal to ... work, what are your expectations ... of me?" she asked quietly.

"Ah, yes. The terms of the deal," Michael said as he grinned and stroked her hair, wishing he could prove his love for her right then and there. But there was much to do before she would be convinced he was sincere. "Just marry me," he said as he cradled her head with one hand. He felt her start when she heard his words, and he smiled.

"But, I thought I already did," she replied, her eyes wide in disbelief. "There was a vicar and ..."

"Exactly. You've fulfilled your end of the bargain," Michael countered happily. "I have not, however." He took a deep breath. "Unfortunately, there is much I must do this evening," he said with a hint of regret.

Olivia stared at him, wondering what he meant by *those* words. "Will doing bodily damage to Edward be included?" she asked in a small voice, a bit of alarm replacing the calm Michael had induced with his words. Part of her wanted the man to suffer for what he had said to her, but another wanted her husband to forgive the man's indiscretion.

A deep chuckle rumbled in Michael's throat. "No, not tonight," he said with a shake of his head as he led her to the dining room door. He leaned down and kissed her quickly. "Perhaps tomorrow," he said with a cocked eyebrow, his grin making it apparent he was teasing. "Now, I do not know about you, but I find myself rather hungry, and I believe dinner was ready a few minutes ago?"

Olivia gasped, her eyes widening in surprise. "Yes," she replied with a nod. "Will you join me?" she asked. Edward had gone upstairs after their earlier conversation, and she hadn't seen him since.

Michael held out his arm and she took it. "Of course," he said. He escorted her to the dining room where they shared a pleasant meal, their conversation about the business deal he and her father had worked out on his last trip to Shipley.

Despite how forthcoming Michael was about his intention to eventually wed her, Olivia was very aware that they did not talk about the earlier events of the evening nor about the issue of Tuesday nights.

When they finished, Michael led her to the door to her bedchamber. "There is much to do before I can retire this evening," he said before he kissed her quickly. "Good night, my love." With that, he turned and descended the stairs, leaving Olivia wondering even more about her odd marriage.

Having finished her simple supper of bread, cheese and an apple, Anna was scraping the crumbs from the small kitchen table when she heard the sound of knocking. She moved to the one window at the front of the apartment above Madame Suzanne's modiste. From her vantage point, she couldn't make out much about the figure below. Although the traffic was still heavy despite the nearly nine o'clock hour, Suzanne had closed the shop so that she could attend that evening's performance at the Drury Lane Theatre.

Perhaps a client wished to pick up an order, Anna figured. Hurrying down the back steps to the shop below, Anna made her way in between the bolts of fabric and past a mannequin to the front of the shop. She was still several feet away from the door when she realized the person knocking wasn't a woman but a man. In the darkness, fear gripped her.

And then, she heard her name called out from the other side of the glass in the front door window.

Anna knew that voice—had known that voice her entire life.

Edward!

She rushed to the door, fumbling with the bolt until she managed to get it undone, and then she fumbled with the door knob, finally managing to get the door open.

"Thank the gods," Edward got out as Anna stared at him.

After an awkward pause of only a moment, Anna flung herself into his arms.

"Edward!" she whispered into his neck. Did he know she had vowed to forget him? Had her thoughts conjured him into existence? *How did he ...?*

She probably shouldn't have been as surprised as she was just then. There was that moment earlier in the day when she'd been hemming Mrs. Cunningham's ball gown, that moment when the woman might have overheard her comment about Edward. She couldn't be sure, but there had been a brief look of ... *something* ... in Mrs. Cunningham's eyes when Anna managed to get her to a chair. When she looked as if she might faint—after the look of fear at hearing about the viscountess had passed. *She must have overheard me!*

Between kisses on her temple and forehead, Edward whispered, "I've come for you, Anna."

Realizing a fashionably dressed couple had paused in their stroll along the street to stare at them in horror, Anna pulled Edward into the shop, making sure to shut and bolt the door before returning to Edward's arms.

"Have you been here the whole time?" he managed to get out, his hand waving to indicate the shop before he settled it on the side of her face.

Anna nodded. "Well, ever since Suzanne moved the store here," she said, moving a thumb along the side of Edward's jawline. "We were in Oxford Street before ..." Her explanation was cut short when Edward took her lips with his, kissing her with the fervor of a thirsty man gulping water after a trek through the desert.

Anna finally returned the kiss, purring with pleasure. "You found me," she said when Edward paused to take a breath.

His lips had moved to her jaw and down the side of her neck before he finally said, "I believe I have visited every ..." He paused to kiss her throat. "Modiste in the West End ..." He kissed the hollow of her throat ... "Except those on *this* side of New Bond Street." After giving her one more kiss beneath an ear, he stepped back a bit, but kept his hands at her waist. "I came earlier this evening, when the shop was still open, but the owner said you were busy in the back."

The comment seemed to surprise Anna until she remembered she had been working on Lady Harvey's ball gown. She regarded Edward with an embarrassed grin. "I have missed you, Edward," she breathed, part of her scolding herself for allowing Edward to just walk in and hold her like this. She should have refused him entrance. Should have turned him away. They couldn't be together. Not how they both wanted to be. Allowing him these intimacies would only prolong the inevitable.

"Likewise," Edward said with a nod. "Which is why I'm taking you away from all this."

Anna's expression changed from surprise at his comment to one of disappointment. "I cannot, Edward," she said with a shake of her head. "I finally have a secure position. Suzanne has been most adamant that I cannot have any men visit ..."

"I mean to make you my wife," Edward interrupted her, pulling her back into his arms.

Anna sighed in exasperation. "You have always meant to make me your wife," she said, a hint of annoyance in her voice. "But we both know that will never happen," she added, fighting back tears. *Good grief!* She'd gone months without a cry and was suddenly spending the day as a watering pot!

"But it has to," Edward countered, feeling a bit of panic at her comment. "I've just come from the bishop's office. I have a special license, and I've an appointment to get married in the morning. And reservations at the Clarendon for the next few nights. The Harvey's ball to attend Thursday night ..."

Shaking her head back and forth, Anna regarded Edward as if he was a candidate for Bedlam. "Perhaps you've had a bit too much to drink this evening," she suggested quietly.

"Not a drop," he claimed, his head shaking the same way

hers was doing. "Well, just a sip of brandy, actually. And I haven't gambled a pence in months."

Anna raised her eyes to his. "I could have sworn you said something about getting married in the morning. Do I ... do I know the lucky lady?" she asked in a hoarse whisper, for tears were streaming down her face, making it hard for her to breathe and even harder to look at the man she'd loved her entire life. If he was getting married, was he here to arrange for her to be his mistress again? For, if that was the case, she would turn him away. And beg him to leave her alone forever.

Taking a step back, Edward regarded Anna for a long time, wondering at her question. "You know her better than anyone, my sweet." Reaching into his waistcoat pocket, he pulled out a gold ring. "You know me better than anyone else. I hope." He took her left hand in his own and slid the ring onto her fourth finger. "It's time we be man and wife. For the rest of our lives. Will you marry me?"

Anna stared at the gold ring on her finger before turning her gaze back to Edward. Then, for the first time in her life, she fainted.

CHAPTER 28

TUESDAY IS HIS BRUISER

April 18, 1815

Olivia awoke Tuesday morning feeling anxious and tired. She'd been relieved when Michael returned the night before, but where had he been? And what had he been doing for the forty minutes or so he'd been gone? *Had he walked to my sister's townhouse?* she wondered, her throat tightening at the thought. He barely gave notice to her news about the wedding gift from the Duchess of Somerset. He had said 'I love you', but he was angry at the time and perhaps not in command of his faculties. He had kissed her sweetly when she wondered about her part in the business deal between him and her father. Then he had explained most of his dealings with her father during dinner, their conversation much like the conversations they had shared at Waterford Hall.

And then he'd said, 'Marry me'. As if they weren't already married. *What was that all about?*

At least she'd told him about his mother's plan to be at the Harvey's ball. He didn't seem to know his mother would be in attendance, she considered. And she'd told Edward about Anna and hoped that he would find her and ask for her hand.

Sarah, her dresser, opened the drapes and went about

pulling various gowns out for her to review, but she had no desire to get out of bed. It was only when there was a knock at the door that she finally sat up in bed. Sarah hurried to answer the door, opening it only a crack before closing it again.

Curious, Olivia pulled the covers off of her and moved to get up. Sarah was almost to the bed, though, holding out a white folded paper. A wax seal with an 'S' stamped in it gave her no hint as to who it was from. She opened it slowly, recognizing the writing even before she read the missive.

Dear Olivia, I hope you are finding your first few days as a wife to be a wonderful experience. I know that when I last saw you, I did not seem happy for you, but I must assure you that I truly am; my unhappiness was due to my not having had the opportunity to speak with you about a most important topic. Please come for tea this morning. I have news I must share and can simply wait no longer to tell you. Yours, Eloisa.

Olivia stared at the note for a very long time. There was no indication as to the nature of the news, but Olivia could only imagine that Eloisa would admit to her *affaire* with Michael. What else could it be? It was Tuesday, after all. *And why is there an 'S' in the seal?* she wondered. "Sarah, I need a walking gown, please. The peacock blue ensemble will do," she finally said.

If Eloisa was going to admit to being Michael's mistress, then Olivia wanted to at least look the part of a well-to-do aristocrat's wife. She promised herself she would not cry nor would she act the least bit surprised by the news. *I know, after all,* she thought. And even before Edward confirmed her suspicions, Olivia was sure in her own heart that her sister had captured her husband's heart. She recalled the look on his face, though, when she had asked him the night before. *Why couldn't he just admit that he had taken her sister as his mistress? Why did he seem so torn by what needed to be said?*

Rich men took mistresses all the time; *why did he seem so ... embarrassed?* she wondered, her brows furrowing. *Was it embarrassment? Or was it wounded pride?* And then, when she was outside the library, she heard Michael deny he had a mistress—and he'd said it as if he'd had to repeat it to Edward several times.

Sarah made a 'tsk' sound and Olivia looked up to find her maid eyeing her. "It does your pretty face no good to be frowning like that, madam," Sarah said with a shake of her head.

Olivia attempted a smile. "No, I suppose not," she replied, getting out of bed and moving to the area behind the ornate dressing screen. Sarah followed her with the gown and under things. "Was it bad news, my lady?" the lilting voice asked as she helped Olivia with her chemise and corset.

"I ... do not know," Olivia answered uncertainly. "But I shall find out soon enough. I am going to see my sister," she announced, her chin held high.

"Oh," Sarah replied, a bit surprised. "Does she live here in London?" she asked, hoping her question wasn't too personal. "Shall I have Jeffers arrange the carriage for you?"

Considering her options, Olivia shook her head. "It depends. How far is it to Green Street from here?"

Sarah shook her head, surprised that her mistress had such a close relative living nearby. "Not far at all. A ten minute walk, I would say," the maid said as she tied Olivia's stocking garters. "And then some depending on which block her home is on."

So, he keeps her close, Olivia thought, her heart suddenly very heavy, the ache from the day before returning to make her feel as if she could not breathe. "Then, I shall walk," Olivia announced as brightly as she could muster.

Sarah glanced up as she held out a pair of pantaloons. "And who shall I ring to accompany you?"

Olivia considered the need for a chaperone and decided for this trip, she would not require one. Although she had promised herself she wouldn't make a scene, she did not want a servant witnessing cruel words, or worse, a cat fight between two sisters.

"I will go by myself," Olivia replied smartly.

"And what about breakfast? Shall I have something brought up?"

"No, thank you," Olivia said with a shake of her head, not wanting to admit it would probably make her sick to eat when she was so anxious. The very last thing she wanted was to cast up her accounts on her sister's floor!

At half past nine, a parasol held in one hand and her reticule clutched in her other, Olivia set off toward Green Street.

She found the small brick townhouse easily; it was modest and not quite what she imagined given Michael's apparent wealth. The door knocker, though, seemed intimidating as its lion's face growled at her. She ignored the visage and pounded it twice, careful to put on a pleasant face. *Smile,* she thought to herself. And she did, when Eloisa answered the door with a huge grin and opened her arms to hug her right there on the stoop!

"Olivia, you've come!" Eloisa exclaimed as she finally let go of her sister. "Or, *Mrs. Cunningham,* I suppose I should call you now," she said with an even more enthusiastic grin. "You look ... divine," she added as she stepped back and cast a glance up and down Olivia's smart gown and pelisse and the matching bonnet.

"Thank you, Eloisa. And thank you for the invitation," Olivia said as she regarded her sister. "I hope I haven't called too early." Her sister wore a simple blue batiste gown and slippers, a very small sapphire pendant on a gold chain, and wire loops in her ear piercings. Not at all what Olivia thought a mistress would wear, she considered, wondering to herself if she expected scarlet satin, ostrich feathers and Egyptian style jewelry.

"Goodness, no. I've been up for hours," Eloisa responded with a wave of her hand.

Olivia though it best to apologize for what happened

when they'd last seen one another. "I am very sorry I was not able to spend time conversing with you when we were last in Shipley.

You seemed ..."

"Preoccupied, I know," Eloisa finished for her. "And I must apologize to you for not taking the time to tell you my news then," she added as she led Olivia to the small parlor and indicated the yellow silk damask settee. "Please have a seat. I will be right back with tea and biscuits."

Olivia watched her sister carefully, not seeing any animosity or anger in her eyes, nor did she hear it in her voice. "May I come with you? I would love to see your home," she said, not wanting to be left alone in the parlor. Left to herself, she was quite certain she would turn into a watering pot.

"Of course!" Eloisa answered happily. "It will not be my home for long, though, but it has been a most comfortable place to live these past ten months. Far better than what I could have been living in, I assure you," she added, her voice still light as she rolled her eyes.

Olivia frowned as she followed her sister to the kitchen and wondered what Eloisa meant by the comment. The townhouse was modest, but modern in design, with its own water pump and faucet and a cold storage box. "Whatever do you mean?" Olivia asked, her frown increasing as she tried to work out Eloisa's odd comment. She watched as her sister busied herself with making tea and placing Dutch biscuits on a plate.

Her sister sighed. "I have much to tell and such good news, too!"

Olivia's mouth opened in surprise. *Good news?* This was not at all what she was expecting. "I could use some. Please tell," Olivia pleaded, following Eloisa back to the parlor. Although the decor in the house was pleasant and light, it was not Eloisa's style, Olivia realized. The place had probably been let with its furnishings and decorations intact.

Eloisa's brows furrowed as she turned to regard Olivia.

"Whatever do *you* mean?" she asked, a frown replacing her lighthearted smile as she placed the tea tray on the low table in front of the settee. She sat down in the chair opposite the settee and lifted the teapot. As she poured, she watched Olivia slowly lower herself onto the settee.

I cannot very well tell her that I know she is my husband's mistress, Olivia realized. "Michael's friend Edward told me some ... unfortunate news yesterday," she said instead, hoping her cheeks weren't as red as they felt. "But, please, share you good news."

Eloisa arched an eyebrow at the mention of Edward, wondering for a moment if he had heard bad news about the woman he had spoken of the day she met him. But when she was told to share her good news, she smiled and held out her left hand. A gold band with a round sapphire decorated her ring finger. "I am getting married," Eloisa announced, barely able to contain her excitement. Her face split into a huge grin as she wriggled in delight.

Her jaw dropping, Olivia stared at her sister and then at the ring for several seconds. "Married?" she repeated, her heart pounding so hard she thought it was showing through the bodice of her gown.

Eloisa was nodding vigorously. "To a banker, yes," she affirmed happily. "It is what I wanted to speak with you about when I came to Shipley. I know I should have spoken with father, but ... I wanted *you* to be the first to know before you left for Wiltshire. I wanted to find out when you could come to London for the wedding. And then ... with everything that happened and *your* wedding and your quick retreat back to town ..." She sighed and shrugged her shoulders. "I didn't want my good news to overshadow your wedding!"

Despite her promise not to cry, tears of happiness and relief began flowing down Olivia's cheeks. "Oh, Eloisa, I am so happy for you," she said as she reached out to take her sister's hand, her bandaged wrist appearing from beneath her sleeve. "But, oh my, who is this man and how long ... how long have you been *engaged?*" she asked, suddenly wondering about the time line of the past few weeks.

Would Eloisa be a mistress to Michael if she was betrothed to another man?

Eloisa's attention was on Olivia's wrist as she gave her a cup of tea and took one for herself. "Just two weeks. I know it is not long, but when Mr. Cunningham introduced us ..."

Olivia choked on her first sip of tea and put the cup down quickly. She cleared her throat as Eloisa handed her a linen napkin. "Mr. Cunningham? You mean *Michael?*" Olivia questioned. *Two weeks?*

"Your husband, yes," Eloisa nodded, a beatific smile on her face as she lifted her teacup. "Olivia, what happened to your wrist?" she asked suddenly, her brows furrowing.

Olivia regarded her arm with a roll of her eyes. "I sprained it when Michael dropped me in the garden Sunday morning," she said before a nervous giggle burbled up. "It's fine, really. Please tell me about this man of yours!"

Eloisa stared at her sister for a long moment, wondering if there was an amusing anecdote to go with the 'being dropped in the garden', but she continued with her own story. "When I met Mr. Huntington, it was as if we both knew immediately we were right for one another. And I rather think Mr. Cunningham knew we would be a perfect match when he introduced us," she claimed, a faraway look coming over her face. "With us both being widowed, and ..."

"Widowed?" Olivia repeated, her brows furrowing in confusion. "You have been married before? When did ... when did *that* happen?" Her head spinning just a bit, Olivia had to take a breath and hold it for a moment.

Eloisa sighed and angled her head to one side. "You mean, Father didn't tell you?" she asked, her eyebrows furrowing. "I suppose I shouldn't be surprised. Father would never approve of a military man for a husband," she murmured.

Olivia shook her head. "He said nothing."

Although Eloisa had originally thought to tell Olivia the

entire truth of her stay in London, she realized just then she had to withhold the worst of her experiences—it would be unfair to tell her *everything*. Better to continue describing the scenario she and Michael had come up with to explain her situation in life. "I was briefly married to an infantryman, William Smith, but he died in France. I was just coming out of mourning when Mr. Cunningham introduced me to his banker. You see, Mr. Huntington was mourning the loss of his wife, and he was missing her terribly. And he asked Cunningham about me—because he wanted an introduction."

Olivia followed the story, suddenly realizing where the 'S' came from in the wax seal on Eloisa's letter. *But why hadn't Father mentioned news of her marriage?* She was supposed to have been a governess for a banker. "Is this Mr. Huntington the banker for whom you were a governess?"

Eloisa's breath caught and she stilled her features, not wanting to think about that day at Lucy Gibbons' brothel in Covent Garden. "No," she said with a shake of her head. "I was never actually a governess," she clarified, her fingers wringing the napkin in her lap. "I actually came to London to ... to get married," she added, knowing she spoke the truth with the admission. She'd never had any intention of accepting an offer from any of the boys in Shipley; she wanted a life in town, and meeting and marrying a man in London seemed the best way to achieve her goal.

"Oh," Olivia replied, feeling a bit lost. "So, your intended. Is he an ... an older gentleman then?" she asked with an arched eyebrow, suddenly imagining a decrepit old man.

Blushing, Eloisa rolled her eyes. "Yes, but only thirty-eight, and quite handsome," she gushed. "Debonaire, I think you would say."

Olivia let out the breath she didn't realize she was holding. "Thirty-eight," she repeated with a nod. *That's not so very old, I suppose,* she thought.

"And he has the most beautiful home in Cavendish Square, and a house in the country near Bath!"

Olivia leaned back a bit. *Cavendish Square.* One of the best addresses in all of London! Her sister's fiancé sounded like an excellent match. "And do you ... feel *affection* for this man?" Olivia ventured, wondering if the arrangement would be a marriage of convenience or one of love.

Taking a deep breath so as to contain her enthusiasm, Eloisa nodded. "Olivia, I *love* him," she said quietly. She leaned forward and took another breath. "And I told him so last night when he gave me this ring and confessed his love for me."

Olivia shook her head in stunned disbelief. "Two weeks?" she repeated again, realizing what that meant for her. "Oh, my," she murmured, suddenly feeling faint. By finding someone to marry Eloisa, it seemed as if Michael had divested himself of his mistress *before* his trip to Shipley.

So why did he come to my bedroom thinking she was Eloisa? Or did he? "Olivia, are you all right?" she finally heard Eloisa ask,

apparently for a second or third time.

Shaking her head a bit, Olivia sat up straight and nodded. "I am," she said, continuing to nod her head. "I am very well, in fact," she said, her face showing a grin that was growing into a very large smile. "I am so very happy for you, Eloisa. You will be marrying for *love!*" She clasped her hands around Eloisa's and squeezed gently.

Eloisa smiled at her sister's response, but the smile faded as she continued to stare at Olivia. "You say that as if you ... as if you did *not*," she murmured, her brow furrowing a bit. "I thought ... I thought you had always ... I thought you felt *affection* for Mr. Cunningham ..."

"I did," Olivia admitted quickly, nodding and taking a deep breath of relief. "I ... I do. Feel affection for him, I mean," she added, her head still spinning a bit. "But our wedding was a bit ..."

"Rushed, I know," Eloisa finished for her, a worried

expression on her face. "Pray tell, what *really* happened?" she whispered as she leaned in closer. "I do not believe Mr. Cunningham ... I do not think him capable ..." She stopped and wondered how much to admit. She could not believe Michael would have ruined her sister, as the servants in the Waterford household seemed to believe. And their father seemed to have known Olivia and Michael would be wed, and soon. But she could not tell her sister what she knew of Michael without exposing herself as having been close to the man for the past year.

"He truly did not *ruin* me," Olivia whispered with a shake of her head. "Although, it seems it was meant to *appear* that way."

Eloisa cocked her head to one side, wondering what her sister meant. "Are you saying his intention was to be *discovered* by father? In your room?" she queried, her shocked expression conveying her surprise. But after thinking about the events of the past two weeks, Eloisa considered that her sister was probably correct. *What had Michael Cunningham been up to?*

"I truly do not know," Olivia muttered with a shrug. "But, enough about me. I want to know all about the man who will be my brother-in-law," she claimed as she leaned forward and helped herself to a biscuit. For, with the relief of knowing her sister was getting married came the realization that she was hungry, both for food and for time with her sister. It was hours before she made her way back to the Cunningham townhouse.

Michael appeared at Gentleman Jackson's boxing parlor in Bond Street at exactly three o'clock, the time requested in the note he'd received from his banker.

Arthur Huntington III was already in the ring. Wearing only breeches, the banker displayed a physique that belied his thirty-eight years as he bounced about, occasionally throwing punches into the air.

Moving quickly to the changing room, Michael stripped his coats and shirt from his body and removed his boots.

Remembering his banker's lack of stockings, he removed his own and walked calmly out to the area which held the fighting ring. He waved in the direction of Jackson himself, nodding when the proprietor acknowledged him with a slight bow.

"Cunningham!" Arthur called out from inside the ring. "So glad you could join me," the older man commented as he watched Michael approach the ring. His face held no humor, though.

"Thank you for the invitation," Michael replied as he climbed into the ring and began to loosen up. "I am at a loss as to the reason for this match, though," he claimed, jabbing his right hook into thin air several times. "We usually don't *schedule* when we spar."

Arthur dropped his arms and strode to Michael, wanting their conversation to go unheard by the few bystanders that hung around the ring. "I believe you to have a claim on Mrs. Eloisa Smith," he replied evenly, holding his chin up so that he might convince Michael he would not back down nor back out of their sparring session.

Frowning, Michael shook his head. "As I said before, I have no claim on the widow." At Arthur's look of disbelief, Michael added, "I admit to helping her where I can, but ..."

"You'll no longer be doing that," Arthur interrupted, his chin back up and his gaze very steady. "I have asked for her hand, and she has agreed to marry me," he stated, a hint of pride—*or was that challenge?*—in his voice.

Michael smiled then, a genuine smile that lit up his eyes and allowed his white teeth to glow in the dim light. "Congratulations, old man," he said happily, punching his banker lightly on the shoulder. "I already wished Mrs. Smith happy when she was in Shipley last week. She came to say you were courting her," he added, punching Arthur lightly on the shoulder again.

Hearing the good news about the impending nuptials from Arthur directly, Michael considered how relieved he felt.

He would no longer have to be Eloisa's protector, no longer have to provide her with pin money and a maid, and he would no longer have to provide her a place to live.

He was free to be married to Olivia.

Arthur held up his fists in front of him, a bit surprised by Michael's reaction to his statement and rather incensed at the mention that his betrothed had spoken to Michael in Shipley. "Shall we then?" he asked, an eyebrow cocking in challenge.

"Oh, of course," Michael replied lightly, holding up his fists in a loose, defensive posture.

Arthur was on the attack immediately, jabbing a roundhouse right into Michael's ribs so hard that Michael was sure one cracked. More surprised from the ferociousness of the punch than the pain that it created, Michael reacted with a series of quick jabs to Arthur's face, connecting with his jaw on only one of them. The banker reeled a bit, but was quick to cover himself as Michael tried a roundhouse to his body.

"I must admit, I didn't know you had proposed to Mrs. Smith," Michael said conversationally as he dodged a series of punches and then was stunned by an uppercut that caught his jaw. *Damn! The man was playing for keeps!* "She mentioned you had asked to court her when she saw me at Waterford Hall last week," he added, feeling the sting of the punch and having a devil of a time hiding it.

"I know," Arthur replied with a curt nod, covering himself as Michael managed to get close with a series of punches, finally hitting the man along the jawline again. Arthur danced back out of the way and shook his head quickly. "I thought it best to ask for her hand while you could not interfere."

Taking a deep breath, Michael made sure to hold his arms up in front of him as Arthur moved in to take some more shots to his body. "But, why would I wish to interfere?" he countered as his left fist crunched into the side of Arthur's arm, sending the man stumbling sideways. "As my sister-in-law, I could only hope she would make an excellent match now that her mourning period is over," he added, gasping for breath as he danced around the banker. "I do hope you'll ask me to stand with you during the ceremony."

But Arthur recovered and managed to slug him hard, first against the side of his chest and again into his forearm before he had a chance to comprehend Michael's words. Breathing heavily, Arthur furrowed his brows and dropped his arms. "Sister-in-law?" he repeated, *sotto voce.*

Michael took the opportunity to lightly punch Arthur in the ribs and then again in the shoulder. "Of course," he replied with a shrug. He returned his arms to their defensive posture. "I was in Shipley to get married to her sister, Olivia Waterford," he explained lightly, his breaths still short.

Panting, Arthur stared at Michael. "You're *married?*" he asked, his expression conveying his shock. He tried a round-house, but it went through air as Michael easily ducked away.

"I *told* you I was getting married. Before I left, remember?"

Arthur Huntington stared at him in disbelief. "You got *married?*" he repeated, his jaw suddenly slack.

"Yes," Michael said with a smile, his head nodding as he tried to ignore the sharp pains he suddenly felt from Arthur's punches. "Olivia and Eloisa are sisters," he added, just in case the banker hadn't figured it out from his earlier comment. "I ... I have been looking after Eloisa at the behest of her father," he lied, hoping the news would force the banker to end the match.

"Indeed?" Arthur replied, a flash of anger mixing with confusion. He rushed at Michael and pummeled him with his fists until Gentleman Jackson himself stepped in and pulled the banker off of Michael. "So, does this mean we're to be *brothers?*" Arthur gasped, bending over to try and catch his breath while Jackson looked over Michael's wounds.

"Uh huh," Michael replied, not wanting to smile; he thought it would hurt too much. "Are we done here?" he asked, deciding he no longer wanted to fight Arthur, especially if the man was going to be his brother-in-law.

Dazed, Arthur nodded, wandering off without another word.

The proprietor watched the banker leave the ring. He turned his attention back to Michael and his wounds. "What the hell was that all about?" he asked as he reached up to check the source of a stream of blood running down Michael's face.

"Just a friendly sparring match," Michael replied as he rolled his eyes. His expression darkened, though, when he saw the blood and realized that some of the punches he had taken had caused damage. There was no doubt he would be left with ugly bruises. He could barely breathe given the pain from the cracked or broken rib. Given the level of discomfort he felt, he rather doubted he would be able to consummate his marriage that night. *Damn!* It would be at least a day or more before he would be recovered enough to bed Olivia. *Double damn!* he thought with a sigh, wincing at the sharp pain his simple curse invoked.

But I am free of my obligation to Eloisa. What a relief!

Olivia quietly opened her bedchamber door and stood motionless for a moment, staring at the end of the hallway. Sure it was Michael she had heard come up the stairs, she ventured into the hall and saw that the door to his bedchamber was ajar. Neither he nor Edward had been at dinner that evening; Michael had sent a reminder note saying he would be home late as he was shopping in Ludgate Hill. Olivia had taken her dinner in the parlor and begun reading *Pride and Prejudice*, becoming so engrossed in the tale she only stopped reading when the clock on the mantle struck ten. Taking the book with her, she retired to her bedchamber

Olivia took a deep breath and willed herself to confront Michael. Moving quickly and as quietly as possible, she hurried to his room, her bare feet soundless on the Aubusson hall carpet. There was movement inside his room; footfalls on the plush carpet, a coat being discarded.

Olivia took a deep breath and stepped into the room, one

hand grasped on the edge of the door as she stood staring at her husband.

Wearing only breeches and his Hessians, his hair tousled from having removed his shirt, Michael was at first a sight to behold. His broad chest and large upper arms could have only belonged to a man who exercised rigorously.

Olivia shivered as she remembered the night he had climbed into her bed and moved his body so that it enveloped hers. Besides the awful odor of ale and cheroot smoke, there was the scent of the laundry soap on the linens and a bit of sandalwood and the scent of *him*. There was the heat of his body as it permeated her night rail, flowing into her very being. The weight of his right arm as it rested on the side of her body and the incredible sensation that coursed through her body as his hand cupped her right breast. Her entire body shivered as she remembered that night.

Just a week ago?

Just a week, she realized. *And yesterday morning.* He had done the same thing, although he hadn't smelled of cheroots and ale, thank goodness. She was sure he would bed her then, but there had been that sudden knock at the door and his hasty departure.

Olivia stood before him now in awe, her gaze finally settling on bruises that were so out of place on a man of such perfection. Without thinking, she moved quickly to stand before him, one hand reaching out to caress the flesh where a blue-green stain was spreading over several ribs.

Surprised when he finally noticed Olivia staring at him, *Is that fright I see in her eyes?* he wondered, Michael stopped and returned the stare, watching her as she approached him. As her hand reached out to touch him, he grimaced, expecting to feel pain from the place where he had allowed Huntington to punch him with his right fist, a roundhouse blow that he thought at the time might have cracked a rib or two. But when Olivia's fingertips finally made contact, the touch was so gentle, his skin shivered as if tickled. His sharp intake of breath caused Olivia to quickly pull her hand away, but he caught it and slowly raised it to his lips. Kissing her knuckles, he continued to watch her as her eyes took in all of him.

"You are hurt. What ... what *happened?*" she gasped as she reached up to his face with her other hand and cupped his cheek. A slight discoloration was appearing where Huntington's left upper cut had caught him cleanly on the jaw.

Michael smiled slightly, relieved that at least smiling didn't hurt too much. "I lost a bare knuckle fight," he said as he cocked an eyebrow. At Olivia's gasp and widened green eyes, he shrugged. "Well, *lost* is a bit of an overstatement," he corrected as he wrapped an arm around Olivia's waist and pulled her against him. She let out squeak of surprise as the front of her body was suddenly pressed against his. "I made sure my opponent won," he whispered as he leaned over and kissed her hair.

"Is he as ... bruised ... as you?" Olivia wondered as she continued to study him, her brow furrowing as her gaze took in the whorls of dark hair on his chest, the shape of his arms as he held her.

Michael grinned and closed his eyes as he considered how to answer. "I can only hope," he replied, kissing her forehead again.

"And why would you allow him to win?" she asked, pushing herself away from his body enough so that she could see his face.

Kissing the hand he still held, Michael considered what to tell her. The truth could hurt her, no doubt, but she seemed to know part of it already. He didn't know if Eloisa had told her anything. If he told Olivia everything, they could get on with their marriage, although he wasn't convinced she would forgive him once she heard his side of the tale. And there was still that damned bet.

Olivia saw Michael's face darken, his eyes take on a faraway look that she suddenly found frightening. Her husband was a bare knuckle boxer. What if her query angered him? Would he hurt her? Would he become so angry he might raise his hand to her? His fists?

Suddenly losing her resolve to ask about Eloisa, Olivia stepped away from him.

"What's wrong?" Michael asked as he realized she was staring at him with an entirely different look in her eye. When he moved to step closer, Olivia took another step back. She realized if she didn't ask him, she would always wonder. She couldn't not *know*. Not anymore. Not when she was married to him. "My sister ... is she ... is she ... *was* she truly your mistress?" she blurted out, tears stinging the edges of her eyes.

Taking a deep breath, Michael slowly shook his head. *How long has she thought that?* he wondered, a flare of anger igniting inside that suddenly replaced the sense of relief he had felt at having completed the sparring match with Huntington. "Edward told you that, didn't he?" he replied in a whisper, one hand coming up to scrub his face before he remembered the punch to his jaw. He winced in pain as his hand made contact, barely aware that Olivia had turned and run from the room.

"Olivia!" he called out, following her with his long strides so that he got to her bedchamber just after she ran through the door. His arm reached up and blocked the slamming door before it could latch, and he pushed on it hard, thinking she would be trying to keep it shut from the other side. But she was already to the bed, collapsed onto the counterpane, her shoulders heaving with her sobs. "She promised she would never tell you," he whispered, knowing even as he said the words that they would be of little comfort.

"She didn't," Olivia replied, her voice muffled by the counterpane. "Edward did, but he ... merely confirmed ..." she replied between sobs, her words nearly lost in the fabric. "*You* did. When you called me 'El'," she finally got out, her breath catching as she continued sobbing.

Michael sighed, wondering when he might have referred to her by the name he sometimes used for Eloisa. After a moment of thought, though, he realized that she was speaking of that night—the night he'd climbed into her bed and was caught by her father and more servants than he was expecting to show up as witnesses to his ruination of Olivia Waterford.

He moved to the side of the bed and pulled a handkerchief from his breeches. Holding it out for her, he whispered, "Actually, I called you 'my beautiful.'"

Olivia gasped and looked up at him from red-rimmed eyes, hesitantly taking the proffered hanky. Reaching down, Michael wrapped his arms around her shoulders and waist, lifting her from the bed while ignoring the stabs of pain where Huntington's fists had made contact. His face softened as he turned Olivia's face toward him and saw the pain and hurt in her eyes. He took her head between his hands and pulled her to him. "I promise you, Olivia, I do not have a mistress," he murmured quietly. He felt her body shake with a sob and wrapped his arms around her shoulders.

When he felt her tears on the skin of his chest, he put his hands on her shoulders and pushed her away enough so that he could see her face. "Until a couple of weeks ago, I was ..." He sighed loudly, not wanting to make the confession but realizing it was necessary. "I was Eloisa's *protector*," he admitted finally, "We were never lovers, Olivia. You are my wife, and I intend to honor my marriage vows."

Olivia buried her face in the space between his shoulder and arm. "I hate you," she sniffled, wrapping her arms around his chest and pulling herself against his body in a way that clearly indicated she did not mean what she'd said.

Michael pursed his lips at her response. The words stung, but her physical reaction was quite at odds to her claim. He kissed her hair and rested his cheek against her head. "Do you suppose there will ever be a time when you could ... not hate me?" he countered, trying hard to keep his voice steady. He felt her head shake against him, and her body trembled again. He took a deep breath, ignoring the stab of pain he felt from the damaged ribs. "So, you don't suppose you will ever feel affection for me?" he whispered, his lips finding her forehead and then her temple, his kisses soft and warm.

Olivia quieted and finally turned her face so that her cheek rested against his chest. "Maybe," she whimpered, sniffling quietly.

Michael's lip curved a bit then. Cupping her cheek with one hand, he kissed her nose and moved his lips to hers, barely brushing them, his breath warm on her face. "I suppose I shall have to wait then," he whispered gently. "Come, let's sit down so that I can explain some things. I owe you that much."

In her despair, Olivia had no strength to fight him, allowing him to lead her to the alcove and the settee therein. As he sat back into one corner and pulled her against him, she was very aware of his bare skin, of his nipple under her thumb as she placed her hand against his chest.

She had dreamt about being this close to him, spent many nights fantasizing about him being in bed next to her, wondered how it would be to touch him, what it would be like to love him—but all those times were under far different circumstances. And those were just daydreams. Just her imagination. Right here, right now, she was truly in Michael Cunningham's arms. His rather large, bare arms. Against his very bare chest.

When Olivia finally nestled her head into the space between his shoulder and chest, Michael sighed. "You sister is getting married," he finally said, not knowing quite where to start.

Olivia nodded and raised her head from his shoulder. "She told me this morning," she whispered, a hitch in her breath breaking up her words. "She said you know the man," she added, her tears finally subsiding. "That you actually introduced them to one another."

Michael placed a hand on the back of her head so that he could pull it back onto his shoulder. "My banker, actually," Michael answered before kissing her on the head. "Arthur Huntington the Third," he added wistfully. "Not a bad bare knuckle fighter in his own right. And he's got ten years on me."

At that, Olivia raised her head to stare at him. "You fought ... you *dueled* over my sister?" she asked, her face reddening as her ire returned.

Surprised she would make that connection, Michael swallowed. "*I* did not. *He* thought that's what we were doing. Remember, I wanted *him* to win," Michael explained in his own defense. At Olivia's confused expression, he went on. "Arthur loves your sister very much. Apparently he's wanted her as his wife for some time now, but he thought I had some kind of claim on her, which, of course, *I do not*, so we had to fight so he could prove his worthiness and his affection for her." At Olivia's continued frown, Michael stared down at her. "As I said, I lost deliberately."

He smiled to himself as he recalled the earlier sparring match, explaining in great detail what had happened, pantomiming some of the moves he'd made against Arthur Huntington and then describing the hits that had resulted in the bruises he now sported, pointing out each one with a self-deprecating tone in his voice.

Olivia's head was spinning just a bit as Michael finished telling his story. "Do you men often do these irrational things when you're in pursuit of a woman?" she asked, her brows still furrowed. A bubble of laughter erupted from Michael, and Olivia found herself smiling in spite of herself as she felt his body convulse against her.

"Irrational, perhaps, but it was ... necessary," he whispered. He thought of all the things he'd done in the last three weeks to ensure his marriage to Olivia would happen in time to meet the deadline he had set for himself.

Irrational?

Yes.

Necessary?

Perhaps not.

Did he regret what he'd done? It was still too early to tell, he decided.

"So, why were you holding my sister's hands and kissing her in the library?"

Michael jerked beneath her, surprised by the question. "You saw that?" he asked, his eyebrows practically in his hairline.

Olivia nodded. "I thought perhaps ... I thought you were proposing marriage," she murmured sadly.

Sighing, Michael rubbed his hand along Olivia's arm. "She had just told me Arthur was courting her. I was wishing her happy," he replied in a whisper. "And I was so relieved, Olivia. I cannot tell you how good it felt to know I no longer had to be her protector."

Relief, indeed. After a quiet moment, the smile disappeared and Olivia pressed her lips together. "So, may I ask how it was you had to provide protection for her in the first place?" She braced herself, thinking he might be embarrassed by her query or that he might simply go quiet and leave her to her overactive imagination. He surprised her by doing neither.

"Do you remember the first time we ever met?" Michael murmured as he leaned back and began stroking her shoulder.

Olivia nodded into his neck. "I was ...sixteen. You saved me from being kissed by Eli Blaylock," she replied, not understanding why he asked.

"I thought you were so pretty."

Olivia inhaled sharply. "You did?"

"Oh, yes. Still do, in fact," he added as he continued to rub her arm with his hand. "And your father knew it immediately. Told me in his study that I wasn't to go near you for three years," he spoke quietly. "It was quite an effective threat."

"It's been ... *five* years," Olivia stated as she lifted her head to look at him, not sure if she believed his claim.

And shouldn't she be offended that he took so long to climb into her bed?

Michael sighed, and he chuckled softly. "As I said, it was

a very effective threat," he repeated. But he sobered a bit. "Over the years, though, I've been a bit put off by the thought of marriage, my love," he answered in a whisper.

My love? Olivia repeated to herself. She rather liked it when he used endearments like that.

"And you never seemed to show any obvious interest in me," he accused with a shrug. "At least, not *that* kind of interest," he amended quickly when he felt her body go rigid.

"I conversed with you during dinner," she countered, a bit too indignant with her response. "I read books to you. I played the piano-forté for you. I walked to Shipley with you."

Michael pretended to ignore the comments. "Your sister was another matter, though."

Olivia stiffened even more as she realized to what he was referring. Eloisa was always quick to offer him tea, to engage him in conversation, to volunteer to serve him first at dinner. Her flirting was a testament to her attraction to the man. If asked directly, Eloisa would admit out loud to having a crush on Michael Cunningham. And although Olivia, too, had a crush on him, she wouldn't admit it.

Sometimes not even to herself.

"Tell me, did your sister wish to come to London because she didn't have any marriage prospects in Shipley?" Michael wondered, the back of one finger brushing along Olivia's neck. She shivered a bit at his touch but left her head resting against his shoulder.

"Eloisa always had admirers in Shipley. And West Grinstead. And all around Horsham," Olivia replied with a shrug. "But she made it very clear before she was even seventeen that she had no intention of marrying a barkeep, or a farmer, or a miner or anyone involved in smelting."

Michael grunted. "That doesn't leave a lot to choose from," he murmured, his fingers combing through the hair near her temple. He felt her smile as she continued to lean against him.

"No, indeed. She wanted a gentleman in town. Nothing

else would do," she sighed, wondering what it was about London that made country girls give up their perfectly acceptable situations and take the risks that some did to have a life in the world's largest city.

"Did you know that I have an older brother?" Michael asked then.

The change in topic caught Olivia off-guard. "Y ... Yes. But what has ...?"

"Patience, my sweet. There is much to tell if you really want to know how I came to be Eloisa's protector." At Olivia's hesitant nod of agreement, Michael continued, "Last May, I received a note from Marcus asking me to meet him at a brothel over in Covent Garden." He felt her body stiffen again at his mention of the brothel. "I just went for the brandy," he added quickly, not wanting her to think that he would indulge in such behavior, even if he was a bachelor. "I'm sure Marcus would have engaged one of the harlots, but he had actually shown up the night before. I read the note a day later than he intended me to."

There was a long minute before he heard her say, "Oh." Then she relaxed back into his arm.

"While I was enjoying my brandy, I noticed a girl crying in the corner. At first glance, I thought she was you ..."

Olivia suddenly pushed herself up from Michael's body and stared at him, her mouth open in shock.

"*Ouch,*" Michael growled as he leaned forward, his free hand going to the large bruise on his rib.

"Oh, I am so sorry," Olivia spoke quickly, pulling her hand away from his chest. Her eyes were as wide at having hurt him as from the implication of his comment. *Serves you right!* she found herself thinking, surprised she could be so spiteful when her husband really was in a good deal of pain.

Michael pulled his leg up and around Olivia so that he could sit up straighter on the settee. "I'll live," he said with a sigh. He wrapped an arm around her shoulder and pulled her against him again. "It was your sister, although she looked very ... *different*," he winced as he recalled the bruise on her cheek and the short petticoat she wore.

Olivia inhaled sharply, her brows furrowing and her face a statement of her confusion. "But, she was a governess ..." *Wait! No, that's not right,* she remembered from her earlier conversation with her sister. *Eloisa said she had come to London to get married.*

"No," Michael stated with a shake of his head. "She came to London *believing* she had landed a position as a governess, but it was a ruse to get her to the brothel. The madame there is quite unscrupulous when it comes to how she acquires her girls," he explained with a sour expression. He paused for several seconds before adding, "Virgins fetch a higher price with certain clients."

Her hand suddenly covering her mouth, Olivia thought at first she would be sick, her breathing quickened so.

When Eloisa announced she'd been offered a position as a governess the year before, Olivia had been stunned. She had been pursuing positions for nearly a year and not been hired while her sister's quick reply to a posting at the local mercantile resulted in an immediate offer. *I was so jealous!* Olivia remembered thinking as she recalled Eloisa's excitement about moving to London.

Seeing her distress, Michael cupped Olivia's cheek with a hand. "She was ... sporting a bruised cheek, but otherwise ... well, she was fine once I paid off the proprietor and got her out of there," he assured her quietly.

Meeting his gaze, Olivia tilted her head. "But she was already ..." She stopped, not knowing what to say. *Ruined* seemed inadequate somehow, especially compared to her own ruination at the hand of Michael.

How had her sister kept this from her? And why hadn't Edward said anything about this when he was telling her everything else?

"She had already lost her virtue, of course," Michael said quietly. "And enough men had probably seen her that night at Lucy's so that she was unable to live a completely respectable life by herself, at least for a few months. But I did what I could," he said quietly.

"Then, *you* bought her the townhouse?" Olivia wondered, realizing now that everything in her sister's life made more sense.

"I leased the house on her behalf. Set her up with a maid ... and although she was very insistent that I should be ... compensated, I suppose one could say, I refused to take her as my mistress," he explained with a sigh, not surprised when Olivia flinched at the last bit. "It wouldn't have been right."

"Did you ... do you ... feel affection for her?" Olivia asked, her hands suddenly trembling as much as her lower lip.

Michael took both her hands in his. "I felt ... *responsible* for her. I was never in love with her," he clarified, his voice very insistent.

Olivia nodded her understanding. "And Mr. Huntington? How did he come to ... meet her?"

Smiling, Michael sat up straighter. "Actually, I arranged that," he said, a bit of pride in his voice. At Olivia's raised eyebrow, he added, "I knew Arthur to be a widower and quite lonely. We talk occasionally at White's and at Gentleman Jackson's, where we fight, and he mentioned a day he'd seen me walking with a woman. He wanted an introduction. Seems he had been sweet on her since the moment he'd seen her shopping. Eloisa always wore black when she appeared in public, so he guessed she was in mourning. He asked about the fate of her husband, and I came up with a plausible story that made your sister seem respectable enough. On a day I knew he would pass us while we were walking, I introduced him to your sister. He subsequently declared his intentions to call on her."

Olivia inhaled and stared at Michael. "Now, what is this about her having been married?" she asked, remembering she was about to gain a brother and needed to know more about her sister's fabricated past. Eloisa had mentioned her marriage to a William Smith, but very few details about the man or their short life together.

"Everything in her life is as you know it except that when she left for London, she married an army infantryman who then went off to France to fight, and he died on the battlefield. Now she's a widow living off her husband's meager pension. And she's just come out of mourning," Michael stated automatically, as if he'd repeated the story several times.

Smiling, Olivia sighed and regarded her husband. "And her married name was truly Smith?" she said with a quirked lip.

Michael grinned. "It was the best she could come up with on short notice."

Olivia rolled her eyes. "And Mr. Huntington believes all this to be ... true?" she asked, deciding perhaps the story was believable enough and far better than hearing her sister had been an unwilling lady of the evening.

"Oh, yes. He's quite taken with her," Michael said with a nod, recalling the look in his banker's eye when he challenged Michael.

"Have you seen the ring he has given her?" Olivia asked, raising her left hand to indicate she meant an engagement ring.

Michael grimaced when he caught sight of the iron ring still on Olivia's finger. "No, but then I have not seen your sister since we were in Shipley," he replied with a shake of his head. "But, I can tell you it had better have a very large gemstone on a very pretty precious metal band," he added emphatically, thinking the banker could afford some finery for his wife-to-be.

"A sapphire," Olivia replied with a nod. "On a gold band. She's very happy. And she says Mr. Huntington seems very in love with her, too." She sighed and sat back in the settee as she considered everything her husband had told her. She frowned. "So, why did you have to fight Mr. Huntington?" Olivia asked suddenly.

A loud sigh emanated from Michael before he leaned back in the settee. "The sparring match was his idea, but I thought it best he prove himself worthy of your sister. I couldn't just pawn her off on him without knowing his true intentions. And I wanted Eloisa to know how much Arthur wants her."

Biting her lower lip, Olivia nodded at the odd logic. "And do *you* believe my sister to ... want Mr. Huntington?" Olivia remembered Eloisa's excitement at her future with the banker, but she wondered if Michael knew of her sister's enthusiasm for a life with the man. She hoped he did.

Michael smiled. "I believe so. She's ... she is in love with him," he stated, his expression not indicating how he felt about it. For at that moment, he felt a great deal of jealousy. Not because Arthur had taken Eloisa from him or because Eloisa loved Arthur instead of him. He was jealous of Arthur because of *how* Eloisa felt about him.

Will Olivia ever truly love me? he wondered suddenly.

He shook himself from his reverie, knowing Olivia was watching him closely. "Arthur will be able to keep her in fine style. And since this is a second marriage for both of them, he plans to get a special license, get married, and introduce her to his friends at a ball given in their honor. I expect that will happen in the next few weeks," he said confidently.

Olivia's eyebrows popped up. Eloisa hadn't mentioned a ball, so Arthur must not have mentioned it to her. "And who is hosting the ball?"

Michael pulled Olivia into his arms and took a deep breath. "I am thinking *we* should," he replied, his manner very guarded.

"But, we have no ballroom!" Olivia replied, her eyes wide with surprise at his suggestion.

Michael regarded her for a moment. "Well, not in this house, but there is one in the family house in Cavendish Square," he said casually.

"Oh," Olivia replied, stunned at the information. *I have a key to the house in Cavendish Square!* "So, you are neighbors with Mr. Huntington?"

Michael nodded. "His house is directly across the square."

Olivia smiled, feeling a sense of relief and calm she hadn't felt in a very long time. "Do you have other family houses besides the one in Mayfair?" she asked, suddenly wondering where the properties of the viscountcy were located.

"A few, I suppose," Michael murmured after he'd given it a bit of thought. "But there is just one in the country in which I would ever live myself," he added quickly. "Iron Creek. The one we talked about at dinner the other night."

"Twenty miles from?" Olivia asked, her hand rubbing lightly over the top of his chest as she remembered them discussing the property over dinner. *A little cottage with twenty rooms on twenty-hundred acres ...* And now that she thought about it, she'd heard mention of that estate before. *Somewhere near home.*

Michael placed his hand over hers and stilled it. "Horsham District, near Crawley Down," he replied, watching her face closely as he said it.

Pushing herself up so that she could see his eyes, Olivia stared at him. "Because of the prize-fighting?" she asked. Her lips quirked, thinking that, of course, he would like living near where he could watch bare-knuckle mills.

Grinning, Michael shook his head, "Well, there is that," he agreed, surprised she would make that connection.

But Olivia's eyes widened as she thought of the areas around home. Of the lands and estates in Horsham. "Is your father truly Viscount Cunningham?" she asked suddenly, her curious expression a source of amusement for Michael but her misplaced hand on his ribs a source of extreme pain.

"Yes, he is," Michael replied with a nod and a wince. "A title my brother shall someday inherit if he does not die before my father, but one I'll probably be stuck with since he seems quite intent on ending up in debtors' prison," he added as he pulled her hand away from its perch on his ribs.

Olivia gasped as she sat up straighter. "Please, forgive me," she said as a hand covered her mouth. "Is there anything I can do?" she asked as her eyes fell again on his worsening bruises.

Michael leaned back into the corner of the settee and closed his eyes. "Tell me you'll host a ball in your sister's honor three weeks after they are wed," he answered evenly, still grimacing from the pain and breathing carefully so as not to make it worse.

"I will," she agreed, realizing Michael was quite serious about the ball. "I'll ask Jeffers to assist me with the plans," she added, her face brightening as she thought about planning her first ball as a married woman. "But you must help me with a list of the people to invite."

"I will," he replied, his arm wrapping around her shoulder and pulling her back to his chest. There was silence for a moment as Michael pondered how to ask Olivia about her feelings for him. If she even had any. *Besides despising me.* "And you?" Michael wondered, his head bent so he could see her face as his fingers caressed her temple and threaded themselves through her long hair. "Who did *you* want?"

Olivia stared back for a moment before tearing her eyes from his. Had she ever wanted anyone other than Michael Cunningham? Had she even *imagined* wanting anyone else? Had she ever imagined herself being held by anyone other than Michael? Had there been anyone else she thought about touching? Holding? Kissing?

You, she thought silently. *It has always been you I wanted.*

And here she was, in his arms being stroked and held and comforted despite her earlier proclamation of hating him and despite her jealous behavior regarding her sister. *He really must have feelings for me or he wouldn't put up with me like this*, she considered. *He has said as much.*

Olivia returned her eyes to his, noting the expectant look on his face. "You," she admitted finally, letting out a breath she'd been holding far too long. "It has always been you ..."

"And not just because I am in such severe pain?" he asked in a quiet voice, heartened by her reply.

She looked up at him and sighed. "I have been bewitched by you since the day I met you," she admitted finally.

Stunned at her response, Michael tried to sit up straighter and winced at the sharp pain it caused. "You have?" he questioned, surprised. "For five years?"

Olivia nodded. "Indeed. You saved me from Eli Blaylock," she said, her tone matter-of-fact. "I feel affection for you, too, if you must know," she added with a sigh.

Michael pulled her closer, wincing when her body pressed against his bruised rib. But he ignored the pain in order to kiss her hard on the lips, to claim her as his own and hold her protectively in his arms. And she allowed it, even returning the kiss after a moment of surprise passed. Lifting her, Michael carried her to the bed and turned so that he could sit on the edge of the mattress. With her head on his shoulder, Olivia found herself sitting on his lap. Holding her with one arm, Michael drew the fingers of his free hand down her arm and captured her hand in his. "I had to know," he whispered, his face angling so that he could kiss her lips, taking her lower lip between his and nibbling gently. His hand moved to the side of her breast, his thumb gently pressing against the nub that he felt under her night rail, rubbing around it until he felt her sharp intake of breath and her eyes lifted to meet his. Her mouth was suddenly against his, her arm wrapped around his neck, her thumb against the space on his jaw just behind the bruise that was still darkening there.

Caught a bit off-guard, Michael finally returned her kiss, pulling her more closely to his body as he allowed his desire for her to take over. The hand that held her breast moved down the soft fabric of her gown to the hem and found the bare skin of her leg. Sliding his open hand up along her calf, around her knee, along the length of her thigh, he felt her break the kiss to gasp quietly. He recaptured her lips, though, and used his tongue to tease her lips and teeth apart as his hand smoothed over her hip, along the side of her waist and under her breast. Her body arched as his thumb found the hardened nipple and the caress of his fingers sent shivers of pleasure through her breasts and her belly.

Desire overwhelmed her. There was a heat building deep inside her, between her thighs and the base of her spine that demanded he do something more. She could feel the hard ridge behind the fall of his breeches. *Why doesn't he take me now?* she wondered, wishing she could feel his flesh inside of her, filling her and soothing the ache that had slowly manifested itself every day since their wedding.

Michael pulled away a bit and then kissed her lightly. "Sleep well, my love," he said quietly, wincing as he stood up with her still in his arms. Turning around, he placed her down on the bed and smoothed her gown down around her legs. *I want her right now*, he thought suddenly, realizing she was ripe and willing to share her bed with him.

Stunned that he would simply stop when he did, Olivia's breath caught as she stared at him. His face was drawn. The bruising on his body was much worse than when she had first seen him only an hour ago. Suddenly understanding his quick dismissal of her, Olivia's desire was replaced by concern. "Should I have Jeffers send for the doctor?" she asked, the worry on her face matching the tone of her voice. She reached over and lightly kissed a bruise on the side of his chest.

Michael closed his eyes and sighed as he felt the pleasurable shiver pass through his body. *Perhaps I could ...* But he was no longer able to breathe without feeling pain. "No," he replied quietly, his head shaking. "I'll be fine. I may even be able to dance at the ball," he added with a forced grin. He leaned over to kiss her on the forehead, the tiredness in his body finally overtaking him. A moment later, he was flat on his back on the bed, sound asleep.

Olivia raised herself on one elbow and surveyed her battered husband. The bruising truly was worse than when she had first seen him in his room, and she found herself becoming more worried. She got out of bed, pulled on her new dressing gown, and yanked the bell for a servant. Then, hurrying to the door, she opened it slightly and waited until a footman appeared at the top of the stairs. He seemed startled to see her, but bowed and said, "Yes, my lady?"

"Do you know if there is any arnica in the house?" she asked urgently, hoping she wouldn't have to send the man next door to the doctor's house. If she applied the pain reliever now, she hoped her husband might sleep sounder and the bruises would heal quicker.

"Right away, madam," the footman replied before bowing and hurrying back down the stairs. Although it seemed as if he was gone for a very long time, Olivia knew it was probably only a few minutes before he reappeared, huffing as he reached the top of the stairs. He hurried to her door, holding out the dark jar.

"Thank you," Olivia said as she took it and nodded to the footman's hasty bow. Grabbing a flannel from near the ewer and basin, she moved to stand next to the bed. Starting with his jaw, she slowly and gently applied the herb and oil ointment to the bruises on Michael's body, working her way down his chest and ribs to a bruise that continued beneath his breeches. Undoing the fastenings, she pulled down the fall of his breeches so she might loosen the garment from around his waist. Despite the slight arousal that was still quite evident beneath his drawers, Olivia was determined to apply the medication wherever he might have been punched. She pulled down his breeches and drawers, finding that, even in his apparently unconscious state, Michael seemed to help with undressing himself.

After she laid his garments aside, she stood and stared at his naked body, a bit frightened but at the same time very drawn to what she saw before her. Even in this relaxed state, his prone body seemed to exude barely contained energy. The long muscles of his thighs were evident in the relief cast by the light from a candle on the night stand. Only the tops of his collarbones were apparent; his thick chest and dark hair hid most of his ribs. His waist was not as pinched in as some of the younger men seemed to sport, but there was no hint of a belly. His arms, very large and muscled from the shoulder to the elbow, hung from broad, sloped shoulders. As her gaze followed the arms to his hands, she smiled when she thought of what it would be like to have those hands on her breasts again.

Shaking herself from her reverie, Olivia returned her attention to his wounds. The bruises did not extend much below his waist, but she quickly applied arnica where they did. When she completed her ministrations, she set aside the medication and turned to regard his manhood. The nearly engorged shaft hovered over a nest of dark curly hair while his testicles rested on his thighs. She was about to reach out and touch him when a candle guttered and went out.

With only one candle left alight, she sighed and pulled the downturned bed linens and blankets from under his legs and covered him, carefully climbing into the bed and covering herself, too. At first, she dared not get close enough to touch his body, but when he stirred and turned slightly on the mattress, she was forced to allow herself to roll against him, the front of her body pressed slightly against the mostly unbruised side of his body. She gingerly lay her right arm atop his torso, her hand cupping over his manhood before she realized what she was touching.

Resisting the urge to pull away, she left her hand there and wondered if he would notice. Soon, though, one of his hands lifted and covered hers, the weight of it pressing her palm down harder on the velvety skin and the curly hair. Several moments later she relaxed enough to allow sleep to take her, vaguely aware of a kiss being placed on the top of her head.

CHAPTER 29

WEDNESDAY BRINGS CONFESSIONS

April 19, 1815

When Eloisa opened the front door to find her sister standing on her stoop, she immediately wondered as to the reason for Olivia's visit. The look of desperation on her younger sister's face made her look much older than her twenty-one years. *Damnation! What's wrong?*

"Please, come in," she invited, stepping aside as Olivia entered the small vestibule. "You look beautiful in that ensemble. That dark green is so becoming," Eloisa offered, wondering if her sister had come with questions. Even accusations, perhaps. It had been seven days since Olivia's quick wedding, nine days since Eloisa accepted Arthur Huntington's offer of marriage. *What could be wrong?* "Would you like tea?" she asked, forcing lightness into the question.

"No, thank you, though," Olivia replied with a shake of her head. "Do you have a moment so that we might ... talk?" She thought the walk to her sister's townhouse would improve her mood and fortify her resolve to ask the questions she felt she must. Instead, it gave her more time to wonder and to imagine the worst.

Her older sister had always been attracted to Michael, had always shown him favor. Now that she'd learned her husband had been Eloisa's protector for the past year— and how he came to be her protector—Olivia was determined to discover if Eloisa still harbored feelings for him. Olivia didn't believe she could stay married to Michael if either of them had feelings for one another, even if Michael did love her, as he claimed that morning, whispering in her ear before he eased himself from the bed and made his way to his own bedchamber in the early morning hours.

Since they hadn't yet consummated their marriage, Olivia was wondering if she could arrange for an annulment. It would be far better to walk away from the marriage now than to live with knowing the awful truth for the rest of her days. She was sure she could still secure a position as a governess. Even the Duchess of Somerset had already arranged for a governess, there were more opportunities for employment in London than in Sussex.

Eloisa sighed and nodded. "Of course," she said as she motioned her sister to the settee in the parlor, thinking that once she was married, she and Olivia could meet like this every morning for tea and share stories of their lives. They could spend their afternoons shopping in New Bond Street and in Oxford Street, enjoy ices at Gunter's Tea Shop in Berkeley Square, have dinner at the Clarendon Hotel. It was the life she had imagined when she'd left Sussex the year before, expecting to have employment as a governess and eventually marrying a gentleman. Although she might have mistaken the details of how she would end up married to a gentleman, she thought the end result well worth what she'd been through.

"Did you ... do you ... do you love him?" Olivia wondered, turning to face her sister, her lower lip trembling as she moved to sit down. Although she wanted to remain standing for this encounter, she found her knees unable to support her any longer. A tooth caught her lip in an effort to stave off the tears she felt pricking her eyes.

Eloisa swallowed a gasp, surprised at how forward her sister was with her question. "If you are speaking of Mr. Huntington, then, yes, Olivia, I do love him. I love him very much," Eloisa stated with an enthusiastic nod. "Indeed, I believe I fell in love with him the moment I first met him. When you meet him, when you see us together, you'll understand."

Olivia frowned and nearly reconsidered why she came. "I was speaking of Michael, of course," she clarified, her sadness suddenly replaced with impatience and a hint of anger.

Michael? Eloisa blushed a deep shade of pink as she considered her sister's query. Although she often wondered if Olivia would eventually learn of how Cunningham had become her protector, she still had to think a moment before responding. "At one time, I believe I did feel affection for Cunningham," she admitted in a very quiet voice, her breaths coming a bit too fast as her head bobbed nervously. *How much do I tell her?* "You know I did—before I ever moved to London. But, Olivia, you must believe me when I say I did not ever feel for him what I do for Mr. Huntington. Arthur is the only man I have ever *loved*," she added quietly. "And I do not believe Mr. Cunningham has ever felt affection for me. Indeed, I have always thought he felt affection for *you*."

Stunned at her sister's comments, Olivia took a deep breath and let it out slowly. "Oh, Eloisa," she whispered, tears starting to well up in the corners of her eyes. If Eloisa truly had no feelings for Michael, and if he loved her as he claimed he did, then Olivia could remain married to him. "There is something you must help me with," Olivia said as she gave Eloisa a pleading look.

Eloisa regarded her sister with a look of surprise. "Whatever it is, I will assist you in any way I can," she promised, wondering at her sister's request. When Olivia did not speak right away, she watched her with a raised eyebrow. "What is it?"

Sighing, Olivia blushed and closed her eyes. "Michael has yet to ... we have not yet consummated our marriage," she whispered, the sound of her voice barely audible. "We have come close. I was sure he was going to last night, but he was so bruised ..." She shook her head. "I do not know ... I wish to know what I should *do* to make him bed me," she stammered, her eyes finally locking on Eloisa's and her cheeks turning crimson.

"Oh," Eloisa responded, a bit of surprise in her voice. Why would her sister expect *her* to know about such things? Did Olivia believe she and Michael had been lovers? She repositioned herself on the settee and thought for a moment. "Well, I have always believed I must never allow a man to see me completely unclothed," she announced loudly, a shake of her head adding force to her statement. At Olivia's stunned expression, she gave a shrug and added, "I am quite modest and, until, well ... I rather doubt I could allow it," she stammered with a shy smile as she turned her attention back to Olivia.

"What are you suggesting?" Olivia wondered, a look of concern appearing on her face.

Eloisa blushed bright red. "Tease him, I suppose. Pretend to be a wanton woman. Take off all of your clothes and then remove all of his and ..."

"Until I am completely naked?" Olivia whispered hoarsely, her eyebrows quite high. She swallowed hard. She had already removed all of Michael's clothing, although certainly not in anticipation of lovemaking. And he had seen her bare breasts. He seemed quite surprised when she allowed him to stare at them. She had wondered at that, wondered at his look of awe and realized she rather liked the expression on him. His stare wasn't lascivious or one of carnal lust but of ... appreciation? Wonder, perhaps? Instead of making her feel exposed and vulnerable, his gaze had made her feel wanted—*desired*, even.

Eloisa shrugged and gave her sister a quick glance. "Yes," she answered, nodding as if to convince herself as much as Olivia. "And until he is, too." She stopped and put a hand over her mouth. "Oh, what am I saying?" she blurted, sure Olivia would be mortified at her suggestion.

But Olivia put a hand to her own mouth and began giggling. "He has a very strong, manly body," she spoke quietly. "I must admit, I saw all of it last night, although he is covered in those awful bruises Mr. Huntington put upon him," she complained with a roll of her eyes. "He may even have a cracked rib!"

Eloisa hissed and shook her head. "As it is with Mr. Huntington! The two are usually just sparring partners, but when Cunningham fought with him yesterday, it was quite obvious from the damage that there was more to it than just a friendly sparring match. And all bruised like that—that will be the way Arthur is after his visits to Gentleman Jackson's," she added with disgust and a shake of her head.

At Olivia's raised eyebrows, Eloisa blushed again, realizing she had given away too much with her description of Arthur's bruised body. "I insisted he show me the wounds when he winced so badly. I had put my arms around him when he was about to leave here yesterday—to give him a farewell kiss— and ..." she shook her head and pushed an errant curl behind her ear, "I made him remove his shirt to show me what Cunningham had done to him. Under the pretext that I might have some salve that would help him heal, of course. And I kissed his bruises and ..." She sighed happily, a wistful look on her face as she stared into space and a soft pink blush spread over her face.

"You made love?" Olivia gasped quietly, a smile of embarrassment appearing along with a pink blush on her own cheeks.

Eloisa shrugged, her face turning a shade darker. "Honestly, I did not mean for it to happen, Olivia, but I knew he ... he was *aroused*," she said in whisper. "And he had just given me the most exquisite necklace," she reached over to the side table and picked up a flat, black velvet box. "Before I knew what was happening, we were kissing, and he was carrying me to my bed, and we were saying wedding vows to one another." She opened the box and showed Olivia a necklace of creamy white pearls, each pearl separated by a small diamond. "I felt so wanton! And yet, I am not the least bit ashamed of myself," she claimed in a whisper. "We are to be married, after all!"

Olivia stared in awe at the string of pearls and then at her sister for a moment. "And has he seen you naked then?" she asked, her eyebrow arching as she teased her sister.

"Every last inch of me," Eloisa replied, a huge grin on her face. "He is a very generous lover. Very protective, very passionate. And I did not allow him to leave here until after I fed him breakfast this morning."

Smiling still, Olivia held her sister's hand. "And when will you wed for keeps?" she asked. She hoped she might bear witness to her sister's wedding.

Eloisa took a deep breath. "He has a special license so that we may wed Friday morning," she replied happily. "He's speaking with a vicar today about an appointment."

Olivia sat back against the settee and grinned. "And whatever shall you wear on such short notice?"

Frowning, Eloisa regarded her sister for a moment. "Oh, dear," she answered, her face suddenly taking on a look of doubt. "I haven't ... I haven't given it any consideration!"

Smiling, Olivia thought for a moment. "If you don't mind wearing a hand-me-down, you could wear the gown I am wearing to the Harvey ball tomorrow night," she suggested, remembering it was once supposed to be a wedding gown. "I promise I won't spill anything on it, although I cannot promise you that someone else won't."

Eloisa grinned as she considered the offer. "Is it ... appropriate?" she asked with a suggestive cock of her eyebrow.

"Oh, yes," Olivia assured her. "Madame Suzanne was making it as a wedding gown for someone else. And your new necklace will be perfect with it, I am sure."

Nodding, Eloisa smiled and said, "Then I accept your most generous offer." She sighed again before wrapping her arms around her sister's shoulders. "And please accept my congratulations on your wedding," Eloisa added quietly. "We never really had a chance to say anything about it while I was in Shipley."

Olivia grinned and returned the hug. "Thank you," she murmured. "You will send word when you know what time you'll be saying your vows?" Olivia wondered as she moved to leave.

Eloisa stood and considered her sister's query. "Will you stand with me?" she asked suddenly. "It's why I went to Shipley. To ask if you would stand with me."

Beaming, Olivia nodded. "Of course, I will. I've nothing to wear, though," she added with a giggle. When she saw the look of happiness on her sister's face, she hugged her. "Come. Let's go shopping in Oxford Street," she suggested. "You'll need some bride clothes for after the wedding!"

Eloisa smiled and nodded in agreement. "We both need some bride clothes," she replied happily. Once she'd fetched her reticule and a shawl, the two sisters left for a very long shopping excursion.

"My mother is in town," Michael commented in a low voice as he regarded Olivia. When he'd knocked on her door and peeked in at her call of "Come in," he found her reading *Pride and Prejudice* in bed, her bare shoulders and arms suggesting she was naked beneath the covers. She quickly set the tome on the night stand and motioned for him to come into the room.

"Did you see her today?" Olivia asked, curious as to why he wouldn't have mentioned it over dinner.

Michael shook his head as he made his way to the side of the bed, his dressing gown loosely tied shut. "I just received a note from her," he replied, wondering if he dare attempt to stay in the room again that night. "It was delivered by one of the footman from the Cavendish house, so she is definitely staying there," he added with a sigh. His gaze lowered to the bed and he fell silent.

"What is it?" Olivia wondered, seeing an odd expression cross his face. The bruises on his face from the day before were already fading so that just a hint of yellow showed on his jawline.

"I did not mean for our wedding to be such a ... slapdash

affair," Michael murmured, his tone apologetic as he stared at the blue draped fabric of the canopy above Olivia's bed. *My mother's bed*, he thought with a frown. "I hadn't given it much thought, seeing as how I've known for so long that you would be my wife," he added in a whisper, turning his head in her direction. Their evening had been very pleasant; a good dinner without Edward—the man hadn't been seen by any of the staff since Monday night—a quiet walk in the garden after the dessert course, a glass of port in the library. And then Olivia had nearly fallen asleep in his arms as Michael held her in the large leather chair and gently caressed her nearly-healed wrist.

Olivia gasped at the odd comment and raised herself up on one elbow, the motion causing the coverlet to slide down. Very aware of a suddenly bared breast, Michael held his breath for a moment in an attempt to remain in control of himself.

"How long have you known that?" Olivia wondered, her brows knitted in a frown.

Michael sat on the edge of the bed and reached over to gently smooth the crease in her brow with the edge of his thumb. He noted how long her lashes were as she closed her eyes at his touch. "Since you were ... sixteen, I suppose," he answered, his thumb sliding down to her temple.

Her eyes opened in surprise. "Sixteen?" she repeated, trying to sit up straighter but forced to remain where she was as Michael pulled back the coverlet and climbed into the bed next to her. He shed his dressing gown as he did so, watching to see what Olivia's reaction would be to his sudden naked-ness and his very apparent arousal.

He remembered waking up naked that morning, though, and realized she had to have undressed him while she applied arnica to his bruises. The medication had done wonders; most of the slight bruises were already fading and the worst ones were changing from the purply-blue to the just-blue stage. Within a few days, there wouldn't be any evidence of his sparring match with Huntington.

But Olivia's attention stayed on his eyes. "How can that be? I was only sixteen the first time you ever ..."

"Indeed," Michael interrupted, settling his head on a pillow and moving to wrap an arm around her shoulders. "From the moment I met you, I thought of you as my intended," he admitted in a quiet voice. "I imagined what a ring would look like on the base of the finger that was bleeding." He pulled that same finger into his mouth, gently suckling it until he noticed the iron ring and grimaced. At Olivia's shocked expression, he let go of her finger and added, "Your father knew right away, of course."

"Whatever do you mean, 'of course'?" Olivia countered as the arm behind her lifted her shoulders and rolled her so that the front of her body was pressed against his unbruised side. Her left arm ended up across his ribs, her hand above the bandage around her wrist finding purchase on his chest. When her fingertips brushed against his nipple, she heard his sudden intake of breath and realized what had caused it. She was contemplating whether to repeat the movement when he said, "He just knew. He ... saw how I looked at you, I suppose, or perhaps he decided ..." He let the sentence trail off, wondering how, indeed, Harold Waterford had realized just how taken Michael was with his daughter. At Olivia's expectant glance, he added, "So he promised you to me."

Olivia stared at Michael for a very long time. His heavy-lidded eyes were unreadable in the dim lamplight, but she sensed he was quite serious. Then she remembered something he'd said the night before. "You said he told you to stay away from me for three years!" she countered, thinking she'd caught him in a lie.

"And then I could have you as my wife when I was ... ready," he stammered, his eyes not quite meeting hers. *Why did I wait?* he wondered just then. If he already knew he wanted Olivia as his wife, he could have made his intentions known to her. He could have at least given her a betrothal ring and secured her agreement to be his wife.

"You didn't tell me that," she murmured, her chin coming to rest on his bare chest.

"I take it, then, that your father did not speak of it either?" Michael whispered, a bit surprised the old curmudgeon had kept his daughter's apparent betrothal a secret from her. But others in their village knew, he was sure. Wouldn't someone have told her?

"He never told me, no," Olivia answered, biting her lip. "I rather wish I'd known," she added, her ire increasing as she considered the wasted effort she'd put into finding a position as a governess. "Had I known, I could have ... I could have better prepared myself ..."

"For the shock of having to marry me?" Michael interrupted, his lip curling in amusement.

"To be a wife to a member of the *ton*," she countered, not appreciating his teasing just then. "I am a daughter of a ... of a tradesman. I didn't attend finishing school in London ..."

"Your father is hardly a tradesman," Michael interrupted, his eyes opening wide. "Your education is more than adequate—you're probably a bit too knowledgeable about the world to be a wife to ... to anyone, let alone a member of the *ton*," he murmured, not meaning for the words to sound offensive. "And, as the second son of a viscount, I had a bit more latitude as to whom I could choose as my wife. The *ton* be damned," he finished, his eyes closing as he settled his head back into the pillow. After a moment, he sighed. "I'm sorry I didn't tell you," he said as he tightened his hold around her shoulders just a bit. "I have been a poor example of a man betrothed. And I've no idea how to be ... how to be a *married* man," he apologized quietly. He lifted his head from the pillow to kiss her forehead before allowing it to fall back into the fluff, his eyes closing even before his head came to rest.

A watery smile appeared on Olivia's lips. She expected he came to her bed to finally make love to her, but when he made no move to do so, she wondered how to broach the subject of her prolonged virtue. Since she could not bring herself to say anything aloud, she began trailing her fingertips over the light dusting of dark hair on his chest and midsection, moving her hand in tiny circles that made their way down his torso. When she brushed against his hardened manhood, she lifted her head from his chest at the very same time he gasped and caught her hand in his, holding it tightly against his arousal.

"You are naked," she accused, her widened eyes indicating surprise.

Michael took a deep breath and held it for a moment. "As are you," he countered, trying to sound nonplussed despite his next breath being more labored than the last. He shut his eyes tightly as he felt her grip on him increase, felt her fingers moving along the velvety length of his shaft, felt her heartbeats against his own, felt his entire body about to explode as he thought of allowing himself the release he so desperately wanted. As much as he considered staying her hand, or removing himself from the bed altogether, or fighting to remain in control, he instead gave into his body's desire.

He would return the favor just as soon as he'd recovered —*tomorrow night, after the ball*, he thought. So, he allowed her to stroke him and tease him, allowed her to kiss his nipples and caress the space above his groin, allowed himself to feel her fingers wrap around his turgid length and slide down his swollen manhood, cup his sac and then return to stroke him from top to bottom in slow, torturous movements until his body demanded he let go. He allowed her to witness his ecstasy. "Olivia..." he started to say before a growl escaped and his entire body tensed, the muscles along his torso tightening as the incredible spasm of pleasure gripped him, as his world went black and his seed spilt onto his flat stomach.

Aware of what was happening, Olivia watched his body, watched his face, heard his labored breathing, felt his hand grip over her fingers and hold them hard against his manhood. She wondered at how such pleasure could appear so painful. Had she looked like this when he'd pleasured just the night before? The sensations had been so intense, so unlike anything she had ever experienced, she could not imagine a greater pleasure. And yet she remembered the ache she'd felt between her thighs, and she wondered.

She loosened her grip and allowed her fingers to travel the length of the taut, silken skin. When her thumb moved over the wet tip, she watched his body's sudden reaction, smiling as she realized how simple it was to pleasure him. Finally, she moved her fingers to the space above his groin, running her fingers through the warm pool of semen. *He is definitely not impotent,* she thought with a satisfied grin, her fingertips circling his naval and then diving back into the dark curlies that surrounded his manhood. When her continued touching and caresses didn't seem to elicit a response from Michael, she looked up toward his face. It seemed softer, more relaxed somehow, the planes not as sharp as they had appeared earlier. Dark lashes lay atop his cheekbones and his breathing was regular. Her grin turned to a frown when she realized why he appeared so relaxed.

Michael had fallen asleep.

Shaking her head as she regarded him, Olivia sighed and lowered her head into the small of his shoulder, settling herself for another day of being a virgin bride.

CHAPTER 30

THURSDAY'S BALL IS A
BETTOR'S GAMBLE

April 20, 1815

Sarah rushed about the bedchamber, pulling out accessories from one set of drawers before hurrying to another set to get something else. Until she had actually seen the ball gown created by Madame Suzanne, she could not comprehend how beautiful fabric could be, how it could drape and be shaped and fall to the floor in such elegant folds. She sighed as she watched Olivia prepare for the ball, proud she'd been allowed to help with her hair and dressing.

Olivia stood in front of the cheval mirror as she pulled on a pair of long white gloves. Having finished her running about, Sarah stood behind and to the side of her. "You look lovely," she sighed quietly. "You will be the prettiest at the ball."

Sarah had spent the better part of the past two hours plaiting tiny braids into Olivia's auburn hair before wrapping the remainder into a stylish chignon. The braids were then wrapped about the seams of the chignon and held in place by a series of evenly spaced hairpins camouflaged with tiny white flowers from the garden. At the last minute, she'd added a few tiny yellow rose buds from a hothouse, their golden color a good match for the gown's cream palette. And then she'd pulled the laces on Olivia's corset with an extra tug so that the tops of her breasts would mound more than just a bit above the neckline of her dress.

Smiling, Olivia took an experimental breath, quite conscious of the tightened corset and the effect it had on her appearance. She turned and winked at her dresser. "Let us hope my husband is of the same opinion." *And his mother,* she thought suddenly, remembering that she would be meeting her mother-in-law at the Harvey's.

Since the woman had only been in town for a day, Olivia had yet to meet her. Had Michael insisted on a public place so that Lady Cunningham would not create a scene upon meeting a daughter-in-law who was not of the *ton?* Or was it truly because Harvey's was convenient, since the viscountess hadn't arrived in London until just the day before and had too much to do?

A knock at the door tore her from her thoughts. She moved to the door, waving Sarah away as she did so. Opening it, she gazed up at Michael, resplendent in his black knit breeches, a red waistcoat made of superfine, and a black topcoat. His snowy white cravat was tied quite fashionably, a garnet pin showing through the folds. The lace-trimmed cuffs that poked out from the ends of the topcoat sleeves were held closed at his wrists with garnet cuff links.

Michael stared at the woman who stood before him. He hadn't expected she would answer the door, and he certainly didn't expect she would be fully dressed and apparently ready to leave. He had been quite prepared to insist she leave with him that instant no matter her state of readiness.

But instead, he stood and simply stared at his wife. Her gown, a pale cream satin confection, displayed the tops of her breasts, the swells above the neckline so enticing, he was afraid some young buck, nay, a whole herd of young bucks would fill her dance card with the intention of spending their dance wishing they could plant their faces into her bosom.

I certainly want to.

The short draped sleeves of her gown fell seductively from her bare shoulders, displaying the satin-soft skin he remembered holding against his body just last night. Candle-light gleamed on her hair, the red highlights outlining the carefully done braids and bun and the shape of the ringlets near her ears.

Olivia looked up at him expectantly, her gloved hand reaching up to caress his jawline just beyond the fading bruise. He leaned his head into her hand and furrowed his brows.

"I ... I was looking for my wife. Perhaps you have seen her?" he asked, his eyes never leaving hers. Nor did they seem to hold any humor despite his teasing comment.

Blushing, Olivia grinned and leaned up to kiss him on the cheek. "Despite what you claimed a few days ago, you are a tease!" she accused, her grin fading as he continued to stare at her. "What is ... wrong?" she whispered, suddenly uncomfortable under his scrutiny. She glanced down at her gown, thinking something must be amiss.

Michael blinked and took a breath, taking both of her hands in his. "It's been said I have behaved very poorly toward you, and I could not agree more," he stated evenly, his eyes downcast. "Miss Olivia," he said very formally, "I would like very much to have your permission to court you, if you would allow me to do so," he stated with a slight bow.

Olivia wondered if he was still teasing, but found herself giving him a curtsy before replying, "I believe ... I would like that very much, sir." Even if Edward had caused a great deal of trouble, the man had at least made Michael aware of his shortcomings with respect to how he treated her.

Michael let go of her hands and reached into his topcoat, pulling out a slim package. Lifting one side of it, a multi-jeweled necklace appeared, held in place around a shaped velvet circle. Several round rubies were interspersed with square emeralds and round sapphires along a delicate gold chain.

"Oh, Michael, it is exquisite!" Olivia breathed as she gingerly reached out to touch one of the jewels, her gloved fingertip barely making contact. Despite the dim lamp light in the hallway, the facets caught the light and shimmered with rich color.

"I would be honored if you would wear it this evening," Michael said quietly, "Although your beauty far exceeds anything I could buy for you," he murmured, kissing her forehead.

Olivia felt the color rise in her face. "Of course, I will wear it," she gushed, carefully removing the necklace from its package. Sarah was suddenly there, undoing the clasp and wrapping it around her neck as if she'd done it a dozen times before. She took the empty package from Michael's hands, and then she was gone.

Michael sighed and then nodded. "I have something else, but ... well, we should be going," he said suddenly, his manner once again all business. He turned and held out his arm for her. "We'll be announced when we arrive, of course, and, I know I should have said something sooner, but ... I confirmed today that my mother will be there," he stammered, his cocked eyebrow indicating he was giving her a warning.

"I know," Olivia replied with a nod. "I must admit, I thought she would pay us a visit before now," she added as she took his arm and walked with him down the hall and to the top of the steps.

Michael remembered her mentioning Lady Cunningham's eminent arrival, but couldn't remember how Olivia had found out his mother would attend the ball. "Who told you she would be there?" he asked. He'd only found out the day before when he received his mother's note announcing her arrival.

"The seamstresses at the modiste where I bought my ball gown. The modiste where Anna works," she added with a lifted brow. "They mentioned Lady Cunningham was due for a fitting when she returned to town," Olivia explained, her expression giving no indication that she was scared nearly to death to meet the woman.

As they descended the stairs, Michael considered her

words and thought about Edward and Anna. If the man had taken his advice, Anna Holdwalter no longer worked for Madame Suzanne. She was probably a customer by now.

He regarded his wife for a long moment. "Whatever she says, Olivia, please know that you have married me, and that I ... I love you, and I will do whatever it takes to see you are treated by my family as if you are a peer of the realm."

Olivia smiled slowly as she glided across the marble floor to the vestibule, aware of Jeffers's look of approval and of Sarah watching them from above. "From what you've said, I think you are more frightened of her than I am," she whispered, her brow arching up.

"That's because I am," Michael replied lightly, the twinkle in his eye a sign of his teasing. He smiled and nodded in Jeffers's direction. The butler came forward with his hat and a great coat, and after donning both, Michael led Olivia down the front steps.

With the help of a footman and Michael, Olivia climbed into the open carriage. Right behind her, Michael wrapped an arm around her shoulders and seated her next to him rather than in the seat across from him.

"Are you sure you are warm enough?" he asked, realizing he hadn't given her a chance to stop for a shawl or mantle.

"Oh, yes, Michael, the night is perfect," she replied with a smile, her fingers moving to touch the jewels at her neck.

"Your gown is beautiful," Michael commented. "Who was your modiste?" he asked as the carriage pulled away from the curb and headed toward Mayfair.

"Madame Suzanne," Olivia replied. "It was to have been a wedding gown for someone who apparently had second thoughts about her groom-to-be," she said lightly, thinking she might have chosen such a gown for her own wedding had she been given the opportunity.

Michael snorted. "Indeed?" he answered, thinking the fit of the gown, the color and the style seemed to suit Olivia as if it had been custom made for her. "I am familiar with that modiste. My mother bought her last traveling ensemble there," he said, a frown coming to his face. "I expect Madame Suzanne knows to send the bill to me?" he half-questioned, thinking the gown to be quite expensive.

Shaking her head, Olivia replied, "Oh, no. I paid for it with some of the pin money you gave me last Sunday."

Michael regarded his wife for a moment, a look of surprise on his face. "You did not have to do that," he said, his brows furrowing to the point that Olivia thought he might be angry.

A look of chagrin on her face, Olivia sighed. "I thought ... I thought that's what pin money was for—to buy gowns and frippery and such," she countered quietly.

Laughing out loud, Michael settled back in the squabs, pulling Olivia closer to him. "And here I thought you would spend your pin money on *books*." He sighed and turned to place a kiss on her temple. "You aren't going to cost me a lot, are you?" he teased, his free hand moving to take one of hers.

Olivia gasped as she considered the implication of his comment. "Did my father imply that I would?" she asked, her ire suddenly up. She wasn't about to admit that she *had* used some of her pin money to buy a book.

Michael regarded her for a moment. "Not at all," he replied, the hand around her shoulder gently rubbing the top of her bare arm. "But that doesn't mean I can't spend what I want on you," he added before he took a deep breath and then sighed rather loudly. "It came to my attention that I never asked you for your hand in marriage," he finally said, his manner most serious.

"Oh?" Olivia replied, swallowing hard. "You must have spoken of it with my father ..."

"I did, in fact," he replied before he reached into his topcoat and pulled out a ring, holding it up so she could see it in the light from the gas lamps they passed. "Here is the reason I missed dinner the night before last," he murmured. "I waited for the jeweler to finish it."

"Michael!" she breathed as she caught site of the sapphire and diamond ring. The stones were mounted on a gold band with the large, round cut sapphire surrounded by a ring of tiny white diamonds. The stones flashed and the gold glimmered with each passing street lamp.

"You're not still wearing that piece of iron, I hope?" Michael said with a hint of disgust, reaching over to slide the ring onto her gloved finger. Over the satin fabric of her glove, the fit was rather snug, but Olivia considered she would be less likely to lose it during the ball. And she would be able to examine it more thoroughly under the candlelight in the ballroom at the Harvey's.

"I most certainly am," she retorted. "I've grown rather fond of it," she added defensively, "Even if it does make my finger turn a bit green."

Michael grinned and continued to hold her hand. "And this one?" he asked, fingering the sapphire with a thumb.

"I am already rather more fond of this one," she admitted, ducking her head a bit in feigned embarrassment. "I shall wear it always," she promised, angling her head so that she could kiss the corner of his mouth. He turned a bit and caught her lips in his, returning her kiss with a deeper one that left her both breathless and aroused.

"Will you be my wife?" Michael asked, his lips moving to her jawline and then down to her neck to briefly take purchase and kiss her. "Please?" he murmured, the word not sounding a bit like a plea.

Olivia sighed and smiled. "So, I suppose that means my attempts to *be* your wife this past week have failed?" she asked, not exactly sure what he implied by the question. *Was this his proposal?*

Sitting up, Michael regarded her with mischievous eyes. "You have failed at nothing. I am the one who must start from the beginning," he replied with a sigh. The carriage suddenly stopped and a liveried footman was opening the door.

Other carriages lined the street in front of the palatial home of the Harvey's, their occupants spilling out onto the lawn. Michael stepped out and turned to assist Olivia, opting to lift her in his arms and carry her out of the carriage and towards the house until they were well onto stone flags leading up to the front door. Olivia squealed with feigned embarrassment when he finally deposited her on solid ground. They were both aware of the stares of nearby guests who were making their way to the large front doors along with them, their silk-covered shoes dampened by the wet grass and mud.

As they climbed the front steps and walked into the huge vestibule, Olivia felt a growing sense of unease. When would she meet Lady Cunningham? And would her mother-in-law deign to welcome her to the family? Or shun her son for having chosen a wife without a title? "Where is the reception line?" she whispered to Michael as he removed his hat and coat.

"There isn't one, which is one of the reasons I prefer this ball over so many others," he replied as he leaned over, his lips touching the edge of her ear as he spoke.

Olivia shivered at the feel of his warm breath on her neck and the feel of his lips on her ear. "Oh," she replied, nearly breathless. "But you will introduce me to our hosts, I hope," she countered.

"I promise I will if we should cross their path," he replied, a smirk on his face. Michael left his top hat and greatcoat with a footman and led Olivia up a wide set of stairs to a landing and another set of stairs. When they reached the middle of the top step, Michael suddenly turned, reached to cup Olivia's face with his free hand, and kissed her. It was a quick kiss, but Olivia colored up, embarrassed that he would do such a thing in the midst of such a public gathering. Her gasp was matched by those who saw Michael's impropriety, but he was grinning when she looked up at him and relaxed a bit.

He turned his attention to a liveried man wearing a white powdered periwig. The man leaned over and listened to Michael. The herald nodded and stepped back, announcing in a loud but clear voice, "The Honorable Michael

Cunningham and The Honorable Mrs. Michael Cunningham."

Olivia inhaled sharply, her gaze directed down onto a huge room full of people who suddenly seemed to turn in unison and look directly at *her*. She was slightly aware of a collective gasp and glanced over at a still grinning Michael. His gaze was on her, but he nodded his head and indicated they needed to descend the steps leading to the ballroom floor. Returning his nod and a self-conscious grin, Olivia allowed him to lead her down the stairs, one quivering hand firmly tucked in the crook of his elbow while her other held her skirts. When they reached the bottom, Olivia took a deep breath of relief. Within seconds, several people were surrounding them, at once eyeing her as they congratulated Michael on his having married.

"You dog, you," a rather tall, older gentleman was saying as he elbowed Michael. Olivia was glad to be on his bruised side, thinking the man would have caused her husband a great deal of pain if he hit Michael's ribs.

And then she recognized the man.

"Ah, Grandby, so good to see you!" Michael said as he slugged the man on the shoulder. "Olivia, this is Milton Grandby, one of my sparring partners," Michael said in introduction.

Olivia curtsied as she gave the man a smile and then leaned in to kiss him on the cheek. "It's an honor to see you again, my lord," she said, a bit surprised that her husband would introduce the Earl of Torrington so casually, even if the man was her godfather.

The earl's face seemed to redden a bit after Olivia's kiss, but no more so than Michael's. Grandby reached out and captured Olivia's gloved hand and kissed the back of it, his eyebrow rising as he took in the sight of the sapphire ring. "You may call me Grandby, milady," he said in a rich baritone, "But if you were not married, I would simply request that you call on me."

Stunned by the overt suggestion, Olivia suppressed the

urge to gasp and look horrified. Or giggle. "As one of your many *goddaughters*, I expect I shall do so as a courtesy," she countered lightly.

The comment had the desired affect on Michael as one of his eyebrow's cocked in understanding. *Grandby was her godfather?* Perhaps Grandby hadn't recognized her. Michael was quick in his response, though. "Watch it, Grandby, or I'll punch you really hard next time we're in the ring," he warned, his arm moving to capture Olivia around the waist and pull her a bit closer to him. Olivia couldn't see the expression on Michael's face, but the tone of his voice was light with amusement.

The Earl of Torrington rolled his eyes. "*Faith!* Olivia Waterford?" he confirmed as he held his hands out toward her shoulders. "The last time I saw you, you were ..." He held the palm of one hand out in front of him. "... Much *shorter*," he claimed, using his other hand to make a fist. "I'll be damned," he said happily, turning his attention back to Michael.

As the earl moved to plant his fist squarely on the side of Michael's shoulder, Olivia sucked in a breath and lifted a gloved hand to intersect the earl's teasing punch. "I beg of you, my lord, save your punches for Gentleman Jackson's," she pleaded lightly, knowing the earl didn't mean to do anything more than lightly punch Michael. She wasn't about to have her husband more bruised than he already was, though.

Grandby's eyes widened as he quickly pulled back his punch. "And she has quick reflexes, too!" he commented, his smile broadening as if he was proud of his goddaughter.

Stunned by his wife's move to prevent him from being punched, Michael captured Olivia's hand and redirected it to his lips, where he bestowed it with a kiss. "And very protective, too," he murmured, an appreciative gaze directed at Olivia.

The earl watched the interplay between Michael and Olivia, saw how her face blushed as Michael regarded her and then redirected his gaze back to the ring on her hand. The viscount's son had done well with his choice of wife. "Know any rich widows I could prey upon this evening?" he asked, his eyes doing a quick sweep of the room. "I rather like this ball as it gives me the opportunity to find someone with whom I can attend all the rest of the events of the Season."

This last remark was directed at Olivia, who still felt the color rising in her cheeks. But having overcome her initial embarrassment at defending her husband, she decided she could suggest one woman she knew was available. "I understand Lady Worthington has called off her wedding," she commented with an arched eyebrow.

This was obviously news to the earl, and to Michael, too, as he turned his head to regard his wife. "Indeed?" Grandby replied quite happily. He glanced at Michael. "What happened?"

Michael shook his head. "This is the first I've heard that Weston is off the hook," he replied, his eyebrow rising to match the earl's. "Olivia?"

The color still high in her cheeks, Olivia bit her lower lip. "I do not wish to gossip ..."

"I *order* you to," Grandby said as he moved closer, his manner suggesting he would do something untoward if she did not tell what she knew.

Olivia dared another quick glance at Michael before turning her attention back to her godfather. "She discovered her fiancé's extreme gambling debts and did not wish for her fortune to be lost in a gaming hell," Olivia stated quickly, deciding she didn't want to find out what the earl had in mind for her if she didn't tell. When she looked back up to find Michael frowning, she added with an apologetic tone, "I am wearing what would have been Lady Worthington's wedding gown."

A look of realization passed over his face, and he sighed. "No wonder you could buy it with your pin money," he whispered, the corner of his mouth rising.

"I'm off then," the earl announced suddenly. "I saw the lady just a moment ago near the lemonade. With luck, I'll be her escort for the rest of this evening. Oh, and congratulations on winning the bet. I owe you some money," he added as he pointed to Michael.

And then he hurried away, leaving the Cunninghams near the bottom of the stairs but with several people ready to take the earl's place. "Congratulations, Cunningham," another gentleman said as he shook Michael's hand. "You won the marriage bet, I see," Baron Whitehall commented as he passed by, his voice suggesting supreme disappointment. "My payment will be at White's in the morning," he added before he disappeared into the crowd.

Olivia gave a curious look in Michael's direction, but he was already shaking hands with another acquaintance. "Sir William, so good to see you," Michael said with a slight bow. "My wife, Olivia," he said with a nod in her direction.

The younger man cocked an eyebrow and regarded Olivia with a half-smile. "Positively delicious, Cunningham. Where *have* you been keeping her?" he asked as he finally returned his attention back to Michael.

Michael bristled at the rake's behavior and his comment. "My wife lived not far from my home, so I have known her a very long time," he answered as civilly as possible.

Sir William seemed surprised by the news, as did Olivia. "Oh," he replied, one eyebrow cocking in a suggestive manner. "Congratulations to you both, then. I'll leave your winnings at White's after tomorrow's supper," he added before moving away and allowing another well-wisher to approach.

Olivia kept a smile on her face but wanted desperately to get Michael alone so she could ask him about his winnings.

As they made their way through the crowded ballroom, Olivia was well aware of eyes turned in their direction, of heads bent together with hands and open fans hiding whispering mouths, of men who nodded at Michael as if he had performed some sort of miracle and of other men who regarded him with derision. She was also aware of a light-headed feeling and a graying around the edge of her vision that portended a fainting spell. Wishing she could hide in the ladies' salon, Olivia tightened her grip on Michael's arm until he was forced to turn his attention to her.

"I do believe I shall have another rather deep bruise on my arm in the morning," Michael said as lightly as he could manage given his teeth were gritting from the increasing pain he felt.

Olivia gasped and released her hold on his arm. "Forgive me," she whispered, her cheeks bright red but her face otherwise too pale.

Michael's brows furrowed as he saw the evidence of her distress. "Are you feeling all right?" he asked, taking her hands in his as she swayed.

Before she could answer, he wrapped an arm around her shoulders, turned and led her through a set of French doors. Within moments, they were in the back garden terrace, Michael nearly carrying her as they made their escape from the ballroom.

The sudden wash of fresh air was a relief, and Olivia took a deep breath, her lungs filling and her vision clearing even as Michael set her on her feet. When she did not immediately return his gaze, Michael lifted her chin with a gloved forefinger. "What is it?" he asked, concern in his voice. "You looked as if you were about to faint!"

Refusing to meet his gaze, Olivia bit her lip. Anger threatened to make her lash out at him. *What kind of wager had he made at White's that could possibly involve me?* she wondered. He'd obviously won the bet. *And how much had he made as a result of winning the bet?*

He'd made a fool of her, she was sure. He had informed the Duchess of Somerset of their marriage even as she was making the final arrangements to be the woman's governess. He must have planned their quick wedding well before it happened. He had obviously known exactly when their nuptials would be long before he climbed into her bed—had probably even arranged it with her father. And he had been her sister's protector for... for nearly a year!

When Olivia finally looked up to meet his gaze, tears threatened, but she swallowed hard and fought to keep herself steady. "It's about the ...," she started to say before she caught the edge of her lower lip with a tooth and looked away. She could feel her face bloom with color, as much from embarrassment as from the extreme heat in the ballroom.

Michael contemplated what to say before he saw her hesitation. The way the edge of her lower lip was caught, as if she was trying to bite back what she was about to say—he'd seen that many times in the past. The familiar gesture made a smile almost come to his face. "Please say it, Olivia," he urged gently, despite not being sure he really wanted to hear what she had to say.

From the comments in the ballroom, he realized she now knew there was a bet involving their wedding. *She must really despise me,* he reckoned as he once again wished he had never agreed to such a wager.

Olivia slowly brought her eyes back to his. "Is this to be a marriage of convenience?" she whispered, a tinge of sadness creeping into her voice.

His breath catching at the question, Michael clamped his lips into a straight line and pondered how to answer. "Some will claim that, I suppose," he began uncertainly, his eyes darting around them to be sure they weren't being overheard before returning their attention to her. "But not me. I admit that, yes, many years ago, I did accept a bet involving *when* I would marry," he continued, squaring his shoulders. "But that ..."

"I despise you," Olivia said in a quiet, clipped tone. "My answer to your marriage proposal is 'no'," she added, remembering she had never given him a response in the carriage.

Michael dropped his finger from her chin and gave a curt nod, her words causing his face to wince as if she'd hit him with an right uppercut to the jaw. "I know," he said quietly.

The wrinkle between Olivia's brow deepened, and he nearly reached out with a thumb to smooth it.

"I will speak with a solicitor tomorrow ..." Olivia started to say as she attempted to remove the ring from her gloved finger, becoming frustrated when it wouldn't budge.

"Whatever for?" Michael interrupted quickly, alarm in his voice.

Her lower lip trembling, Olivia fought back tears. "About an annulment, of course," she said quietly, trying hard to avoid having to look at him. She would lose her resolve if she locked her gaze with his. Lose herself in his brown eyes and allow herself to be gathered into his arms and be kissed as if he owned her, body and soul.

"But, you cannot," Michael countered, his voice taking on a note of desperation.

"I must," Olivia replied. "You will be quite relieved to be rid of me, I am sure ..."

"I will not!"

"It should be quite a simple matter. Especially since we've not consummated our marriage," Olivia went on, ignoring his protests.

"Not yet, but I plan to later this evening ..."

"And if I send a dispatch to the Duchess of Somerset at first light, I yet may be able to secure the position of governess." She tried again to remove the ring, nearly stamping her foot when the ring conspired to stay right where it was.

"But, that's not possible," Michael interrupted, shaking his head firmly.

"And why ever not?" Olivia countered, indignation clearly defined in the set of her jaw.

"Because I made it quite clear to my sister that she wasn't to hire you," he fired back, finding it difficult to keep the volume of his voice as low as possible.

Olivia's head snapped up to regard Michael, her mouth open in astonishment.

Sister?

"She won't go against my wishes, especially now that she finally has a sister. She has been dying to meet you ... as my *wife* .., and I shall not deny her the privilege," Michael vowed with a shake of his head, his stance softening just a bit.

Her breaths shallow and her vision graying, Olivia turned around and began walking, rather unsteadily, away from him.

"Olivia," Michael pleaded, following her retreating figure to the edge of the garden terrace flagstones. He stood directly behind her, so close he could hear her ragged breaths. "Please believe me when I tell you that I always intended to marry you," he whispered hoarsely.

Tears gathering in the corners of her eyes, Olivia stood erect and took a deep breath, desperate to get air into her lungs before the sobs could start. "And the wager?" she asked quietly.

Michael rested a hand on her arm and slid it down until his hand closed around hers, covering the ring. "I forgot about the bet until after we were to be wed," he said, his head leaning over her shoulder, his lips suddenly very close to her neck. Olivia felt his warm breath wash over her skin, and she inhaled quickly.

"Why ever did you make such a bet in the first place?" she asked, a bit of anger still in her voice. "You've made a fool of me!"

"I did not," he replied quickly, "And you're not. I have made sure everyone at White's—and I'll make sure everyone here tonight—*knows* that you were my intended all along." His lips took purchase on her neck while one hand moved to rest on her other shoulder, its warmth seeping into her suddenly chilled skin. Olivia closed her eyes and allowed him the kiss, but tried hard not to simply give up and lean against his hard body for support.

"Sir Richard started that damned bet many years ago, and ... I believe it took on a life of its own as my twenty-eighth birthday approached. I wasn't obviously courting anyone, so I am sure it looked like easy money to anyone reading the betting book at White's."

Leaning her head to one side, Olivia gave him a sideways glance. "If you knew you were going to ask for my hand, why didn't you just ... why didn't you just *ask* me? Why did you wait so long?" she whispered in wonder, a tear finally trailing down her cheek.

Michael gently turned her around, wrapping his arms loosely about her waist and pulling her so that she was nearly pressed against him. "I was trying to make my fortune in the world. Unlike other sons of aristocrats, I cannot count on an inheritance. My older brother has a penchant for gambling. And losing. And ... I ... I lost track of time," he explained as he took a deep breath. At her raised eyebrow, he continued, his head shaking from side to side. "I lost track of how old I was. And a few weeks ago, I was in Wiltshire visiting my sister. She thought I was there to announce my impending nuptials, and I thought I was there just to visit, and the next thing I knew..." His voice trailed off as he continued to shake his head from side to side. "I couldn't simply ask for your hand."

"Why ever not?" Olivia demanded, another tear escaping her eye.

Michael reached up to brush away the droplet with his thumb. "I had an obligation to your sister—to make arrangements for her to be settled," he said in his defense. He rolled his eyes as he made the statement, very aware of Olivia's wince at the mention of her sister. "The reading of the banns would have required three weeks. You would have wanted a real wedding. A few months to plan it..."

"No," Olivia replied with a quick shake of her head. "A vicar would have been fine," she countered quickly. "It ... it *was* fine," she amended as she took a quick breath to stave off a sob.

Taken aback, Michael sighed heavily. "I honestly thought my only option was ... was to ruin you," he murmured. At Olivia's expression of shock, he added, "Actually, it was Elizabeth's idea."

Olivia closed her mouth and swallowed, incredulous.

"The Duchess of Somerset suggested you *ruin* me?" she whispered in disbelief. "A *duchess* actually suggested such a course of action?" the rhetorical question coming out with a good deal of doubt.

"Yes," Michael affirmed with a quick nod. "Well, she was suggesting it as my *sister* first, I suppose. Not as a duchess," he added, a bit uncertain as to Elizabeth's motivation. His sister wanted a governess, but she obviously wanted a sister more. "Those children for whom you would have been a governess are now your nieces and nephews," he added suddenly.

Olivia blinked. "I'm an aunt," she whispered, her voice soft.

"And, trust me, as boisterous as they are, you're much better off as their aunt," Michael continued, grinning suddenly. He sobered quickly, though. "Truly, I didn't want to ruin you ..."

"Well, it worked," Olivia acknowledged with a short nod, her response not giving away whether she was impressed with the plan or not, nor if her opinion of the Duchess of Somerset had changed now that she knew it was the duchess who had recommended Michael's course of action.

"But not *well*," Michael quickly replied as he placed his hands on either side of her face. "If I had it all to do over again, Olivia, please know that I would have courted you properly, and then I would have asked for your hand, and then I would have given you a proper ring and had a proper room readied for you that would have been far more beautiful than the purple room that Edward showed you." He paused as he noticed her surprised expression at the mention of the salon. "It is truly your bedchamber, you know," he said, leaning over to kiss her hair.

Sniffling, Olivia sighed. "Not Anna's?" she replied, a wrinkle appearing between her eyebrows.

Michael moved his thumb over the wrinkle and smoothed it. "I had it decorated for you before we were wed, and then," he rolled his eyes and kept his face bent up before continuing, "In my hurry to see Sir Richard, I forgot that Jeffers cannot always see colors quite right, and he took you to my mother's bedchamber instead of to the room I had decorated for you."

Her smile broadening, Olivia regarded him for several seconds before she reached up a hand to cup his jaw. "'Tis a beautiful room," she whispered. "Like a room for a ..."

"A room for a queen," Michael matched her comment, kissing her forehead and then tipping her chin up so that he could capture her lips in a kiss. He pulled away after a moment and regarded her in the moonlight.

"What else would you have done, Michael?" she asked, reaching up with a gloved finger to wipe away another tear.

Michael lowered his head so that his forehead rested against hers. "I would have taken you to the bed in your purple room and made mad, passionate love to you for our entire wedding night," he intoned, his eyes closing as he said the words.

Olivia's eyelashes fluttered against his cheekbones. "You can still do that, at least," she whispered, her face coloring up as she realized what she was suggesting.

A grin split Michael's face and he pulled her all the way against his body. "Yes, I can still do that," he agreed happily.

The sound of a throat being cleared startled them. They released their hold on one another and turned in unison to stare at their interloper.

"Sir Richard!" Michael said in surprise.

An impeccably dressed man not much older than Michael stood resting his hands on the top of a rather ornate cane. "I'm here to make the acquaintance of the woman who helped you win your bet, damn you," Sir Richard said with a teasing grin. "And here I find you in what could be considered a scandalous liaison in the Harvey's garden. This *is* your wife, I hope?"

Michael winced at the words, but Olivia was smiling, obviously recognizing the man. At the moment, Sir Richard looked like the devil incarnate, with his black hair, sinister eyebrows and a grin that was closer to a sneer than a smile. "Olivia, I'd like you to meet my *other* business partner, Sir Richard Waggoner," Michael said as the older man gave a leg and Olivia curtsied.

"I am very pleased to see you again, Sir Richard," Olivia said as she held out her hand, hoping she sounded sincere even though she found herself feeling a bit annoyed at the interruption. And she was very tempted to take that very same hand and slap the man very hard across one of his perfect cheeks. If she wasn't married to the son of a viscount ... and if she hadn't recognized Richard Waggoner to be one of her father's friends ... she wouldn't have bit back the rest of what she was about to say.

Sir Richard brushed his lips over the back of her gloved hand and regarded her for a moment before returning his attention to Michael. "Waterford finally let you have his daughter, then?" he said with a bit of amusement.

Stunned by the comment, Michael took a quick look at Olivia before returning his attention to his friend. "He practically promised her to me years ago," Michael said in his own defense. "And what makes you think Waterford let me have her?"

Sir Richard was grinning. "Harold and I play faro at the club when he's in town. He's quite fond of you. Always wanted you as a son," he said, even though his attention was on Olivia as he said the words.

Olivia dared a glance in Michael's direction, wondering if Sir Richard's information was news to her husband. The surprise in his reaction seemed to indicate it was, indeed, news.

"Really?" Michael replied, his eyebrows cocking. "He never mentioned it to me," he lied, his head shaking back and forth a bit. *At least, he did not say it in so many words*, he reconsidered.

His friend pulled an envelope from inside his waistcoat. "I believe this will make us even," Sir Richard said as he started to hand the envelope to Michael. "Best hundred pounds I've spent this year," he commented, turning to hold the envelope in front of Olivia. "Take it darling. You've earned it, waiting all this time for this fool to make his move."

Grinning shyly, Olivia took the envelope and thanked Sir Richard. "May I use it to buy his wedding gift?" she asked, her voice low so that Michael couldn't quite hear her query.

"Absolutely not," Sir Richard replied with a snort. "You must use it for the most useless piece of frippery you can find, I should think." He made a quarter turn and seemed to listen for a moment. "Or you might use it for his birthday gift. He turns eight-and-twenty tomorrow, you probably know by now." He seemed to pause again as if he was listening. "I must leave you two lovebirds. I have promised the next set to someone quite gorgeous." He gave a nod and Michael and Olivia returned the gesture.

Her head suddenly swimming again, Olivia stepped back a bit to keep her balance and the sense of falling consumed her for a very long second before she was suddenly pressed against the front of Michael, his arms pulling her forward and capturing her in his embrace.

"Are you feeling faint *again*?" he asked as he slid his hand down the back of the bodice of her dress.

Olivia felt his warm hand pressed hard against her skin, his fingers dancing a bit beneath the upper edge of the back of her dress. Just as she felt a sharp tug—the tie of her corset was suddenly undone and the laces loosened—she was able to take a deep breath. 'What a relief," she breathed, continuing to rest her head against Michael's chest as she inhaled fresh air and the scent of him. "I won't ask how you learned that trick," she murmured as she handed him the envelope. "I believe this is yours," she said with a cocked eyebrow.

Michael regarded the envelope before returning his attention to Olivia, his face taking on a look of disbelief. "Oh, so now I am the most useless piece of frippery you can find?" he teased as he snatched the envelope from her gloved hand and shoved it into a coat pocket.

Olivia considered how to reply before she gave him a brilliant smile. "Happy birthday," she whispered, standing up on tip toes to give him a kiss on the corner of his mouth.

He did not immediately acknowledge her kiss as his hand remained down her back for a few moments, his other hand joining it as he apparently refastened the corset strings before he finally, very slowly, slid his hands back up to the nape of her neck. His lips captured hers in quick but thorough kiss— a kiss from which Olivia was sure she would have fainted dead away had he not loosened her stays. "We need to rejoin the other guests," he whispered softly, pressing his lips to her forehead.

"Of course," Olivia replied, stepping away from him and taking his arm and another deep breath.

They made their way back to the ballroom, biding their time as they strolled along the garden terrace until they were through the double-wide doors. They moved through the growing throng of guests and towards the table of champagne.

Lady Harvey would be quite proud of the crush her ball had become. Several couples approached, offering congratulations and doing their best not to seem overly curious about Olivia. She felt relief when they finally reached the table laden with glasses of champagne. She took the glass that Michael offered and they touched rims before taking a sip.

"Is this your second ball?" Michael guessed as he leaned toward her, using the guise of the room's increased noise level as an excuse to put his nose near her ear.

Olivia demurred and rolled her eyes. "I have been to every district ball since I was sixteen and every assembly since I was born," she replied, leaning up to answer so that her lips were near his jaw. Michael took the opportunity to kiss her again, making Olivia blush. "You are shameless!" she whispered loudly, shocked he would do such a thing with so many people nearby.

"He always has been, m'dear," a woman commented as she seemed to appear from nowhere. About forty or so, she wore a stunning gown in gold satin and gold velvet, cut to fit her perfectly. Her hair was swept up in a flawless chignon that sported a gold ostrich feather held in place with a gold comb. Long, gold earbobs dangled on either side, matching the gold of the many chains that hung about her neck, several bedecked with emeralds.

Her most stunning accessory, though, was the man on whose arm she arrived. He was the spitting image of Michael, although his hair was nearly white and he sported a much straighter nose. Olivia smiled at the couple and wondered why the woman would say such a thing when, at the same time, she felt Michael's arm tense under her grasp.

"Mother. *Father?*" Michael stated as he bowed his head, obviously surprised by their sudden appearance.

"Lord and Lady Cunningham, I would like you to meet my wife, Olivia," he said formally just after taking his mother's gloved hand and kissing the back of it.

He moved to shake his father's hand, but the older man smiled and pulled his son into a hug. "Congratulations, son," Mark Cunningham said, his face beaming. "I see Waterford finally let you have his daughter," he whispered before he reached over and took Olivia's hand, kissing the back of it and then raising an eyebrow at the sight of the ring. "I see my son inherited my taste for beautiful women," he commented, his glance going from Olivia to his wife. Violet Cunningham blushed like a schoolgirl, her fan suddenly open and beating the air about her face.

Olivia immediately curtsied and allowed her in-laws to regard her, then felt her face flush as their gazes lingered a bit too long. Lady Cunningham bent her head to one side. "My dear, I have been waiting for this day for far too long. I am so very pleased to meet you," she said to Olivia before returning her attention to her son. "Yesterday, I was informed that I had borne a *magnificent man*," she announced, her face very serious as she made the statement, her fan still fluttering.

Michael blinked a couple of times as he regarded his mother and then stole a glance at his father. He simply shrugged. Then he turned to glance at his wife. *Magnificent?* he wondered. From where had his mother heard this?

Olivia cringed inwardly, remembering what she'd told Madame Suzanne and the seamstresses to say on her behalf when Lady Cunningham returned for her fitting.

The viscountess returned her attention to Olivia. "I must thank you for your kind words, especially since you hadn't yet met me."

"You are most welcome, my lady," Olivia said with a nod, still not certain of the woman's mood. *Or perhaps, she is teasing me,* she considered, although there wasn't a hint of humor about the woman.

Lady Cunningham sighed, not quite sure what to make of her daughter-in-law. "It is rather hard for me to believe an assessment of 'magnificent' can be bestowed upon someone you have not known very long," she commented, her head cocked in a manner suggesting she was challenging Olivia's opinion of Michael.

"Violet," Lord Cunningham spoke in a low tone, patting a hand over the one that was perched on his arm. "She knows her man," he whispered. From his manner, it was apparent he knew far more about his daughter-in-law than did his wife.

"Mother," Michael tried to interject, but Olivia squeezed his arm. Hard.

"Oh, I assure you I knew it when I first met him," Olivia responded brightly, leaning toward the older couple so that she could be heard over the din. "How long has it been, Michael? Five years since you rescued me from that rake?" she remarked as she turned her attention to Michael. At his affirming nod, she returned her attention to his parents. "And he has continued to prove himself worthy of that description since our wedding last week," she added, glancing up at Michael to find him staring at her with a mix of adoration and confusion.

Lady Cunningham blinked, obviously surprised by the news. "You waited five years for my son to ask for your hand?" she asked, the question sounding as if she thought

Olivia to be out of her right mind. "But what ... what if he hadn't come through with an offer? You could have been left on the shelf!"

"Violet ..." Lord Cunningham spoke quietly, the warning in his voice going unheard by the younger couple. His wife immediately covered her mouth with a gloved hand, a blush rising to redden her cheeks.

Olivia felt her own cheeks color again and wondered if she was being tested by the viscountess. "I believe the wait was necessary as I rather doubt my father would have allowed me to marry any sooner," she replied lightly, hoping the response didn't sound like the white lie it might be.

Her father had never said anything to her about when she could wed or when he expected her to get offers. And she'd spent the last year thinking she was nearly on the shelf. Arranging to be a governess was simply the means to make her own way in life and not be a burden to her parents.

How could she know Michael Cunningham had other plans?

Feeling a bit spiteful, she added, "But I assure you, had I been on the shelf, I would not have collected any dust. If I wasn't married to your son, I would be your daughter's governess." Michael's arm under her hand jerked a bit, making her wonder if he found her jibe amusing or an insult.

Dumbfounded by this bit of news, the viscountess stared at Olivia and then turned her attention onto her son and then to her husband, as if she needed confirmation. The viscount chuckled in reply, the expression and sound so much like Michael that Olivia could barely contain her amusement.

"'Tis true. I had to fight Elizabeth for her," Michael stated, a teasing gleam in his eye.

A smile finally graced Lady Cunningham's face. "And I'll bet ten pounds she left a few marks on you, you scoundrel!" She turned her attention back to Olivia. "I never actually gamble, but it's rather fun to pretend, don't you think?" she asked in a conspiratorial whisper, her lips curling up.

Olivia caught her own lower lip with a tooth and wondered at the sudden change in Lady Cunningham's mood. Formidable, yes, but she was also a woman of good humor. "My money was on the duchess," Olivia replied with a wink.

"As was mine," Lord Cunningham intoned, his teasing grin still firmly in place.

The smiling viscountess turned her attention on her son. "Oh, Michael, why didn't you *tell* me?" she scolded him, her manner suggesting she was just a bit peeved with him. She kept her voice low as to prevent nearby couples from overhearing her chastise her son.

Sighing, Michael shrugged. *Why not, indeed?* He could have staved off years of queries from his mother had he just made it known he had *someone* in mind to be his wife. Of course, that would have required he admit to himself that he felt affection for Olivia Waterford—something he'd only realized when Elizabeth made him aware of her own plans for Olivia. "I did not wish to raise your hopes when I wasn't sure the lady would accept my offer," he countered defensively.

Mark Cunningham pulled his wife a bit closer to him, a move that seemed to embarrass her just a bit. "You did well to keep your promise to your mother," the viscount commented lightly. "Your good news simply adds to ours. Instead of another trip to Italy, your mother will be joining me at the estate house in Horsham," he announced with a nod. "We plan to leave for the country house next week."

Michael's eyebrows shot up as he stared at his mother. "No more Continent?" he asked, shocked at the news. *What of Parliament?*

Violet Cunningham was blushing, her head shaking a bit. "Not for a few years at least," she agreed. "I am actually looking forward to spending more time in Horsham. I rather miss living on the river, and I think I like the country life much better than life in a filthy city."

When Michael returned his attention to his father, the man leaned in and said, "She keeps thinking I have taken a mistress. Every time she comes to the house in Horsham, she seems to arrive when I am merely hosting one or another of my cousins."

Michael's eyebrows shot up as he remembered telling his mother about Colette when he escorted her to the ball in Crawley. "As I recall, cousin Colette was the one that started it," he whispered.

"She and two of her sisters have since married and moved out, thank the gods. I was about to commit one or two of the seven deadly sins if they had not." His father sobered a bit, though. "We have news of your brother," he said with a sigh, casting a glance at Olivia as if he regretted including her in announcement. He wondered if she knew anything of the rake that was Michael's brother.

Michael stiffened, not sure what to expect his father to say. "Indeed?"

Mark nodded. "Seems Marcus realized he will not last long here in London. His gambling debts have finally caught up with him. He has this very day boarded a ship bound for America," Lord Cunningham stated, his manner suggesting he was in agreement with what his eldest son had done.

"Death threats can be very effective that way," Lady Cunningham whispered sadly, her comment overheard by only Olivia, who merely nodded her understanding.

"He has formally relinquished his duty as first son," Lord Cunningham continued. "Claims he wants nothing to do with managing the Cunningham lands. That means, of course, that you will inherit the viscountcy upon my death."

Michael stood very still as Olivia placed a hand over the one she already held in the crook of his arm, her head leaning against his shoulder for a moment as she considered the viscount's announcement. Michael took a deep breath and nodded, a bit surprised by his brother's move.

Marcus would not be bankrupting the viscountcy after all, he realized.

And that meant that with decent estate management and the investments he already had in place, Michael would no longer have to develop business deals to pay his way in the world.

"I shall endeavor to do as well as you have, Father," Michael stated with a solemn nod. "But I hardly expect I'll be having to inherit your duties for another thirty years or so," he added with a gleam in his eye.

Lord Cunningham grinned at his son's comment. "Do not get too comfortable in that terrace you call home," he said jovially. "I am considering travel. I plan to take your mother on the Grand Tour of the Continent and leave you in charge of everything."

Violet Cunningham gasped at her husband's comment, obviously the first she'd heard of any travel plans. She wondered what moved Mark Cunningham to send word that he wished her to return to England from this latest trip sooner than she planned. When she arrived at the house in Mayfair two days ago, Mark was there to greet her, treating her as if she was his long-lost love.

Perhaps she was spending too much time away from England, Violet realized.

Having never *not* been in love with her husband, Violet Cunningham agreed to his suggestion that she stay with him —whether he was in London for Parliament or Horsham for estate matters.

The conversations of the crowd around them suddenly quieted and the four turned to follow the gazes of the other guests. At the top of the stairs stood a very tall and regal Edward Seward and, on his arm, a lithe, tall, dark-haired woman. Although not showing any nervousness, she seemed to avoid the gaze of the crowd by simply staring over their heads, giving her an air of superiority. "Anna!" Olivia breathed, loudly enough for both Michael and the Cunninghams to hear.

"Well, I'll be damned," Michael whispered, his arm suddenly tensing under Olivia's. He barely noticed his curse and did not apologize for it. "He really did go through with it."

Olivia tore her gaze from the couple to give her husband a sideways glance, not for overhearing his curse but for what his statement implied. *Michael knew Edward would seek out his love after what had happened Monday evening.* Perhaps he, too, had encouraged Edward to follow his heart. *And I told Edward where he could find her,* she thought happily. "They will marry for love," she murmured, not intending for Michael to hear.

"If they haven't already." He seemed to stiffen suddenly, leaving Olivia to wonder if she had somehow offended him with the remark.

"She is a regal beauty," Lady Cunningham remarked as she closed her fan and held it against her cheek. "And very familiar. Is she the daughter of an earl perhaps?" she asked, directing her query to Michael.

"She is not a daughter of a peer of the realm," he replied quietly, "But as to who she is ..." He let the sentence trail off.

The announcer's voice called out over the quieting ballroom, "The Honorable Edward Seward and his wife, the Honorable Mrs. Edward Seward."

A collective gasp could be heard around the room. Murmurs of "Who is she?" and "When did *he* marry?" filtered to Olivia's ears. She glanced at Michael and then noticed his mother's attention on her.

"You seemed to recognize her, too," Lady Cunningham accused, an eyebrow arching in surprise. "From where do we know her?" she asked, pinning Olivia with a gaze emphasized by a bob of the gold ostrich feather arcing from the top of her head.

"Violet," Lord Cunningham's low voice said in a warning tone. Lady Cunningham glanced at her husband and nodded her head as if to acknowledge that her query was improper.

Taking a deep breath, Olivia considered how to describe what she knew of the woman who had so completely stolen Edward Seward's heart. "Anna was one of the seamstresses that helped to create your gown—and mine," Olivia replied quietly. "She works ... used to work at Madame Suzanne's modiste."

Staring in shock, Lady Cunningham gave no reply but turned her attention back to the couple, now descending the staircase as if they were part of England's royalty.

Olivia looked up at Michael and tilted her head in the direction of the staircase.

"Please forgive us," Michael said to his parents as he placed a hand over the one that Olivia had on his arm. "I really must speak with Edward," he said, and then he moved them in the direction of the staircase even before Olivia could curtsy to her in-laws.

"It was an honor to meet you. Can you come for dinner Sunday?" Olivia tried to say as she was swept along through the crush. The music had resumed and several couples were moving away from the staircase toward the dance floor.

The younger Cunninghams reached Edward and Anna as they took the last few steps. "Congratulations!" Olivia blurted to Anna before she could even acknowledge Edward. "You look divine!" Indeed, the seamstress looked the part of the wife of a spare heir. Her brunette hair was piled in loose curls on the top of her head with spiral tendrils on either side of her temples. Rubies adorned each ear and were spread in tiny beads on a gold chain across the base of her swan-like neck. Layers of pale pink chiffon floated beneath a fitted bodice of pink satin. Long white gloves could not hide her slender fingers nor their nervousness as Anna gripped Edward's arm.

At the sight of Olivia, Anna's eyes widened. "Mrs. Cunningham!" she said, moving to take Olivia's hand with her free one.

Michael's brow quirked as he regarded Edward, and the new groom caught the look. "Did you take my advice?" Michael wondered as the women exchanged their greetings.

"I took Olivia's as to the wedding and yours as to where to spend the past few days," Edward replied, his head bobbing. "I love her, and I could care less what my family thinks," he added, *sotto voce*. Stepping back a bit, he said in a louder voice, "Anna, I wish to present my very best friend, Michael Cunningham and his new wife, Olivia."

Michael gave a leg to Anna's curtsy. "Very pleased to finally meet you. I hope you found the accommodations suitable at the Clarendon Hotel?" he asked, directing his question to Edward.

The taller man smiled before replying, "Most accommodating. And very discreet. Anna and I exchanged vows Tuesday morning before a bishop, and this is the first the denizens of London know of our union."

Anna's face displayed a blush at her husband's account of their quick marriage. "I fear Madame Suzanne would be most displeased with me leaving her employ except that Edward ordered an entire wardrobe for me as he was taking me away from the modiste," she explained, mostly to Olivia. "I did not have the heart to tell him I already have beautiful gowns I made in the hopes that he would one day come for me."

Olivia felt tears prick the edges of her eyes when she heard Anna's words. "I am so very glad he found you," she whispered to Anna.

The young woman's eyes widened at Olivia's comment. "I have *you* to thank for that," she whispered back. "I do hope you have forgiven Edward his ... impropriety," she added, leaning in so that her whisper could only be heard by Olivia. "The naughty boy told me what he did."

Smiling demurely, Olivia nodded. "Of course. He was only trying to help."

Anna leaned over so that her lips were very near to Olivia's ear. "But it was entirely unnecessary! Mr. Cunningham made it very clear to my husband that he loves you dearly—that he always has, and that he had no intention of keeping a mistress—so Edward's trick was very cruel to you," Anna confided, her eyes taking on a worried look as she pulled away from Olivia. "I was quite incensed with him when he told me what he'd done."

Olivia regarded Anna with a bit of surprise and wonder. *So, Michael admitted his love for me to his best friend? Then, surely he must love me.* "Do forgive him," Olivia whispered, her lips quivering as she returned her attention to what Michael was saying.

"Have you decided where you'll live?" Michael queried Edward, deciding he really didn't want to know what the women were discussing.

The issue of where these newlyweds would live hadn't come up Tuesday morning when Edward left to find his Anna. Edward had seemed so nervous about the prospect of marrying his beloved seamstress, Michael did not wish to burden the man with thoughts beyond getting married.

His father's pronouncement about taking over the duties of the viscountcy meant Michael and Olivia would probably be moving to Horsham very soon.

Olivia exchanged glances with Anna and Edward before looking up at Michael. "Why not at the townhouse?" she asked, afraid that perhaps Michael had declared they could not share the home. "I would so like them to live with us. I would have another woman with whom to learn how to be the wife of an aristocrat!" She turned her gaze back to the beautiful seamstress, hoping to find her of a similar opinion.

"The arrangement is agreeable with me, of course," Michael countered with a shrug, "But I believe it is up to Edward and Anna as to where they wish to live."

Edward pulled his bride closer to his side. "All in good time, my friends. It will be at least a few months before Anna and I settle down," he said with a cocked eyebrow. "I'm taking her with me to Italy and Greece for a very long honeymoon."

Michael and Olivia exchanged quick glances, mischief apparent in both sets of eyes. "Then we shall have to make the most of the terrace while you are away," Michael replied with a cocked eyebrow. "And when you are back, we'll simply move to Horsham."

. . .

L *ater that evening ...*

Olivia hurried into the purple room, removing her gloves even before she'd closed the door behind her. Although she considered ringing for Sarah to help her out of her dress, petticoats, and corset, she resisted in the hopes that Michael would arrive before she was completely undressed.

Tease him, her sister had said.

Olivia took a deep breath and slowed her movements, remembering her ball gown would be Eloisa's wedding dress.

She carefully pulled it over her head and draped it on the only chair. Peeling off her petticoats, she suddenly felt liberated. She hoped Michael would arrive in the next moment or so. Her heart beating hard, she loosened the ties of the corset. Before long, she had wriggled out of it and was left in her chemise, stockings and slippers.

Standing in front of the cheval mirror, she pulled off the chemise and regarded her nearly naked body. Her suddenly swollen breasts felt heavy, their tips hardening in anticipation. The stockings were tied with garters near the tops of her thighs, and she wondered if she should remove them completely. Instead, she pulled the rose buds from her hair along with the pins that held the braids and chignon in place. Her hair cascaded down past her shoulders as she shook it out, its red highlights catching the candlelight along with the jewels of the necklace. Putting one foot up on the bench at the end of the bed, she bent over a bit to untie a garter. The sound of a sharply inhaled breath reached her, and she froze.

"Please, do not scream," Michael spoke quietly from where he stood leaning against the panel door, his hands behind his back. The latch and lock clicked into place as Olivia turned her head slowly to regard him. Michael had removed his topcoat and waistcoat, and his cravat was hanging off one shoulder, apparently forgotten when he'd quietly entered the salon.

She straightened, but left her foot resting on the bench, her knee bent enough so that her leg hid the dark space between the top of her thighs. Her hands moved to rest on her hips, and she could almost hear Michael as he suddenly swallowed—hard.

"You'll have to kiss me, then," she ordered, her head cocking to one side as she watched his eyes travel the length of her body and back up to her face.

Michael stood frozen in place, the sight of his nearly naked wife an erotic surprise that both delighted and frightened him. As he stared, she slowly lowered her foot to the floor and turned to face him. *She is allowing me to see her nude,* he thought suddenly, *just as I dreamed she would.* Her upturned breasts, topped with their hardened nipples, were framed with waves of her mahogany hair until she slowly pushed it away from one side and over her shoulder. His gaze followed the curve of her hip and thigh, the sweep of her long legs still sheathed in their translucent stockings, up to the darker area between the tops of her thighs where his hand had been the night before, along the line of her arm as her hand rested on her hip.

"I should warn you that I have intentions to do far more than kiss you," Michael murmured and moved quickly to embrace her, one arm pulling her against him and the other cupping the side of her face. His lips captured hers, and he kissed her, more gently than his quick moves would suggest.

The kiss deepened, and Olivia's body seemed to melt and mold to fit against the front of his as she returned the kiss. Soon, though, he allowed her to take a breath as he moved his lips to her jawline, to her neck, to the lobes of her ears, where he suckled for a moment, sending shivers through her body. He was only slightly aware of her fingers undoing the buttons of his shirt, the fastenings of his breeches, until she had pulled down the fall and placed her hand against his hardened manhood.

His lips let go of her ear as his body spasmed. A low moan escaped him as he felt Olivia's other hand slide slowly over his chest and around to his back, her bare breasts pressed hard against him.

Shrugging the shirt off his body and arms, he slid one hand down past the small of her back and over her bottom to cup one globe. Olivia grinned and gasped as his other hand slid around her shoulder and to the side of a breast, lifting the mound, gently kneading it before he pressed his thumb against the hardened bud, circling it until he heard her breath catch, felt her body liquefy, watched her bee-stung lips open for his hungry mouth. Her entire body trembled, her breaths coming more quickly as he moved his lips to suckle the other nipple.

Her fingers combed through his hair as she kissed his temple and ears. The shivers of pleasure increased to waves, and she cried out his name as he continued to lick and suckle her.

When he finally let go and returned his lips to hers, Olivia was no longer standing before him but was held up, her body lifted by his large hands under her bottom and the back of her thighs. She gasped as the tip of one finger caressed the warm, wet folds between her legs as she wrapped them around his hips.

He carried her to the bed, his lips never leaving hers. And in a single movement, she was suddenly on her back, her hair splayed out across the linens, her legs no longer anchored on his body but bent slightly as she dug her heels into the mattress as she pushed herself farther onto the bed. Michael removed his breeches and stockings, all the while keeping his eyes locked on hers. He was aware of her entire body trembling, shivering as if she was cold.

"I have never done this before," he murmured suddenly, his motions slowing as he realized he, too, was trembling.

Olivia gave him an incredulous look, her eyebrows arching in a manner that suggested she did not believe him. "Neither have I," she whispered as she watched him climb onto the bed and hover over her. He rested on one elbow and shook his head.

"I have never bedded a virgin," he clarified, his hand sliding ever so lightly down the front of her body as he leaned down to kiss her. His lips took hers as the hand moved up and spread out over her breast and then slid down the front of her body, lightly caressing her belly and hips before moving toward her center.

"Oh," Olivia replied, a bit surprised by the confession. "You look as if you ..."

"I do not wish to hurt you," he said quietly, his lips moving down to her breast and her belly, while his hand reached the space between her thighs.

She spread her legs a bit and allowed his probing fingers to touch her inner thighs. His hand continued its journey to the space in the soft, wet folds of her womanhood, his middle finger finding the engorged nub therein. Touching it lightly, he thrilled when she writhed next to him, her chest rising from the bed. Rubbing several fingers around the tender spot, he watched as her head fell back and she began to moan.

He didn't realize how close he'd brought her to the brink until one of her knees was suddenly against his thigh and he heard her whisper, "It will not be so bad." She panted quietly, and then she cried out in ecstasy as one of his fingers found her sheath and slid in easily. He pulled it out slowly as her back arced and her breath caught. He added another finger and watched her as her chest heaved, her breasts so full and her nipples so hard that the sight of them alone made it almost impossible for him not to allow the release his body craved.

Olivia placed a hand against his face and lifted her lips to his as his fingers were making their slow journey out of her. "Come into me now, I beg you," she whispered, her breaths coming faster.

Michael regarded her for only a moment, surprised by her plea. *She's begging me to bed her*, he realized, his heart soaring. *She must feel affection for me!* He positioned himself so his knees were between her legs. She lifted hers and moved her hands to his bottom, pulling on his buttocks until the tip of his manhood, wet and hard and silken, rested against her wet folds. Closing his eyes, Michael slowly drew himself back and then, when he knew he could hold on no longer, he opened his eyes and entered her slowly, very slowly, all the while watching her face to be sure he did not cause her too much pain.

Aware of something keeping him from her, he stopped his movement. But one of Olivia's hands moved to touch the back of his manhood, stroked his sac, while her other hand suddenly pulled hard on his bottom, and his cock was impaling her, filling her and making her arc her back and gasp with pain or pleasure, he could not tell. He grunted at the sudden grip on his manhood as it slid inside her hot, wet haven, amazed at how her body took him in and continued to do so when he tried to pull out just a bit. Her gasps and whimpers excited him, and he increased his thrusts, deepening his penetration into her over and over until he marveled at the looming ecstasy he knew he was about to experience.

With his release imminent, he tried to pull himself out. But Olivia's hands gripped his buttocks and pulled him back into her, hard. The climax caught him, gripped him, and he called out her name, his mouth coming down onto one of her shoulders so that he might stifle the sound as flames of pleasure burned through him and a curtain of black descended.

Olivia arced her back again at the sensations that coursed through her body, at the feeling of liquid warmth that filled her, the incredible waves of pleasure that were just beginning to subside. She was left trembling, her entire body visibly shaking as if she was chilled despite the intense heat of his body where it was pressed against hers.

After a moment, the only sounds were of her quiet whimpers and Michael's labored breathing against her neck. She wrapped her arms around his shoulders and clung to him, felt his body shivering despite the waves of heat she felt wash over her.

"Are you cold?" Michael whispered, feeling her trembling body while at the same time realizing his own body was doing the same.

"No," Olivia replied, drowsily, her arm sliding over his shoulder to pull him back down to her chest. "I am blissfully warm." He was still inside her, although the sensation of fullness had subsided and his heartbeat had slowed somewhat. She could feel his slowing breaths against her neck and thought perhaps he had fallen asleep. *How can he sleep?* she wondered, her body still thrumming, occasional shocks of pleasure still coursing through her body.

Relaxing a bit, she slid her feet down his legs to rest on his calves. She kissed his forehead. *Will it be like this every time?* she wondered, reveling in the sensations and the closeness and the security she felt. *His seed is in me,* she realized then, a small smile touching her lips.

Michael tried to raise his head again but gave up and allowed her to hold him against her. "Did I ... did it hurt?"

Purring, Olivia wondered how to respond. It *had* hurt, but she hadn't been frightened, and he'd seen to it she was prepared for his manhood. And then the pain had subsided and was replaced by that sense of fullness. "A bit, but your lovemaking was ... exquisite," she murmured, her beatific expression enough to assuage his fears.

"I've never ...," Michael started to whisper and then went quiet. *I am still inside her,* he thought, remembering how she had prevented him from pulling out of her as euphoria overtook his body. *My seed is in her.*

"Never, what?" Olivia whispered, her hand going to the side of his head as her fingers spread out to caress his hair.

"I have never allowed myself to ... to release my seed inside a woman before," he stuttered, wondering why he thought it important that she know that about him.

Olivia considered his confession for a moment. "So, you probably have no illegitimate children running about?" she whispered, hoping the relief she felt at this news did not color her voice.

"None," he agreed, his head shifting as if he was shaking his head. "Do you suppose you might ... give me a child or two or ..?" his voice trailed off as if he had fallen asleep.

Olivia smiled broadly before turning to kiss his forehead. "As many as you wish, as long as you continue to visit me in my bedchamber," she replied, wondering how often he might do so.

"Then, would it be all right if I stayed the night right here? he asked, his voice sounding very far way. "I rather think I shall want to visit you again this evening."

Olivia suppressed a giggle. "You had best, since I will not allow you to leave," she murmured, still combing her fingers through his dark hair. She heard his muffled chuckle and then found herself being lifted as he rolled to lay beneath her, his cock still firmly inside her body. She whimpered and then settled her head into the small of his shoulder, aware that he kissed her hair as he wrapped his arms around her body and pulled her legs so that they rested on either side of his legs.

"Will you miss your Tues ..?" Olivia stopped, chiding herself for nearly asking him what she'd wondered since Edward had told her of Michael's evenings with her sister. Despite Eloisa's assurances that she no longer had feelings for Michael, Olivia couldn't help but feel a bit of uncertainty. What if Eloisa's new love proved fleeting? What if Huntington discovered Eloisa's secret and left her? Eloisa would require a protector; Michael, no doubt, would step in and resume his former duty.

Michael was regarding her with a raised eyebrow, poised for her to complete her question. "Will I miss my ..?" he repeated quietly, holding the last word for effect. For a moment, his face was unreadable, but a hint of bemusement replaced his quizzical expression.

"Tuesday nights?" Olivia finished, not realizing she was holding her breath.

There.

She'd said it aloud.

She had no idea how he would respond. With indignation? He was her husband, after all—he could do as he liked. Or would he be angry? Perhaps she should be fearful of ever bringing up the topic. She'd never felt he would strike out at her or do her harm, though. Perhaps he would be apologetic.

He had been the self-appointed protector of the daughter of his business partner and had kept the arrangement completely secret from him and the rest of the family. While doing so, he had protected the family from certain scandal. Olivia fought the urge to avert her eyes, to beg forgiveness and claim she did not want to know the answer.

But she *wanted* to know.

This was her husband. A man who had stood beside her merely a week ago and claimed in his vows to love and honor her. To love her in sickness and health. To forsake all others...

Settling his shoulders into the mattress and emitting a long sigh as he did so, Michael stared at the fabric of the overhead canopy and contemplated how to respond. He had to admit to himself that he usually looked forward to Tuesdays. He liked the short walks to Eloisa's townhouse, even in mid-January. He liked the attention that Eloisa had bestowed on him as she removed his topcoat and took his hat in the tiny vestibule. He appreciated the tea and biscuits she had ready in the small parlor. He liked the dinners she prepared for him and sometimes enjoyed the conversation they shared whilst eating. He liked the glass of port she poured for him when dinner was finished.

But, most of all, he liked that for the entire time he was with her, he could pretend she was someone else. He could imagine he was with the woman who now lay atop him. So ... would he miss those Tuesday nights? he wondered, his lips curving up at the edges. "No," he said quietly, gazing at Olivia. He reached out a hand and cupped her cheek as his head rocked back and forth on the pillow. "Not one bit," he admitted, both to himself and to her.

Olivia's eyes widened. There was sincerity in how he

replied, she realized. "No?" she repeated in a whisper. A tooth caught her lower lip in a effort to stave off the tears she could feel pricking the corners of her eyes.

With some difficulty, Michael lifted himself onto one elbow and smiled. "How can I when I know that the Tuesday nights to come will be so much better?" he murmured, his thumb stroking the hair near her face.

Finally taking a deep breath, Olivia stared at her husband, a curtain of mahogany hair covering one eye. "Better?" she repeated, not grasping his meaning.

With her bee-stung lips, Michael couldn't resist the urge to kiss her again. *She looks so wanton*, he thought. "You'll be *real*," he replied before pulling her face to his and kissing her gently. "You are real. I won't have to pretend it's *you* who I am spending the evening with." He relaxed back onto the bed so that he could use both hands to stroke her face and her arms and her hair.

"Pretend?"

His lips were against hers again, though, and she had to concentrate on his tongue and the feel of his lips and the way his hand had dropped from her cheek to her breast and then moved back up to push her hair away from her face. They stared at one another when the sudden kiss ended.

"I never understood Edward's fascination with Anna," Michael said quietly as he stroked Olivia's hair, his fingers following the waves of mahogany to their ends.

Olivia widened her eyes and regarded Michael with a quizzical expression, her brow furrowing just a bit. "He is not fascinated by her," she replied quietly. "He's in *love* with her. He always wished for her to be his wife."

"As I was saying," Michael continued, cupping her cheek with a hand and stroking her hair with the other. "I never understood it ... until now," he added, his lips pressing against her forehead and then moving to her temple and then to her jaw.

"Now?" Olivia whispered, wondering what had enlightened him.

"Yes. I was always a bit fascinated by you," he whispered, his lips moving to her neck and one arm moving to her back.

"Oh?" she replied, her eyes closing as she allowed herself to be held atop him by his powerful arm.

"I have always felt affection for you, to be sure," Michael continued, his tongue moving in to stroke the hollow of her throat, his arm moving her body as he rolled them onto their sides. "Olivia, my beautiful," he whispered. "I love you, and I do believe I have since the moment my eyes beheld you," he murmured. Sighing, he moved himself so that she was no longer pressed onto him. She moaned as he carefully pulled himself out of her and rolled onto his back, his exhaustion from their lovemaking complete.

Sighing, Olivia considered his words, and then she stiffened as she realized what he had just said.

My beautiful. I love you. Not *El, I love you* as she'd heard that night he'd climbed into her bed and startled her from sleep.

He really wasn't looking for Eloisa's room that night then, she realized, remembering his vehement denial Tuesday night. *And I did not believe him,* she thought sadly.

"If I had known it was you ... when you came into my room last week, I would not have ... I would not have shouted as I did," she whispered then, taking his hand and pressing it against her breast much like he had done when he'd crawled into her bed.

Michael opened his eyes a bit and considered her comment. "But then, we would not have been discovered and ... we wouldn't be married." At the moment, he found he couldn't imagine such a scenario.

"Oh, I think we would be," Olivia countered, her fingers caressing the back of his hand. "You would have had to ask me for my hand and explained why you wanted to marry quickly." Her comment was met with silence, and Olivia wondered what he was thinking. "And I would have accommodated you quite willingly, I think," she continued, "Once you explained that you had sorted things with your sister and already had my father's blessing."

At Michael's continued silence, she lifted her head and regarded him, sighing when she realized he was sound asleep. The hand that rested on her breast gently let go its hold and moved to wrap around her hand, covering it completely. Olivia relaxed into the side of his body and finally allowed herself to sleep.

CHAPTER 31

FRIDAY IS FOR BIRTHDAYS
AND WEDDING VOWS

April 21, 1815, 3:00 a.m.
The smell of smoke from a guttering candle brought Michael to a sudden wakening, and he nearly sat up as he sniffed the air. Satisfied the room wasn't on fire, he relaxed back into the pillows before determining he wasn't in his own room.

The warm body pressed against him stirred, and he smiled as he remembered where he was. His body certainly knew, he realized as he glanced down at his erect manhood. As he watched, Olivia reached out with a finger and drew it down the hardened shaft, barely touching the velvety skin. Michael inhaled sharply and growled, and she quickly pulled her hand away from him. He captured it in his own and moved it back, pressing it against him so that her thumb was on his moistened tip. "Are you .. sore?" he whispered, noticing the blood stain on the bed linen next to where she lay pressed against him. *I have taken her maidenhead,* he thought with an odd mix of satisfaction and sadness.

"I do not believe so," she murmured, desire for him mounting deep inside as she held him and rubbed her thumb over his engorged cock. The space between her thighs seemed to throb, demanding he do something. Before she could ask if he would touch her there as he had the night before,

Michael raised himself on one elbow and cupped one breast with his free hand. His mouth was on hers in an instant, his lips gently pushing hers apart so that his tongue could sweep over her teeth. And then his lips let go to gently nip her lower lip before they moved down to her other breast. His tongue teased the nipple into a hardened nub and he suckled it until he heard Olivia's whimpered plea.

Lowering himself onto her body, he pushed himself down the front of her, drawing his tongue over her belly and down to the top of one thigh, becoming more excited when he heard her soft cries. She spread her legs and lifted one knee, all the while begging him to touch her. Michael wrapped an arm around the upraised thigh, kissing the inside of the tender flesh, drawing his tongue down to the wet folds between her legs. The tip of his tongue sought out its prey, found the engorged nub that would bring her to ecstasy when his tongue touched it.

Olivia gasped and jerked a bit when he made contact, but he pressed his lips around the red fruit and suckled it gently, careful not to bruise it as his lips kissed it and his tongue lightly flicked across it. Olivia's quiet cries increased, arousing so much desire in Michael that he was sure he would climax before he could even enter her wet sheath.

With one quick swipe with the blade of his tongue, Olivia arced her back and cried out his name, the pleasure so intense she thought she might faint. And then, in a deft movement she was barely aware of, Michael was suddenly inside her, filling her and slowly pulling out and pushing into her. With each thrust, she felt his muscles bunch beneath her fingers as she held onto his back. With each thrust, she arced her back so he could push deeper into her wet warmth. With each thrust, her hands moved lower on his back. And with the last thrust, her hands gripped his buttocks and his entire body spasmed.

Michael called out her name as the world around him went black while Olivia held her breath, knowing her own wave of pleasure was about to crash down deep inside.

"Michael!" she whispered, holding onto his body as she rode the wave and allowed it to break and send her floating into an exquisite abyss. She hung there for some time—seconds, minutes, hours—she did not know, but she finally surfaced and took a deep breath.

She was suddenly aware of how her body shivered as she held her husband against her. Her thighs were pinned against the sides of his legs, his solidity providing the only anchor she could cling to in her moment of ecstasy. Tears streamed down the sides of her temples, although she had no idea why she would be crying. And she understood at that very moment how it was a man could *own* a woman.

She had just given herself, body and soul, to her husband.

3 *:45 a.m.*
When Michael finally stirred, he pushed one of her legs gently down the length of his body and then rolled so that Olivia lay atop him. Wrapping his arms around her, he placed her head onto his shoulder and kissed her hair. "Comfortable?" he asked quietly, his voice sleepy.

"Mmm," Olivia murmured in reply. "Happy birthday," she added in a quiet whisper, realizing it must be nearly morning.

"Thank you," he replied with an embarrassed grin. He watched her in the dim candlelight, aware she wasn't yet asleep. "A penny for your thoughts," he whispered, his lips curling up as he watched her eyes meet his.

"I have decided to accept your offer of marriage," she replied, her voice cracking just a bit as she made the admission. "I love you."

Michael stared at her for several seconds, not quite believing what he'd heard. "A penny is suddenly worth a million pounds," he remarked, a smile spreading over his face. "I believe this is the best birthday I have ever had," he murmured sleepily.

As he closed his eyes, his last thought was, *Why the hell did I wait so long to marry?*

10:15 a.m. at Eloisa's townhouse

"So ...," Eloisa spoke breathlessly. "What do you think of him?"

Olivia felt her cheeks flush and wished she could hide her obvious embarrassment. "He is very ... thoughtful," she said hesitantly, not wanting to admit that she found the night with her husband to be the most exciting and pleasurable night of her life. "I believe we shall have a very good life together."

Eloisa's face fell as she regarded her sister. "*Thoughtful?*" she repeated as she noticed her sister's red face. "He did make *love* to you, did he not?" she asked, her brows furrowing. She turned to allow Olivia to button up the ball gown.

Olivia had come at ten with the dress, apologizing for her late arrival and looking as if she'd been up most of the night. But in her defense, Olivia had attended a ball and probably not arrived home until after one or two in the morning. And in true nervous bride fashion, Eloisa had been too anxious to sleep and stayed up entirely too late finishing the needlework on the wedding sampler, back stitching 'Arthur' and 'Eloisa' as well as today's date into the banner portion of the wall hanging.

Olivia took a deep breath and let it out slowly. "He's a magnificent man, actually," she admitted then, smiling. "I had no idea how ... *pleasurable* being with a man could be," she added, her breaths coming faster as she spoke. "He kisses as if his very life depends on it. He knows exactly how to touch me. I think I nearly fainted at least twice. And his tongue was ..." She stopped speaking, suddenly aware of what she was saying and not at all comfortable with telling her sister *everything*.

Eloisa smiled broadly and turned to face her sister, her own face coloring as Olivia continued her description. Her own experiences with Arthur had been rather pleasurable. "Indeed. Arthur is ... so *skilled*," she whispered in reply. "And so generous. He requires that I have my pleasure before he will take his own," she said with a raised eyebrow.

Olivia regarded her sister for a moment. "So, you have spent another night in bed with him then?" she asked, a quirk on the edge of her mouth. It had taken a week for her marriage to be consummated but her sister and future brother-in-law had managed to spend two entire nights together before their wedding day!

A bright pink flush colored her sister's face. "Yes. We weren't going to share his bed until tonight, but ... we'd had dinner at the Clarendon Hotel—with champagne—and his bruises weren't as painful, and he took me on a tour of his house in Mayfair. Oh, Olivia, his home is so beautiful. Very tastefully decorated, beautiful furnishings, and I'll have my very own bedchamber and dressing area," she gushed, recalling the details of the mansion for which she was about to become a mistress.

Her eyebrows rising, Olivia considered her sister's good fortune. "The Clarendon?" she repeated, knowing a dinner there could cost several pounds, as could the champagne.

Eloisa nodded. "It was divine. I thanked him profusely, and he promised we could go there at least once a month!"

Olivia smiled, remembering what Michael had told her about her sister's first day in London. It was only fair the girl be allowed to live a better life now.

A knock at the front door had the two women startled. "'Tis time," Olivia said as she left Eloisa's room. She quickly descended the stairs and hurried to answer the door, opening it to find Michael and an older, thinner but very handsome man standing on the stoop. The two were dressed smartly in superfine morning suits, their red brocade waistcoats a vibrant contrast to the gray of their topcoats. Each held a black top hat in black kid-gloved hands, although the older man's hands gave away his nervousness. Black Hessians, polished to perfection, completed their wedding attire. "Please come in. She's nearly ready," Olivia blurted as she stepped aside to allow the men into the house.

When Michael stepped over the threshold, she stood on tiptoe intending to kiss him on the cheek. He instead wrapped his arms around her shoulders and kissed her on the mouth, causing her to blush a bright red.

"Hello, my beautiful Olivia," he whispered before releasing his hold on her. He seemed not the least bit embarrassed by his show of affection in front of their guest, and Olivia was sure she felt the beginning of an erection when she was suddenly pressed against him.

She returned the kiss, even though she was quite embarrassed at being kissed in front of her sister's intended. She wondered if Michael might be putting on a show in order to further prove he had no claim on Eloisa Waterford. "Hello, darling," she whispered with a grin as she motioned with her head toward her future brother-in-law.

Michael took the hint. "Arthur Huntington, may I present my wife and your bride's sister, Olivia," he said with a wave of his hand and a slight bow.

Olivia couldn't help but smile and blush as she curtsied to Arthur's deep bow.

"It is an honor to meet my new sister," Arthur intoned, his excitement apparent. "I must tell you that I was most relieved to find out that you *existed*, for I feared for some time that your husband was a contender for your sister's heart," he said lightly.

Cocking her head to one side, Olivia smiled brightly. "Not to worry, Mr. Huntington," she replied quickly. "My sister is quite in love with you."

It was Arthur's turn to look surprised and then show a bit of relief, his face coloring up a bit as he gave Michael a quick glance. "As I am with her, I can assure you. And please, do call me 'Arthur'," he added with a nod.

Olivia considered the man for a moment, smiling at his easy demeanor. *Eloisa has done well for herself*, she thought.

"And what have you done with the vicar?" Olivia wondered when a third man didn't appear behind them.

"He's meeting us at the church near Cavendish Square," Michael replied, holding his chronometer in one hand. He gazed at his wife, his eyes traveling to the floor and back up to her face before he added, "And after the ceremony we're going to Berkeley Square for Italian ices. If you would like to, of course," he added, realizing he should probably ask her if she wished to be included in the post-wedding plans.

Olivia beamed. "At Gunter's Tea Shop?" she clarified, never having been to the confectioner's shop.

"Indeed," Arthur replied happily. "The bergamot pear ice is your sister's favorite treat, and I intend to spoil her by making sure she has it at least once a week," he vowed, his chest puffed out proudly.

Olivia and Michael exchanged glances. "I'll fetch the bride and then we can be on our way," Olivia offered as she moved toward the stairs.

"Your new gown is lovely," Michael called out, grinning when Olivia looked over her shoulder with a surprised look. She and Eloisa had visited several shops before finding the taupe satin gown, its shade perfectly complimenting the cream of her ball gown and its style nearly identical. The matching parasols, leaning against the wall in the vestibule, were intended for walks around their squares and the occasional shopping trip, but Olivia realized that, on this sunny day, they would be perfect when riding in the barouche that would take them to the ceremony in Cavendish Square and then to Berkeley Square for ices.

"Are you ready?" Olivia asked as she entered Eloisa's bedchamber, smiling as she took in the sight of her older sister in the ball gown she'd been wearing only hours earlier. "You look ... like a bride!" she breathed, tears threatening in the corners of her eyes.

Eloisa turned from the cheval mirror, holding the string of pearls Arthur had given her. "Almost," she whispered in reply, her hands trembling so that she could not undo the clasp of the necklace. "I am so nervous." A large trunk was packed and ready for a footman to take to the Cavendish Square house; all the other items in the townhouse were part of the property. Once Arthur and Eloisa were settled in their home, Michael and Olivia would head to Crawley Down to spend a month at Iron Creek.

The plans, discussed just that morning when the two awoke at daylight, seemed as if they'd been scheduled for months. In fact, despite being married for only a week, Olivia felt as if her union to Michael Cunningham had been in place much longer. She was confident enough to speak about anything with him and comfortable enough to allow him to see her naked, even in daylight. And, although he seemed to share the same comfort in speaking with her, he was a bit more modest about appearing nude in front of her in the light of day.

8:00 a.m., earlier that day
"I am not as handsome in body as you are beautiful in yours," Michael said in his own defense as he pulled his shirt over his head before trying to leave their marriage bed that morning.

Olivia smiled at that, a slight flush coloring her face. "I find your body very handsome, certainly more so than the bodies of the Grecian statuary in the back garden," she argued, holding her head up from the bed on her hand, her elbow pressed into the mattress as she watched him.

Michael paused in his attempt to get out of bed. "You've looked at the nude statues in the garden?" he asked, his eyebrows dancing as he asked the question, a clear sign he intended to tease her about the subject.

"Indeed," Olivia answered with a cocked eyebrow, not the least bit embarrassed. "And there isn't a one of them I would want in bed with me." After a short pause and a snort from Michael, she added, "Besides, their pricks are far too small."

His mouth, open in shock at her comment, suddenly closed and he settled back into bed. "*You* are a wanton woman!" he accused in a hoarse whisper, covering himself with the counterpane. There wasn't a hint of amusement in his tone. "Tell me, how is it that you are not ... modest... with me?" he asked, remembering that her sister was quite modest the day he helped her dress for their walk to meet Arthur. But Olivia had never covered herself nor asked that the lamplight be extinguished when she was unclothed.

Olivia considered his question, her face coloring up a bit. "I have imagined you making love to me many times over the past few years," she replied in a whisper, "So, I suppose I thought you had already seen me ... nude," she reasoned, wondering if he was really as shocked as his accusation would indicate.

Michael considered her words, taking them as a compliment and feeling quite satisfied with himself. "And ... how did I do in your mind's eye?" he asked then, surprised that she had fantasies about him.

Perhaps even on the same nights he was fantasizing about her.

Olivia regarded him for a moment, aware of what he might be thinking. "Reality is far better," she answered as she climbed atop him, kissing him quite thoroughly.

1 *0:30 a.m.*
"Here, allow me," Olivia said with a grin as she took the jewelry and fastened it around Eloisa's neck. "This is so beautiful with the gown," she said as she admired the string of pearls in the mirror's reflection. The matching earbobs were already in place, their tiny diamonds providing a bit of sparkle against the smooth, matte surface of the pearls. "Your groom is here. He is quite a catch, I think. Are you ready?"

Eloisa nodded, glad to hear her sister's approval. "As I'll ever be," she replied. She followed Olivia down the steps to the parlor and was shocked when Arthur kissed her on the mouth in front of her sister and Michael. "Arthur!" she admonished him, her face coloring to a deep pink.

"Good morning, my princess," he replied, not about to show the least bit of embarrassment given the display of affection put on by Michael and Olivia only moments before. "You are the most beautiful bride I could hope for," he whispered, kissing her temple and giving her a hug about the shoulders. "Are you ready to become Mrs. Arthur Huntington?"

Eloisa beamed, her eyes filling with tears. "Oh, yes!" she replied with a nod.

3:30 p.m.
"You are so beautiful when you are in ecstasy," Michael whispered, wrapping an arm under Olivia and pulling her so that she was resting against him, her head in the small of his shoulder. Only moments before they had returned from having ices at Gunter's, Michael driving a single horse that pulled his fashionable curricle back to Grosvenor Square while one of Arthur Huntington's grooms drove the newlyweds' barouche to Arthur's house in Cavendish Square, its occupants no doubt currently enjoying the same afternoon delight in which the Cunninghams were engaging.

The short wedding ceremony, nearly identical to the one Michael and Olivia experienced the week before, seemed more solemn, more serious somehow, but Olivia figured it was just because she followed this one word for word, when her own had been such a blur she could hardly remember any of the details. As witnesses, she and Michael had held hands throughout, occasionally glancing at one another. And when the vicar pronounced Eloisa and Arthur husband and wife, it was Olivia and Michael who kissed one another.

Olivia wrapped an arm over his chest and slid a leg between his, the top of her thigh touching him suggestively. "And how often might I be that beautiful?" she teased, her fingertips circling his nipples and tickling him where the crisp curls hovered over his chest.

Inhaling sharply, Michael captured her hand in his and brought it to his lips. "I should think at least every Friday night," he replied, his teasing smile hidden from her.

Frowning, Olivia lifted her head and regarded him, wondering if he was being serious. "What about Monday nights?" she asked, her lower lip pouting just a bit.

Michael sighed and did not respond right away, his eyelids heavy and sleep about to take him away from her. "Monday nights, yes," he whispered. "And Thursdays, and ..." His voice trailed off and Olivia smiled as she rested her head on his shoulder.

"And Tuesday nights?" she asked, her hand still held by his and resting on his chin.

His lips captured the end of her fingers and suckled them. "Since I have been pretending to make love to you on Tuesday nights for a year, I believe it is high time you were here for it," he whispered as he lifted himself on one elbow to look down on her.

Olivia smiled at his comment and turned to kiss his bicep. "Then I will not miss it for anything," she replied sleepily, her hand cupping the side of his head.

Michael leaned over her and kissed her softly. "Neither will I," he murmured before laying back in the pillows. He was asleep in a moment.

Despite the frissons that still coursed through her body, Olivia sighed happily. "I think I will like Tuesday nights the best," she murmured. She was soon sound asleep.

EXCERPT

Read on for an excerpt from Linda Rae Sande's
Book 2 of "The Sons of the Aristocracy" Series
The Widowed Countess

"You cannot go to breakfast dressed like that, my lady," Missy announced just as the perfectly coiffed Clarinda was about to open her bedchamber door. Wondering what Missy meant by the proclamation, Lady Norwick looked down and realized she only wore her chemise and corset under a silk dressing gown. A black kerseymere gown was spread out on the bed. Black silk stockings dribbled over the edge of the mattress, and a pair of black slippers were on the floor beneath. Black would be the extent of her wardrobe for a long time to come, she realized.

"Oh," Clarinda managed to get out before her shoulders slumped. *Good grief!* Had she really almost left her bedchamber wearing nothing more than a dressing grown? Well, so what if she had? No one would even notice what she was wearing given the elaborate hair style Missy had managed to create!

Once Missy had her dressed, Clarinda once again announced she had every intention of *eating* and then made her way downstairs to the breakfast room. Moving through the doorway, she smelled the kippers long before she realized they were on the sideboard.

And on the plate in front of Daniel Fitzwilliam.

Her stomach suddenly roiling, Clarinda gasped and hurried through the room, passing her startled brother-in-law and holding a hand against her belly as she mumbled an, "Excuse me," and disappeared into the butler's pantry. She found a chamber pot underneath the silver cabinet just in time.

Well, it wasn't really a chamber pot, she realized too late. The rather large and elaborately decorated soup tureen worked just as well, though.

"My lady! Are you unwell?"

Clarinda whirled around to find Rosie, one of the main floor servants, carrying a stack of dishes through the butler's pantry. The sudden motion did little to settle Clarinda's stomach, but at least the smell of fish didn't reach her here. "I'll be quite fine, thank you," Clarinda answered as she finished wiping her lips with her hanky.

But Rosie's eyes widened. "My lady! You look like you've seen a ghost!"

Gasping, Clarinda's own eyes widened. *Damnation! Was it that apparent she'd been visited by David?* she wondered as she straightened and put one hand up to her face. "Oh?" she ventured as calmly as she could manage, wondering what gave it away.

"You're quite pale, my lady," Rosie said as she put down the dishes. "Should I have Porter send for the physician?"

Swallowing hard, Clarinda considered the offer. There really was no need to have Dr. Collins come over when she already knew *why* she felt sick. All he would do is confirm her state of impending motherhood and probably attach a few leeches to her. She shuddered at the image of the slimy things on her skin, deciding the thought alone made her sicker than the smell of kippers in the next room. "No, Rosie, that won't be necessary," she managed to get out before she inhaled a deep, cleansing breath. "I'm feeling better already, although I do think I'll just make my way back to the hallway using a different route," she said as she left the butler's pantry from the direction the maid had come.

"Yes, my lady," Rosie reluctantly replied as she bobbed a curtsy. "May I say, my lady, your hair looks very nice today."

Clarinda fought the urge to look up. "Thank you, Rosie." Once again very hungry, Clarinda wanted nothing more than to have breakfast, but the thought of going back into the breakfast parlor was rather unappetizing. Not only did it smell like kippers, but *Daniel* was in there. She thought he'd been reading *The Times*—at least, he'd been holding up a newspaper as he ate, she remembered—so perhaps he hadn't even noticed her quick trip through the room. To him, she probably just looked like a black whirling dervish, although she was sure her skirts created a breeze that probably ruffled his dark, silky, wavy hair. She was quite sure he hadn't taken his attention away from the newspaper, though. But from the very brief glimpse she'd had of him, he was still the epitome of David in appearance. So handsome, so fit, so very much a *man*.

"So the mere sight of me makes you *ill*, does it?"

Clarinda had just come around the corner from the servant's hall into the main hall, nearly colliding with Daniel as she did so. As tall as David and just as developed across the shoulders and chest, he made for an imposing figure. And, at the moment, a rather frightening one.

"Daniel!" she gasped, stopping suddenly, one hand pressed to her bosom. After another loud heartbeat, she took another breath. "No," she added with a shake of her head when she realized what he'd said. She could feel ... was that *anger* emanating from his body? "I just cannot bear the odor of..."

"Oh, so now I smell bad?" he countered, his eye blazing with barely contained fury.

Taking an involuntary step backward, Clarinda dropped her hands to her sides, allowing her fists to clench. "You don't. Truly. But the *kippers* do," she managed to get out in a voice that belied the sudden embarrassment that colored her face.

There was a very long pause as the two regarded one another. Clarinda's hands unclenched and Daniel's stance seem to relax just a bit.

"Kippers?" he replied, one eyebrow cocking into an expression that suggested disbelief.

"Kippers, yes," Clarinda acknowledged with a nod, her face still red with embarrassment. Of all the things to happen when she was faced with the prospect of seeing Daniel for the first time in three years, she never would have expected to feel nauseous and have to cast up her accounts, especially in front of a servant.

Daniel blinked, a mannerism Clarinda found very similar to the way David would sometimes react when she said something that befuddled him. Which, now that she thought about it, was quite frequently.

"Not because you find the sight of me somehow ... repugnant?" This last was delivered in a voice that suggested Daniel Fitzwilliam still didn't believe her.

It was Clarinda's turn to blink. "No! Of course not," she replied with a bit too much emphasis.

Daniel seemed to take a step backward, even though his feet did not move an inch. "You do not find the sight of me to be ... repugnant?"

Clarinda's mouth opened in astonishment. *How can this man be so thick?* she wondered, fighting to keep her annoyance from showing on her face. She took a deep breath as she gazed at David's identical twin, looking for any sign of *something* that was different from her late husband. "Since you look *exactly* like the man I married, and since I found that man to be quite *handsome*, I have to admit I could never find the sight of *you* repugnant," she said in a careful, measured tone, thoroughly explaining her reasoning in the hopes her brother-in-law would understand. Then she found herself hoping she wasn't going to have to deal with Daniel's newly inflated ego, which had probably grown several times larger given her adamant assurance that he was handsome.

Damnation, though. He *was* handsome. There were a few differences between him and David, she now was coming to realize, although none of them were differences a casual acquaintance would notice. The little scar near his eye, the one he'd suffered at the point of a bayonet during one of the wars in France, gave him a rakish air. And given his hair was just a shade darker and held just a bit more wave than David's did—probably because David spent more time out of doors—she would have to admit that Daniel was just a bit more handsome than David. *Damn, damn, double damn!* she thought, not able to tear her eyes away from David's twin.

Daniel's mouth began opening and then closing, over and over, as if he was about to say something and then suddenly thought better of it. Clarinda thought he looked somewhat like the tropical fish Lord Everly kept in the large glass tank in his library. "But ... I thought you ... despised me," he finally managed to get out.

Clarinda's brows furrowed, a little wrinkle developing between them. "Only because ... because you despise *me*," she countered, rather surprised he would voice the sentiment and she would bother to reply.

"I do not!" Daniel exclaimed, his protest a bit too loud. He reached out with a finger and poked her right between her brows, as if he was curious about the little wrinkle that had appeared there and thought he could simply press it away with a push of his fingertip.

Pulling his finger away, he stared at that spot, mesmerized. "You really need to stop doing whatever it is that creates that little ..." He pointed at the fold between her brows using the same finger he'd poked her with before, adding, "Or you'll find it will be permanent," he stated with a finality that suggested he was an expert on such abnormalities. "At least, that's what Mother is always telling me about mine."

The feel of his finger touching her sent a shock wave through Clarinda. She might have found it rather pleasant, except something akin to a volcano had began to build deep inside of her, with its molten lava heat and steam churning and rumbling. Although the rumbling was probably due to her hunger pangs, Clarinda realized the rest—the suppressed anger over his impertinent comment, the outrage she felt at his having poked her, the sudden desire to see him uncomfortable—was about to erupt all over Daniel Fitzwilliam. *Pity the man who witnesses a volcanic eruption in the home he is expected to occupy for the next several years*, Clarinda found herself thinking, knowing just then she would have to gain the upper hand on this poor excuse for a man *right now*.

But then Daniel's last comment and the denial made just before it worked to tamp down the volcano. She felt the steam inside her suddenly dissipate. *He doesn't despise me?* she wondered in awe.

"You're doing it again," Daniel murmured as he kept his eye on the furrow between her brows. "It's rather ... cute when *you* do it, though," he added, his words sounding as if he were in awe rather than pointing out an ugly feature on her otherwise beautiful face.

She is still so beautiful, he thought as his gaze took in her oval face with the perfect complexion, the high cheekbones, pert nose and aquamarine eyes that seemed to see right into his soul. The lashes that surrounded those eyes were dark like her hair, and curved so they seemed to sweep through the air as they fell over the light blue-green of her eyes. When they lifted, it was like a curtain rising to reveal the aquamarine jewels of her countenance.

Her maid had obviously become adept at dressing her hair. The elaborate coiffure would have been suitable for a ball at Carleton House. He noticed how she had a tooth caught in her lower lip, the plump flesh bent in just a bit where it made contact. And she was watching him as if she was trying to solve a puzzle. *She is more beautiful than she was when we cursed one another all those years ago.*

At the moment, he couldn't even remember *why* they had cursed one another. Couldn't remember what had brought on the accusations that caused her face to redden and her anger to erupt so forcefully. *Like a volcano*, he thought, *all steam and molten lava roiling out of her.* And then she'd slapped him. Even today, he could feel the sting of that open-handed hit. *Like a steam burn*, he remembered. He could feel the force behind it as her arm swung hard and impacted him like shrapnel from an explosion. He was sure it had hurt her more than it did him, but if it did, he never saw Clarinda flinch.

ABOUT THE AUTHOR

A former technical writer and author of twenty-four historical romances, Linda Rae Sande enjoys researching the Regency era and ancient Greece.

A fan of action-adventure movies, she can frequently be found at the local cinema. Although she no longer has any tropical fish, she follows the San Jose Sharks and makes her home in Cody, Wyoming.

For more information:
www.lindaraesande.com
Sign up for Linda Rae's newsletter:
Regency Romance with a Twist
Follow Linda Rae's blog:
Regency Romance with a Twist

9 780989 397353